T0058674

A DARK LURE

ALSO BY LORETH ANNE WHITE

Snowy Creek
The Slow Burn of Silence

Sahara Kings
The Sheik's Command
Sheik's Revenge
Surgeon Sheik's Rescue
Guarding the Princess
"Sheik's Captive," in *Desert Knights* with Linda Conrad

Wild Country
Manhunter
Cold Case Affair

Shadow Soldiers
The Heart of a Mercenary
A Sultan's Ransom
Rules of Re-Engagement
Seducing the Mercenary
The Heart of a Renegade

More by Loreth Anne White
Melting the Ice
Safe Passage
The Sheik Who Loved Me
Breaking Free
Her 24-Hour Protector
The Missing Colton
The Perfect Outsider
"Saving Christmas," in the *Covert Christmas* anthology
"Letters to Ellie," a novella in the *SEAL of My Dreams* anthology

LORETH ANNE WHITE

A DARK LURE

Montlake
Romance

This is a work of fiction. Names, characters, organizations, places, events, and incidents are either products of the author's imagination or are used fictitiously.

Text copyright © 2015 Loreth Anne White

All rights reserved.

No part of this book may be reproduced, or stored in a retrieval system, or transmitted in any form or by any means, electronic, mechanical, photocopying, recording, or otherwise, without express written permission of the publisher.

Published by Montlake Romance, Seattle

www.apub.com

Amazon, the Amazon logo, and Montlake Romance are trademarks of Amazon.com, Inc., or its affiliates.

ISBN-13: 9781477828731
ISBN-10: 1477828737

Cover design by Marc J. Cohen

Library of Congress Control Number: 2014956690

Printed in the United States of America

For Tom and Jennifer Cole.

Thank you for so generously sharing

your slice of Big Bar paradise with us.

CHAPTER 1

Wednesday. Five days to Thanksgiving.

The library in the East End was quiet. Only 4:00 p.m. and already almost full dark outside, low cloud and a fine Pacific Northwest drizzle cloaking the city, traffic a watery blur behind the rain-streaked windows. He'd crossed the US border into Canada at the Peace Arch around noon, using a NEXUS card.

Now he sat at a computer station at the back of the long room, the bill of his ball cap pulled low over his brow. His clothing was purposefully generic—denim jacket, jeans, work boots. He'd chosen the East End because it was a place of blue collars and transients: street people, the homeless, humans who'd fallen through cracks in society. It was a landscape into which he could blend as effortlessly as a buck melting into a backdrop of dry thicket.

He opened up a social media page and scanned for new posts. Nothing fresh. Or at least, nothing that interested him.

He clicked open another page, and then another. Still no responses to the posts he'd made from Portland two days ago. Before exiting each social media page he typed this message:

Still searching for my biological parents. I am eleven years old. Female. Born July 17 at Watt Lake, British Columbia . . .

For his own social media profile he'd uploaded a photo of a dark-haired kid that he copied off some mother's Facebook site. It was the same image he used for all the adoption reunion sites he'd been routinely trawling since his release from an Arizona correctional facility a month ago.

Computer proficiency was something he'd accomplished while doing time for involuntary manslaughter. In prison he'd also learned from an inmate about the proliferation of these adoption search and reunion pages on social media. He'd had no access to the Internet while inside, but upon his release he'd immediately conducted a traditional Internet search for "Sarah Baker." He'd found not one single online reference to Sarah Baker in the past eight years. Yes, there were others out there with the same name, but no sign of the Sarah he wanted. The countless archived newspaper articles, the feature stories that mentioned her, all seemed to have come to a screeching halt eight years ago. As if her slate had been wiped clean.

As if Sarah Baker had simply ceased to exist.

Or, she'd changed her name, taken on a new identity, was trying to hide.

That was when, on a hunch, he'd turned to the adoption sites.

On these public pages, without oversight or restriction, adopted children of all ages, along with the parents of kids surrendered for adoption, were seeking out and finding estranged biological relatives. He'd read the commentary of experts who claimed that while this new phenomenon was moving families toward more transparency, it also raised new questions. Pitfalls that authorities in the field hadn't yet figured out how to handle.

For him it was a hunter's wet dream.

At every opportunity on his way up to the border he'd stopped at libraries and Internet cafés. Casting out his lines. Dangling his lures like delicate dry flies, ever so gently, upon the surfaces of cyber pools and eddies where he felt his prey might be lurking in shadows, holding against the currents. Waiting.

Watching for a . . . He stilled as something snared his attention.

Mother looking for eleven-year-old.

Quickly he clicked on the link. Not a match. Wrong birth date. Wrong physical type. He rubbed the whiskers on his jaw—the hair dye irritated his skin. Overall this was a crapshoot. Perhaps she'd already reconnected with the kid. Maybe she didn't want to know. Maybe she was happily married, had moved on. Or was dead.

But a hunter, a good hunter, possessed patience. He trusted his gut, and he always knew the mind and habits of his prey. Psychological profiling cut two ways. And he knew Sarah Baker.

He'd owned Sarah Baker.

He'd studied her for nine careful months before trapping her.

She'd been fully his for another five and a half months. Until he'd taken a risk born of hubris. A stupid mistake.

Words from his childhood sifted suddenly like smoke through his mind . . .

The only time you ever take a shot at last light, boy, is if you're confident it's going to be a clean kill shot, or you must be prepared to track down your wounded animal through the dark. Alone. You finish that job no matter what, no matter how many days or nights it takes, no matter how hungry or tired you get, you hear me, boy?

He'd prolonged the pleasure of his last spring hunt too long. He'd waited until very last light to take his final kill shot. He'd missed. She'd fired back and wounded him instead. And she'd slipped into the blackness of the forest.

But he felt in his bones that after she'd licked her wounds, Sarah Baker would come looking, if she hadn't already. Motherhood was a powerful lure. And compassion, curiosity, openness— all her weaknesses. It was how he'd gotten her in the first place.

He opened another page. More messages. All sorts. Mothers, fathers, aunts, brothers, cousins, kids, searching for their castaway blood. Some searches were being conducted on behalf of others. Other times it was for themselves. It bemused him, really, this deep-seated craving in humans for a sense of family, belonging, identity. Roots. Home. To be wanted, needed, to understand why someone might have chosen to toss them aside as babies.

He was about to shut down the last page when a response to his last post suddenly blipped through.

His heart kicked.

I had a daughter born at Watt Lake Community Hospital. She would be turning twelve next summer. Dark hair. Green eyes. A small heart-shaped birthmark behind her left knee. Do you feel this could be you?

The reply came from a user called FisherGirl. Quickly, he clicked through to FisherGirl's profile. No photo. Just an image of a trout leaping on the end of a line, droplets glittering in sunshine. No public access to her timeline or other information. But there she was, live, online, right now. He felt the gentle underwater tug, the nibble on his line.

Well, fuck me.

This made sense. Made fucking sense. He'd first discovered Sarah Baker behind the counter of a sporting goods store up in Watt Lake, a store owned by her husband's family. Sarah had been an expert angler and a hunter, adept at tracking both animal and man. It was her wilderness survival skill set that had really excited him. After the others he'd wanted a real challenge. He'd wanted to up the ante, pique the thrill. He'd gotten what he wanted, and then some.

Gamos, he whispered to himself. His mother once told him that in the context of hunting, the word *game* was derived from the ancient Greek word *gamos,* meaning a marriage or conjoining of hunter and prey. And yes, when he hunted, that was the way he craved it—a relationship, an emotional connection with his quarry. Personal. An irrevocable union.

And it's not a game until both sides know they're playing . . .

A soft blush of adrenaline heated his blood, and his cock stirred, pressing against his fly in a gentle, pulsing ache.

Calm. Breathe. Don't jerk the line. Don't try and set the hook. This is not a wild, leaping salmon. This is a trout. A delicate, elusive, cold-water fighting fish. Piscivorous, more predatory than most, but you want to let her run, dive deep, think she's still free . . .

He could almost feel the virtual fly line, wet and spooling from his fingers, hear the whirr of a reel. A connection had been made, a dialogue had begun between him and something wild. Something that could be his—if he played it right.

He typed:

Yes! I do have dark hair and green eyes, and a small birthmark behind my left knee . . .

He waited. The silence in the library swelled and pressed against his ears. A man coughed. A foghorn moaned outside in the mist-choked Burrard.

Then suddenly:

Could you please contact me privately at FisherGirl@gmail.com?

His mouth went dry. Quickly he opened his anonymous online e-mail account and fired off a message:

How will I know if you're my mother? Can you send me a picture? Do you still live in Watt Lake? What's your name? Why did you give your baby away? Who was the father? I'm very excited.

The response was almost instantaneous.

Due to circumstances beyond my control I was forced to surrender my baby in a closed, private adoption, arranged through an agent. I don't know where my daughter went, and would love to know how she is doing. I now go by the name of Olivia West. I work as a ranch manager and fishing guide at Broken Bar Ranch in the Cariboo. Below is a link to the ranch website. In the staff section you'll find a photo of me. Do your adoptive parents know you're searching for your birth parents?

Quickly he clicked on the link provided in the e-mail.

The Broken Bar Ranch website filled the screen. He opened the "About Us" link. Staff photos came up.

He scrolled rapidly, stopped at a photo. Enlarged it. His heart slammed against his ribs. He couldn't breathe.

It's her.

Not one shred of a doubt.

Shit. He went dizzy, almost blinded by a delirious injection of pure, sweet, hot adrenaline. He tried to swallow. Yes, she'd changed. Matured. The lines of her features had grown finer, a little more angular around the chin, the look in her eyes a little cooler, not quite as obviously guileless. But there was no mistaking that thick chestnut hair, the basic oval shape of her face. The full mouth. Those wide-set eyes the color of forest moss. Heat prickled over his skin.

He touched the screen lightly with fingertips. Sarah Baker. His wounded deer. Now calling herself Olivia West. He tried the new name out mentally on his tongue. *Olivia . . .*

"Excuse me?"

He freaking jumped out of his skin. His gaze shot up to the source of the interruption. A young woman. Big blue eyes.

"Will you be at this computer station much longer?" she said. "I do have it booked."

He held her eyes, heart thumping, and slowly he curved his lips into a smile. "Just give me a minute to shut down, okay?"

A blush washed softly up her neck and into her cheeks. And in that moment he knew that while he'd also changed, while prison had aged and worn him lean, driven lines deep into his features, he still had it. That smooth voice. The capacity to charm. To put a seductive lure into his gaze.

"No worries," she said. "Thank you. I . . . I'll just wait over there." She seated herself on a chair not far behind him. He felt her presence, possibilities. But he had a target now. A plan was forming.

Maneuvering his shoulder to block the young woman's sightline, he opened the website's FAQ page and jotted the lodge directions onto a piece of paper. It was a five- to six-hour drive north, up into the high interior plateau. According to the FAQs, the Broken Bar Ranch was open until the end of the Canadian Thanksgiving weekend, after which it shut down for winter. He didn't have much time. The first big snows and freeze would soon be upon the Cariboo region, and he didn't know if Olivia West would stay.

It struck him suddenly—the irony, the utter perfection of the timing. As if a sign. It was this time of year, almost to the day, that he'd taken her twelve years ago, the Sunday afternoon right before Thanksgiving, on the cusp of the first really big winter snowfall. Like the bears itching to go into hibernation, he'd always been able to scent the coming of the first snowfall. He heard it in the whispering in the trees, saw it in the slant of light, tasted the metallic tinge on the breeze. And he knew, like the bears making for their dens knew, that if he moved right on the edge of the first big storm, the coming snow would blanket and hide his tracks. For the remainder of the winter he'd be safe, holed up where no one could trace him to his lair.

He reread her e-mail, started to type an answer, then hesitated over the blinking cursor. Engage further? No. He had what he needed. Didn't want to make her suspicious. Let her think the "kid" had spooked and vanished.

He shut down his accounts, exited the web pages, cleared the cache, and left the computer station to the waiting young woman. Tucking the piece of paper with the ranch address into his inside pocket, he pulled up the collar of his denim jacket, pushed open the library door. He stepped out into the cool, misty drizzle on Hastings. Bending his head into the rain, hands in pockets, he joined the throng of commuters spilling out from the buildings and scurrying home for the day.

Fresh purpose fueled his stride as he made for his truck and camper parked two blocks down. It was time to go home—all the way home. Time to finally finish the hunt. After so many years in a tiny prison cell he once again had the wild taste of freedom on his tongue. The mountains and forests, the cool, clear air beckoned.

A memory snaked suddenly through his mind, drawing him back in time.

He's eleven years old, exhausted from a hunt, sitting on his mother's lap. She strokes his hair, which is long and unruly, and she's surrounded by her ubiquitous books. His father sits on the opposite side of the crackling fire, smoking his pipe, watching them both with hard, narrow eyes. His mother's voice sifts into his consciousness . . .

Man stands apart from animal, Eugene, my sweet. For man, a hunt is not always about subsistence. Often it's the pure thrill of the chase that's the foremost lure. It's about sensation—that unique combination of anticipation, mental alertness, tension, and physical exertion . . . Her hand moves slowly down his body to his thigh, and her voice drops to a warm whisper of breath at his ear . . . *The hunt can be almost mythical in its exhilaration. Delicious . . .* Her fingers brush the inside of his thigh, and his little penis stirs.

His father grunts, lurches up from the chair, and points his pipe at his wife . . . *Cut the crap, why don't you? He* lost *the fucking animal—there's no fucking* thrill *in that!* His father shifts his fierce gaze to his son . . .

It's your duty, boy, your goddamn duty to track down a gut-shot deer. You don't stop, you hear . . . you don't goddamn stop tracking until you've bagged the prey you've hurt. You make it yours. You take ownership. You don't let this happen again, you hear? If you can't fucking get a clean shot, you don't squeeze that trigger at last light.

A foghorn sounded, jerking Eugene's mind back to the present. Mist from the gray waters of the Burrard swirled up in thick, tattered swaths, billowing along the brick and cobbled streets of the old quarter. He shrugged a little deeper into his jacket.

Your goddamn duty, you hear . . .
To finish the kill.

—

Blood boomed in Gage Burton's ears as he stared at his computer screen, waiting for a response.

Could it be? After all these years, he'd finally got a strike?

Seconds ticked by. Then minutes.

Nothing more came through.

But he'd felt it. A nibble on his line, and then it was gone. No further response to his e-mail.

He typed again, hands trembling.

If you're interested in talking further, please do e-mail me back, no obligations. All I need to know is that my child has found a warm and loving home.

He hit "Send." Waited. More minutes ticked by.

Nothing.

Perspiration beaded along his lip, and Gage dragged his palm over his balding head. He glanced at the papers scattered across his desk—newspaper clippings from the *Watt Lake Gazette*, articles run twelve years ago. Old crime scene photos showing clinical images of exhumed skeletal remains, desecrated bodies. Rotting skulls. Missing tongues. Gaping eye sockets. There were photos of steel grappling hooks in the meat shed where the Watt Lake Killer had hung, gutted, flayed, and bled out his victims like slaughtered deer. Photos of the shed where he'd done his butchering, images of a generator-powered freezer that had revealed unspeakable horrors. Pictures of the shack beside the shed where he'd shackled and roped his victims alive, where he sexually abused and fed and kept them over the winter before setting them out for a spring hunt.

Gage drew closer a photograph of the Watt Lake Killer's last victim.

Sarah Jane Baker.

Twenty-five at the time. The young wife of Ethan Baker, daughter of prominent Watt Lake pastor Jim Vanlorne. Sarah Baker had been taken, as the others had, in the hours preceding the first big storm of the season. She, like the others, had been chained and overwintered in that shack. And then, at the sound of returning geese, he'd armed her and released her into the wild.

For there is no hunting like the hunting of an armed man . . .

These words, Sarah had revealed in interviews with police later, the killer had whispered into her ear. He'd quoted to her from the works of Thoreau, Hemingway, Blackwood.

A well-read man.

Unlike Sebastian George, the man who'd been caught, charged, tried, and convicted for the murders.

Despite all the evidence, Gage could not believe they'd put away the right guy. He'd been hunting him ever since, in his spare time, nights. A secret obsession. Because he'd made a pledge all those years ago. A pledge for justice.

He'd been keeping tabs on Sarah Baker ever since. It was his belief that the real Watt Lake Killer might one day return for her.

Gage blew out a chestful of air. Still no response to his e-mail. He opened up several of the other accounts he'd created and checked to see if there were any fresh hits on his posts there.

Zip.

He dragged his hand down over his mouth, doubt and fear braiding with dark excitement. He could *sense* him out there, on the other end of a computer. The killer. Listening, waiting.

The door opened suddenly. "Dad?"

He jumped. Adrenaline slammed. He swore, getting up fast, scrabbling to gather up the newspaper clippings, crime scene photos, notes.

"Tori, dammit. Knock. How many times have I told you!"

His daughter's gaze shot to the papers clutched in his hands, then to the computer, then settled on his face. "What are you doing?"

"What do you want, Tori?"

She glowered at him in silence for a beat.

"It's Aunt Louise," she snapped. "On the phone. Didn't you hear it ring?"

Accusation. Anger. So much negativity since Melody died. Since Tori lost her mother and he'd lost his wife, his best friend, his crutch. His reason for life itself.

"Thank you," he said, holding her gaze, waiting for her to leave.

She exited and slammed the door. Footfalls stomped off down the passage.

Jesus, he hadn't even heard the phone . . . *Sharpen up. Focus.* He picked up the phone, cleared his throat.

"Lou, hey. How're you doing?"

"More important, how are *you*?" His older sister's voice was all businesslike, par for the course. "I thought I'd hear from you this week, Gage, after your last appointment. How did it go? Can they operate?"

They couldn't. Both Melody and he had already known this before her accident.

He glanced out the window. Darkness was full. So early at this time of year. Rain squiggled in watery worms against the black reflection of the windows.

"I blew the appointment off," he said.

Silence hung for a few beats.

"I was busy, Lou."

"Shit," she said softly. Then came a muffled sound, as though she'd covered the receiver with her hand in order to quietly blow her nose. "You have an obligation to Tori, you know, to stay on top of this."

"I have plenty of time—"

"How much, exactly? Something could go wrong any day. You don't know how it's going to manifest. You've already been forced into early retirement because of . . ." Her voice faded, falling just short of mentioning his blackouts at work.

The few mistakes he'd made during a key homicide investigation had raised red flags with brass. He'd lost periods of time, found himself in places without knowing how he'd gotten there. He'd physically laid into a punk-ass drug dealer in the interrogation room last week and hadn't even known what triggered him, or what he'd been doing. One minute he'd been present, the next he was being yanked off the scumbag. Questions about his health had been formally raised. Next came the issue of early retirement versus long-term disability leave. This goddamn illness was robbing him of his life even as he walked.

"Look, all I'm saying is that you need to manage this, because if Tori—"

"I will. I just have some things I need to take care of first."

"Like what?"

"Loose ends."

His sister sighed heavily. "And how is Tori doing? You've told her, right?"

"Not yet."

"Gage—"

"Enough. I'm her father, and I know that she's not ready. Especially since the incident at school—"

"*What* incident?"

"She had a bit of a dustup with another student, set fire to the kid's books in the school cafeteria."

"I'm packing a bag right now. I'm heading to the airport for a standby flight. Ben and the kids can manage without me for a while. At least I can be there for Tori, when you do tell her."

"No."

"She'll also need time to assimilate the fact that she's going to have to come and live with us. I don't think—"

"Louise, stop. I know you mean well. I know you'll be there for Tori when it happens. But right now I'm as strong as a bloody ox. I'm clearheaded. I'm *fine*. I've got my big retirement bash to attend night after tomorrow, and I've taken her out of school. We're going to—"

"You've *what*?"

He closed his eyes for a moment, pinched the bridge of his nose. "It was either that or risk some other mishap and an expulsion. Besides, I want to spend some time with her. I want to go away for the Thanksgiving weekend, make some good, final memories with her, different memories," he said softly. "She's suffering from her own guilt over Melody's accident. We need to work through that before I tell her what's going on with me. Just give us a little while, okay?"

This time he heard his sister clearly sniffling and blowing her nose. It sliced him. Lou, his capable, businesslike older sister, was crying.

"I don't understand life, either, Lou," he said quietly. "I don't know why we get dealt the cards we do. Tori got a bad hand. The bloody joker in the pack. But that's the one she's got, and I need to fix some things, tie up those loose ends for her before I go."

Silence—a long, long beat of silence.

Gage stared at his sorry-ass reflection in the black, rain-streaked window. Outwardly he still looked strong, muscles bulked from hours in the gym, fit from running long distance. This beautiful house in Kits, the view of the ocean, they'd thought they had it all. Great kid. Decent careers. Love. Respect. A perfect and delicate glass ball.

And then it shattered.

He'd gotten the diagnosis. Melody had made it seem manageable. She was going to be there with him every step of the way. And once it was over, Tori would still have had a mother. Their daughter would not have to be alone.

Then Melody went and skied into a tree well on Cypress Mountain after the last big spring snowstorm. She'd suffocated, trapped upside down under mounds of pristine white powder while Tori had struggled to yank her mother out by her skis and boots. When Melody died she'd taken with her all the light and heart and energy in their lives. Without Melody . . . it was like removing the battery from an appliance. Just didn't work. Both he and Tori had started to crumble under the confusion. The rage. The unjustness. The utter gaping maw of loss.

"Give us until after Thanksgiving," he said quietly.

His sister inhaled shakily. "So where are you going for this trip?"

"Not far. A few hours' drive into the interior."

"Call me when you get back, okay?"

"You got it." He said good-bye. But as he was about to hang up, he heard a soft click. As if a phone receiver in another part of the house had been set gently into its cradle.

Gage flung open his office door and marched down the passage.

"Tori!" He opened her bedroom door. No sign of her. "Tori? Where are you?"

He heard the water in the shower. He saw the phone receiver in its cradle. Relief punched through him. For a gut-sickening moment he'd thought she'd heard them on the phone.

———

Eugene climbed into his truck cab. A set of Washington State plates lay upside down on the floor of the passenger side. It was safer to keep the plates than trash them where someone might find them.

He fired the ignition and flicked on the windshield wipers. Pulling out into the stream of traffic, wipers clacking, he headed over the congested Lions Gate Bridge, bumper-to-bumper traffic. Once clear of the bridge he aimed for the ramp onto the highway that would take him north into the mountains.

A *thump thump thump* sounded in the camper on the back of the truck. His blood pressure spiked. Irritability crawled over his skin. The drugs he'd given her were wearing off earlier and earlier now as she built tolerance.

He glanced up into his rearview mirror, which ordinarily afforded him a glimpse through the cab's rear window into the camper via another small window. But it was dark, rain squiggling down the pane, refracting light from traffic. She was securely bound but must have found a way to kick at the boards with her heels.

Thump thump . . . thumpy-thump came the noise again. This was one fucking determined piece of baggage he'd been carting around.

There always came a time when the fresh meat grew stale. She hadn't even been fresh to begin with. Mustn't rush with the disposal, though. He needed to do this right. He needed to send a very special message.

. . . It's not a game until both sides know they're playing . . .

A smile curved his lips as it suddenly occurred to him exactly what he would do, how he'd gradually make Sarah Baker aware that she was once again prey, being hunted. He moistened his lips, recalling the bittersweet, salty taste of raw fear on Sarah Baker's skin.

CHAPTER 2

Thursday. Four days to Thanksgiving.

Olivia spurred her horse into a gallop up the ridge, hair streaming behind her, wind drawing tears from her eyes. She should have brought gloves—her fingers were frozen. But she adored the sensation of the chill autumn air against bare skin. Ace, her German shepherd, lagged far behind, guided by the sound of Spirit's thudding hooves. Cresting the ridge, she reined in her mare just in time.

The sky to the west was streaked with violent shades of fuchsia and saffron, and the army of black spruce marching across the spine of the west esker was backlit by the setting sun. It looked as though the trees themselves were afire. As she watched the shimmering ball of fire sink slowly into the horizon, the wind shifted suddenly and temperatures dropped. Coyotes began yipping, their chorus of cries echoing into the distant Marble mountains. The sun disappeared, and the world turned tones of pearlescent gray. The coyotes fell suddenly silent. A chill rippled over her skin, and the fine hairs on her arms rose.

It never ceased to hold her wonder, this nightly show, this clockwork ritual of light shifting into dark and the response of the wild. This big, open sky. The miles upon miles of endless forests and the smooth, glacier-formed hills of this high interior plateau. This place, this ranch was where she had finally found a sense of peace. Of home.

To her mind this ridge afforded the best vantage point of Broken Bar Ranch at sunset. From here, golden fields rolled all the way down to the turquoise lake. Cattle usually grazed these lands, but the last of the herd had been recently sold, as had most of the horses—a stark reminder of the change that was upon this place.

She could count three small fishing boats still on the water. They were heading slowly back toward the campsite on the west shore as the water turned pewter. The Marble range to the south was dusted with the first skiffs of snow, and the aspen leaves had turned gold. Thanksgiving weekend was upon them. This would be the last weekend that fly fishers—the diehards who didn't mind the freezing temperatures at night—would try to eke a few more hours of angling from the year. Winter was creeping down from those mountains fast, quietly closing an icy fist around the wilderness. Within weeks, days even, the forests would be white and frozen, and Broken Bar would be closed to guests, cut off from the world.

If it were her place, she would open the ranch for winter stays, offering sleigh rides, cross-country skiing, snowshoeing, and snowmobiling along the miles upon miles of wilderness trails. There would be ice skating and hockey games on the lake. Big bonfires at night. She'd provide a cowboy country-style Christmas dinner complete with a ranch-raised turkey dinner, vegetables harvested from the kitchen gardens, and a nightly roaring fire in the giant hearth. She'd lace sparkling white lights around the big blue spruce that stood sentinel in front of the old lodge house. Broken Bar was picture-perfect for it. Olivia felt a small pang in her chest, a poignant longing for Christmases and Thanksgivings past, the warmth of large family gatherings. A life she once had. But she was no longer that person, could never be. And there was no way she was going to be a victim about it.

Not anymore.

The victim role had near killed her. She was a different person now.

Yet this time of year, this tremulous window between fall and winter, was always a bit of a struggle. The scents of autumn, the sounds of geese migrating, the first shots of the fall hunt cracking through the hills still got to her, filled her with unspecified dread, whisperings of unforgotten fear. She also felt, at this time of year, the sharp chasm of loss. A mother's loss of her child. And questions would fill her.

Where are you now, my baby girl? Are you happy? Safe?

Her mood shifted, and her attention turned toward the smoke curling up from the rock chimney of the big old lodge house in the distance. Dr. Halliday's black SUV was still parked outside.

The ranch belonged to Old Man Myron McDonough. It had been in his family since the mid-1800s, since his ancestors had homesteaded this Cariboo land. The way Adele Carrick, his longtime housekeeper, told it, Broken Bar had been a thriving cattle and guest ranch business up until the accident twenty-three years ago that had taken Myron's wife, Grace, and their youngest son, Jimmie. From that point Myron had begun to draw into himself, growing harder, gruffer, coarser, wilder, and the ranch business had started a long slide into disrepair. His two older kids had left, and no longer returned to visit.

And now that Myron had taken ill, he was further scaling back what was left of the ranch and fishing business. Since his diagnosis last winter, the last of the cattle and almost all the horses had been sold. Guests no longer stayed inside the lodge. Only the cabins and campsites were rented, spring through fall. Horseback trail rides had stopped last season, the wranglers and grooms laid off, all but one who cared for the handful of remaining horses. The remainder of the staff had been trimmed down to a housekeeper, a chef and kitchen assistant, seasonal wait staff and bartender, part-time cleaners, a seasonal farmhand, the groom, and her. The office and fly shop manager had been let go last week with a promise that her job would open again next summer. But there was a question whether Myron would even be around next summer.

Wind gusted hair across Olivia's face. She could almost taste the coming snow in the air this evening—a faint metallic tinge, and she felt a sense of things closing in.

She wanted to catch the doc before he left. She was about to whistle for Ace, who'd gone snuffling after some critter, when the rumbling noise of a large rig coming along the logging road carried across the lake. She squinted into the distance. A fine line of dirt was rising like spindrift above the trees on the opposite side of the water. It sounded like a diesel engine hauling a trailer. It was probably heading to the campsite.

She'd let whoever it was settle into the campsite, and if they didn't come around to the office to check themselves in later tonight, she'd swing by first thing in the morning. She didn't want to miss Halliday, and his SUV was pulling out from the lodge parking lot now.

Giving a sharp whistle for Ace, Olivia nudged Spirit into a trot down the ridge. By the time she reached the dirt road, Halliday's vehicle was already nearing the cattle grid, a cloud of dirt boiling behind him. She spurred Spirit into a gallop to head him off at the arched entranceway, hooves thudding on the dry ground. Halliday's vehicle slowed as he saw her. He came to stop under the arch with the big bleached bull moose antlers. Olivia reined her mare in. Spirit sidestepped, snorting into cool evening air.

The doc opened his door, got out.

"Liv."

She jumped down from the saddle and led Spirit toward him.

"I'm glad I caught you," she said, a little breathless. "How is he?"

The doc reached up and took Spirit's bridle. He scratched the mare's forehead, then he sighed, looked away. Wind gusted. For a moment he watched Ace sniffing about his vehicle tires, then met her eyes again. Olivia's heart sank at what she saw there.

"I spoke with the oncologist this morning—the results of his CT scan came in. The cancer has spread rapidly. There are masses matting his lungs, along his spine, in his liver. He's in a great deal of pain, Liv. He's going to need round-the-clock palliative care. There are decisions that will need to be made."

Her chest went tight. "How soon?"

"As soon as possible." He hesitated. "Myron could take a turn for the worse any second now. Or it could take longer. Much will depend on how badly the old badger wants to hang in and battle the pain. His son and daughter should be informed, and we all know that Myron isn't going to do that himself."

"I don't think he ever stopped blaming Cole for Grace and Jimmie's deaths," she said quietly.

The doc nodded. "I've known this family for years, and that accident changed everything. Myron's bitterness toward his boy is part of who he is now. Lord knows there's no love lost on Cole's side, either. Still, if it were my father, I'd want to know. I'd want the choice of saying good-bye, of maybe making amends as best I could." He hesitated. "Myron might take it better if it came from you—if you called them."

"Me?"

"You're his friend."

"But you're an older friend, Doc."

"I'd do it, but I'd really prefer not to alienate him right now. I'm going to need his trust as we head into this next phase of his health management. You know what he can be like."

Olivia exhaled, pressure crushing into her chest at the thought of losing Myron, of losing her place on this ranch. Her home. As the cold wind gusted she felt it again, that sense of a dark cold closing in. Things coming full circle.

Her mind strayed to the framed photographs hanging in Myron's library. The fact they hung there at all showed he had some feeling for his remaining children.

"I don't know his kids," she said softly. "I've never spoken to them."

"Liv, *someone* needs to do it."

———

Deep in thought, under the glow of the kerosene lamp hanging from the barn rafters, Olivia groomed and watered Spirit and put her in her stall for the night. She then returned to her cabin, where she fed Ace. Beneath a steaming shower she gathered her thoughts before dressing warmly and going up to the lodge to talk to Myron. Ace followed, leaves crunching underfoot as they made their way along the narrow path that led from her cabin through a dense grove of trembling aspen, then up over the lawn toward the three-story log house.

The porch and interior lights spilled yellow and welcoming into the darkness. She climbed the wood stairs, scuffed her cowboy boots on the mat, and pushed open the great big wooden door.

As she entered the stone-tiled entrance hall, Adele bustled past with a laden tray. She started at the sight of Olivia and came to an abrupt halt at the base of the sweeping wood staircase.

"Oh, it's you," she said, looking oddly flustered. "I . . . was just taking Mr. McDonough's supper up. He's taking it in the library tonight."

"No one booked for the lodge dinner?" Olivia hung her jacket over one of the antler hooks near the door. A wrought-iron chandelier strung from the vaulted ceiling above cast a faceted light over the entrance hall. To her right lay the open-plan living room where guests were welcome to sit by the fire, watch TV, or use the computer station or pool table. A small bar in the living area opened at mealtimes. Beyond that were the dining area and kitchen.

"Not tonight," said the housekeeper. "But we do have reservations for Friday and the rest of the weekend."

While guests no longer stayed in the upstairs rooms, the lodge still opened for dining, depending on reservations from guests staying in the cabins or campsite. But from what Dr. Halliday was saying, the kitchen would probably not be reopening again next summer. This was likely the last weekend for the ranch guests ever. The thought was sobering.

"Here," Olivia said, reaching out. "Let me take that up for you. I need to speak to him anyway."

The housekeeper handed her the tray.

"How's he doing?"

"Full of piss and vinegar, if that's what you mean."

It brought a smile to Olivia's face. "Well, that's a good sign. You might as well head on home. I'll sit with him while he eats, then clean up the kitchen after."

Adele regarded her for a moment, an unreadable look entering her eyes. She reached behind her back to untie her apron. "If that's what you want, then. I'll just finish up and be gone."

Irascible as Adele could be, she was indispensable to this place, and to Old Man McDonough. Olivia wondered what the woman would do when he died.

She found the library door slightly ajar, and edged it open farther with the tray.

A fire had been lit and crackled in the hearth. Myron was in his wheelchair watching out the window, his back to the door. Ace made straight for the hearth.

"Hey, Old Man."

He turned, and his craggy face crumpled into a grin beneath his shock of steel-gray hair. "Livia!" He rolled his wheelchair around.

He'd been a great, big, gruff mountain of a man before this disease had felled him. He still reminded Olivia of an old Sean Connery and Harrison Ford bundled into one. With a bushy pirate's beard.

"Hungry?" She held up the tray.

He wheeled over to the hearth. "Bring it to the table by the fire. Pour a drink. Join me?"

"I think I might."

She set the tray on a small table next to the fire and went to the buffet, where she poured a whisky for each of them. She placed the bottle on the table next to Myron where he could reach it, and seated herself in a big leather chair on the opposite side of the hearth. She sipped her scotch, watching him bring the soupspoon to his mouth. His tremors had worsened. Soup spilled. His complexion had taken on a sallow pallor, and beneath his whiskers his cheeks appeared sunken. His eyes were rheumy, the whites yellowing. A great big hollow filled her stomach.

"What's eating you, Olivia?"

She cast a reflexive glance up to the large photographic study of Myron's son hanging in pride of place above the river rock fireplace. Cole McDonough seemed to peer down at her with the same deep-set, moody, probing gray eyes as his father's. Where Myron's hair had grayed, Cole's was still wild and dark, his skin deeply sun-browned.

It was an iconic study of him shot at a Nanga Parbat base camp. He exuded a rugged virility, a devil-may-care attitude. The photo had been used for an *Outside* magazine cover some years ago, a publication to which Cole had contributed a firsthand account of a tragic Taliban attack on Nanga Parbat climbers, which he later expanded into a book. It had subsequently been made into a movie. One of two to his credit.

Cole was an ex-military psychology and philosophy scholar turned war correspondent turned narrative nonfiction adventure writer. A literary adrenaline-seeking junkie who lived life on the razor's edge of death, and sought to psychologically deconstruct others who did, too. It was the underlying theme in all of his works—why men and women did extreme things, why some people survived against all odds, yet others perished. She'd read the jackets of his books lining Myron's shelves.

His was a narcissistic pursuit. Olivia had decided this some time ago. She resented the very idea of him—maybe because she envied his freedom, his ability to live life with such full-throttle lust.

Myron's gaze followed hers up to the portrait. His hand holding the spoon stilled.

"What is it?" he said.

Olivia cleared her throat. "Where is he now?"

"Cole?"

"Yes. And Jane. Is Jane still in London, with her family?"

Myron slowly set his spoon down and reached for his whisky tumbler. He took a deep, long swig and closed his eyes. "You've been speaking to Halliday?"

"Yes."

He said nothing. The fire popped, cracked. Ace rolled onto his back, tongue lolling out the side of his mouth, relaxed as the puppy he once was.

"He told me," she said.

Myron opened his eyes. "What, exactly?"

"That you'll need to make decisions about palliative care. He said someone should call Cole and Jane, let them know what's happening."

His thatch of gray brows lowered, and his eyes narrowed to flint. Very quietly, he said, "Over my dead body."

"What over your dead body, Myron?" she said, just as quietly. "Getting nursing care? Going into a hospice, or someone calling your kids?"

"All of it." He downed the remainder of his whisky, reached for the bottle beside him and sloshed another three fingers into the crystal. She knew he was on a lot of medication. Drinking like that was probably not a good idea. But good for what, if one was dying anyway?

"I don't give a pig's ass what the fine doctor says. If I'm going to die, I'm going to do it right here. On *my* terms. On my ranch, in my own goddamn home. Where I've lived my entire goddamn life. Where I brought my wife. Where we had babies . . ." His voice faltered, leaving unspoken words hanging in the void.

Where my wife died. Where my youngest son died . . . where my family fell apart . . .

The firelight caught a glint in his eyes.

Olivia set her glass down and leaned forward, arms resting on her knees.

"Myron, if you don't move into a place where they can care for you, you'll need in-home nursing—"

His palm shot up. "Stop. Don't even think about it. The day I need a nurse to wipe my ass, brush my teeth, and empty my bedpan is the day I die. Dignity. Goddamn dignity. Is that too much to ask?"

"Your children should know. They have a right to—"

"Enough!" He slammed his glass down, cheeks reddening. "No way in hell. I will *not* have those two squabbling over their inheritance, trying to sell this ranch out from under my feet. And they will try, mark my words."

"You can't be so sure they—"

"Of course I can. Cole doesn't give a rat's prick what happens to Broken Bar or to his old man. And I don't need him here, rubbing my face in it. They can have the ranch when I'm dead, when my ashes are scattered and my memorial cairn has been placed up on that glacial ridge alongside Grace's and Jimmie's. Then my ghost can haunt them." He paused, looking suddenly bone tired but no less determined. "You'll do it for me. Scatter my ashes, sort out that stone cairn."

She rubbed her brow, stole another look at the photo above the fireplace. "Where is he now?"

Silence.

She turned to look at Myron. An odd expression had overcome his features. His shoulders had rolled inward, compressing him into his chair. In his eyes she detected regret.

Olivia felt a sharp tug of emotion.

If it were my father I'd want to know. I'd want the choice of saying good-bye . . .

Was it possible to set certain wrongs right? Was it foolhardy to even attempt to do so when anger, bitterness, regret, blame were all so deeply rooted in the soil of one's psyche, each twisting so tightly over the other that if you tried to extract one root, the whole tree died?

"He's in Havana," he said finally. "Drowning his sorrows."

Surprise rippled through her. "Havana, Cuba? How do you know?"

He gave a halfhearted shrug and looked away, staring into the flames, his veined hands resting limp on the arms of his chair. The fact that he even knew where Cole was told Olivia he still cared. At least a little. And she was besieged with a sense that Myron needed to do this—to make peace with his son. His daughter, too.

Or was it Olivia's subterranean guilt about her own estranged family that was fueling this sentiment? She swallowed, forcing herself to remain present. Bad things happened when she allowed her thoughts to feather back into the past.

"What sorrows?" she said quietly.

Still refusing to give Olivia his eyes, he said, "Cole seems to have come to a standstill after his woman and her kid left him."

"I . . . didn't know he had a family. Was he married?"

"Common-law partner. Holly. She had a son, Ty, from a previous marriage. She returned to her ex after some horrendous incident with Cole in the Sudan that endangered her kid's life. Took the boy with her, back to his father. The boy would be eight now."

"How do you know all this?"

"Read about it in that magazine he writes for. He has a knack for that, you know—living his own life to the extreme, chasing the storm, at the expense of those around him. Cole never even brought Holly or Ty home—I never met them." Myron gave a harsh snort. "Then again, Cole stopped calling Broken Bar 'home' a long, long time ago."

"What happened in the Sudan?"

Myron waved his hand, brushing the whole thing away like a bad smell. "Don't want to talk about it." He cleared his throat, then said, "Jimmie was also eight. When Cole drove him into the river."

A chill washed over Olivia. She was overcome by an eerie sense of time warping and weaving and replicating like the double-helix strands of DNA.

Myron fell silent, his mind seemingly drifting away on some sea of secret sorrow, buoyed by booze and painkillers.

She stole another look at Cole's image above the fireplace.

"All things have their season, Liv," Myron said, his words thick and slurring slightly now. "Each life has a cycle. One makes one's choices and bears one's punishment. Even this ranch . . . maybe it is time. The end of an era. The end of the McDonough legacy." He reached for his glass, swirled the dregs with a shaky hand, watching as the liquid refracted firelight. "It's unrealistic to expect my progeny will carry it on." He cleared his throat and continued.

"Even if someone did want to start running cows again, the financial outlay would be huge. But the guest and tourism business—that could be year-round. The lodge could be full again. With some work the cabins could be refurbished, go a little higher end, bring greater yield per guest. There's a market for that sort of thing now. German tourists. Asians. Brits. This wilderness gives them something they simply cannot find back home."

She stared at the Old Man. It was fatigue, whisky, painkillers talking, yet it afforded her a rare window into his thoughts, one she had not expected.

"I had no idea you'd even thought about it—a winter business."

"It would never work."

"But it *could*. If there was a will." She couldn't help saying it. This was something she'd dreamed about so often that she'd even created spreadsheets, broken down potential staffing costs, called around for quotes and estimates, because . . . well, because she didn't have a life, that was why. This place had become her life. Because she'd had a stupid fantasy that she might one day present Myron with the paperwork and formally propose something. But then had come his diagnosis.

"I could see a higher-end lodge experience," she said. "Expansion of the guided trips—even horseback rides to fish the steelhead runs up in the Tahkena River; float-plane companies flying in executive guests; excellent organic and ranch-grown produce, top-end cuisine. Fresh lake trout, venison from the forests. Add to that a winter experience with a focus on Christmas. I believe it would work. I *know* it would."

He regarded her for a long while, an inscrutable look entering his eyes. He shook his head.

"Forget it." He set his glass down and wheeled himself across the carpet, the effort twisting his features. "I need to hit the sack early tonight. Can I leave you to lock up?"

She came to her feet, took the handles of his chair.

"No. I can do this myself."

But this time she overrode him. "Forget about it, Old Man. I need you to live a few more days." She pushed him toward the library door.

"Why do I let you boss me around like this?"

"'Cause I'm nice," she said with a smile. "And I don't cost much." She wheeled him out into the hall and up to the small elevator that had been installed last spring. She reached over to press the elevator button.

"You come from a ranching background yourself, don't you, Liv?"

She tensed. "You've never asked about my past."

"But you do—the hunting, fishing, horsemanship, it has to come from somewhere. Where's home to you, Olivia? Were you raised in BC? Another province?"

The elevator doors opened.

She hesitated. Trapped. She owed him some kind of truth after all he'd done for her. Myron had made it so easy for her to stay here on Broken Bar, to fit in, to begin to heal, to finally find a measure of peace. And it was easy because he never *did* ask where she was from, beyond the basic résumé stuff when he first hired her. He'd seen the scars on her wrists. But not once had he ever mentioned them. This was a man who knew about secrets, and reasons for keeping them.

"Yes." She wheeled him into the elevator and pressed the button for the third floor. The doors closed, and the elevator hummed upward. "A ranch. Farther north."

He was silent, thank God, as she steered him out the elevator and along the corridor to his room, a corner suite that afforded him views over the lake and the mountains to the south, and the rolling aspen-dotted hills to the west.

"Thanks," he said as they reached his bedroom door. "I can handle it from here."

"You sure?"

"Not goddamn dead yet. Like I told you, the day I need someone to brush my teeth, wipe my ass, put me to bed in diapers, is the day I stop living."

She snorted. Yet an uneasiness coiled in her gut at the look of determined ferocity in the Old Man's eyes—she feared suddenly he might take his own life, on his own terms. Using all those pills.

"Well . . ." She hesitated, reluctant to leave him alone. "Night, then." She started down the passage.

He startled her by calling after her. "Why do you do this, Olivia?"

She turned. "Do what?"

"Push a dying old man around. Humor him. What do you want from me?"

A bolt of hurt cracked through her.

"Don't, Myron," she said quietly. "Do not think you can push me away too, now. I'm not that easy."

He glowered at her, his hands fisting on the armrests of his chair. "You think I pushed my kids away? You think I alienated my own son—is that what you think?"

"Did you?"

He spun his chair around and wheeled himself through the door into his room. "Go to hell, Liv." He slammed the door behind him.

"Been there," she yelled back at him. "Done that!"

Silence.

Damn the old bastard.

"I know your game, Myron!" she called through his door. "You're too damn weak to man up to your own emotions, that's what! Compromise takes too much work, so you just cut everyone off!"

No response. Just the old grandfather clock ticktocking down the hall.

Olivia muttered a curse as she turned and stomped down the passage. She clattered down the massive three-story staircase, memories suddenly hounding her on the way down. She'd cut off her own family, her ex, her community. All she had left was a dying old man for whom she cared far too much, and Ace and Spirit. That was the extent of her family now. Home was her tiny log cabin on the lake in a grove of trees with no electricity or computer to connect her to the outside world, and it was not even hers. It would go to Cole and Jane, probably sooner than later.

It was all going to shit under her feet.

Buck up, buttercup, you've come through worse. Nothing you can do about the old man dying . . .

But there was something. She stalled outside the library. There was one little thing she could still do. She could call his children. She could give them the choice to come home. To say good-bye. To bridge the gap of broken years. She could give them a chance she never got.

She could give Myron the chance to say he was sorry.

———

Olivia strode through the library to the annex at the back that served as Myron's study. The fire was dying to glowing embers. Ace was still there in front of it, sleeping like the dead. Inside the study, Myron's dark wood desk was cluttered with papers. A fat manila envelope rested atop the clutter. On it was scrawled "Last Will and Testament." Another stark reminder that things were coming to an end.

She opened the top left desk drawer, from which she'd once seen Myron take his Rolodex. Inside the drawer, next to the Rolodex, was a hardcover book with a bookmark between the pages. Surprise washed through her. It was Cole McDonough's most recent publication—a work of narrative nonfiction titled simply *Survivors*.

She opened the cover, read the inside jacket.

Why does one person miraculously survive against all odds, while others perish when all they had to do was wait to be rescued? In this examination of the psychology of survival, Cole McDonough dissects true, bone-chilling encounters with death to expose a surprising set of traits that explain why certain individuals can avoid fatal panic, and go from victim to survivor . . .

Olivia's chest tightened with complex emotions. She liked to think of herself as a survivor—one who'd outlasted and outwitted the Watt Lake butcher. But had she? His evil still touched her deep inside. On some level she knew she'd always be struggling to outrun him, the memories. The person she once was. Maybe Olivia was the survivor, but Sarah Baker was not. Because he'd killed Sarah. And she'd helped him.

Olivia decided to borrow the book. She was sure Myron wouldn't mind.

She flicked through his Rolodex, found the entries for Jane and Cole, scribbled them down on a piece of paper. Whether the cell numbers were current or not, she'd soon find out. Replacing the Rolodex, she closed the drawer. As she did, she knocked over a small brass figurine. It clunked loudly to the wood floor. She cursed, picked it up and set it straight. Then stilled as a noise came from the library. Her pulse quickened.

"Hello?" She entered the library cautiously. "Who's there?"

A soft scuffling sounded in the hall. Ace wasn't on the mat. Tension quickened through Olivia. She moved fast and quietly as a cat, suddenly acutely aware of the hunting blade she habitually wore sheathed at her hip.

She entered the hallway. A figure moved around the corner and under the staircase. Olivia caught the flash of a pale blue dress.

"Adele? Is that you?"

The housekeeper stepped out from behind the staircase, Ace behind her. Flustered, she smoothed her skirt.

Anger spurted through Olivia, fired by adrenaline. She *hated* being scared. Fear brought the possibility of flashbacks.

"Was that you in the library?" she said too brusquely, heart thudding.

"No . . . I mean, yes," Adele said. "I saw that Mr. McDonough's dinner tray was still there. I cleaned it up and was just going to leave for the night when I thought I heard someone moving in his study." Her gaze dropped to the piece of paper and book in Olivia's hand.

"It was me," Olivia said curtly, stuffing the paper with the phone numbers into the back pocket of her jeans.

"Yes. Well, good. I . . . thought it might have been an intruder. I'd better be on my way." She bustled to the front door, grabbed her coat from the hook. She punched her arms into the sleeves, then hesitated.

"Did you find what you needed, then? In Mr. McDonough's study."

Suspicion unfurled in Olivia. "Yes. Thank you."

Adele waited a minute. Olivia said nothing.

"Good night, then."

"I'll follow you out," Olivia said, grabbing her own jacket and a flashlight from the shelf.

She locked the front door behind her while Adele made her way around the side of the house where she parked her Subaru. Olivia heard the engine start. From the porch she watched the housekeeper's vehicle heading down the dirt driveway, headlights' twin beams disappearing into the blackness. Above, the sky was a dark vault pricked with stars.

As the sound of the Subaru engine faded into the void of wilderness, a heavy, cold silence descended, and a strange unease settled over Olivia's shoulders.

She flicked on the flashlight and crossed the lawn with Ace at her heels. As they entered the unlit grove of aspens, dead leaves and dry grasses rustling and whispering about them in the night breeze, she heard the sharp crack of a twig.

She froze.

Another crack.

Olivia stuffed the book down the front of her jacket and bent down to grab Ace's collar. She panned her flashlight around into the shadows. Ace growled. Her heart beat faster. She waited, listened.

Nothing more. Just the clapping and whispering and rustling of dead leaves and dry branches. Yet the sense of being watched from the darkness remained acute.

Still holding on to Ace, she ran her beam through the trees again, expecting the reflecting gleam of green eyes. Or red. Depending on whether it was a night-vision animal or something warm blooded.

But she could discern nothing but shadow and darkness. Keeping a firm grasp on Ace's collar, she quickly made her way to her cabin. Ace didn't stand a chance against coyotes or a bear. He didn't stand a chance against much at all, going blind and lame as he was.

Once inside she lit the kerosene lamps and a candle. Warm light quavered into her small living area. She immediately felt more relaxed.

Olivia reached for the dead bolt on the door, hesitated, then dropped her hand. She suffered from panic attacks when confined. She also *refused* to be scared out here. Sebastian George was dead, and not locking her cabin door was her statement of freedom, her personal line of triumph in the sand. Yet she stood there, rubbing her arms, nausea churning her gut. Why feel like this now? As if something dark was coming? It was Myron's looming death— that's what it had to be.

Drawing the blinds, she stoked up what remained of the glowing embers in the woodstove and set a pot of soup onto the stove. Ace curled up on his mat in front of the fire. Checking her watch, she figured it would be close to midnight in Cuba, and about six a.m. in London.

It was both too late and too early to call.

She paced her open-plan living area, still rubbing her arms. A nervous tic.

To hell with it. Myron could be dead tomorrow. She unsheathed the stubby satellite phone on her belt—a small Globalstar GSP-1700, one of her few indulgences. She didn't spend much on clothes, barely anything on makeup. She rarely went into town, unless for chores. Her extravagances were expensive bamboo rods, fly-tying equipment, pricey fly line and reels. And she owned and carried a sat phone, not because cell reception out here was crap, not because she wanted contact with the outside world. But despite her proclamations otherwise, despite the fact she refused to be a victim, or afraid, a dark permanent thing had lodged deep inside her psyche—she wanted a way to call for help, wherever she was. In spite of her bravado, she never again would be totally cut off without a safety line.

First she dialed Jane's number in London. Her call went straight to voice mail. She hung up, pausing as she heard something outside. She listened carefully, that dark feeling closing tighter around her. She glanced at Ace—her radar. But her dog was sound asleep. She dialed the number for Cole McDonough.

He picked up on the fifth ring.

CHAPTER 3

Florida Keys. Black's Marina Bar.
Thursday, almost midnight.

The night was sultry, the bar crowded. Windows were flung open wide to the salt air, but it did little to dissipate the smoky, jazz-filled atmosphere. Perspiration gleamed on the dark skin of the Cuban expat jazz musicians crowded upon the tiny stage, and on the faces of patrons who laughed, and whispered, and drank and swayed to the palpable beats on the marina's tiny dance floor.

A female vocalist took the mike. Lovingly. And began to sing, her voice low and dark and full with mystery and ancient heat. Sensuality burned like heavy incense into the air as the couples on the floor moved with the rhythm of her voice. Candles trembled in jars, and the floor seemed to shift a little under Cole's chair.

Or perhaps it was the booze. And the weed they'd smoked on the boat. He blinked, trying to marshal his consciousness. His lids were heavy. He sat nursing a beer at a small round table with his old mate from the war trenches, Gavin Black, a photojournalist who'd packed it all in to open this dockside bar in the Keys and run fishing charters on his boat. He and Gav had been up before dawn, and they'd fished until after dark. They were sunburned and salt-stung, and their muscles ached in a good way.

Gav had lured Cole stateside a month ago, claiming he needed a hand with his fishing gig. It was a lie.

What Gav Black really wanted was to save Cole from himself. Word was out that he was wasting away in Havana bars and beds, trying to write some ass-crap about Hemingway's need for risk.

The vocalist, Cole realized through his booze fog, was singing about a sinner-man who was trying to run from the devil. Rather than focusing on the words, he squinted at the woman's features through the haze. Her skin was ebony, her eyes were low lidded, and her lips, voluptuous, seemed to make slow love to the microphone. She reminded him of a face he'd seen in the Sudan. Which in turn reminded him of Holly and Ty. His skin felt hot.

"You need to find yourself a new story, mate," Gavin said, reaching for his beer, watching him closely.

Cole glanced at his friend. Gav's face was blurry around the edges.

"I'm done." Cole raised his hand and motioned for a server to bring them another round. "I might as well face it—the muse, she has left." His voice felt thick. His words came out slurred.

Gav leaned forward, his tanned and powerful forearms resting on the small round table, a tattoo flexing under hard muscle—a tat to commemorate Afghanistan. Cole had first met Gav Black in the Hindu Kush. His photojournalism had shocked the world. Gav used to do with pictures what Cole could only hope to achieve with words.

"What about tackling that piece you always wanted to do on Zambian witch doctors and the black-market trade in human body parts? It'll take your mind off stuff."

Stuff.

Anger swelled softly into his drunkenness, a kind of black, torpid acrimony that had more to do with self-loathing and self-recrimination than anything else right now. Probably self-indulgence, too. On some level he knew this. He knew Gav was right. He needed to find something that fired the old juices. But he just couldn't reach that level of interest in anything anymore. His pursuit of story no longer felt noble. He didn't see the point in telling his tales to the world. Not since the paradigm of his experience had shifted in the Sudan.

"What did you go and sit in Cuba for, anyway? Some idiot homage to Hemingway—was that seriously your idea for your next book? Because it's been done. A thousand times over. You're better than that."

"Why don't you fuck the hell off." He punched his hand higher into the air, motioning irritably again for the barkeep, pointing at the empty bottles in front of them. "If I wanted a shrink I'd get one."

A server came weaving through the thick crowd toward their table with two more bottles of beer.

But Gav's gaze continued to bore into Cole's. "Why do you think I opened this place in the Keys, called it quits? You think you have sole proprietorship over suffering? 'Cause you don't, mate. The work can bite anyone in the ass."

The server placed two full bottles in front of them, smiled. Cole reached immediately for his drink and raised his bottle.

"Cheers. Best escape from 'stuff' is right here." He took a deep, cold, frothy swig from his bottle.

A phone rang as he swallowed—he heard it ringing somewhere, along the edges of his consciousness, under the music, below the pulse of a drum. The smell of sweat and salt was thick. His skin, his shirt were wet.

"It's yours," Gav said.

"What?"

"Your cell." His buddy nodded to the phone buzzing along the surface of the table. "It's for you."

Cole stared at it, slightly bemused someone was even calling him. He reached for it, fumbled to connect the call, put it to his ear.

"Yeah."

"Cole McDonough?"

A voice. Female. Noise in the bar was too loud. He put his finger into his other ear.

"Who's this?"

"My name is Olivia West. I'm the Broken Bar Ranch manager, and I'm calling about your father, Myron. He's . . ."—her voice cut out, then back in—". . . decisions . . . doctor says . . ."

"Hello? You're breaking up. What did you say?"

". . . needs . . . come home . . ."

"Hang on a sec."

He glanced at Gavin. "Gonna take this outside." He stood, stumbled, caught himself on the table, swore. He pushed through a throng of glistening dancers and patrons huddled by the door.

Outside it was just as hot. He could hear distant surf crashing on the barrier reef, and he could scent something sweet and flowery in the humidity. The face of the big clock on the marina store glowed just after midnight.

A group of women, ebony skin glistening, bright, tight dresses, offered him glittering white smiles, laughing and making lewd suggestions as they passed him. The promise of sex drifted in their wake. More mindless, fucking, hedonistic sex . . .

He stumbled over to the boardwalk railing, leaned his hand against it for balance, and put the phone back to his ear.

"Who did you say you were?" His words came out slurred. Phosphorescence shimmered on the surface of the heaving ocean.

"The ranch manager, Olivia West. Your father needs his family. He's dying."

Cole's brain stalled.

"Excuse me?"

"The doctors say he doesn't have long. The cancer has returned full force. He'll need to move into some sort of palliative care very soon, which means there are decisions to be made."

"I spoke to Jane, my sister, the other day. She said he's fine . . . he told her that he was . . . fine."

"Other day? What day was that?"

He sank his fingers into his hair, thick and stiff with humidity and salt. Needed a cut. He hadn't bothered since . . . he couldn't remember when. A month ago? How many months had passed since Holly had walked out on him? How many months since Ty had gone back to his father . . .

"Are you there?"

"Ah . . . yeah. Look, I don't know who the fuck you are. But—"

Anger lashed into the woman's voice. "Your own father is dying. I thought you might like to know. I thought you might like a chance to say good-bye. But if you don't the hell care, if you think sitting in some Cuban bar—"

"Florida. I'm in Florida."

"Whatever. Wherever you're wallowing in your own self-pity, drinking yourself into a stupor every night is not going to bring your family back to you. You're no survivor, you know that? You know dick about surviving. All you know is your own narcissistic pursuit."

Shock, then drunken rage, imploded into his stupor.

"Who . . . who the *fuck* do you think you are?" he yelled into his phone. "Who are you to get off on talking about my—"

But the phone went dead.

"Hello? . . . Hello?"

Silence.

Shit. The woman had hung up on him. Shaking with adrenaline, anger, he hit the button to recall the last number. Nothing happened. He examined his phone. Battery was dead. He glanced out over the shimmering, heaving ocean and swore again. Now he couldn't even find the number of this woman to call her back. What did she say her name was? Olivia?

He pocketed his phone and placed both hands on the railing, steadying his thoughts. He stood for a moment, abstractedly watching the heave and pull of the sea under the command of a fat yellow gibbous moon.

His father was dying. Was it true?

Sometime last year Jane had mentioned he had cancer, but she'd also pointed out that their father was strong. Nothing to worry about at this point. Had it under control. Would his father even tell Jane if he was going downhill? No. No, the hell he would. When *had* he actually spoken to Jane? She'd called him a ways back.

Cole scrubbed his hand hard over his forehead as he tried to recall why Jane had called. Right. She'd phoned to ask if he was prepared to sign some digital letter of intent, something to do with the sale of the ranch. He'd been drunk. Par for the course. He'd told her he didn't care what happened to the ranch, that she and his father could do whatever they wanted with the land.

She'd then e-mailed him a document full of tiny print. He hadn't bothered reading the thing before signing it with an e-signature.

But now that he actually thought about it, there was no way his dad would want to offload that precious ranch of his. Not while he was alive.

Had Jane known at the time that their father's health was failing? Was she trying to cash in on the farm already?

That would be Jane. No surprises there.

Cole pushed himself off the railing, started weaving down the boardwalk. A cab. He needed a cab.

His buddy came running out of the bar behind him. "Cole! Wait up!" He caught up and grabbed Cole's arm as he was crossing the road.

"Where are you going?"

Cole turned to face his mate. And Gavin stilled as he caught sight of his friend's face under the street lamp.

"Jesus. What happened?"

Cole stood there, swaying a little, trying to pull into place the jigsaw pieces that had exploded through his head with that call.

"I've got to get back to the motel, charge my phone. I need to call my sister."

"Who was that on the phone? Everything okay?"

No. It was not. His father was dying.

. . . you're wallowing in your own self-pity . . . drinking yourself into a stupor every night is not going to bring your family back to you. You're no survivor, you know that? You know dick about surviving . . .

Who was this woman, and where did she get off passing judgment on him? What did *she* know about survivors? Or the family he'd lost?

"My father is dying," he said quietly, a coolness and clarity crawling into the periphery of his muddied brain. "And I'm not even sure how I feel about that, but I need a favor. Take me back to the motel. I need to pick up some gear, my passport. Get me to the airport."

"You're drunk."

"And I'll be half sober by the time I get on a standby flight. By the time I land at YVR, I'll be clear as glass."

From Vancouver International he'd need to get up to Pemberton, where he'd left his Piper Cub with a friend who rented his and Holly's old house there. From there he'd fly into the Cariboo. As the intent formed in his mind it hit him—he was making a decision to go home. For the first time in thirteen years. The prodigal son was returning.

"At least you *will* sober up. Don't know how many more nights like this you could tolerate before you kill yourself. Who was it? On the phone?"

"Some woman called Olivia."

Gavin regarded him steadily. "Some woman called Olivia probably just saved your sorry ass, you know that? Come, let's go."

———

Olivia sat in her bed, flicking irritably through Cole's book while Ace snored at her feet. He'd cut her off, the bastard. Under a thumping sense of personal affront, she felt pity for Myron. She'd come to believe this would be good for him—to make peace. Maybe it would have even been good for his son. Waste of bloody time.

Something caught her eye in the text. She brought the page closer, read the words.

> Survival is a journey. It is the quest that underlies all Story. No matter the geography, or culture, or era, in one form or another, the story of survival is the same story we listen to, riveted, around the flames of the hunter's fire. Or hear from the mouth of the astronaut returned from a burning spaceship, or from the woman who trumped cancer. We listen in the hopes of learning what magic they used to conquer a great beast, to deliver a decisive victory, to make it alone down the peaks of Everest alive . . .

She flipped to the back jacket of the book. There was another photo of him.

In this image his steel-gray eyes were tempered by a glint of what appeared to be amusement. The photo had been shot in some African locale. His skin was tanned dark, and a half-smile played across his wide, sculpted mouth. As if he knew a secret. Perhaps the secret of feeling alive. She swallowed, feeling an odd sensation as she once again noted the genetic echoes between son and the father for whom she cared so deeply. And it hit square between the eyes why she disliked this man.

It wasn't that he seemed to exude a screw-you, rugged in-your-face alpha virility. Nor was it the way he seemed to flip a bird at caution. It wasn't that she envied his courage to bite into life so fully and zestfully—no, it was none of that.

It was a slow-dawning admission that she was attracted to him. In a way that felt dangerous to her. And it was not just his looks but his mind. She was turned on by the masculine beauty of his prose, the clean, muscular sentences that bespoke a latent empathy in the author. He was an acute observer of the world and human nature in it.

The idea of a man like Cole McDonough was both alluring and threatening. Olivia set the book aside and turned off her kerosene lantern. It was a good thing he wasn't coming. She'd rather not face him. She didn't want to find any man attractive again. Seeing revulsion in her own husband's eyes when he'd perfunctorily tried to make love to her after she'd healed had crushed her.

She had no intention of even getting close to putting herself through that debasing kind of humiliation ever again.

———

Eugene watched the small light in her cabin go out. Wind whispered cold about his ears, and a wolf howled in the distant black hills. Hairs rose along his arms at the haunting sound. His thoughts turned to home. Wilderness. Freedom. Yes, he could taste it. After all this time she—all of it—was finally within reach. He could fulfill his purpose, go back to the beginning, end it where it had all started. He liked the sense of destiny in this. It had the right patterns.

He'd arrived just before sunset today. He'd scoped out the campsite, the cabins, the stables, the lodge. He now had a decent sense of the lay of the land. There weren't many people about. Once darkness had come, he'd gone up to the lodge and watched the lighted windows for a while, trying to get a handle on how many people stayed there, worked there.

That's when he'd caught sight of her through a big picture window on the second floor, talking to a gray-bearded man in a wheelchair. He'd known it was her in a blinding instant.

Known it with every fiber of his being. It was in the color and fall of her hair. The shape of her face. The way she angled her head to the right as she talked. It was in the line of her neck, the curve of her chin.

He knew Sarah Baker more intimately than any man ever would. He knew the taste of her mouth, the taste of her most intimate parts, the taste of her blood and meat. He swallowed at this thought. She was inside him, part of him.

Already he'd catalogued much about how she handled herself out here. He'd seen the sheathed fixed-blade knife on her belt. Her dog wasn't young and looked as though it navigated primarily by scent. She moved with confidence through the dark, but the slightest crack of a twig brought fear, fast. She was quick. Alert. Which meant, surely, that she still remembered him well. She still carried with her a fear he'd put there. He smiled quietly.

The nearby cabin through the trees appeared vacant. No telephone lines led into her cabin. No satellite dish was mounted on her roof. He couldn't see hydro wires, either. She carried a phone on her belt. It was likely reliant on the cell tower he'd seen in the mountains when he came in. There were landlines to the lodge house, and a big dish on the roof. The dish was most likely for television. Possibly Internet. Apart from those lines, this whole area was likely dependent on that one tower for cell coverage. This worked in his favor. Especially with the coming snow that he could taste on the night breeze.

Adrenaline rustled through him.

But the game was not on. Yet.

It wasn't a game until she knew she was playing.

They probably hadn't got his message yet—there'd been nothing on the radio today, nor in the papers he'd perused at the gas station in Clinton on his way up to Broken Bar. But it shouldn't be long now until his message was found. And what a message it was.

He'd strung the body up in a grove of cottonwoods just off the road.

He would drive back into town maybe tomorrow or the next day, pick up a newspaper and other supplies he'd need. A few more days, and she would be his.

An owl hooted softly. Wings *fwopped* invisibly through trees. He waited until the mantle of night was cold and heavy upon him, until frost began to glitter on grass in the rising moonlight. Until the constellations had moved across the sky, then he sifted like a ghost back into the shadows.

He'd return in the morning, bearing the first little gift. It was time his presence began to whisper around the periphery of her consciousness.

CHAPTER 4

O'Hare International. Friday.

Cole lugged his duffel bag toward a coffee stand, questioning his motivations for having boarded the plane in the first place.

He'd snagged a flight four hours after Gavin dropped him at the small Keys airport. In Miami it'd taken three hours to score a standby seat to Vancouver with a layover at O'Hare. Outside the terminal windows dawn was a soft orange streak along the Chicago horizon. A mother of a headache dogged him. He felt surreal, as if suspended in a dreamscape between day and night as he chased time westward. Part of him began to think he'd imagined Olivia West's phone call in a drunken delirium.

He ordered a double-shot of espresso and headed off to find his gate. This was a mistake. He was the last person on earth his father would want to see, especially if the old codger was weak. His old man detested showing weakness. Especially to his son.

A trickier, darker thought snaked through him as he took a sip from his cardboard cup—given his absence for so many years, suddenly showing up on the ranch now that his father was apparently dying was going to smack of Machiavellian opportunism. The last goddamn thing Cole wanted was to let his father think he needed, or wanted, anything from him. Like an inheritance. A share of the ranch. He meant what he'd told Jane—they could do what they liked with the place, and its ghosts.

Cole found a seat near his gate and opened up his laptop, head pounding, brain thick. While it fired up, he called Jane in London. She hadn't picked up when he'd tried before departing Miami.

This time she answered on the third ring.

"Jane speaking," she said in her adopted, clipped-Brit accent. His sister could be such a fraud.

"It's Cole. Did you know that Dad was dying? Is it true?"

There was a moment of dead air.

Cole cursed inwardly. "Goddammit, Jane, you *knew*?"

A sigh. "No. Not really. Not until I got a call from his manager at some ungodly hour this morning about Dad needing hospice care. It was a shock, to be honest. All I knew was that he had the cancer, but he'd told me he was fine after the chemo. He'd said he was in remission. Appears he was lying—which is nothing new. Always 'fine, all fine,' you know how he is. I've been trying to reach you. Where are you?"

He inhaled deeply as he watched a father and his boys pushing bags. It made him think of Ty. Holly. Lost chances. "O'Hare. I'm going home."

"What?"

"I got on a plane, and I'm going home."

"I . . . well . . . I . . . no, this is good." She cleared her throat. "This actually works out really well, because Toddy and I can't get away right at this moment. It's a bit tricky with the ambassador position possibly coming up in Belgium. Once you're at the ranch you can let me know how Dad really is, and whether things are as serious as his manager claims, and whether I need to come."

Cole closed his eyes, pinched the bridge of his nose. He counted to ten, then said, "Who is this ranch manager, anyway, this Olivia West? Do you know anything about her?"

Another odd hesitation. "She works on the ranch as a fishing guide and general farmhand, I believe. This was the first time I've actually spoken to her." She wavered. "Listen, about Dad's will—"

"Jesus, Jane, stop. Right now."

"But you're still on board, right? To sell the ranch?"

"I don't know where they found you, do you know that? When you called me in Havana about selling, I was under the impression . . ." He swore under his breath. He couldn't even remember what Jane had really been going on about. He had zip idea what she'd gotten him to sign.

"Why *did* you call me about selling? If you thought everything was fine with Dad?"

"Because Clayton Forbes contacted me with that proposal, that's why." Her voice was sharp, defensive suddenly. "He was sounding me out on the hypothetical possibilities because—well, because I'm easier to talk to than our father is, let's face it. He was hoping I'd massage things in the right direction if I—we—were interested."

"Interested in what, exactly?"

"You're kidding me, right? You signed the document."

"I don't remember what I signed."

"You were blind drunk, probably, that's why."

"Humor me, Jane. Refresh my memory."

She muttered a curse. "Forbes wanted to get a read on our family because an incredibly exciting opportunity came up for a major real estate development. He wanted to be certain where you and I stood on selling the ranch before he entered more serious negotiations with financiers, and before he started commissioning plans, environmental impact studies, that sort of thing."

"Securing financing? Planning? For *Broken Bar*?"

"Yes. For a big high-end commercial development and private estates."

His head reeled. "Dad would *never* agree with that. Ever."

"But we agree."

"It's not ours to sell."

"Oh, spare me, Cole. Dad's ill. No one lives forever. I'm a pragmatist, that's all, and so is Clayton. He knows Dad will leave us the property. And I know you want nothing to do with the place, so what's the problem?"

Dark feelings sifted through Cole at the thought of Clayton Forbes. His nemesis at school. Forbes had always had a cunning, duplicitous, aggressive approach to life, and people.

"What did I sign?"

"A document of intent to enter into good-faith negotiations with Forbes Development Company when we inherit Broken Bar."

Shit. He pinched the bridge of his nose harder.

A call came over the intercom. His flight was boarding.

"I've got to go. I'll call you when I get there."

"Wait. There's one other thing. Clayton believes Dad's ranch manager is exerting undue influence on him in his frail state. He thinks she's gunning for her own share of the inheritance, if not all of it, and if that ever happened, she would not be willing to sell. The whole deal would fall through."

"And Forbes believes this why?" He watched the first-class passengers lining up. His ticket said *D*. Cheap seat.

"I don't know. He called me about it and suggested we do something."

"When did he call?"

"Oh, I don't know, Cole, recently."

"Like this morning? After the news that Dad will need to move into palliative care?"

"Listen, I also need to run. Kids have a school field trip. Just call me when you get there and let me know how Dad is. And check this Olivia woman out, okay? Apparently no one really knows what her background is, or where she comes from. She's young and very attractive, and Dad seems smitten." She hung up.

He blew out a chestful of air. Christ, what had he just landed himself in? Myron McDonough being smitten by a younger woman was an improbability, given the way he'd clung so bitterly to the loss of his wife. But what did Cole know—it had been thirteen years since he'd last seen his father. His mind turned instantly to the creased photograph he always carried in his wallet, to the reason he'd fallen afoul of his father's affections all those years ago, but he quickly shunted thoughts of Jimmie and his mom to the back of his mind. He didn't want to dwell there, but at the same time, he knew going back meant also having to face those memories.

As the next seating section was called up, Cole quickly turned his attention to his laptop and pulled up the Broken Bar Ranch website. He found the staff page and clicked on Olivia West's photograph and bio. Her image filled his screen.

Cowgirl. Devoid of makeup. Clear green eyes that brought to mind the colors of spruce forests and moss. Direct gaze. Vitality exuded from her features. Her hair was a warm chestnut color and fell in thick waves onto her shoulders. Full, pretty mouth. She wore a red-and-white bandana around her neck, checked button-down shirt, cowboy hat. She was attractive, in an understated, athletic way. Her blurb stated that she'd worked as a fishing guide up north. Yukon. Alaska. Northwest Territories. She'd cooked at remote logging camps and worked at a cattle ranch in northern Alberta. She'd been at Broken Bar for the past three years.

Cole dug a little deeper, following links to the camps mentioned in her bio. It all stood up on the surface, but his sister was right. He could find no online reference to this particular Olivia West prior to eight years ago. No social media links. Zip. He heard his seating section being called and closed his laptop, grabbed his bag. As he joined the queue to board, Olivia's words taunted him . . .

. . . *You're no survivor, you know that? You know dick about surviving. All you know is your own narcissistic pursuit* . . .

What did *she* know about survivors that made her so angry

with him? While he knew squat about her, she certainly knew personal things about him, and she'd judged and found him wanting. Curiosity nibbled at him.

He handed over his passport and boarding pass.

A woman with a mystery past? Exerting undue influence over his tough-ass father—the man who'd put his dead wife on a pedestal to the detriment of the rest of the family? It was unlikely.

Just as unlikely as him going home after all these years.

———

Broken Bar Ranch. Friday. Dawn.

Temperatures had dropped below freezing during the night. Down near the dock, red rose hips and dead leaves sparkled with diamonds of hoarfrost. The sun hadn't yet broken over the mountains, and mist rose in ghostly tendrils off the mirror-still lake. Trout darted in shallows beneath the untroubled surface.

Early morning gunshots cracked through the hills, echoing through the valley. Olivia huddled deeper into her down jacket, frosted grass crunching beneath her boots as she tramped out a half-mile track for Ace to follow, dropping scented articles at intervals along the way—bits and pieces of fabric, a leather glove, some wood, plastic bag ties, a hair clip . . . items she'd stashed under her sheet while she slept so that they'd absorb her scent. She was still pissed at Cole McDonough's rudeness. Arrogant, self-indulgent, narcissistic drunk. What kind of man had zero interest in his dying father?

Yet she remained selfishly relieved he wasn't coming.

Once the track was laid, Olivia circled around and back to her cabin. She stomped up the three steps onto her small porch that looked out over the misty lake. A loon quavered out on the water.

Behind the door Ace was snuffling, whining.

"Whoa, old boy," she said as he tried to nose through the door the instant she opened it a crack. "Go wait on your mat."

He dutifully obeyed, panting, watching her with milky eyes as she took out his tracking line and harness.

Crouching down near the door, harness and line in hand, she called him over. "Okay, boy, you wanna track? Huh? Come on then!"

Ace squiggled excitedly over. Her heart did a funny little squeeze as he tried to lick her face while she clipped on his tracking harness. She loved him with all her heart. He was about eight years old now—not ancient for a German shepherd by any means, but he'd had a rocky start in life, and it was showing. His teeth were ground down to nubs, and he was having some trouble with his hips. He was also going blind.

She'd found him just over three years ago along a deactivated logging road shortly after she'd released herself from hospital. The bandages around her wrists had been fresh, and she'd gone straight from the hospital to the liquor store. Her goal had been to drive out into the wilderness, get drunk, and end her life properly this time, where no good Samaritan who happened to be a paramedic could rescue her again in the nick of time.

She'd made good inroads into a bottle of vodka and shouldn't have been behind a wheel at all. But it was almost winter, the logging roads empty, and she was driving to nowhere when she'd slowed at the sight of a matted brown-and-black shape lying on the side of the road. She'd thought it was wildlife roadkill at first. But something made her stop.

With shock she'd realized it was a dog and it was alive—a bag of bones in mangy fur, unable to walk, with eyes so beseeching it had clean broken her in two. Carefully she'd felt the animal's body and had detected fractured bones. She'd carried the dirty, stinking, flea-ridden pile to her truck. Shoving the half-empty vodka bottle off the seat, she'd used her jacket to make a bed on the passenger side where she could rest her hand on the dog as she drove.

Then she'd turned her truck around and steered back toward civilization in search of a vet.

Ace had been the U-turn in her life. He'd forced her to act outside of herself, given her a simple purpose.

The vet figured the dog was about four years old but said it was hard to tell given his malnutrition. He'd been chained probably most of his life, a rope still partially embedded in flesh around his neck. That had slayed her. She knew what that felt like. And from that moment she'd known she could never let this dog down.

Ace had saved her. Ace gave her unconditional love. And she gave it back in buckets. Loving had started to mend the dead things inside her.

She'd been forced to secure a motel room in that tiny northern town where she could wait for Ace to heal enough, where the vet could follow through on treatment. It was in the town's only diner that she'd found a newspaper on the table declaring that Sebastian George—the Watt Lake Killer—had been found hanged in his cell. She'd sat stunned until the waitress asked if she was okay.

It was then that she'd decided Ace was her charm. Her guardian angel. Because in that same newspaper was Myron's employment ad, seeking a fishing guide at Broken Bar Ranch, something for which she was uniquely qualified. The job came with a cabin right on the lake. It was seasonal with an option for long-term, year-round employment if the right applicant was willing to take on additional winter responsibilities with the horses. It was the perfect place for Ace to run free.

For her to start over, yet again, this time with the knowledge *he* was gone. Dead and burned to ash in some prison crematorium.

She'd bundled Ace into her truck, driven south, and found Myron, who had looked beyond the obvious mess she must have been, and hired her. She'd discovered a measure of peace and friendship on Broken Bar. She'd found a home.

Ace, the ranch, and Myron had formed the skeleton, the backbone, from which she'd been able to flesh out a new life. Now she was losing Myron, and in all likelihood her home, too. Even Ace was fading slowly. She wondered if she'd crumple into a formless puddle without those bones to prop her up.

She led Ace out the door and down toward the lake where she'd stamped out a scent pad for the start of his track. He pulled energetically against the line.

The vet in Clinton said he'd probably go fully blind within the year. And while he was proficient in air-scenting search games, where he worked off-lead looking for human scent, with his failing sight she was worried he might run himself blindly over a cliff or into some other kind of physical danger, so she'd started him on on-line tracking, where he needed to slow down and drop his nose in order to work meticulously from footprint to footprint. Mostly this was just for fun. Their bonding time. And it jibed with a passion Olivia had always had for tracking both game and man.

She opened a large plastic ziplock bag containing a sweatshirt she'd worn earlier, and held it down for Ace to smell.

"This, Ace, find *this*."

He nosed into the bag, cataloguing the scent he was being asked to follow, then sniffed the ground looking for a match, circulating air loudly through his nasal passages. As he hit the scent pad she'd stomped out, he muscled into his harness and was off, nose low to the ground, zigzagging from footprint to footprint in the frosty grass.

She held the line and trotted behind him, her own breath crystallizing into white mist. They moved first along the lakeshore, and then up into a field where she'd laid a box track, and then a ladder track. He handled the corners on the box expertly, and Olivia watched for the negative in her dog—the moment he lost the scent at the end of the ladder track. As soon as she saw it in his body posture, she raised the tracking line high, letting him work in a wide arc until she saw from his posture that he'd picked up the scent from the top of the next ladder.

"Good boy, Ace. Good tracking," she panted as she trotted behind him.

He slowed and suddenly lay down. Between his paws at the tip of his nose was a glove, the first article she'd dropped.

"Yes! Way to go, boy!" She picked up the glove and slipped it into her sling pouch, then held her hand to the ground again. "Track, boy. Keep going."

They entered a stand of skeletal deadfall—pine trees that had been killed by the beetle blight, dry and crackling and eerie. Two huge deer, gray, startled at the sight of them and crashed through the dead brush into a swampy area.

With each article Ace alerted on, she gave hearty encouragement. They'd been going almost a quarter mile when they crested a ridge and Olivia caught sight of a second track through frosted grass.

Man track.

She slowed to study the trace. Boot prints. Big.

From the flagging of the grass, the person, probably male, had headed in the same direction she'd been going when she'd laid Ace's track. She guessed the prints to be about size twelve. Someone with a long stride. And the flagging was fresh. She lifted her gaze, following the line of the track. It perfectly paralleled her complex box and ladder track. Hairs prickled up the back of her neck.

She told herself it was coincidence.

"Let's go, Ace, keep at it," she said softly.

But as he shouldered back into the harness, a chill lingered. Something was off. Ace came to another article on his track, sniffed it, and then passed over it.

"Whoa, easy up, boy. Back up. You missed one." She restrained him as she crouched down to gather up the missed article. A scarf. Not hers.

Not her scent. It was why he hadn't alerted.

The scarf was a soft cashmere thing woven in tones of burnt orange, gold, and ochre, with stylized images of cacti and mesas. A tiny tag sewn into the seam said *Handwoven by Lulu Designs, Arizona.* The chill deepened into her bones. She glanced up.

Ace sat expectant, panting. Her attention shifted back to the boot prints paralleling her track on the left, then to the dark spruce forest into which they were headed.

The sun was still not up yet, the shadows black among the trees. She scrutinized the shadows for a sign of movement.

Nothing.

Slowly she turned in a circle, carefully cataloguing her surroundings. Above her a hawk flew. She recognized the *fwap fwap fwap* rhythm of the wings.

A duck made a panicky *frappity frappity frappity* sound. A ruffed grouse was similar. A crow's feathers produced another kind of sound against currents of air. Out on the lake a fish jumped and slapped on water. All normal.

Once more she scanned the trees. And this time she felt suddenly ice cold. There *was* something in those trees, dark, tangible, and it was watching her. She felt it in her gut.

Twelve years ago she should have trusted her gut.

She trusted it now.

"Okay, Ace," she whispered as she crouched down, removed his harness, and clipped his regular lead onto his collar. "We're done. Let's go back, boy."

He looked confused as she led him briskly up to a path that was clear of trees and from which she would be visible from the lodge windows.

As they hit the path, the sun cracked over the horizon, and color spooled in warm shades of yellow and red across the fields. Steam began to rise instantly from the grass as hoarfrost started to melt. The lake shimmered from a flat gray color into a deep turquoise green, and the ranch looked suddenly like a chocolate-box-perfect image of autumn, complete with white-barked aspen and shivering gold leaves. And from the rise, she could see boats heading out from the campground. Tension lifted from her shoulders.

Her fears suddenly seemed absurd. And as her spirits rose, Olivia's thoughts turned to the hot coffee she'd left brewing and the breakfast she'd eat before heading out on her rounds.

But as she and Ace approached their cabin, she noticed something on the mat outside the door. She climbed the stairs, taking a moment to register what it was.

A small basket of wild blueberries.

Words, unbidden, curled like smoke into her mind, his voice thick velvet over gravel. Intelligent, seductive, alluring. Dark . . .

There are some beautiful wild blueberries in a patch down at the river bend, Sarah . . . They'd make a gorgeous Thanksgiving pie . . .

Her mouth went dry. Her world narrowed. Her hands started to shake.

A crack of gunfire shot through the hills. Sweat broke out over her skin in spite of the morning chill, time spiraling back with a sickening nausea. She saw his eyes. Watching her. Pale amber like a mountain cat. Lucent like fireweed honey. Rimmed with thick, dark lashes. His smile—teeth so white and perfect. Wild black curls the color of a raven's feathers. *Sarah . . .*

No.

She braced her hands on the railing of her porch.

Stop.

No flashbacks.

You're not *a victim. Not a prisoner of the past. No memories allowed. He's dead. Gone. You're safe. Sarah has gone with him. You are Olivia. This is your haven. No one can take this from you now. No looking back . . .*

Anger fired slowly back into her veins. She scooped up the basket of berries and opened her door. Once inside, she stoked the fire in the stove to a ferocious roar. She fed Ace his breakfast and poured a stiff coffee. Taking a hot, welcoming sip, she let it scald down her throat, the sensation forcing her firmly back into the present.

Stay calm. Stay focused.

There was a simple explanation for the scarf and blueberries. Had to be. She'd find it.

Coffee consumed, Ace done with his breakfast, she grabbed the scarf and basket of berries and marched up to the lodge.

———

From the shelves of the sporting goods and logging supply store he selected rope, bolt cutters, duct tape, a fly-tying vise, forceps, packets of beaver back hair, some brightly dyed cock's hackle, grouse feathers, a roll of lime-green surveyor's tape, a packet of shiny red beads, size 1/0 and 2/0 looped eye hooks, and a spool of holographic thread. He then added to his selection a field skinning knife with a slight hump to the blade. The blade was an odd-look-ing leaf shape, but once the tip was inserted under an animal's belly hide, all one need do was rock the hand back and the skin would peel away like butter. This skinning knife would complement the all-purpose knife already in his possession in the camper. It would have made things a lot more pleasurable at Birkenhead the night before last.

On his way up he'd managed to liberate from a hunter's camp a scoped, bolt-action Remington .308, and a 12-gauge, pump-action Winchester Model 12, along with several boxes of ammunition. Guns were tightly regulated in this country—buying one without requisite documentation was out of the question. He was content with these acquisitions. The rifle had good heft, ideal for hunting deer in thick timber. He'd keep the shotgun and give the rifle to her, like the last time he'd set her out for a hunt. Yes, it would be challenging. Yes, he could lose his own life. But that made for a real hunt. A hunter should always face possible death when up against worthy prey.

The woman behind the counter was charming and flirtatious as she rang up his purchases and took his credit card. She chatted about the bad weather coming and the big buck her brother had bagged over the weekend. Eugene smiled and held her eyes. He watched her cheeks warm and her pupils dilate in response. It reminded him of the girl in the library. But there was only one woman for him now. One game left.

From the sporting goods store he made his way to a small supermarket, where he bought food. He perused the newspaper and magazine rack.

No news about the body. His message was not out yet.

He'd make the one-hour trip to Clinton to check the papers again tomorrow.

———

The housekeeper was ferrying a basket of linen up the big wooden staircase when Olivia entered the hallway.

"Adele?" she called up the stairs, "Did you leave this basket of berries outside my cabin door for me?"

Adele halted midway and frowned down at Olivia. "No, why? Is everything all right?"

Olivia hesitated, feeling suddenly self-conscious. "I . . . was just wondering. There's no note."

"Jason brought some fruit and veg boxes up from the Clinton market this morning. He has wild mushrooms, too—maybe he or Nella left them."

Relief washed through Olivia. Yes, of course it was probably Jason or Nella. She'd cracked for some reason. She was making connections that were not there.

"I'll ask them. Thanks. And if anyone comes looking for a scarf, I found this down in the field near the abandoned wrangler cabins." She held it up for Adele to see.

The housekeeper nodded and continued on her way up the stairs.

Olivia made straight for the big kitchen. Pushing open the door, she was assailed by a warm, hearthy-home feeling. Something delicious was steaming away on the gas stove. Copper and stainless steel pots hung from cedar beams above an island with a thick wood counter. Herbs frothed in clay containers along the large sunny windowsill.

Grace, Myron's deceased wife, had designed this kitchen when they'd first opened the ranch house to guests. Myron never came in here. He said her presence lingered here, even after all these years.

Olivia set the basket of berries on the wood table.

"Jason?" she called out the chef's name as she hooked the scarf around the back of her neck and peered into the pantry. It was empty. He couldn't be far, given the bubbling pots.

She went out the back door into the fenced kitchen garden. Jason Chan was not there, either. Neither was his young daughter, Nella.

As she re-entered the kitchen a muffled thud came from the walk-in cooler. The cooler door was partially open, chill air seeping out like smoke.

She stared at the door, going cold.

Another thud.

"Jason?" She called, heading toward the door even as her stomach tightened with an urge to flee. She drew the door open wider, stepped inside. A side of dead animal swung suddenly and hit her in the shoulder.

"Shit!" She jumped back, pulse jackhammering.

The half deer carcass swayed back and forth, hook creaking on the overhead rail system. Behind the side of animal hung two butchered turkeys and some other wild game. She fixated on the deer. Skinned, veined. White sinew.

Sweat broke out over her skin. In her mind she saw a woman's partially flayed body hanging by the neck from a meat hook. The woman had red hair on her head, red pubic hair. Bile rose in her throat.

"Olivia?" Jason appeared from behind the dead animal. "I was just getting this one out to butcher for the venison stew on the menu tomorrow tonight. We have a nice crowd coming for the Friday dinner."

Her gaze remained riveted on the meat hook. Blood drained from her head. She swayed, her world spiraling down into a black memory tunnel. She couldn't breathe.

She stepped backward, catching her heel and stumbling.

"Liv?" He caught her arm. "You okay?"

"I . . . I'm fine." She spun around and quickly exited the meat locker, her pulse racing.

Jason followed, consternation creasing his brow. "You look deathly pale," he said as she grasped the back of a chair to ground herself. "You sure you're all right?"

She heard geese honking—the sound coming through the kitchen door she'd left open. Suddenly in her mind it was spring. She could smell it. She could smell human blood.

No!

The geese are flocking south. It's fall. You're on Broken Bar. All is fine, dammit. Fine.

She gripped the back of the chair tightly, hanging her head down a minute, fighting to stay present. "I . . . I'm okay. Just give me a minute."

Do not let the flashbacks back in. You cannot allow them to take over again . . .

Blood flowed back into her head. She felt her cheeks warm. Slowly, she put her head upright and forced a smile. "I'm sorry about that. I must be coming down with a bug or something. Felt dizzy for a minute."

"Can I get you a glass of water? Some juice?" Concern filled his dark narrow eyes.

"No. Thanks. I just wanted to say thank you for those blueberries you left outside my door this morning."

Jason glanced at the basket of berries on the table. "I didn't leave those."

Something inside her went still.

"Maybe Nella did?" Her voice came out tight.

"I don't know." His brow furrowed deeper as he regarded her. "Is it important? I can try and find her and ask—she's probably out feeding the chickens or watching Brannigan with the horses."

"Oh, no thanks." She forced a light laugh that didn't come out so light.

"I did bring up a couple of trays from Clinton, so she might have."

"Tell her I said thanks, will you? I'll just grab a coffee and an apple for Spirit and get out of your hair."

Feeling Jason's eyes on her, she poured another big mug of coffee from the pot on the counter, snagged an apple from the bowl on the table, and made her way to the office off the guest living room.

Ace was already in the office, sleeping in his basket in a puddle of yellow sunshine. She checked e-mail for any new reservations that might have come via the website. There were none.

Apart from the late drop-ins, this was likely the end of the guests for the season.

She listened to voice mail and scanned the dining reservations book to see how many would be coming for meals over the weekend.

Before heading out, she checked the daily weather report. Surprise rippled through her. There was a big storm in the short-term forecast. Precipitation was expected in the form of snow, which could start falling by Monday afternoon. Up to two feet was predicted. It looked as though winter would be arriving early this year, right on the back of the long weekend. She'd have to warn guests. There was no plow service out here—a big dump would render the dirt roads impassable. They could be cut off for days.

Grabbing the campsite reservations book, credit card processor, and the cash pouch from the safe, she whistled for Ace and headed out the door. She helped Ace up into the cab and drove over to the stables where Brannigan, the groom, routinely chopped, bundled, and stacked wood for the campsite.

After checking on Spirit and feeding her the apple, Olivia donned her gloves, dropped the tailgate, and started tossing wood bundles into the bed of her truck. Working up a sweat, she wiped her brow with the back of her sleeve. This was good. She felt more solid already. The sun was climbing and temperatures warming fast. Whatever had assailed her earlier this morning—it was over. Done.

When she arrived at the campground she saw there were new occupants in two of the sites. The first site had a gray Ford truck parked across the entrance. Olivia left Ace in her vehicle, rounded the Ford truck, and headed down a small path to where a camper, which had been jacked off the truck, was positioned closer to the shore. Next to the camper a generator chugged away, powering a small freezer. There was no one here. She was about to go back up to the entrance and jot down the Ford's plate number when she caught sight of blood streaking down the side of the freezer. She froze.

A buzzing started in her ears.

Blackness mushroomed through her mind, swallowing her vision down to tiny pinpricks of light. And suddenly she could smell *him*. He was behind her, his hot breath whispering against her cheek, into her ear.

Gamos, *Sarah. It's a marriage . . . we are conjoined . . .*

Olivia swung around, heart jackhammering.

The lodgepole pines towered above. Branches black against the sky. The dark trees seemed to swirl around her, faster, faster, a dizzying kaleidoscope of bright and black. Branches whispered and swayed. Again she saw the purplish-white body of a redheaded woman swinging from a creaking hook.

She saw the glint of the knife.

Through the cracks of her shed, she saw *him* hacking hunks of meat from the body, putting the chunks into the freezer, blood streaking down the side.

Olivia braced her hand against the picnic table. She fought to draw a breath. But she was hyperventilating. Quickly she made her way back up to her truck. The wind gusted. Branches swayed.

Sarah . . . Ssssssarah . . .

She reached her truck, yanked open the door, and shoved Ace aside. She climbed in, slammed the door. She sat for a moment, hands shaking, sweat prickling over her skin.

Olivia. Your name is Olivia West. He's dead. You cannot allow the flashbacks back in. You cannot go back there.

Reaching forward, she fired the ignition. Gravel spewed out behind her as she hit the gas, and her truck fishtailed. She drove too fast around the lake, dust boiling behind her. When she reached the lodge, her shirt was drenched. Her hands still trembled. The taste in her mouth was sour.

It was happening again. The flashbacks. And it was going to get worse unless she found a way to stop it.

CHAPTER 5

Late Friday afternoon. Vancouver.

A knock sounded at the front door. Tori ran to open it. Sergeant Mac Yakima stood there, dressed in jeans, leather jacket.

"Hey, kiddo," he said with a warm smile. "I've come to pick up your dad for his big retirement party."

"He doesn't want to retire."

Mac stared. Stalemate. He cleared his throat. "Sure he does." He bent down. "Don't tell him, but we got him one of those Sage spey rods he's always wanted. He's been itching to dust off those tackle boxes. Fishing nirvana awaits."

"He's only fifty-six," Tori said. "People don't retire at fifty-six unless there's something wrong."

"How about you tell him I'm here?" Mac followed her inside.

"Dad!" she yelled up the hall steps. "Sergeant Mac is here."

She stomped through to sit in front of the TV, but she could see them through the arched doorway.

Emotion roiled, tightened. Tori clamped her arms tightly over her stomach. She loved her dad. But she'd loved her mother more than the entire world. It was her fault her mom had died, that she hadn't been able to pull her out of the tree well. Her eyes burned, memories rearing up inside her—her mom's legs kicking as Tori had tugged on her ski boots. More and more snow falling into the hole and landing on top of her mom each time she tried to help her move. Then the whole load of snow from the tree above had come avalanching down on top of them both. Like it was yesterday she could feel the spasming in her mother's legs, then the sudden, terrible limpness. Tori had screamed for help as more snow came down, muffling her pleas.

"You all set for the big night?" Mac slapped her dad on the back.

Tori, pretending to watch the TV, slid her gaze over to them in the hall. She could tell it was all false, that backslappery.

"What happened to your hand?" Mac said.

Her father held up his right hand. It was bandaged. Tori hadn't noticed that before. "Scraped it last night while moving a bookshelf."

She frowned. She hadn't heard her dad moving any bookshelf. Then again, she'd been locked in her room listening to music.

Her father peeked into the living room. "You sure you don't want the sitter to come over, Tori?"

"I'm almost twelve," she snapped, refusing to look at him. She glared at the television instead. But she knew why her father was asking—he was worried about her state of mind after that thing at school.

"Not sure what time I'll be back, kiddo. Don't stay up, okay?"

She didn't reply.

As they exited the front door she heard her father say, "I can still drive myself, you know."

A hearty laugh came from Mac. "Not after we're done with you tonight, you won't." The door banged shut. She heard their footsteps crunching past the window, saw the tops of their heads.

Tori got up, went to the window.

She watched them climb into Mac's car, back out of the driveway, and pull away. When she was certain they were gone, she hurried upstairs to her father's office. The door didn't have a lock. She pushed it open, her pulse quickening as she made for the filing cabinet where she'd seen her dad stuff that concertina file with newspaper cuttings and crime scene photos. He'd tried to hide them from her, but one had fallen to the floor. A black-and-white photo of a woman's naked body. She yanked at the drawer of his file cabinet. It was locked. She scrabbled in her father's desk drawers. No key anywhere.

She stood there, thinking. Her father had changed. Everything had changed since Mom died. He was hiding all sorts of things, growing weird and short-tempered and increasingly distant. It made her mad. It made her feel like he was forgetting Mom. Forgetting her. Forgetting the family they once were. A recklessness fueled by hurt fired through her.

She booted up his computer, then froze as she heard tires crackling on the wet street outside. But the vehicle went past their driveway.

His computer was password protected, and nothing she entered into the box worked. She shut the computer down, turned in the swivel chair, thinking again. She got up and made quickly for the adjoining room that had served as her mother's study.

Opening the door cautiously, she stepped inside.

It was cold, the heat turned off.

She could still scent her mother's perfume in here. Her lotion. There were books everywhere. Her laptop sat on a small desk with trinkets she'd collected over the years. A bay window let in lots of light despite the stormy sky outside. A reading bench covered with cushions in a pink-and-green cabbage rose pattern ran the length of the window.

The room was pretty. Soft and gentle, spiked with accents of livid fuchsia, which underlined the playfulness in her mother and reminded Tori of the sparkle in her eyes. The slight smile that had so often played across her mouth.

Her mother was—had been—a successful novelist. And it was in this gentle, calming place that she wrote some very dark books of fiction, mysteries and thrillers that reviewers said were ripped from the headlines and usually based on true crimes. The stories had actual sex in them. Violence. She hadn't been allowed to read them, but she'd found them in the public library, and online, and read them anyway.

Tori's English teacher had told her she'd inherited her mother's talent for writing. Others told her she looked like her mom, and that she was so like her mom in so many other ways. She'd informed everyone she, too, would be a writer some day. Her eyes burned as she touched her mother's things. She picked up a framed photo of the three of them. The three musketeers, her dad used to call them. Tori's mind drifted to the pastor's words in church, at the funeral, how he spoke about her mother being in a *better* place. With God.

What kind of God did this? Stole away the people you loved most? Why should it be a *better* place?

Heartsore, Tori replaced the photo and curled up on the window bench where her mother used to read to her. Clutching a small pillow tightly to her chest, she watched the rain outside. The sky was heavy and battleship gray. She couldn't see the mountains on the other side of the water. Foghorns sounded repeatedly.

Curling tighter around the soft pillow, she drifted into sleep, bad dreams haunting her. She woke with the start of a scream. Her heart raced. It was getting dark out. Shivering, she got off the bench to lift the lid and find the soft afghan her mother had knitted.

Inside the bench box, lying atop the neatly folded afghan, were the printed pages of a manuscript secured with a rubber band. Tori clicked on the lamp and lifted out the manuscript. She read the title page.

The Pledge
By Melody Vanderbilt

Tori's breath caught. She hadn't opened this bench since the accident—she'd never seen this manuscript. Tentatively, she touched the words, black ink on white. More eternal than flesh. Words her mother had put on paper. Words that had outlived her. And Tori's chest felt as though it would burst in pain. Her mom once told her that words were like magic, like ancient runes, symbols, that, if you knew how to unlock and decode them, conjured stories—people and pictures in your mind.

Is this what you were working on when you left us, Mom?

A tear plopped onto the page. It left a gray mark and startled her—she hadn't even felt it coming. She slipped the rubber band off the manuscript and lifted the title page. The dedication page lay underneath.

For my dear Tori, a story for the day you are ready. I will always love you, more than you will ever know . . .

Tori's heart banged as she read the words. Almost subconsciously she closed the bench box and climbed back on top. Wrapping the afghan around her shoulders, she began to read:

Prologue

It started, as all dialogues do, when a path crosses that of another. Whether in silence, or greeting, a glance, a touch, you are changed, irrevocably, by an interaction. Some exchanges are as subtle as the touch of an iridescent damselfly alighting on the back of your hand. Some are seismic, rocking your world, fissuring into your very foundations and setting you on a new path. That moment came for Sarah when he first entered the store.

The bell chimed, and in came a cool gust of air. Sensing something unusual had entered, she glanced up.

From across the store his eyes locked onto her face—the kind of full-on stare that made her stomach jump. Ordinarily she'd smile, offer a greeting, but this time she instinctively averted her gaze and continued with her bookkeeping. Yet she could sense his gaze on her, rude, brazen, probing as he approached the counter where she worked.

"Morning."

She was forced to look up into eerily pale amber eyes. They brought to mind a mountain lion. A wild predator.

He smiled. It was bewitching. It twisted something low and hot in her belly. His hair was black as ink, unkempt. Not unpleasantly so. He reminded her a bit of that actor, Rufus Sewell. Same kind of curls. Similar intensity. He was tall. Sun-browned. High cheekbones. Beautiful fingers, strong hands.

She helped him choose beads—silver, red—thread, hair, feathers, hooks. As she rang up his purchases, he allowed his hand to touch hers.

And in that secret moment she was a little thrilled that Ethan wasn't in the store with her that afternoon. You know those moments? You mean nothing by them. You will never cheat. But they fire a spark in you. They make the world feel wonderful. They make you feel like a vital, sexual being. Basically, they make you feel alive.

In retrospect, she believed that was the moment he first selected her. Culled her from a pack. Like a wolf singled its target out from a herd.

He took his time. He played with her. He returned twice each week from the end of the summer into the chill of fall. Nearly always on those afternoons when Ethan was away. She liked to imagine he watched for those opportunities.

Little did she know. For he did watch. He planned. Everything.

Then, when Thanksgiving was almost upon them, he told her how the steelhead were running up the Stina River.

She tied him a fly, using a pattern she'd designed, one that had given her untold luck with those silvery fish, those fighting steelhead. She was anxious for his return.

"Does it have a name?" he said, when she gave it to him.

"The Predator." She smiled. A little embarrassed.

His eyes turned dark, and her heart beat faster. His voice dipped low. "It's a fine name."

He regarded her for several heavy, silent beats. She felt an atavistic pull, the hairs on her arms rising toward him, as if in electrical attraction. He leaned closer and her mouth turned dry. And he told her about the wild blueberries. Down by the bend in the river.

She took the lure.

She went in search of the berries.

She never came home.

Tori's pulse raced as she quickly lifted the page and laid it upside down on the bench beside her. She started reading the next page.

Olivia opened the gate to the chicken coop and stepped inside. The birds cluttered and clucked around her boots. Ace lay outside the fence, head between his paws, watching intently as she poured feed into the trays. The sun would be setting soon. The wind had shifted, and colors were warm in the low-angled light. But inside she felt cold. It was as if the inky poison of the past had seeped in through cracks that had opened in her mental armor, and now she was going to have a devil of a time ridding herself of it all again.

As she emptied the last of the feed and exited the coop, her phone buzzed at her hip. She extracted it from its sheath, didn't recognize the caller ID. "Olivia," she said as she latched the gate closed.

"The east field still functional as an airstrip?" It was a male voice against a noisy backdrop of an engine or something. She stalled, hand on gate.

"Excuse me?"

"Can you still land a plane on the east field?" he yelled over the noise.

"Who *is* this?"

"Hey, you're the one who called me. It's Cole McDonough."

Shock slashed through her. "You're *coming*? When?"

"ETA two minutes, if you can give me an all-clear on that field."

East field? She looked up as she suddenly heard a distant drone—the buzz of a small plane. "You're coming by air?"

"How's that field?"

Shit. "I don't know. I mean . . . what do you need to land?"

"There used to be a dirt track running east-west on the back field behind the stables, up by the old barn. I'll circle in the air, take a look-see from above. But if you could take a run out there and clear out any cattle, then raise your arms and give me an all clear—"

"No livestock. Not anymore."

But the call had cut out.

The buzz grew louder. She shaded her eyes. A tiny sparkle appeared on the distant horizon, reflecting the setting sunlight. Her heart kicked.

"Ace! Hop! Quick!" She helped him up into the front seat, jumped into the truck, fired the ignition. She barreled down the rutted road, dirt roiling out behind her, stones spitting out in her wake. She slowed, barely, to rumble over a cattle grid, after which she swung a sharp right up onto an old dirt track that climbed a rise to the east field. She popped out onto a plateau of land.

Olivia hit the brakes, and stared out over the golden field, grasses bending softly in the breeze. She had no idea whether one could land a plane on this. Depended on the craft. And the only planes that did fly into this area tended to land with pontoons on a lake.

She wound down her window, heard the increasing hum of an engine. She shielded her eyes again.

A tiny yellow single-prop plane grew out of the horizon. Tension skittered through her. She exited her truck, went out into full view.

———

Vancouver. Friday. Almost sunset.

Gage's retirement party was at the yacht club, the same club where he, Melody, and Tori used to keep their kayaks. Correction. The kayaks were still stored here, all three of them. A family unit. Waiting for a summer that was never going to come again. Hard to believe she'd been gone six months already. As he entered the club Gage felt the loss as raw as if it were yesterday.

The place was packed with law enforcement and support personnel, most from homicide. Floor-to-ceiling windows ran the length of the room and looked out over the yachts in the marina and into the misty inlet beyond. Lights glowed in halos from the tankers that lurked in the Burrard. Behind those mists, on the other side of the inlet, rose the mountains where Melody had died. On a clear day he could see that mountain from their house. He saw those mountains from nearly everywhere he went on the mainland.

Someone had hired a music duo with a fiddle and flute. Irish tunes. Again, he was reminded viscerally of Melody, their love, their honeymoon in Ireland.

Drinks flowed liberally. There was much laughter and chatter and speeches and backslapping. But Gage felt weirdly detached. It was now just over forty-eight hours since he'd hooked a response with his adoption Internet lure, and he'd heard nothing more since. It was winding him wire tight, messing with his head. If the Watt Lake Killer was out there, if it was he who'd taken the bait, he now had information on how to find Olivia West.

Would he act on it?

How soon?

Where was he now? How far away? He glanced at his watch, worried also about Tori. That incident at school, the dark violence he'd glimpsed in his kid, had rocked him hard. Perhaps it had been a mistake to leave her home alone tonight. There was no goddamn manual for this shit.

Where are you, Melody? Are you looking down, watching me going through this charade? Help me with Tori . . .

The afternoon leaned into evening. Beer. Food. Music and voices growing louder. Garish smiling faces that seemed to leer in and out of his consciousness. People congratulating him. On fucking what? Being forced out early? Losing his mental faculties to a point he'd become a problem on the job? How much did any one of these people here really know about his reasons for retiring?

They presented him with a handcrafted spey rod. He'd always wanted to work on his spey casting. It was part of what he and Melody had been planning to do—load up the camper, tour the continent when Tori went to university. Fucking bucket list. He plastered a smile onto his face. Cracked jokes.

Deputy Commissioner Hank Gonzales got up and clinked his glass with a spoon. Silence fell in the room. Outside the foghorns continued their plaintive moans into the mists. Rain beat against the windows, wind rattling halyards against masts outside and straining the yachts against their moorings.

"I have had the pleasure, the honor, of knowing Gage Burton since our first days of training at Depot Division."

Gage's neck muscles tightened. Bastard was going to use this occasion to parallel their careers, and who wouldn't fail to notice that while they'd trained together as rookies, Gonzales had become head honcho boss of E Division while he was still working as a homicide detective.

"Burton and I crossed career paths again when he was serving as staff sergeant at Watt Lake and I was on a task force to hunt down the Watt Lake Killer, as the media dubbed him back then."

Laughs. People actually laughed.

Blood pounded in Gage's head. His hand tightened around his beer mug. Mac Yakima placed his hand on his forearm. Gage shot him a glance.

"Cheers," Mac whispered, holding up his glass. "Drink up. It will drown him out."

"Fuck him," Gage muttered under his breath.

"Water under the bridge, okay? Let it be."

Gage nodded, but everything inside him resisted.

Mac was one of the few cops who knew just how much Gage's head-butting with Gonzales over the Watt Lake investigation had cost him in career terms.

"And now—" Gonzales raised his glass. "Here we are, back full circle, Burton and I in the same detachment." He smiled. "It's been a good run. And here's to some big-ass steelhead on that new rod, Burton."

Someone banged an empty mug on a table. "Speech, speech!" Fists joined in the banging.

But as Gage pushed himself to his feet, several cell phones in the room began to ring simultaneously. His gaze darted around the crowd as members began answering their phones. All IHit guys.

And there was only one reason the Integrated Homicide Investigation Team was called into action. Suspicious death.

Someone leaned over and tapped Commissioner Gonzales on the shoulder. He bent his head, listening. Commish Gonzales then glanced up at Gage.

"Hey," Gage said, raising both his hands. "No worries. I've never been big on speeches." He forced a smile.

Several members started leaving. Others came up to Gage to bid him farewell before they left. *Good luck, good to see you. Have a good life.* They shook his hands, slapped his shoulder. But while they smiled he read something different in their eyes. They felt sorry for him. They were glad it wasn't them. They were excited about this new call.

Mac came up to his side. "Gage, buddy, I'm sorry. Got to go. We'll catch up later?"

"What was the call, Mac?"

Mac hesitated.

"Oh, for Chrissakes, I'm not even out the goddamn door yet."

A strange look crossed Mac's features, and a chill sense of foreboding sank into Gage's bones. He clamped his hand firmly on his mate's arm.

"Tell me," he said.

Mac swallowed, his gaze flicking around the crowd as if to see who might be watching him spill. "A body, female. Middle-aged. Found in Mount Currie, along the Birkenhead River."

Mount Currie was native land—a route that led into the interior. To where Broken Bar Ranch was located. The Watt Lake Killer had aboriginal ties—his hunts, his kills, had all been on native land.

A buzz began in his ears.

His desperation must have showed because compassion softened Mac's black eyes. "Come, I'll walk you out. I'll get Martinello to drive you home."

They exited the door. Rain was coming down like a bead curtain. "How was the body displayed?" Gage asked.

Mac's features tightened. He hesitated again.

"Jesus, Mac," Gage said. "A morsel on my retirement, please?"

Mac rubbed his brow. "Vic was found hanging from a tree by her neck. Been disemboweled, partially flayed."

Gage's heart went *whump whump whump*.

"Come, let's get out of the rain—there's Martinello pulling up." Mac raised his hand to summon Martinello closer.

"Hung by the neck? How? A hook?"

Mac leaned down as constable Jan Martinello lowered her cruiser window.

"Can you give Burton a ride home?"

"Who found her?" Gage demanded.

Mac opened the passenger door for Gage. "Two kids."

Perspiration prickled over Gage's skin, mixing with rain. "Any ID on the vic?"

"That's all I've got at this point." Mac waited for Gage to get into the car.

"It's him," he said. "It's his signature. The hook. The flayed skin. The gutting."

"Sebastian George is dead, Gage."

Silence shimmered, thick, hot. Rain came down harder.

"What if we had the wrong guy—or what if he had a partner?"

"This could be anything. A copycat. Another hunter." Mac gave him a patronizing and pitying look, the kind of look people gave an Alzheimer's patient, or a kid not old enough to understand. "Go home, Gage. Get some sleep. Go on your fishing trip with Tori. She needs you now. You have a kid to think about."

Yeah. I do. I have Tori to think about. I'm thinking about her right now. I want to get this bastard so I can leave a safer world for her . . .

"Sergeant Burton?" It was Martinello calling out from the driver's seat. "You getting in?"

Gage gritted his jaw, climbed into the passenger seat, slammed the door shut.

"I've been tasked with the pleasure of driving you home," Martinello said as she pulled out of the parking lot.

She was young. Typical cop. Hair pulled back into a tight ponytail. Clean complexion. Very little makeup. He felt resentful of her age, her potential, the smugness that came with youth.

"You okay, sir?"

"Yeah. Can you go any faster? Take a left here, quicker route." He tapped his knee with his hand.

"You sure you're okay, sir?"

"I need to get home."

Martinello shot him a hot glance.

It was *him*. He was back—Gage knew it. That murder—it *had* to be him. He'd been lying low somewhere for years, maybe even incarcerated for another crime, but he was back. The game was on. Gage could feel it. He had to finish this. The clock was ticking.

————

Friday evening. Sunset. Broken Bar Ranch.

Cole banked his small two-seater Piper PA-18 Super Cub over endless, rolling forest, much of it red-brown and dead from the pine beetle blight. In clear-cuts the skeletons of decimated pines had been stacked in pyres, waiting to be burned as soon as the weather turned wet. Through the valleys silvery streams and rivers meandered. A bear startled and galloped for cover as the plane buzzed overhead.

Cole crested a high esker ridge formed by ancient glaciers, and the ranch came suddenly into view. He caught his breath at the sight of the startling aqua-blue, crystal-clear waters and white marl shoals of Broken Bar Lake. Mist rose from the churning river at the outflow, water tumbling down into a narrow rocky canyon. Cole tensed—a muscle memory. That river held dark memories. It had changed everything.

He banked again, following the smooth, curved mounds of glacial ridges that were gold with grass. Wisps of smoke rose from campfires among the trees at the west end of the lake. A few boats and float tubes dotted the waters. Fresh skiffs of snow covered the Marble range. He was overcome with a sense of timelessness. He'd forgotten just how clean, beautiful, unspoiled this wilderness around the ranch was.

He saw the old lodge house with its big chimney, the small cabins nested among alders and aspen, the barn where he used to tinker with engines, where he'd rebuilt his vintage truck. The old wrangler quarters were covered in vines, the roofs caving in, the grass around them grown tall. Something caught in his chest.

Home.

It had been a long time. In more ways than one. Cole wondered if sometimes you traveled so far away from home that it wasn't possible to find your way back. If he had to pinpoint it, this place had ceased being a real home since the day of the accident. Since his father rejected him.

A dark tightness filled his chest.

He'd returned to BC often enough during the past decade. He and Holly had bought a house in Pemberton. They'd rented the house while traveling the world in search of his stories, staying in the suite whenever they were back. But they hadn't come up to Broken Bar. He'd never brought Ty and Holly here. Cole had felt no need to see his father, not since their truly epic bust-up thirteen years ago.

He started the descent. He didn't have to stay long. He'd check on his father, help organize the palliative care, if that's what was needed, make any decisions required for the continued functioning of the ranch until Jane organized the sale. Then he was out of here. Duty done.

Coming in for the landing, it struck him—the fields were devoid of livestock. Not a cow to be seen anywhere on the ranch. He saw a rust-red truck parked on the east field. A woman stood beside it, hair blowing in the wind. Olivia. She raised a hand up high, giving him the all clear.

He brought his craft in.

CHAPTER 6

Olivia tensed as she held her hair back off her face—the wings of the little yellow single-prop plane were seesawing in high crosswinds, and it was coming toward the ground at a startling angle.

Fat tires smacked the dirt road with an explosion of soft glacial dirt. The bush plane bumbled along the track, a cone of silt roiling out behind it. She blinked into the blowing grit as the craft came to an abrupt halt. The cloud of dust overtook and enveloped the plane. The prop slowed then stopped.

Anxiety twisted through her.

The cockpit side flap dropped open.

A man, tall, climbed out. He raised his hand in greeting, then reached behind the pilot seat. He hefted out a military-style duffel bag. Closing the door flap, he ducked out from under the wings and slung his gear up onto a broad shoulder.

With a long easy stride, a smooth roll of the shoulders, he closed the distance to where Olivia waited alongside her truck. He was dressed in a dark-brown leather jacket that looked worn. Vintage. WWII bomber style with a sheepskin ruff and lining. His jeans were faded in places that screamed masculinity. His boots were scuffed.

He brought to mind paramilitary figures. A guy with authority, one who exuded a command presence.

Not surprising. This was a man who wrote about alpha men. Extreme risk takers. Conquerors of the world's tallest peaks and remotest poles. He walked the walk, climbed the mountains, flew the skies. Yet in spite of his apparent machismo, his written words bespoke a sensitive view of the world. A beautiful mind.

Ace barked from inside the truck as he neared.

Her pulse quickened, little moth wings of nerves fluttering in her stomach. She wiped her hands on her jeans, thinking of all the negative emotions she'd directed toward him, his rudeness on the phone. Up close, in the flesh, he was even more formidable, more vital than anything in those photographs. A chiseled, tanned echo of his dying father. A mountain of a man.

"You must be Olivia." He reached forward to shake her hand. "Cole McDonough."

Her spine stiffened instinctively as she held out her hand. His grip was unapologetically firm. Calloused palms. Warm hands. As his gaze met hers, a sharp crackle of electricity shot through her body. His eyes were deep-set under a prominent brow and fringed by heavy lashes. And they were intense. Moody like a thundercloud. His chin was strong, darkly shadowed with stubble, his brown hair tousled. Everything about this man radiated a kind of feral aggression and power, yet there was fatigue in the craggy lines that fanned out from his eyes and bracketed his mouth. His deeply sun-browned skin seemed to belie a paleness, a quiet exhaustion beneath.

She cleared her throat. "Pleased to meet you," she lied, firming her own grip, asserting her space, her place on this ranch. "And this is Ace," she said of her dog, who was now sticking his head out the window and lolling his tongue out in anticipation of a greeting.

Cole held on to her hand a fraction longer. "How's my father?"

She glimpsed real concern in his eyes. It threw her slightly. It messed with her prejudiced animosity toward him.

"In a great deal of pain," she said quietly. "But he's stoic about it. You know he can be . . ." She paused. "Then again, maybe you don't."

His features darkened. He released her hand. "And I presume you do. After all, you've lived here what? A whole three years?"

She felt something tighten reflexively inside her.

"Thanks for coming out to meet me," he said, scanning the surroundings. "Would you mind giving me a ride to the house?" His voice was low toned, velvet over gravel. Her stomach tightened. A voice like that had cost her everything.

She glanced at the plane, and it struck her, given the ease with which he'd just landed, and those little fat-ass tundra tires: Cole McDonough could have brought this thing down just about anywhere on the ranch. "You didn't need me to scope out the landing at all, did you? You just called me because you wanted a chauffeur."

His lips curved slightly. Irritation sparked in her, and she latched fast onto it. It was a safety mechanism. It was easier to put up walls than deal with her very primal gut reaction to this man.

"Admittedly it would have been a bit of a walk—I can't bring this puppy down much closer to the lodge because of the hydro wires and phone lines. More so, I was worried about livestock."

"We no longer run cattle," she said, words clipped. "Just a few horses and chickens left. Since Myron took ill last spring the place has gone downhill. Guests no longer stay in the lodge house. Only the cabins and the campsites open during season. Staff has been cut down to core."

His brows rose slightly in interest.

She glanced at the plane again.

"It'll be fine there. I'll sort it out later."

"Fine." She yanked open the driver's door of her truck and scooted Ace into the middle of the seat. "As long as you don't mind my stopping by the campsite first—I have some guests who need to be checked in. I missed seeing them this morning."

"I'd rather go straight to the house."

She stilled, hand on the door. "After thirteen years you can't wait a half hour?" She couldn't help it. The words just came out. He'd made her jump to his bidding. He was here to stick Myron into a hospice, carve up and sell this ranch. Make her find a new home. And she was drawing her own line in the sand.

He regarded her, a silent energy coming from him in waves. He dipped his gaze, taking her in, head to boot. Absorbing her. She shifted uncomfortably, aware suddenly of her hidden scars, her latent shortcomings. Her shame. Her need for distance from people.

"Olivia," he said quietly, his voice deep, resonant. It curled through her like seductive smoke, and she hated him for it. It scared her. Her reaction to him. Everything about this guy. He took up too much space—too much of *her* space.

"I don't know who you really are," he said quietly, "or what your exact role is on this ranch, or what your relationship is to my father, or why you have clearly prejudged and taken a disliking to me, but *you* were the one who phoned *me*, remember? When you told me that my father was dying, there was a very real sense of urgency. I went directly from the bar to the airport, and I slept on a plastic seat until they could get me on a plane. Then I flew to Vancouver, drove up to Pemberton, got my plane, and flew directly here. I've been in transit for almost twenty-four hours. I'm beat. And you might have noticed I could do with a shower. But I'll concede." He hefted his duffel into the back of her truck. It landed with a soft thud on top of the wood she had piled in there.

"Come. Let's go do your chores first." He went round to the passenger side and opened the door, got in.

She opened her mouth in shock, leaned into the cab. Ace was trying to lick his face. "What do you mean about my relationship with your father?"

"My sister said you and he might be involved."

"*What?* Is that what you really think, that I'm in some kind of relationship with your *father*?"

"Get in, Olivia. I'm tired."

"Jesus," she muttered as she climbed in, slammed the door, and fired the ignition. "I'm taking you back to the lodge first."

"I'd rather you got your cash from the guests."

"Forget it. I'd rather offload you." She rammed the vehicle into gear and hit the gas, spitting up dirt. They bombed down the hill, grass ticking against the undercarriage, her hands tightly gripping the wheel. "Maybe if you'd come home in the last thirteen years you'd know your father better, and you wouldn't make such goddamn offensive insinuations. Because you would *know* he'd never look at anyone other than your mother."

"Right. I forgot. My mother who's been dead twenty-three years. He holds so tightly to that bitterness he can't let anyone else in. Not even his kids." He closed his eyes, leaned his head back against the headrest. "Glad to hear you've gotten through his bitter crust."

She shot him a look, dumbfounded.

"I don't owe you any explanations," she snapped. "I don't owe you a thing." She spun the wheel sharply and barreled too fast over the cattle grid. The vehicle juddered like a machine gun, forcing him to sit upright and curse.

Cole stole a quick glance at her profile. She was prickly all right, but also easy on the eyes. Pretty, full mouth set in a tight line. Thick hair that fell to her shoulders. Like her photo on the ranch website, she was dressed cowgirl-style in worn jeans, button-down flannel shirt over a white T-shirt, boots that had seen the business end of a barn. He'd noticed right away how her ass fitted into those jeans, her slim, long legs. What red-blooded male wouldn't notice? She was lean and fit looking with a soft tan that offset her haunting green eyes.

The color of her eyes made him think of the *National Geographic* photos Holly had shot of a young Bedouin woman. His mind darkened as he was reminded of Holly's photojournalism. His own work. The Sudan. The politics.

Holly's son. His little family. Lost to him.

Nausea and the thought of a drink washed through him.

She swung the truck onto the main road that led to the lodge, dislodging Ace, who slid along the seat into him. Cole put his arm around the German shepherd, holding the dog steady as they juddered over another grid. "It's okay, big guy. I've got you." He scratched behind the dog's ears.

Olivia shot him a withering look.

She had a mother of a hunting knife secured at her hip, along with a holster of bear spray and a phone on her belt. His guess was this was a capable woman. No wedding band. No jewelry at all. Her words on the phone came to mind.

Wherever you're wallowing in your own self-pity, drinking yourself into a stupor every night is not going to bring your family back to you. You're no survivor, you know that?

Resentment and curiosity curdled through him. She knew things about him. She knew about Holly and Ty. About his time spent "wallowing" in Havana bars. Things that could only have come from his father. Which meant those two *were* close. At least on some level. He could see a confident, capable, and yes—very sexually attractive—woman like this managing to appeal to the old man's aging ego. Or could he? She was right in that his father had always put his mother on a pedestal. Then again Cole hadn't been home to see his father in a long while. Things could have changed.

He was too tired to dig at it all right now. He needed sleep. Food. A hot shower. And he needed to get his first meeting with his father over and done.

He wound down the window and let the cool wind wash over

his face as he turned to look out at the rolling fields. Empty fields. Dotted with stands of ghostly white-barked aspens, gold leaves blowing free from the branches in the wind. Fences sagged in disrepair. The old wrangler cabins listed with sunken-in roofs. Swallows darted in a cloud out from the rotting eaves.

She was right. This place had fallen into a state of sad dilapidation. No one had told him it was this bad. But why should he expect different?

They neared the lodge house. It too looked like it could use some love—a power wash, a fresh coat of paint on the shutters. Cole tensed as she pulled up in front of the big porch. She hit the brakes hard, jerking him forward.

"There," she said coolly. "Looks like you made it home in time for supper." She waited for him to get out, engine running, her hands fisting the wheel.

He suddenly noticed the scars on the insides of her wrists. They were puckered and ran lengthways up into her sleeves. Scars that meant business.

She flinched as she saw him notice, then looked away, out the window.

He swallowed, off-kilter suddenly. Tension inside the cab was thick. He opened his door, got out, and reached into the truck bed for his gear.

"Where are you going?" he said, leaning back into the door. "You don't take dinner at the lodge?"

"Not tonight. I'm going to park my truck and then go to my cabin." She refused to face him.

He closed the passenger door. She pulled off, leaving him in a cloud of dust.

Curiosity rustled through him as he watched her go.

Cole slung his duffel over his shoulder, and turned to take in the lodge. A carved bear statue still stood guard at the base of the stairs. The old swing seat was still on the porch, but with fresh cushions. A cocktail of memories churned through him. He was in the last year of his thirties, yet he still felt a twinge of boyhood trepidation at walking into that childhood home. Facing his father.

Odd how life played those tricks on a grown man. He'd lived a rich life so far, had his own family for a while. Lost them. But the boy always lurked inside the man. And with that thought came the weight of exhaustion, failure. As if the past decades of his life had meant nothing.

He jogged up the porch steps and entered the hall, stepping back in time. The big rack of antlers was still being used to hang coats. The stuffed moose head, an animal his grandfather had taken down in the Sumas swamp, still peered down from the archway that led into the living area. A fire crackled in the living room hearth, and he could smell polish on the stone floor tiles.

"Cole McDonough! My good Lord!"

He swung around at the sound of a voice from his childhood. "Mrs. Carrick," he said with a smile. "You're still here. And you haven't changed a day."

"Of course I'm still here. And I'm Adele to you now, young lad," she said with a smile, clutching a basket of folded laundry against her chest. "Why, *look* at you." She came forward, as if she might set the basket down and give him a hug, but she restrained herself. Mrs. Carrick wasn't a hugger—never had been.

"I . . . had no idea you were coming. Does your father know?"

"Not yet. Where is he?"

She looked a little flustered. "He took a late nap today. He wasn't feeling well. I was about to go wake him for supper."

"Let me do that."

"Uh . . . perhaps you should wait until he's dressed and comes down. I imagine he'd like to be in fighting form when he sees you."

"I imagine he would."

Her face reddened suddenly. "I mean—"

Cole smiled. "He still in the same room?"

"Yes, the one at the end of the hall on the third floor."

He took the stairs, two at a time.

———

Tori turned over another page, filled with a voyeuristic salaciousness, her heart beating faster as she read more of her mother's work.

In the early days of that winter she sometimes heard choppers thudding behind the low cloud. That was the most devastating, hearing them searching for her, knowing her family and friends were worried.

She knew there would be search dogs, too. Big groups of volunteers on ground teams. She wondered if they'd found her fallen basket of berries, seen signs of her scuffle when he'd put the sack over her head. She doubted it. She'd told no one where she'd been headed that afternoon. And a snowstorm had blown in that night. The snow hadn't let up for days afterward. Any whisper of a trace would've been buried deep under that first thick, smooth blanket of the season.

Then one day came silence—they'd stopped looking. It was her new reality. Deadening winter silence. Darkness. If she'd thought that hearing them search was the worst, it wasn't. It was this. They'd given up on her. And aloneness was suddenly suffocating.

A light died inside her during those first days of silence. She went numb to his abuse, to the things she glimpsed through the cracks in the chinking of the shed where she was chained and roped to the wall. She knew she wasn't the first he'd kept in there, on that pile of stinking bearskins and burlap sacks. There'd been at least one other. She'd seen her gutted body hanging on the hook outside the neighboring shed. The body had red hair. He took it down after a freeze, and she heard chopping and thudding and, once, the sound of a saw. She wondered if the body on the hook was the redheaded forestry worker who'd gone missing last fall.

She wondered if there would be another woman taken next fall. If he'd kill her before that, and hang her on that hook, too.

As the daylight grew shorter, she tried to figure out whether it was Christmas yet. She tried to imagine how Ethan was handling things, how her mother and father, her friends were doing. Did they go into the store and speak about her in soft, sorrowful tones?

Occasionally over the months she heard a small bush plane up high. She'd listen and scream inside her heart for help, pray for some miracle.

And then something did happen.

She became certain that she was carrying a child. Ethan and she had been trying for almost a year to get pregnant, and she'd undergone fertility treatments. Before she was taken she'd skipped a period. She'd felt changes in her body. She'd made a doctor's appointment to have it confirmed. An appointment she'd been forced to miss. But now she had proof. Her belly was rounding, going hard. Her breasts were swelling, becoming tender, her nipples darkening. This dawning realization changed everything. She had part of Ethan with her.

She was no longer alone.

She had a beating little heart inside her belly. A baby—their baby. And by God she was going to live. She would do whatever it took in the Lord's or the devil's name to survive now. She would kill that bastard. She would be a master of restraint while he fucked and hurt her—because when she fought him and screamed, he got off on it, and just hurt her more. She would wait for exactly the right moment.

She would not end up on that meat hook . . .

Tori lifted the manuscript page and placed it upside down on the growing stack of others already read. Rain ticked against the windowpane. Wind gusted.

She knew it wouldn't be long before he noticed her belly growing. She needed a plan for that . . .

So engrossed was Tori, so ensnared by her mother's fictional world, that she didn't register fully the sound of a vehicle entering the driveway. The front door downstairs banged, and her father's boots clattered up the stairs.

She froze.

"Tori!" Her dad's voice boomed down the hallway. "Where are you?"

She quickly scrambled to gather up the pages. They fluttered to the floor.

The door to her mother's office swung open and her father loomed in the doorway. A range of emotions raced across his face as his gaze dropped to the manuscript in her hands, the loose pages on the carpet.

"What the—" He strode in.

Tori shrank back on the bench, hiding the rest of the manuscript with her body. His face reddened. His eyes turned bright. He didn't look right. His neck muscles corded, and his hands fisted like hams. Suddenly, for the first time in her entire life, she felt afraid of her dad.

"What in the hell do you think you're doing in here!" He snatched a handful of pages off the floor, glared at them.

"I miss her," she snapped. "I wanted to be with her things!"

"What *is* this?" He lunged for the rest of the manuscript behind her.

She yanked it out of his reach. "No!"

He swung up his hand. His face was twisted, dark red. His eyes gleamed with moisture.

She cringed back against the window. "Please . . . don't hit me, Dad!"

It was as if her words pulled a plug out of him. His mouth opened, and his features went slack. He lowered his hand slowly and stared at her in silence for several beats, as if refocusing. Then, deflated, he sank onto the bench beside her. He bent forward, scrubbed his hands hard over his face.

"Jesus . . . I'm so sorry, Tori. Please, just give me that manuscript. You have no right to be in here, in her office."

But Tori scooted farther back, pressing herself between the corner of the wall and the bay window. She curled herself into a ball over the pages. "It's mine," she said. "Mom dedicated it to me. It says so right on the front page. 'For my dear Tori, a story for the day you are ready. I . . . I . . .'" She choked on the next words. "'I will always love you.'"

Surprise chased over his face. Then worry entered his eyes, and his features steeled with fresh determination. "She meant it, Tori. *One day*—not yet, not now."

"*Why?*" she screamed. "Why not *now?*"

He reached for the pages again. She jerked them away as his hand closed on the corner of the dedication page. It tore. A jagged line right through their hearts. They stared at each other in pulsing, electric, palpating silence. This tangible metaphor of their lives ripped in their hands, their little nuclear family, rent apart by the two people who loved Melody the most.

Her dad swallowed.

"I *hate* you!"

"Tori," he said quietly, darkly. "This was something that your mother was working on. It's not ready yet. She was going to finish it, and let you read it when you were older."

"She's not going to finish it now, is she?"

They both stared at each other. Wind gusted and raindrops plopped against the dark window. Branches brushed and scratched at the eaves.

"It's . . . adult material," he said. "There's violence."

"I read adult books. I've read Mom's others. I got them from the library. I read *sex.*" She spat the word at him, shaking inside. "What do you think? I'm almost twelve. I know thirteen- and fourteen-year-olds from school who *have* sex. Julia Borsos did it with Harlan. Did you know that? Did you know that's why I punched her face and burned her books, because I hate her guts because Harlan was *my* boyfriend. And she took him away because she's a slut, and she can do that. And I wouldn't. Do you think I don't understand the mechanics of sex? And death—I was there when Mom died. She died in *my* hands. I . . . I couldn't pull her out. I felt her struggling to live . . . it . . . was my fault." Her eyes burned, and a tear trickled down her cheek.

He blanched. Another squall of raindrops beat against the window.

"You need to give me those pages, kiddo," he said, his voice going thick, his own eyes filling with emotion.

He took them gently out of her hands. She let him. She had to. She was worried about enraging him again. In that terrible moment when she'd thought he might strike her, she'd glimpsed in his face the same tightness, the same hot glitter, the same black, blinding rage that had consumed her when she'd found out about Julia and Harlan. A terrible, frightening sort of violence that had turned her into an animal over which she'd had no control.

"Thank you."

"I really do hate you," she whispered. Tears washing softly down her face now. "You were going to hit me."

He reached out with his arm. "Come here."

He put his arm around her shoulders, tried to gather her against himself like he used to when she was little. She pulled away, squirmed, but his grip tightened. He forced her into a great big bear hug, and he would not let go. His familiar dad smell wrapped around her, stirring warm childhood memories. And in a few beats she felt her muscles give. A sob racked through her body.

He stroked her hair, rocking her gently as she sobbed. And sobbed. Until she was dry. Then she just leaned into her dad's body, feeling like she used to when she was a child, when she'd needed her dad. When he could stop all the evil in her world. When she would race into his arms when he came home, and he'd lift her all the way up to the ceiling and spin her around and around in laughing circles.

She felt a wetness against her brow. And with shock Tori realized her big cop dad, the detective who hunted down killers and stuck them in prison, the man who'd protected her all her life, was crying. Hurt. Vulnerable.

Inside Tori went dead still.

That was perhaps the most terrifyingly alone feeling of all—realizing her dad was not invincible. That he was as lost as she was.

And he was sick.

There was something terribly wrong with him. She'd heard him talking to Aunt Lou on the phone, and she was too afraid to ask him, to make it real, to let him know that she'd eavesdropped.

"I miss her too, sweetie. God, I miss her too."

She bit her lip hard.

He moved hair back from her face, looked deep into her eyes.

"I'm going to take you away, okay?" he whispered. "Just me and you. We're going to go away for the Thanksgiving weekend. We can eat someone else's turkey dinner. Make some new holiday memories. We can stay longer than the weekend if we want, not worry about school. Spend some time together again. Get away from the city, out of this rain. We'll leave tomorrow, okay, at first light? I'll have the truck and camper ready." He cleared his throat. "Come, let's get you some dinner and into bed. Early start tomorrow. I'll clean up here."

"Where are we going?"

"A place called Broken Bar Ranch," he murmured against her hair.

—

Cole pushed open the door quietly and stepped into his father's room. His attention shot immediately to the wheelchair next to the bed. Shock plunged through him. He had no idea his father was in a chair. The indignity of that wheelchair had to be killing a man like his dad. A man who once used to stride this land, hunt these forests, fish these streams . . .

His gaze shifted to a drip and oxygen machine against the wall, then settled on his father's shape in the bed. He was snoring great big bear snores, but he was a gray shadow of the man he'd once been. His cheeks appeared hollowed, very lined. His skin was rough in texture and sallow, his bushy beard unkempt. Perspiration sheened his face. He seemed vulnerable in sleep.

Cole walked quietly over to the window that looked toward the lake and mountains in the distance. He dug his hands deep into his pockets as he studied the view. He felt exhausted suddenly.

He caught sight of Olivia below, walking across the grass toward the alders. She had a slight awkwardness to her gait, a bit of a limp.

His father stirred behind him. Cole's pulse kicked. He shot a glance at the bedroom door that he'd left slightly ajar. He should leave, quickly, before his father woke, giving him some dignity.

But as he carefully crossed the room, a floorboard creaked beneath his weight. Cole stilled. Too late. His father's eyes popped open.

"Who's there? Who is that!" His father blinked as he tried to focus. "Cole?"

"Hey, Dad. Yeah, it's me."

A myriad of emotions chased over the old man's features, from shock to pleasure, confusion, then firming into tight anger. His fists balled the sheets as he fought to sit up.

"What in the hell are *you* doing here?"

"Thought I'd stop by, see how you were."

His father struggled to get himself into a position where he could lean back against the headboard, but as soon as he did, he sucked air in sharply and doubled over in pain. He groped blindly for the bedside table, fumbling and knocking over a container of pills.

Cole surged instantly to the bedside and caught the bottle

from falling off the edge. He handed the container to his father, then tried to help him sit back up.

"Get your hands off me." He smacked Cole away and fought himself up back into a sitting position. "You come to check on your inheritance? Did you talk to Forbes on your way up about selling?" He battled with gnarled joints to open his pills. His eyes, once such a piercing, clear gray, were rheumy and bloodshot.

"That's not—"

"Who did this? Who called you? Halliday?"

"Olivia."

"Shit." He looked away. Then he swore again as he tried once more to open his pills.

"Need some help with that?" Cole nodded to the pill container.

"Get the hell out of here. I don't need any help."

Cole's heart beat hard against his ribs, tension rising in his gut. He remained, silent, watching his dad struggle with the pills.

"What're you standing there for—what do you want?" his father said again. "What the *fuck* did Olivia tell you that made you leave Cuba?"

"Florida—I was in the Keys. She told me you were dying."

Myron stared. Silence hung. Then he reached over and bashed the intercom button on the wall next to his bed with the base of his fist "Carrick! Where in the hell are you, woman. Get upstairs. *Now*."

He managed to pop the lid off his pills. He fisted a couple and stuffed them into his mouth. With shaking hands he reached for the glass of water on the stand.

Cole handed the glass to him. His father stilled as their eyes met. He helped his dad drink. The old man closed his eyes, inhaling deeply, as if awaiting the effect of the medication. Cole read the label. Big-gun painkillers.

Eyes still closed, perspiration beading on his brow, his father said, "Is Jane here, too? Have the two of you cut a deal to sell this place before I'm cold in my bloody grave?"

Cole blew out a chestful of air, guilt twisting through him. "Would you stop beating that drum for a moment—I don't want this place. I don't care what you do with it."

Myron's eyes flared open. With the back of his fist, he hammered at the intercom button next to his bed again, repeatedly, angrily, in frustration, pain.

"Get me Mrs. Carrick," he barked. "Tell Olivia I want to see her. Now. Where is she?"

"I saw her heading down through the trees."

His father winced, then took a deep, slow breath.

Adele Carrick entered the room.

"Thank God, woman," his father muttered. "Pass me my clothes, please. And get my son out of my bedroom. Give me some dignity and space here."

She hesitated, glanced at Cole, then bustled about the room, gathering clothes.

"Shall we get you ready for dinner, then, Mr. McDonough?"

"Not hungry. Just get him out."

"Shall I prepare one of the lodge bedrooms for Cole?"

"He can have the empty staff cabin. Give him the keys." He looked at his son. "You'll prefer the privacy, I'm sure."

Cole stepped outside the door, adrenaline hammering through his blood. From the passageway he heard his father muttering, "Thirteen goddamn years and he's standing there next to my bed while I'm sleeping. The prodigal son returned. No warning, nothing . . ."

Cole started down the passage toward the stairwell.

What in the hell was he doing here anyway? It was a mistake. On so many levels.

Adele came out, closing the door softly behind her. She caught up to him. "I'm so sorry, Mr. McDonough."

"It's Cole, please. You make me sound like my father. And it's fine—I didn't expect less."

"He's in a lot of pain. He's not thinking clearly. He asked if you would meet him in the library tomorrow at eleven."

"Right." He snorted. "A formal meeting."

"Come, I'll give you those cabin keys. They're in the office downstairs."

———

Eugene sensed the subtle shift in the weather. He could taste the coming snow on his tongue. *Tick tock, nature's clock.* He hummed softly—a refrain from Beethoven's *Fidelio*—as he wound shimmering purple thread around the hook secured in the vise clamped to the camper table. His mother used to like Beethoven, Bach, Mozart, Händel. Some Wagner. She used to play operas on vinyl records using an old turntable powered by solar energy and water from the creek. Totally self-sustainable they'd been.

He threaded one of the red beads and wound it onto the body he was creating around the hook. He added two more beads. Once the beads were securely tied, he dabbed them with a clear nail varnish he'd found in the bunk box beside the mattress. He shifted to a strain from Mozart's *Don Giovanni* as he shredded pieces of lime-green surveyor's tape.

Sarah would like this gift.

CHAPTER 7

Vancouver. Saturday morning. Two days to Thanksgiving.

The day dawned in shades of gray, and rain fell in a soft mist. From her upstairs bedroom window Tori watched her dad in the driveway. He was jacking up the camper so he could drive his Dodge Ram under it. He didn't look sick. She wondered what could be wrong with him. Memories sliced through her—his big bear hugs. Him laughing at Mom's jokes. A strange feeling tightened in her chest, and she was filled with a moment of compassion. He missed his wife. She'd seen real pain in his eyes yesterday. And now he looked so alone out there in the dark, wet morning. Alone like she felt. Her hands tightened on the windowsill.

He'd told her to pack her bags, and her gear was on her bed ready to go. She figured he'd be another twenty minutes at least, getting the camper hiked up and secured properly on the bed of the truck.

She took her digital reader and cord into her mother's office and quickly powered up her mom's laptop.

A dialogue box popped up asking for a password. She cursed, racking her brain for ideas. On a whim she entered her own name into the box. *Victoria.*

It opened.

Tori stared.

Her own name had unlocked the private world into her mother's computer. Emotion stung her eyes. Love, a huge aching hole of it, burned in her chest. She heard the big diesel engine of her dad's truck rumble to life. He'd be reversing it under the camper now. Her heart hammered. She didn't have long. Hurriedly she did a computer search for the title of her mother's draft manuscript: *The Pledge*.

Her father had locked the paper copy away, but there had to be a digital version in here.

Bingo. There it was.

Her hands started to shake a little as she plugged in her USB cord and connected her e-reader to the laptop. She hit the keys to send the manuscript to her e-reader. The truck's engine went suddenly silent. She tensed.

The file transferred. Pulse racing, Tori disconnected her digital reader.

The downstairs door banged.

"Tori! You ready?"

She closed down the computer, and, grabbing her e-reader, she ran softly on socked feet out the door and down the passage. Leaning over the banister, she called down the stairs. "I'll be down in a sec, Dad."

"I'm just hooking up the trailer now, then we're good to go."

Mouth dry, hands clammy, she hurried to her room, closed the door. She checked her e-reader. It was there—her mother's last work in progress was safely stashed inside her device. She was going to be able to take something of her mother with her. She was going to read her last words. Tori closed her eyes, clutching the reader to her chest. And she mouthed the words: *Thank you.*

———

Cole was awake before sunrise. Last night he'd showered, shaved, and crashed like the dead. This morning he was a new man—without a hangover for the first time in six months, something of a stranger to himself. He made coffee in the small kitchenette that overlooked the lake. The staff cabin was tiny but warm from the woodstove, and Adele had seen to it that there were basic supplies in the cupboards and fridge. Propane heated the water in the bathroom and at the kitchen sink, but there was no electricity. Internet access was apparently available via the sat dish on the lodge roof. He'd be able to charge his laptop in the lodge and work down here. If he found the inspiration.

He shrugged into his jacket, took his mug, and stepped out onto the small porch. He sipped his coffee, listening to the loons. From here he could glimpse the other staff cabin through the trees.

The sun was just peeping over the ridge, the first gold rays hitting the snow on the Marble range. Ribbons of yellow deciduous foliage cut through the dense green décolletage of the mountains, and the air was delicate with cold. He could feel the whisperings of winter creeping silently over the high plateau.

He'd missed the sharp definition of seasons while in Africa, Cuba, Pakistan, Afghanistan. He'd always loved this time of year, when salmon came home to spawn, silvery and red in shining water. When the leaves turned gold and crackled underfoot, and hoarfrost grew on berry branches. When the scent of wood smoke mingled with the fragrance of pine. Memories, a bittersweet mix, filled Cole's mind as he sipped his brew.

What now? He stood at a crossroads. Sober, he now had to face what he'd been avoiding—finding a way to move forward. To write again. A new story. Something that interested him.

He stilled as the door of the other cabin opened. Out came Ace followed by Olivia. She marched determinedly over the frosted grass. Long legs. Slim jeans. A thick down vest over her long-sleeved sweater. Her ponytail swung jauntily.

"Morning!" he called.

She stopped dead in her tracks. Stared.

Ace gamboled over and up onto his porch. Cole bent down and ruffled the dog's fur.

Olivia came across the grass. "What are you doing in the staff cabin?"

"Apparently I like the privacy."

"Myron said that?"

"He doesn't want me in his house." He sipped from his mug, watching her.

She stared up at him. This morning her eyes were the color of the lake—a pale green made luminescent by the underwater white marl shoals. Her cheeks and nose were pinked with cold. She seemed to be reevaluating him, taking in his cleaned-up appearance.

"I'm sorry," she said softly.

He shrugged. "I knew it wasn't going to be a cakewalk."

"Why *did* you come, then?"

He snorted. "Good question. I was on a plane before I had a chance to sober up and change my mind. So, what's on the ranch work agenda this morning?"

Her shoulders stiffened slightly. This was her turf, and he was muscling in.

"I never got around to checking those campsite guests in yesterday. And I need to clean up the bins, put in new garbage bags, that sort of thing."

"I'll come."

"What?"

"I'll give you a hand."

A wariness snapped through her eyes. He could see her walls shooting back up.

"Come on, humor me. Show me the lay of the land, how the ranch works. I'm not so bad to be around." He set his mug down on the railing, reached over and shut his door. Jogging down the stairs, he zipped up his jacket.

She frowned. "I'd rather do it alone."

"What? You don't want interference from the ranch heirs? Feel like we're taking over too soon?"

"You're as blunt as your father is, you know that?" she said crisply. "No wonder you two don't get on."

He felt the corners of his mouth curve into a smile in spite of himself.

Her gaze held his—a subtle challenge with an underlying flicker of unease. She huffed, spun around, and began to walk up the path. He followed her through the aspen grove. Gold leaves quivered and fell like rain upon them. Their breath misted in clouds.

They reached her truck, which was parked outside the lodge. She helped Ace up into the cab.

"His hips giving him trouble?" Cole said.

"The vet thinks he might have early signs of degenerative myelopathy. It's a progressive thing with no cure. I'll just pick up my stuff from the office."

Cole climbed in beside Ace while Olivia unlocked the office from the outside door. She exited carrying a box of brochures, a book, and a credit card reader. She shoved these onto the seat between her and Ace and stuck her keys in the ignition.

"Apart from being banished to the staff cabin, how did it go with Myron yesterday?" she asked as she fired the engine and put the truck in gear.

He leaned back against the headrest. "It didn't go. He threw me out at first sight and set up a formal meeting with me in the library for eleven this morning."

She cast him a quick glance as she pulled out onto the dirt track. He looked again at the scars on her wrists and wondered about her past, where she came from. Again, her words from the phone call dogged him.

You know dick about surviving . . .

"Do the campsite guests still approach via the logging road on the other side of the lake?" he said.

"Yeah. Sometimes they'll come all the way around and check themselves in. Mostly I just swing by once or twice a day and register them on-site. The cabin guests need to come past the lodge office."

At the campsite entrance she stopped the truck, reached across him, and popped open the glove compartment. He caught her scent. Clean, soapy. Fresh. It brought to mind shampoos with names like *Rainwater* or *Forest Spring*. She removed a pair of work gloves from the compartment, slipped them on, got out of the truck. He followed.

She reached into the bed of the truck and hefted out a large sandwich board. It was yellow with black text that warned of bears in the area.

"Want help?" he said as she lugged the signboard a few feet down the road. Wind was picking up and washing through the swaying pines with the sound of a river.

"I'm good." She placed the sign where the road forked. One side led to the small beach and picnic area, the other to the boat launch and campsites. Cole leaned against the truck, watching her, reabsorbing this place that was once so much a part of his life.

She definitely had an awkward gait—he wondered about that. She wore no ring, demonstrated no overt sign of being attached to a man, yet she was a close friend of his cantankerous father.

Cole was an astute observer, a cataloguer of facts, a reader of micro signs. It was a skill he'd honed over years of investigative reporting. Some called his powers of observation and memory uncanny, but it had made him damn good at his job. He could see through smoke and mirrors to the heart of a situation where others got sidetracked.

And he was seeing a woman who was trying to hide. It raised questions in his mind. Hide from what? Where did she come from prior to eight years ago? Had she tried to kill herself? Why? When? What exactly was she to his father, to this ranch? What would she do when his father died and this place was sold?

She pulled off her gloves as she approached the truck, her ponytail lifting in the wind.

"Still getting problem bears in the fall?" he said with a nod to the sign.

"More so over the last two seasons." She opened the driver's door and got in. He climbed back into the passenger's side. "There's a sow with two cubs-of-the-year who have been getting into garbage. Repeat offenders. We also had one get into the chickens last week."

She started the ignition, and headed toward the concrete boat ramp.

A man in waders was tinkering with his boat on the ramp. He glanced up and waved. Olivia stopped the truck. She hesitated, then said to Cole. "He's an old regular. I'm just going to say hi."

He watched her walk down to the ramp. Ace whined and licked his face again. Cole noticed for the first time the cloudiness in the hound's eyes. He peered closer. "Hey, bud, you losing your sight, boy? You wanna go see what she's up to?"

His tail thumped.

Cole helped Ace out of the truck, and they followed Olivia down the ramp to where she was talking to a craggy-faced, sun-browned man in his late sixties.

"The trout biting?" Cole called out as he approached.

"Got totally skunked this morning," the old guy said as he pushed up to his feet. "They're no longer feeding off the marl—the colder weather at night has driven them into deep water. I think they're on glass worms now, which makes it tricky to lure them with anything else. They get suspicious." He grinned, showing missing front teeth. "But I got two over twenty inches yesterday."

He reached for the rope at the prow of his boat, began hauling it up the ramp. Cole helped him.

Once the boat was on the trailer, the man dusted his hands off on his waders. "I'm thinking of heading up to Forest Lake Monday. Maybe I can get a window in there." He chuckled, then coughed, a hacking, rattling sound in his chest. "Before the big freeze and the snow blows in."

"It looks like that might be early this year," Olivia said. "A weather warning has been issued for late Monday. You might want to think of heading home before it barrels in. This is Barney," she said to Cole. "He's one of our regulars." She smiled. It put a dimple into her left cheek, and a lambency into her mossy eyes, and it punched straight into his gut. He stared. Bewitched suddenly. The light in her eyes faded, her features sobering as she noticed his reaction. She looked away. When she spoke again, her voice was changed, lower. "Barney, this is Cole McDonough, Myron's son."

The old man scrubbed his grizzled beard. "Well, I never. *Myron's* boy?"

Cole gave a half smile. "Haven't been called that in a while."

The old fisherman continued to scratch his whiskers, studying Cole intently. "You have his genes all right. You been gone a long time . . . over ten or twelve years or something? Before I met Myron and started coming here, that's for sure."

Cole glanced at Olivia. She was watching him closely, too.

"It's been a while," he said.

"That was quite some movie, that *Hunt for the Wild*."

Surprise rippled through Cole. "You saw it?"

"Hell, yeah. Who in Clinton *didn't* see it? Myron brought a DVD down to the Cariboo Hotel. He sprang for beers and moose burgers on the house. He brought copies of the books along, too. Door prizes, he called them. We watched on the large screen in the bar. That was some party." He shook his head, grinning a mad, gap-toothed grin.

Cole stared at Barney, his chest suddenly tight.

"Well, it's been really good to meet you, son." Barney reached out and gave Cole a hearty handshake and a slap on the shoulder. Another smoker's cough rattled through his lungs. "Stop by for a drink, you hear? Myron used to do that before that chair took him. We'd cast a few lines together, tie a few flies." He coughed again. "Damp weather is coming, all right. Hits my chest right here." He thumped his sternum. "My rig is parked at number twenty-seven, right on the water. Like I said, I'm here until Monday, if that storm holds." He jerked his head toward the sky. A bank of dark cloud was building low on the southern horizon.

On the way back to the truck, Cole couldn't help saying it.

"I didn't know."

She opened the truck door, bent down, and wrapped her arms around Ace's belly. She hefted him into the truck. "Know what?"

"That my father even saw the film. He never wrote or called to mention it."

She ducked into the driver's seat and started the engine. "He's seen both movies that were made from your books. Did you ever call to tell him they were showing?"

He met her probing gaze, said nothing.

She gave a shrug. "He's got every single one of your books in his library. The *Hunt for the Wild* poster hangs in his office."

Cole swallowed, looked out his window, and cursed softly. He'd been hoping this would be simple. In and out. That his father's anger and barriers would make it so. But this? No, he had not expected this.

Olivia drove about a hundred meters and pulled up at a neat gravel clearing where two wooden outhouses flanked an information sign, two garbage bins, and a tap. She got out, pinned a new bear warning on the notice board, and replenished the box that held pamphlets. She returned to the truck for her gloves, then began to empty the full garbage bag from the first bin. She dumped it into the bed of the truck. Cole got out, came up behind her, and as she tried to heave the last bag out the bin, he took it from her.

Their arms brushed. Their eyes met.

Her mouth was so close. He could almost imagine the feel of her full lips against his. His pulse quickened as he saw the darkness of sexual attraction in her eyes.

"I can manage." Her voice came out hoarse.

"You brought me along," he said quietly. "The least you could do now is let me help."

She relented, letting him lug the heavy bag of garbage to the truck.

She grabbed fresh rolls of toilet paper and replenished the stash in the outhouses. Then she hauled a rake from the back of her truck, and with fast movements she began to smooth out the gravel. Cole restocked the bins with fresh bags, and Ace watched them both from the truck.

Sneaking a sideways glance at him, she tossed the rake back into the truck and climbed back into the driver's seat, where she waited for him.

He got in, patted Ace, and gave her a grin. "So, what's next?"

Her mouth tightened, and she refused to meet his eyes as she restarted the truck. "Check in the newcomers, see if anyone wants firewood. Let campers who haven't gone out for the day know there's a storm coming Monday night."

She drew up to a wide gravel area along the waterfront, which was occupied by fifth-wheel RVs and trucks. Awnings stretched out over picnic tables that were draped with plastic cloths. One table boasted a vase of fake flowers. Generators chugged, and the scent of wood smoke and bacon and coffee filled the air. Camp chairs had been positioned to afford a view of the lake, while others ringed the fire pits. A small satellite dish sat atop the corner of one RV.

"So much for old-fashioned tenting and peace and quiet in the woods," he said, taking in the scene.

"It's mostly what we get these days. Especially at this time of year when temperatures drop below freezing at night. These guys are equipped with everything including gas furnaces. Mostly retired couples, or single guys obsessed with hunting and fishing, like Barney, eking the last drops out of a season." She reached for the clipboard on the dash, checked the vehicle registrations against her list.

A couple sitting in chairs at one of the fire pits waved as their black poodle lunged at the end of his line, trying in vain to yap. He'd been de-barked, poor bugger.

The old man got creakily up from his chair and ambled toward the truck, travel mug in hand. The woman shaded her eyes, watching them.

Olivia put her elbow out the window. "Morning."

The dog lunged again, making a hoarse but valiant effort to warn them off.

"Top of the morning to you, too. I see there's some nasty weather building," the man said with a nod to the south horizon. "Think it'll hold until after the weekend?"

"Forecast says so, but if it changes, I'll let you know. You still planning on staying until Tuesday?"

"We'll play it by ear, keep an eye on that weather."

"How's the fishing?"

"Trout have turned skittish. Went out at first light—not a thing. Will give it a shot again this afternoon."

"Sounds like they're onto the glass worms," she said. "Any sign of the bears?"

"They came through the barbecue pits during the night— knocked over two chairs."

"After the meat drippings, I bet. You guys need any firewood?"

"We're good."

They moved on.

Farther along the lakeshore the campsites were small and nestled deep among tall evergreens and willow scrub with peekaboo views of the water. Olivia checked off three vehicle registrations against her book. She seemed to tense as they approached the next site.

A gray Ford truck was parked across the entrance. She slowed, bit her lip.

"What initially brought you out to Broken Bar?" Cole said casually.

"I was looking for a change."

"Change from what?"

Her eyes narrowed slightly. He could see her pulse racing above the bandana around her neck. The scarf was a different color from the one she'd been wearing yesterday.

"From the north." She reached for her clipboard, cash pouch, and credit card reader. "The job advertised was for a fishing guide, but it's morphed into general ranch duties as staff has been laid off. I used to guide on the lake as well as do the trail rides. The rides stopped when most of the horses were sold last year. And of course everyone associated with the cattle has gone."

"A lot of work, ranching. Might be best to sell it."

Her gaze flashed to his. "Yeah, right. Seems no one is up for the job. End of an era and all that."

His jaw steeled. He thought of the generations of McDonoughs who had farmed this land. "You're fond of this place."

"It's my home. I hate to lose it."

"Where was home before this? Where did you grow up?"

Her gaze probed his, as if searching for the trick in his question. "Look, you can talk to your father about what he wants from this ranch, and from me as an employee. Beyond that, I don't see my role here as being your business." She hesitated before getting out of the truck again. "For what it's worth, Cole, Myron insisted I did *not* let you or Jane know that he was dying."

"Yeah. He made *that* clear."

"He figured you'd both . . ." She wavered. "He said he didn't want you and Jane squabbling over inheritance and trying to sell the place out from under him while he was still alive. He'd rather you messed with the ranch once he was dead, and he wouldn't have to witness what you did."

Cole held her gaze, a dark twist of anger threading through his guilt. He'd already signed papers. Jane was already moving ahead. He made a mental note to deal with Jane and those papers when he got back to his cabin. "So, why did you go against his wishes, then? Why *did* you call me?"

She heaved out a heavy breath. "Okay, I'm just going to say this straight. In spite of his protestations, I had a gut feeling Myron needed to see his kids. You especially."

He raised his brow. "Meaning?"

"I believe he needs to atone, for . . . whatever it was that happened between you and him. He needs to make his peace." She swallowed. "I felt it might be good for him. Maybe even both of you. To say sorry."

"And you call *me* blunt?"

"You asked."

"My old man doesn't want to atone, Olivia. He doesn't want anything to do with me. He hasn't wanted anything to do with me or Jane since—"

"Since after the accident. I heard. But sometimes people are broken and don't know how to mend because they aren't able to say what they need or deeply want. Sometimes you get to a point in life where you realize you've made a terrible mistake and you desperately need to fix it, but it's so deep and bitterly ingrained you can't start."

"Well, I never," he whispered, his gaze lasering hers. "What are we now, the ranch psychotherapist? We're all going to hold hands and sing 'Kumbaya' before he dies?"

She glowered at him, her face reddening. "Well, fuck you, too," she whispered. "I've said my piece. Calling you probably was a mistake. I'll get you back to the lodge as soon as I'm done, then you can do the hell what you want and clear out of here."

She got out, slammed the door, marched toward the gray Ford parked across the site entrance.

He got out behind her. "Olivia—"

"Spare me."

He hurried over, reached for her arm.

She spun around, a wild heat crackling in her eyes. Electricity pulsed between them. Trees swished in a gust of wind, raining down dead needles.

"I like him, okay. I *like* Myron. He's been a dear friend. He . . ." An unexpected surge of moisture glittered into her eyes. She paused, glanced away, corralling her emotions. When she spoke again her voice was level.

"He gave me a job. He gave me and Ace a place to stay when we both needed it most. I *owe* him. He's dying and I feel powerless, and just wanted to help. Calling you was the least I could do. Now that I've gotten that off my chest, do with it what you will." She turned, took two paces away, then swung back to face him, as if she was unable to drop it. "I had a harebrained notion you were somehow better than this, you know that?"

"Better than what?"

"I thought you might be big enough to take the initiative, to say sorry, make peace . . . before he passes."

"Where on earth did you get *that* idea?"

"From your book, the way you write. I thought you had this . . . this view of the world that was somehow deep. That you cared about meaning." Her eyes crackled with light. "But I was wrong. You're a fraud."

She turned her back on him and stomped around the back of the Ford, disappearing down a track behind dense brush.

Cole stared after her, dumbstruck. Wind swirled and rushed through the pines, as if whispering with memories, with the susurrating voices of the dead. He dragged his hand through his hair. She was right about one thing. This was a mistake.

And he was wrong about another thing—this woman was not some Machiavellian seductress after an inheritance. Her feelings for his father felt genuine. And his cantankerous beast of a dad appeared to have helped a woman who Cole now believed was hiding a big-ass wound. A woman who'd maybe tried to kill herself because of it.

I'll be damned.

He inhaled deeply, a strange surge of emotion in his chest. But as he was about to return to wait with Ace in the truck, a scream pierced the air.

Olivia?

Cole raced down the path, adrenaline busting through him. He rounded the bush and saw her on the ground next to a picnic table. White-faced. Blood trickled down her temple. Looming over her was a tall bearded man with an ax in his hand.

CHAPTER 8

Eyes of pale amber trapped hers. Lion eyes. Hungry, consuming.

His eyes.

His scent filled her brain. His coldness, his evil, crawled alive over her skin. Bile rose in the back of her throat, and her heart hammered. A tunnel of dark tightened around her, blocking out the ranch, the sky. All she could see was him. She was naked again. On the bearskin. Rope around her neck.

"Olivia!" Cole's voice broke through.

She blinked, scrambled rapidly backward in the dirt, butted up against the picnic bench. Panic flared. She fought to pull herself into focus. To stay present.

The man with the ax took a step back as Cole rushed up to her and dropped to his knees. He cupped her face.

"Are you all right?" His eyes were bright with concern, adrenaline. He fired a brief glance at the man before returning full attention to her. "What happened?"

"I . . . I came around the back of the camper and he just appeared from behind it, with the ax. I got a fright, that's all."

I lurched straight into a full goddamn flashback . . .

Cole took her arm, helped her up. She wobbled to her feet, dusted off her jeans.

"I'm so sorry for my overreaction," she said to the man. "You spooked the hell out of me. I must have tripped over my own feet."

She put her hand to her temple. Her fingers came away with blood. Confusion chased through her. "I . . . must have hit my head on the picnic table."

Cole felt the corner of the table. "There's a nail end sticking out. You probably caught it. Let me take a look."

"No! No, I'm fine." She gathered up her fallen book, money pouch, and card reader. "Please, let me try again," she said to the man, giving a light laugh that sounded false even to her own ears. "I'm Olivia, the ranch manager. I saw that you got in yesterday afternoon."

Sorry was an understatement. She was mortified. Her whole body, her insides were shaking. She was an idiot to have returned so soon, when the blood on this man's freezer had come close to triggering her first full flashback in years. It didn't help that his eyes happened to be the identical color as Sebastian's. Same height, too. Something about him . . . She shook herself.

She was in a worse way than she'd thought. Her eerie experience while tracking, the basket of berries, that episode in the kitchen cooler with the deer carcass—it had all conspired to plunge her back into the past again. Over the last three years she'd begun to believe she'd fucking slayed the flashbacks. This was a devastating blow.

The man regarded her steadily. He was wiry-strong with a shock of steel-gray hair, thick beard and mustache that hid his mouth and much of his face. Dark patches stained the thighs of his jeans. His fingernails were black. Dirt. Maybe blood. Fear spurted afresh. She cleared her throat.

"You got in yesterday?" she prompted.

The man cast a glance at Cole, and something in his face darkened as the atmosphere between the two men seemed to shift. Again Olivia was touched by a sense of brooding malevolence. She swallowed, trying to push it away, knowing it was a fabrication of her own mind.

He's dead. Gone. This is just your brain playing tricks . . .

Cole placed his hand momentarily at the small of her back. Surprise then relief shocked through her. His touch was grounding. Her eyes burned. As much as she fought for independence, as distant as she kept herself physically from people, she was profoundly grateful to have someone at her back right now.

"Got in around sunset yesterday," the man said. His voice was hoarse and whispery, like that of a heavy smoker. Or a de-barked dog.

"And how many nights will you be staying?"

"Until after Thanksgiving."

"Just so you know, there's a storm coming. Snow could start falling by Monday night."

"Snow?"

"There's no plow service. You could be stranded. I'll keep campers informed as I get more weather updates." She cleared her throat again. "The site is twenty bucks per night. Wood is five dollars extra. Let me know if you need any, and I'll deliver a bundle each morning."

"Got my own wood." He propped his ax against the picnic bench and fished his wallet out from the back pocket of his jeans.

Out of the corner of her eye she noted Cole scrutinizing the ax blade, the camper, the freezer. The blood streaks down the side.

She entered the dates into her book as the man dug a wad of notes out of his wallet and peeled off the requisite amount. "I'll pay up to Tuesday, then you won't have to come back."

Suited her fine.

"Thank you." She took the cash from him. He allowed his hand to linger against hers. Olivia's gaze shot up to his. He smiled, a slash of white teeth through facial hair.

Like his teeth . . .

She counted the money quickly, zipped it into her cash pouch, then handed him a brochure. "There's a map, everything you need in there. We do dinners up at the lodge. You need to reserve before noon on the day. And we have a Thanksgiving special on Sunday night. Turkey. The works."

"I'm good. Thanks." He took the pamphlet, holding her eyes.

"It's probably best if you wipe that blood off your freezer," she said. "It'll bring in the bears."

"Gotcha."

"Well, enjoy your stay." As she moved, she caught sight of the bow inside his camper. "Bow hunting?"

"The only kind," he replied with another hint of a smile. Flat eyes. "I like a real hunt."

"Bow-hunting regs are in there, too." She nodded at the brochure in his hands. "No hunting on ranch land. The ranch border is denoted on the map. Conservation officer comes by every couple of days or so, checks permits, tags."

She started up the path to her truck.

"You just bagged something fresh?" Cole said.

Olivia swung around. Cole was looking at the blood on the freezer, hands in his pockets.

A hawk shrieked up high, and small birds scattered from trees.

"Deer," the man said.

"In the Marble foothills?"

"Canyon. Got him on the way up."

Cole nodded. "Enjoy your stay." He joined Olivia, and they rounded the Ford together. She jotted down the BC plate number.

Back in her own truck, Ace nuzzled against Olivia. He was stressed and trying to sniff the fresh blood on her brow. She inhaled deeply. "It's okay, boy." She dropped down the truck visor and peered into the small mirror, dabbing at the blood with a tissue from the glove box. It wasn't a bad gash. Nothing some disinfectant and butterfly bandages wouldn't fix. But she was going to have a mother of a purple egg.

Cole climbed in beside her.

"Want me to look at that?"

She shook her head, balled up the tissue, stuffed it into the cup holder, and started the engine. She was still trembling as she drove to the next site, about a hundred yards farther down the lake.

"He's off."

"That guy? Yeah. We get weird ones sometimes."

"You okay?"

She nodded.

"You're going to have a nice lump on your head."

She snorted.

"He really spooked you, huh?"

Olivia felt her walls slamming up. "It was the ax, I guess. Startled me, coming around the camper with it in his hand like that."

She drew up at the entrance to the next site. Gray Ford trucks appeared to be the choice *du jour*, but the one parked in this site had a long box, and the camper was affixed to it. Two fold-up chairs flanked the fire pit. There were also two plates, two mugs, and two sets of knives and forks on the picnic table. The boat had been removed from the trailer and floated in the water, roped to a snag jutting out from the low bank.

"So what *do* you do with the troublesome guests, or, say, a big rowdy bunch of drunk guys? The cops are at least an hour out—where do you get backup?"

She sat for moment, sighed, then pulled a wry mouth. His gaze went to her lips, and she was suddenly conscious of the subtle electricity that seemed to radiate from him.

"I haven't really had a problem to date—this campsite gig wasn't part of my job until last summer." She carefully pushed flyaway strands of hair away from her cut. "I've got my knife, bear spray. Bear bangers. Radio. Sat phone." She wasn't going to mention the illegal Smith and Wesson stashed behind the truck seat that she'd bought from a logger up north. "And Ace."

He smiled. The warmth in his features was instant, and the friendly lines that fanned out from his deep gray eyes tugged at something deep in her chest. She hadn't seen him smile yet. It stole her thoughts. The cab suddenly felt smaller, the air closer. A soft panic flickered through her stomach—a very different kind of fear from what she'd just experienced in the last campsite.

"Yeah," he said. "A killer German shepherd, with bad eyesight and gimpy joints."

Ace licked his face in ignorant approval. But Cole saw something in hers—a glimpse of just how deeply losing Ace would cut her.

"I'm sorry," he said.

She shrugged. "It's true. He's going blind. His back legs will give him trouble sooner or later. I should probably stop him from following me when I go riding."

"How old is he?"

"Not old enough to have these problems, but he had a rough start." She opened the door. "One more to check in."

———

Cole followed Olivia down into the campsite, thinking this was a vulnerable job for a lone woman. It stirred something protective in him, along with an unexpected sense of responsibility, proprietorship.

"Anyone home?" She knocked on the camper door.

The door opened. A man with white-blond hair in a close brush cut smiled and put his finger to his lips. "Wife is sleeping," he whispered as he came lightly down the rickety metal stairs, agile for his size. He stood about six-foot-two. He sported a neatly clipped mustache and Balbo beard with a soul patch. His blue eyes sparkled, and his skin was bronzed by sun. He had the look of a buff but gaunt vegan—virile. He drew them toward the picnic table, out of earshot of his wife in the camper. Cole guessed him to be in late fifties, early sixties.

Olivia appeared edgy in his presence. Mr. Axman back there had spooked her good.

"I'm Olivia," she said. "De facto ranch manager. This is Cole. He grew up here."

The man reached out and shook their hands in turn. Solid, confident grip.

"Algor Sorenson. I was going to come around to the lodge later to check in. We arrived yesterday evening. My wife, Mary, is sleeping in."

Olivia quoted the rates and asked how long the couple planned on staying.

"I'd like to wing it day to day, if that's okay with you?" he said, glancing at the lake. "As long as the fish are biting we'll hang in." He gave an easy smile. Bright white teeth.

Olivia's gaze flickered. She cast her eyes down, entered the guest details. "Probably a good idea," she said as she copied down the truck registration. "Big storm in the forecast. Could blow in early, and if it does, roads will become impassable for a while. Right now it's supposed to hit Monday night. I'll come around and let everyone know if that changes. How would you like to pay? Credit or cash?"

Cole noted she wouldn't meet the man's eyes. Her hands were still trembling.

The guest gave Olivia his credit card. She glanced at the name on the card, ran it through her reader, and handed him the portable device so he could punch in his PIN.

"Do you need any wood for tonight?"

"Love some."

Cole jogged back to the truck to retrieve a bundle. He carried it back, cataloguing Sorenson's gear.

Olivia was explaining the dinner reservation procedure and Thanksgiving meal.

Sorenson smiled, hands in pockets. "My wife and I like to do a turkey in the camper oven. Small one. Did one last year in Moab."

"You originally from Washington?" Cole said, dumping the wood next to the fire pit and dusting his hands off on his jeans.

"Excuse me?"

"Saw your ham radio operator's plate on the back of the camper—I'm also a licensed operator."

"Oh, that. Yes." His eyes flickered. "My wife. She's the radio buff. I let her at it. Not my thing."

"Well, enjoy your stay," Olivia said.

As they drove the rest of the circular road through the campground, Cole noted it was only the few sites along the water that were occupied. The rest of the big campground was empty, desolate looking.

"Does it fill up in the summer?"

She shook her head. She was pale. Compassion mushroomed softly through him, and he realized he liked this prickly woman. Olivia West was rekindling his interest. He wanted to know more about her, what made her tick, how she'd gotten those scars.

Cole fell quiet, watching the lake, the forest. Memories of Jimmie and him playing here washed through his mind.

"How could you tell?" she said suddenly.

"Tell what?"

"That he was originally from Washington—Sorenson had BC registration on his truck."

"Each amateur radio license plate comes with a unique call sign that has a prefix showing where it was issued. It's like that all over the world—you can look the sign number up and find out who the ham operator is. There's software you can use to track their movements on a map if they have their radios on. Ordinarily, if someone from the States moves here, they'd get a new Canadian call sign."

"I guess his wife came from the States. Oh, shit—" She hit the brakes suddenly and backed up to where the ranch boundary fence had been recently cut and peeled back to create an opening the width of two vehicles. Tire tracks led through the hole into the dark, muddy, dense forest beyond.

"Bloody poachers." She wound down her window to examine the vandalism. "Or squatters. That's the old deactivated road that goes into the otter marsh and out the back."

"I know," he said quietly. "Jimmie and I used to play in that swamp, much to my mother's chagrin."

"I'll need to come back and fix that."

"I'll do it," he said.

She shot him a glance.

He blew out a heavy breath. "While I'm here. I'll do it."

"This is my job, my—"

"And it is my father's place. I don't like you doing this stuff alone. It's not safe. Those vehicle tracks look recent. Someone could still be in there. And likely armed, given that it's open season."

She stared at him, an odd look entering her eyes.

He shrugged. "Call me chauvinist if you want."

She didn't call him anything. She drove back in silence.

When they returned to the lodge, Cole hung up his jacket and saw that a fire was already crackling in the living room hearth. Two girls sat reading on the long sofa in front the fire, one on either end, as if they didn't know each other. A robust balding man with broad shoulders stood with his back to them, hands deep in his pockets as he watched the news on a large flat-screen television mounted on the back wall.

"Looks like we have new guests to check in," Olivia said as she hung her jacket next to his in the hall.

She made her way into the living area. Cole glanced at his watch. It was still too early to go to the library and wait for his dad. He followed Olivia.

As she neared the man, a "Breaking News" banner flared across the big television screen. The program cut instantly to an anchorwoman in the CBC newsroom. The man reached over and bumped up the sound. The anchor's voice blared loudly into the room.

"We interrupt this broadcast to bring you breaking news out of Mount Currie," the anchor said. "Please be warned, sensitive viewers will find the following material disturbing. A woman's body was found hanging by the neck from a tree yesterday afternoon, alongside the Birkenhead River in Mount Currie, a First Nations community about thirty minutes north of the popular Snowy Creek ski resort. The Lower Mainland's integrated homicide team has taken over the case and is currently on scene, assisting both local and tribal police."

Olivia stalled, body rigid.

The two girls on the sofa spun around to watch.

"CBC reporter Mike Stone is currently on site. What can you tell us at this point, Mike?"

The footage cut to a reporter in a blue windbreaker in front of trees yellow with fall leaves.

"Two teens from Mount Currie were out fishing yesterday afternoon when they made a very gruesome find," said the male reporter into his mike, looking a bit shaken himself. Cole stepped closer.

"They came across a woman's naked body hanging by the neck from a tree. Police are not commenting at this point other than to say the death is suspicious. But I spoke with Joshua Philips, a cousin of one of the teens who made the discovery. And again, a warning to sensitive viewers, the following information is disturbing. Joshua, can you tell us what your cousins found?"

The camera focused on a young man in a fleece jacket. He was bloodless under his naturally tawny complexion, his black hair ruffling in the wind. "My cousin and his friend were going to check out the spawning coho when they came across it hanging in a stand of cottonwoods."

"By 'it' you mean the body?" said the reporter.

The young man nodded. "It . . . was gutted. At first my cousin thought it was a deer being field dressed by some hunter. But it was a woman, hanging by her neck from a big metal hook. Her eyes had been gouged out, and her entrails were spilling out."

Olivia made a strange sound. She stumbled sideways, reached for the back of a chair. Cole's gaze darted between Olivia and the TV.

"Homicide and forensics arrived at the scene from Vancouver late yesterday evening," the reporter said. "The area has since been cordoned off, and tents have been erected over the site, where investigators have been working through the night with the aid of klieg lights. No one can get closer than where I'm standing here, and police are not saying if the body has been identified."

Olivia's knees buckled, and she slumped to the ground.

Cole surged instantly to her side. The man in front of the TV spun around, shock on his face. He stared at Olivia.

"Turn that thing off, now!" Cole barked at him as he helped Olivia up into a wingback chair. "And get those kids out of here, for God's sake."

"Tori," the man demanded of one of the girls. He sounded shaken. "Go into the office. Wait there. And take your friend." He reached for the television controls, turning it off as his daughter skulked through the door into the office. The other girl hurried into the kitchen.

Olivia was sheet-white, her skin cold, clammy, her breathing shallow. Cole felt for her pulse. It was racing. Irregular.

Adele rushed out of the kitchen. "Dear God, what happened? Nella said Olivia fainted."

"Put your head down," he told Olivia. "Right down, between your knees. Adele, can you bring her something sweet to drink?"

"Can I help?" the man said.

"If you could just wait in the office," Cole said. "Someone will be with you guys shortly."

"Here." Adele returned with a glass of orange juice.

"Drink this," Cole said.

Olivia lifted her head slowly. "I . . . I'm okay." Perspiration gleamed on waxy skin. Her hand went to the cut on her head. Her pupils were dilated. She looked confused. She was having trouble breathing.

Cole set the glass down, reached for the bandana around her neck, began to untie it.

"No!" Her hands clamped fast over his. Her eyes flared wide. "Please, don't."

"You need to breathe properly." He pushed her hands away and removed the bandana. Cole's blood turned ice-cold.

A vicious, ragged, ropey scar ringed her neck like a dog's collar.

Adele gasped softly. Her eyes shot to Cole, horror in her face.

CHAPTER 9

Adele leaned over and whispered into Cole's ear. "Jason, the chef, said Olivia had what he thought was a panic episode in the kitchen yesterday."

"Thanks." He glanced up at the housekeeper. "I wonder if you could leave us alone a minute?"

Her eyes narrowed. Her gaze flitted to Olivia. "Sure. I . . . I'll be in the kitchen if you need me."

"Look at me, Olivia," he said softly. "Focus. Here, have some juice."

"I don't want any. I said I'm fine." The spirit in her eyes had been broken. She looked frightened, vulnerable. Compassion crushed through his chest.

He placed his hand on her knee, but her body snapped wire tight and her eyes shot back to his.

He moved a lock of hair away from the crack she'd taken on the skull. "Talk to me."

"Don't," she said through her teeth. "Please . . . do not touch me."

He removed his hand, surprise, confusion rippling through him. She scrabbled quickly for the bandana at her side and hooked it back around her neck.

"Please, leave me alone. Thank you," she said, attempting to retie the ends of her bandana with trembling fingers, but she kept fumbling the knot.

"Let me do that."

"No."

Moving her hands aside, he overruled her and tied the knot gently, repositioning the fabric to nicely cover her scar.

"There." He smiled.

She swallowed, her eyes glimmering suddenly with moisture, her hands fisting tightly on her knees.

"It was shocking news," he offered. "Visceral stuff. They should have given better warning further out. Those kids shouldn't have seen it, either."

She broke his gaze, looked away, visibly struggling to marshal her emotions. She cleared her throat, squared her shoulders, then met his eyes again. Her control had returned.

"Thanks." The fight had crackled back into her eyes. "I've been feeling a bit off lately. I think I might be coming down with a bug. I should attend to the guest in the office." She came to her feet, bracing herself a moment on the back of the chair.

"I can do that," he said.

"You have a meeting with your father shortly." She held his gaze, as if daring him to ask about her neck scar, to voice the thoughts and questions she had to know were crowding his mind. He said nothing.

She turned abruptly and strode toward the office, shoulders square, her boots clicking on the wooden floor. Cole watched her disappear into the door. He blew out a chestful of air and scrubbed his brow.

No wonder this woman had walls. She'd most likely tried to kill herself, as evidenced by the scars on her wrist. And she'd had something terribly violent happen to her neck—something she was desperate to hide. She also had issues with physical proximity and being touched.

Cole went into the kitchen, where he introduced himself to Jason and his daughter, Nella, and he asked about Olivia's panic incident yesterday.

"It was the deer meat in the freezer that set her off, I think," Jason said. "I was pushing it along the rack and bumped it into her."

The words of the newscast played through Cole's mind.

It was . . . gutted. At first they thought it was a deer. But it was a woman, hanging by the neck . . .

"She did say that she hadn't been feeling well, so maybe she's coming down with something." Jason turned suddenly to his daughter. "I forgot to ask you, Nella. Liv was fretting over a basket of berries left outside her cabin door when she came in here yesterday—did you leave them for her?"

Nella, who was sitting drawing at the kitchen table, shook her head and eyed Cole warily.

"You look like him," she said suddenly.

"Who?" Cole asked.

"Mr. McDonough."

A smile curved over his mouth. "I *am* Mr. McDonough."

"I mean, you look like your father. In the old photos in his office, when he was younger. I bet you'll be just like him when you're old, too."

His smile faded a little.

———

Olivia entered the office. The guest had his back to her as he examined the fishing lures for sale under the glass counter. Mounted on the office wall behind the counter were framed photographs of previous Broken Bar guests, many of them regulars, holding wild silvery trout, big grins on their faces. The wall with the door to the outside boasted windows that looked over the lawn and the lake beyond.

An elk's head dominated the wall opposite the counter. The stuffed animal owned a massive rack of antlers and eerily realistic glass eyes that seemed to track Olivia whenever she worked in here. If she had her way, she'd have gotten rid of it long ago. Once upon a time, before her abduction, she didn't mind this sort of thing— these trophies of the dead. Now she was strictly a catch-and-release gal herself. If she hunted at all, or kept fish, it was for food.

Out of nowhere, a dark memory—*his* voice—smoked into her mind.

. . . We all have it, Sarah. Blood lust. That primordial thrill that comes from a chase, the hot rush of pleasure when you make that kill . . .

She wiped her damp palms on her jeans. PTSD sucked. It was a dragon that lived inside her own head, shaking loose more and more nightmarish memories, each one prompting another like dominoes tumbling.

. . . It was a woman, hanging by her neck from a big metal hook. Her eyes had been gouged out . . .

That murder on the news was heinous. But it had nothing to do with *him*. Or her past. He was dead. Gone.

"Good morning," she said crisply.

The guest spun around.

Olivia forced a smile. "I apologize for that little episode back there. My name is Olivia West. How can I help you?"

He returned her smile, but his dark blue eyes quietly assessed her. He was big. Fit-looking, balding. Maybe late fifties. Broad shoulders, hands like hams, thighs of a lumberjack. He wore jeans and a casual fleece jacket over a white T-shirt. He exuded an air of capability.

"Gage Burton," he said, reaching forward to shake her hand. She noted the gold wedding band, his solid grip, the power in his arms and shoulders, the way laugh lines crinkled around his eyes. He had a good vibe. She liked him immediately.

"Some nice flies here." He nodded to the counter. "Who tied them?"

"Most of them I designed myself. They're lures specific to this lake, or to the local rivers."

"I'd like to give some of them a try. We—my daughter and I—were wondering if you have any cabins available for the long weekend. We did drive around to the campsite first, but thought we'd shoot over and see if you had a cabin."

The girl who'd been sitting in the living room earlier suddenly appeared from behind the rack of postcards in the corner. Dark-haired and sullen, she held her shoulders in a hunch and regarded Olivia in heavy silence.

Gage held out his hand. "This is Tori."

"Hey, Tori." Olivia forced another smile. "Had a long drive?"

The kid turned abruptly and shoved out the door. The bell chimed, and the door swung shut silently behind her. She stomped down onto the lawn. Ace, who was lying on the grass in the sun outside, got up and wiggled over to her. Tori bent over to scratch the dog's head.

"I'm sorry," Gage said quietly. "She lost her mother six months ago, and she's"—he hesitated—"we're both having a hard time coming to terms with it. We have a long road ahead yet. Things were . . ." He cleared his throat. "Thanksgiving would be rough at home. I thought some country air, wilderness, fishing, making some new memories together, might help." Gage regarded her intently as he spoke. As if he were still weighing her. "I left it late, though. I should have planned ahead properly."

"I'm so sorry for your loss."

He smiled, rueful. "I don't need sympathy. Just a cabin."

The hurt on his face, the sudden visceral aura of loss around him, it got her in the gut. Olivia stole a quick glance at the black-haired girl outside. Tori was now kicking at stones. She'd given up on Ace, who was waiting at the glass door, looking to come in. Olivia went over and opened the door. Ace made for his basket.

"How old is Tori?"

"Eleven. But she likes to call it 'almost twelve.'"

"Must be a rough age to lose a mother, just as you're about to head into your teens."

"It is. She's a sensitive child to begin with. Very smart, creative, but also an introvert. She doesn't make friends easily, and her mother was her closest companion. She's been hitting out at the world in an effort to hide her pain, so I apologize for her behavior in advance." He paused. "My wife and I used to fish together. And I . . ." Embarrassed, he dragged his big palm over his head, eyes gleaming. "I'm sorry. I've . . . that's more than you need to know."

"We can do a cabin," she said quickly, uncomfortable at the rawness of emotion in this powerful-looking man. "We have a two-bedroom available, and a one-bedroom with a pullout in the living area." She went behind the counter, showed him the rate card. "The cabins all come with a wood-burning stove, a small kitchenette. Hot water via propane. There's no electricity or phone lines. We supply the wood. It's stacked on the deck."

"We'll take the two-bed," he said, perusing the rate card. "For the full weekend, including Monday night."

"I should mention we're expecting possible snow on Monday or Tuesday. Roads could become impassable for a few days if a serious storm sets in."

His eyes flared up, met hers. Something flickered through them. "That's okay. We'll take the cabin until Monday night, play it by ear if necessary."

Olivia entered his name into the computer and gave him the spiel about meals at the lodge.

"Here's the menu for tonight." She slid another card over the glass-topped counter. "It's casual dining. Guests sit together at several tables. It gives people a chance to meet others if they want. And this is a map of the ranch. Your cabin is here." She marked it with an X in marker pen. "The Buckeye cabin. We have boats for guest use. The dock is right here." She marked it on the map. "Life jackets are in the boat shed on the beach, near the gazebo."

"Thank you." He gathered up the pieces of information she'd given him.

"I should mention that cell reception is spotty and weather dependent, but there are certain areas on the lawn in front of your cabin where you can pick up a signal from the tower."

"Gotcha." He hesitated. "That was some nasty news on television."

She glanced up, held his gaze for a moment. "Yes, it was. Do you have a credit card? For the reservation?"

There was a beat of silence. He took out his wallet, handed her his card. "I might as well just pay up front and be done."

She processed his card, gave him the receipt.

"Could we reserve for dinner tonight, too?"

"Absolutely. I'll put you down. Jason, our chef, has venison on the menu."

He opened the door, gave her a nod. Olivia watched as he walked down the lawn to join his daughter. He put his arm around his kid's shoulders, but she jerked away.

They walked toward their truck and camper, together but apart. The child's black hair was dead straight and reached almost to her waist. It shimmered blue-black in the sunlight.

Olivia swallowed, a strange feeling washing over her skin.

An elusive memory, like a fingernail against glass, *tick tick ticked* against the surface of her mind, trying to get in.

———

Cole stared at the enlarged framed photo of himself mounted above the hearth, in pride of place in the library—the old cover shot for *Outside* magazine. He went to the bookshelves. Olivia was right; his father had copies of his works. He picked up one of several framed photographs of Jane and her family displayed on the shelves.

Olivia's words sifted into his mind.

... I had a gut feeling Myron needed to see his kids. You especially ... I believe he needs to atone, for whatever it was that happened between you and him. He needs to make his peace. I felt it might be good for him. Maybe even both of you. To say sorry ...

If Cole knew one thing about his dad, it was pride. Do-it-all-himself machismo. A genetic inability to admit he was wrong. Or say sorry.

... I bet you'll be just like him when you're old, too ...

From the mouths of babes. *Likeness lies in wait,* he thought as he set the frame down and walked over to the window.

From the window he watched the guest who was in the living room earlier crossing the lawn. The man tried to put his arm around his daughter. She shrugged him off. They climbed into their truck and disappeared around the trees.

His mind turned to Ty, a memory of walking with his arm around his stepson's shoulders. Ty would be just a little younger than that girl now. A sharp pain shot through his temple. Cole pressed his hands down flat onto the windowsill, drawing in a deep breath. What he'd give to have a second chance, to walk down to that very lake with Ty, fishing rods in hand.

He wanted to tell that man and his daughter that nothing lasted forever, that they must use each moment, each day, as a rare gift. That they must never allow the cloak of hubris and self-indulgence to stop them from appreciating, nurturing, protecting those closest to them.

Out from under the eaves below came Olivia with Ace at her heels. She lugged a roll of wire toward her truck, a tool pouch around her hips. Her chestnut hair shone in the sunlight as it lifted with the wind. Gold leaves chased over the lawn in her wake. She hefted the coil of wire into the back of her truck. He cursed softly.

She was going to fix that fence. He checked his watch, wondering if he had time to get down there and help her before his father showed up.

But as he looked at his watch, the library door swung open. His father rolled his chair in.

Cole was gut-punched by the sight of his dad crumpled into that chair, the gray pallor and strain in his sunken face. But his eyes were sharp and hot under their thatch of brow.

"I made a decision," he said brusquely, pushing himself over to the fire, and wheeling around to face him. "Olivia needs to hear this, too. Go fetch her."

Cole bristled but held his cool. "She's gone about her business."

"We have two-way radios. In the office. She carries one in her truck. We use channel four. Tell her I need to see her. Now."

"You doing okay?"

"How the fuck does it look like I'm doing? Just go get Olivia."

———

"What's eating you, Tori?" Gage said as he parked their rig outside the little log cabin. The sign over the porch said "The Buckeye."

"I don't like her."

"Olivia? Why not?"

"Why do *you* like her?" she snapped, eyes flashing. "I could see that you did. What about Mom?"

She threw open the door, jumped down, and marched across the lawn, her shoulders and brow thrust forward like a stubborn little fish battling upstream. She clumped up the wooden stairs and onto the small wraparound porch. She'd gained weight over the past months, and her skin was bad.

Despair wrapped around Gage.

There was no manual for this. No checklist he could follow that would help his daughter with her sudden weight gain, her spotty complexion. Her anger. Her guilt. He'd tried taking her to a therapist, but Tori called the guy an idiot and refused to go back.

God, he needed a therapist himself—he missed Melody more than he had words for.

He got out of the truck and walked slowly out onto the grass rise in front of the cabin. He looked out over the aquamarine lake toward the snow-dusted mountains in the distance. The air out here was so cool and clean you could drink it.

Was *he* out there somewhere?

Wind whispered suddenly through the lodgepole pines, yellow leaves skittering across the grass. A chill tickled over his skin. With it came a thread of fear. Could he control this? Could he keep them all safe?

Or had he set something utterly reckless in motion? Fear deepened. A different kind of fear—a question about the soundness of his own mind, his own grasp on reality.

No. You're fine. You're doing the right thing. For Tori.

For Sarah.

His mind turned again to Sarah—Olivia. Gage had been worried she might recognize him, but his fears appeared groundless. He hadn't been directly involved with her case. The big honchos had come up from Surrey, formed a federal task force, and taken it over. But Watt Lake had been his detachment. He'd been the boss there, and he'd been privy to investigation details. He'd watched the Sebastian George interrogations, and he'd looked in on most of the interviews with Sarah.

His appearance had also been very different back then. He'd been lean, bordering on thin, with a trademark handlebar moustache and a full head of neatly trimmed dark hair.

Time wrought big changes on some people, very little on others.

He took out his cell and found a hillock in front of the cabin where he managed to pick up a few bars of reception.

He dialed Mac Yakima's number. He wanted to know if they'd

learned anything more about the Birkenhead homicide. His call flipped straight to voice mail. He pocketed his phone and went into the cabin. The interior was cozy. Clean. Rustic. Tori was behind a closed door in one of the bedrooms. He built a fire in the cast-iron stove, and once it was crackling, he knocked on her door.

"Tori?"

She made a muffled sound.

"I'm going to take a walk, okay? Take a recon of the area."

No response.

"Don't go anywhere until I get back. If you need something to eat, it's in the camper."

Silence.

—

Cole found the two-way radio in a charger on the office counter. Beside it was a copy of today's *Province*. The front-page headline was about the Birkenhead murder. Above it, in bold block letters, was written Olivia West's name and the ranch address.

Cole scanned the story. In the middle of the text was a teaser for a related op-ed piece on page six. Cole turned to page six. Nestled there, between the pages, was a plastic ziplock baggie containing a lurid, lime-green fishing lure with three red eyes.

Frowning, he picked up the bag and studied the lure. It wasn't a trout fly—too big. More likely for winter steelhead or big fighting salmon.

He keyed the radio. "Olivia, this is Cole for Olivia." He released the key, waited as he continued to examine the fly. It was an unusual design.

Static crackled.

He keyed the radio again. "Olivia? You out there?"

"What is it?" Her voice came through, irritable.

"My father has demanded to see you."

"What?"

"Myron. He wants to see you."

"*Now?*"

"Yes, now. Before he has a heart attack. Wants both of us in the library to announce something." *Summoned like bloody schoolkids.*

She muttered a curse then said, "Tell him I'll be there in ten."

He stuck the packet with the fly back into page six and gathered up the newspaper addressed to her. He'd give it to her upstairs.

———

Olivia tossed the radio onto the truck seat and stared at the hole in the fencing, a roll of wire in her gloved hand. She was reluctant to be here alone, but she was also determined to do it alone, to stand up to her fear. To draw a line with Cole. He ate up way too much of her space.

And now he wanted her back at the lodge. Jump. Just like that. The McDonough men had summoned.

Her face heated. In the few hours that Cole had been on Broken Bar Ranch he'd learned things about her no one else knew, or had seen. The memory of his touch at the small of her back washed through her, and she clenched her jaw, hating the fact she'd welcomed it. Needed it. Taken comfort in having someone at her back.

She hated that she found him physically attractive. She told herself she could deal with that. It was the compassion, the pity, the kindness she couldn't handle. It made her feel like Sarah Baker again. An outcast. A rape victim. A curiosity.

She whirled around and dumped the wire back into the truck bed and marched round to the driver's side. But she stopped short as she noticed fresh boot prints in the black mud atop the tire tracks. They hadn't been here when she'd come through with Cole.

A cool whisper threaded through her. They were the same size as the prints that had followed her own track yesterday. Her gaze shot to the hole in the fence. Both the prints and the tire tracks led into deep forest. Again she was touched by a sense of being watched. She swallowed.

Then cursed. Opening her door, she scooted Ace over, climbed in, removed her gloves, and rubbed her hands hard over her face. Once she'd felt so safe here. She'd begun to believe she could actually be normal.

How could her world have changed so fast?

———

Olivia pushed open the library door, her tool belt still slung at her hips—she wasn't planning on staying long. She'd hear Myron out, then return to fix that fence. She was determined to do it. The bruise on her temple throbbed under the butterfly bandage she'd applied.

Myron hunkered in his chair by the fire. Cole looked uncomfortable in the wingback opposite him. Father and son. Past and present. The imagery was suddenly stark and caught her by surprise.

"What's so urgent?" she said to Myron.

"You shouldn't have done it. I told you not to call him." Myron jerked his head toward his son.

Cole's jaw stiffened. Even seated, his posture was combative, yet controlled.

"Look, it's done, Myron," she said coolly. "And I'm sorry—it was a mistake. But I know what it's like not having closure, not being able to say good-bye. And I thought . . ." Emotion snared her out of left field. She cleared her throat. "I'm done meddling. You two sort yourselves out. The ranch still needs running." She turned to leave.

"Wait. I summoned you here because you *both* need to hear this. I'm leaving the ranch to Olivia in trust."

She froze, turned back slowly. "Excuse me?"

Myron turned his attention to Cole. "And since you've taken the trouble to finally come home now that I'm kicking the bucket, you can be the one to phone Jane and make damn sure she knows this as well."

Myron wheeled yet closer to his son, his eyes boring into him, his hands clenched tight on his chair wheels. "I called Norton Pickett, my estate lawyer, about an hour ago. I've asked him to draw up a new will, and to bring me copies to sign as soon as he's done. Broken Bar Ranch goes in trust to Olivia. For as long as she wants to live here— until she leaves the ranch, or she dies—it's hers. Everything. She does what she wants to the place. You, or Jane, or Clayton Forbes and his vultures, can't touch a thing. And I know Forbes is after this place. I know you and Jane both want to sell to him."

Olivia stared. Cole didn't speak.

The fire crackled, and the *tick tock* of the library clock grew loud. A shutter began to bang rhythmically in the increasing wind.

"What do you mean by 'in trust'?" Cole said finally.

Myron repeated himself slowly. "For as long as Olivia wants to live here and manage the Broken Bar Ranch, it's hers to run. Until she dies. Or until she leaves of her own volition. After that it can go to you and Jane. If you outlive her."

A soft noise sounded at the door behind Olivia. She swung around.

Adele stood white-faced in the doorway with a heavy tray in her hands. "Ah, sorry, I . . . uh . . . I have the tea and sandwiches you wanted brought up, Mr. McDonough."

"Put it over there," Myron snapped, pointing at the buffet.

She bustled over, moved aside a newspaper that was on the buffet, and set the tray down. The noises of teacups rattling and sandwich plates being set out was unnaturally loud as all waited in tense silence for the housekeeper to leave.

"Close the door when you go, Adele."

"Of course, Mr. McDonough."

She cast a quick glance over her shoulder, briefly meeting Cole's eyes before she exited the library door.

As soon as the door was shut, Olivia said, "You're not thinking clearly, Myron. You're under a lot of medication, and this is—"

"Goddammit, girl, I don't have brain damage. I'm thinking more clearly than I have in years. I debated this at length last night. It's done. Nothing you can do to change it, either."

"It's *not* done. You just said yourself that Pickett has yet to draw up the papers. You haven't signed anything yet."

"It's as good as signed," he said. "Pickett should have the paperwork here by this evening. He understands the sensitive time factor."

She threw a desperate look at Cole. "*Say* something. This is your inheritance. *Your* land."

"It's not his goddamn land," Myron interjected. "He left this place years ago. He can't just waltz back in now that I'm at death's door."

"There is—"

"Olivia," Cole said quietly. "Let it go. This cuts much deeper than the will. This is about me and my father and what happened twenty-three years ago. He blames me for killing my mother and brother."

"I will *not* let it go, dammit!" she snapped, heat riding high into her cheeks. "I won't accept this. I don't want this ranch. I can't take it from you."

Cole gave a derisive snort. "That's certainly not what Jane thinks. She's convinced you've been using your feminine wiles to exert undue influence over our ailing father in his vulnerable state."

Her jaw dropped. "And you believe that?"

"Well, it clearly looks like Jane was on to something, given *this* recent development."

"You *bastard*. You're just attacking me to rile your father. You're better than this."

His mouth flattened, and he regarded her with silent equanimity.

Anger pounded into her chest. "I don't give a damn what you or your sister think about me, Cole McDonough." She spun to face Myron. "And you—I won't take the ranch from you or your children. You're being a jerk."

"What is it that you think belongs to them, anyway? This land? This *home*? They left both. They just want some developer's windfall. And you? You've got nowhere to go. I know you love this place. I know what you could do with it. You could make Grace's dreams come true, turn this place into a year-round destination."

"Right," Cole said quietly. "It's all about Mother. Always has been."

"My resignation will be on your desk tomorrow," Olivia said. "I'm not getting involved in some family legal squabble. You're forcing me to leave."

Myron grunted. "And where exactly will you go? You have no friends, woman. Apart from a dying old man, an irascible sod who let his whole family slip away."

Cole's gaze darted to his father, his brow rising as if this was the first time he'd ever heard his father admit any culpability in the dissolution of their family.

"This is not about me, Myron. This is you trying to hurt your son, and him lashing back at you. It's about stupid old battle lines between two macho assholes who can't the hell see that those lines don't mean a thing anymore."

Myron gasped, doubled over in his chair as if he'd been punched in the abdomen. His face contorted, turned puce. His breaths came out in wheezes. He hit the arm of his chair, as if trying to speak.

"His pills!" Cole barked, lurching up and lunging for the pitcher of water at his father's side. "On the buffet. Get them."

Cole sloshed water into a glass.

Olivia rushed to the buffet, grabbed the pills, knocking a newspaper onto the floor. The headline blared up at her.

"Birkenhead murder—echoes of the Watt Lake Killer?"

A ringing began in her ears.

"Pills, dammit! Now!"

She hurried over, handed Cole the pills.

"How many?" Cole said to her, popping the cap, anxiety, adrenaline burning in his eyes.

But she couldn't think. The ringing in her head grew loud. She felt herself going distant. His father held up two fingers. Cole shook two pills into his palm, put them in the old man's mouth, brought the water glass to his lips.

Myron spluttered. Swallowed. Coughed. He clenched his armrests, his head bent forward and his eyes scrunched tightly as he waited for the medication to take effect. Gradually his breathing eased, and his whole face seemed to change. Tension melted from Cole's shoulders. Olivia watched, numb, unable to fully absorb the present. She swallowed, walked woodenly back to the buffet, picked up the newspaper from the floor.

Her name was printed in block letters across the top of the headline. Her gaze dropped to the teaser for the op-ed piece. She opened the paper to page six.

On some distant level she felt Cole watching her.

Something fell out of the pages and landed at her feet. A small plastic bag. She bent down, retrieved it.

Inside was a large fishing lure. Tied with lime-green surveyor's tape. Three glossy red eyes. Shimmering holographic thread around a barbed hook on a leader.

The ringing in her ears rose to a screeching cacophony. Sweat prickled across her lip.

"Where . . . did this come from?" Her voice came out in a hoarse whisper.

"It was inside the newspaper like that when it was delivered to the office this morning," Cole said, standing behind his father, his hand resting protectively on the back of the wheelchair. "I brought it upstairs."

"We don't get delivery."

"I just assumed it was delivered. It has your name and the ranch address on it."

She stared at the lure. "It was *inside* the office?"

"On the counter."

Blood drained from her head. Nausea washed up into her throat.

"It's not possible," she whispered.

"What's not possible? What's the problem, Olivia?"

"Did you see who left it in there?"

"I have no idea who left it. Whoever it was must have come in between the time you left and the time I got down there to use the radio."

It's not possible. It can't be him. He's dead . . .

She turned, and, clutching the paper and the packet with the lure, she walked woodenly, a zombie, one foot carefully placed in front of the other, like a drunk focused on looking sober.

She opened the door. Stepped out. Shut it quietly behind her.

CHAPTER 10

"What upset her like that?" Myron said.

"Beyond your leaving her the ranch and me acting like a jerk? I think it was that story in the paper about a murder." Cole frowned at the closed door that Olivia had just exited so oddly. "It was breaking on television news downstairs. When she saw it, it was like she'd taken a twelve-gauge slug to the chest. Collapsed to the floor."

"What murder?"

"Two teens found the naked body of a woman hanging from a tree by her neck. She'd been gutted like a deer. Entrails hanging out, eyes removed."

Myron stared, worry etching into his features. "Do they know who did it?"

"Cops aren't saying much. But there was an op-ed piece in the paper suggesting the murder had echoes of the Watt Lake killings from over a decade ago."

Myron's eyes narrowed sharply, an intensity boiling up around him. "And in the packet—what was in that packet she had in her hands?"

"A fishing lure. Someone must have left it for her tucked inside the paper. The paper had her name on it."

"Go," Myron said quietly, urgently. "Go after her." He rolled his chair aggressively toward the door as if he would get up and run after the woman himself if his legs would bend to his will. "Don't leave her alone like that." His eyes flared to Cole. "You saw the scars on her wrists?" He pointed at the door. "That woman tried to kill herself once already, and it wasn't long before she came here. When she arrived on Broken Bar those scars were livid and raw. This news has something to do with her past. It's reminding her of something."

Cole hesitated, then moved quickly out the door and into the passage. He leaned over the stairwell banister. "Olivia?" he called down the stairs.

The front door banged shut.

Cole clattered down after her.

His father yelled from the landing. "Just don't press her too hard—you'll spook her! She's feral that way!"

———

Fuckfuckfuck.

Olivia stormed down the lawn, hand fisted around the newspaper and lure. Her single goal was to reach her cabin, fast, shut her door to the world—to the dark nightmares chasing her into the grove of alders. As she entered the trees, the paper-white bark with black streaks looked suddenly ominous. Leaves clattered and laughed at her in the mounting wind. They blew against her skin, edges dry and sharp.

She'd fought within inches of her life to bury the person she once was, to lock naïve, stupid, victimized Sarah Baker into the basement of her soul, throw away the key. She'd struggled into this new identity. This new life.

Now, some bizarre set of coincidences were cracking open the locks, forcing her to look down into that fathomless abyss of her past again.

Her eyes burned. Her muscles wound wire tight. *Fuck this.*

That's all it was—coincidences. Had to be. Because *he* was dead. The Watt Lake Killer was ash.

The *Province* journalist was sensation-mongering by mining any similarities. The murder on the Birkenhead had *nothing* to do with Sebastian George. It was just not possible. And if there *were* any echoes in the signature display of the body, it was a copycat. Some sicko who'd gotten the idea from a serial murderer who'd gone before him and made national headlines.

Those boot prints paralleling her track this morning? Simply an angler or hunter or hiker setting out for the day. The Arizona scarf found atop her own tracks could have blown there after having been dropped by a woman on a dawn walk. That basket of wild blueberries outside her door? She still had to ask Nella about those. Probably Nella's thank-you token for helping with her homework last week.

Her mind was just drawing stupid parallels. Wind gusted, clattering another rain of small dead leaves down onto her and Ace. She sucked in a deep, shaky breath as she negotiated the path that narrowed and twisted deeper into the trees. It was just this time of year. The strong scents of autumn, the coming snow, the sounds of the geese flying south, the echoes of gunshots, deer season, the sense of winter closing its fist around the wilderness—it was *always* a tricky time.

Scents, images could trigger flashbacks. The therapist had told her so.

It's time . . . time for the hunt, Sarah . . .

She fisted the paper tighter, trying to block out his voice.

The Predator . . . it's a fine name . . .

So why *had* someone left a duplicate of that very same fly tucked inside a story referencing the Watt Lake killings? In a newspaper with her name on it? Terror surged afresh in her chest. Her throat tightened. She moved faster.

Behind her she heard the thud of footfalls. Coming fast. Someone running—chasing her.

Panic was instant. The urge to flee overrode her brain. She was back in the forest, racing blindly, not along any path, but deep into the trees, weaving through branches, stumbling wildly over roots, breath rasping in her throat. In the distance of her mind she registered a dog barking furiously. Branches, twigs cracked. The footfalls came closer. Hard breathing behind her . . .

She had to hide, find the bear den. Sweat dampened her skin. The thudding behind grew louder, faster. He attacked, grabbing her arm, spinning her around. She jerked free, and in a heartbeat, she'd dropped the newspaper, and her hunting knife was unsheathed. She gripped the hilt, blade up, primed for an upward thrust into the liver, under ribs. She went into a crouch, swayed the knife slowly, menacing him back. Sweat dripped into her eyes. Her heart beat so loud she couldn't hear anything else now but her blood against her eardrums.

Sebastian's eyes lasered hers. He was smiling. His shining black curls ruffled in the wind. He came closer, closer . . .

. . . *It's not a game until everyone knows they are playing, Sarah, my sweet . . . the prey must be aware of the hunter . . .*

"Don't. Move," she growled through her teeth. "Not another goddamn foot forward or I'll rip your throat out."

He stopped advancing. Slowly he put both hands up. Palms out. "Olivia?" he said quietly. "Focus. It's me. Cole. Cole McDonough. Myron's son. You're safe, fine. It's all fine. Olivia? Can you hear me?"

Olivia.

Her name.

New name.

Not Sarah.

"It's okay," he said. "Come back to me."

Her vision returned, slowly spiraling outward from tiny pinpricks, taking in reality, the bigger picture. Shock slammed through her as she stared at Cole. Ace growled at his heels, confused. Like she was. She started to shake violently, the kind of great big palsied shudders that come from being transported from one reality to another.

"Here," he said, holding out his hand. "Give me that knife."

Still uneasy, she swallowed and took a step backward, sheathed it herself. She took another step back, wiped her upper lip with the back of her hand, and bumped hard up against the trunk of a tree. Panic slammed. Her brain went black. She fought with all her might against the compulsion to flee again, fought to remain present. But a fresh kind of terror licked through her stomach— she was losing her mind again. Like before.

"Focus." His voice was low, gravelly. His stormy gray eyes were intense, filled with concern.

He came closer. Her heart beat even faster, the drive to escape almost blinding. She couldn't breathe.

He reached out, placed a hand firmly on each of her shoulders. Large, steadying hands. He held her still. Somewhere in the distance of her mind Olivia registered warmth. Solidity. Safety. A sense of being protected.

He slid his hands down her arms and took her fingers in his. Slowly he drew her toward him. Wrapping his arms around her, he held her shuddering body tightly against his. So tight she couldn't move. So tight she couldn't fight.

He stroked her hair. Her eyes burned with emotion. The scent of him filled her senses. The hardness, the heat of his body, his rough stubble against her stirred things inside her she thought long dead. She tried to resist this need, tried to go numb. But his care, his physical comforting, exploded a fierce desperation in her chest—a need to be held, cherished by another human. Loved. Just accepted.

She fought these new feelings because they brought a whole other set of fears. But she couldn't. A coal had been ignited, and it burned down deep.

He held her until her breathing slowed and became regular. Until the rigidity in her muscles softened. Then he cupped her face and made her look up into his eyes. His mouth was so close. His pulse thrummed in his neck.

She stared up at him. This handsome man. This man of wild places. He was making her feel again, and she didn't know which was more terrifying.

"You were having a flashback or something," he said softly. "Tell me what's going on, Olivia."

Her gaze darted around, seeking a way to escape the questions. To escape everything. She swallowed.

"I know PTSD, Olivia." He paused. "There's no shame in it. That's one thing they tell soldiers. No shame. No need to try and hide it."

Shame.

How could he ever know the tricky depths of the shame she felt because she'd been Sebastian's rape victim? Because she'd attracted him. Because she'd fallen for his tricks. Because she'd thought he was handsome, charming. Nice.

Embarrassment washed through her. How could he know how sullied and dirtied and utterly humiliated she'd been made to feel by her own husband? Her own father and mother. Her community. She'd become the "other." Tainted. Something that people hid in a closet or cast away rather than confront the darkness of humanity, their own weaknesses and fears.

He bent down, picked up the newspaper and lure she must have dropped when she pulled her knife.

He handed them back to her. She took the paper and packet from him, mouth dry.

"You going to tell me what's going on?"

She glanced away again, then flashed back to meet his gaze. Barbed wire crawled around her as her resolve firmed. He'd cut too close to her bone. He knew and had seen too much. And she could not open further. She could *not* be Sarah Baker in his eyes, anyone's eyes.

"I'll tell you what's going on." She pointed in the direction of the lodge house. "Your father is throwing me into combat with you and your sister, and as much as I care for that old badger, as much as I want for him to die in peace, I don't want *this*. *I* refuse to have anything to do with his inheritance crap."

"Olivia," he said quietly, pinning her with his gaze, using her name to bring her down. And she hated it. Him. For making her want things again that she couldn't have without exposing her truth. Without unveiling her scars, her past, her humiliation. Without having to be that victim again.

"I apologize for what I said. It was dumb-ass. You can't stop Myron McDonough when he gets a burr under his saddle. You just need to ride it out. And believe me, I speak from a lifetime of experience. Trust me on this."

Trust.

She didn't even know *how* to trust. Not anymore.

"Besides, this isn't about the will. Are you going to tell me what really happened? Was it that news story? That lure?"

She flattened her mouth, looked away, heart slamming so hard against her ribs she thought it would bust free. "It's nothing." The words were lame. But she had no energy to find better ones. She just needed to get out of this guy's orbit, which was sucking her in. "I'm fine."

She turned woodenly and picked her way through the trees and back up to the path, clutching the newspaper. Ace followed.

"Don't treat me like a fool, Olivia!" he called after her. "You're just confusing the issue here."

She kept walking.

"Don't you dare write me off like this. Who do you think I am? Some worthless piece of shit? Some asshole who couldn't hold on to his own family? What did you call me—a narcissistic fool?"

She stalled, her back to him.

"That murder upset you." He came up through the trees toward her. "It triggered some PTSD thing. What can we do to help? Are you in some kind of trouble?"

"No," she said, refusing to turn around. "I'm not in trouble."

He's dead. I'm going to be fine.

"Olivia."

Wind rustled.

He waited.

She moistened her lips. She'd rather leave Broken Bar than expose her past. Before the media came storming again, on the back of rumblings of a new Watt Lake Killer. Before people started looking at her in that old way. Like some freak of survival. Before Ethan and her family could find her. She would not—*could not*—come clean about this. It would undermine everything she'd built. And if it meant shutting this man out, so be it.

"I'm fine." She resumed her march down the narrow path, Ace following loyally behind her. "And don't bother to come after me again," she called out over her shoulder. "Because there's nothing in it for you, understand? If your father goes through with this, my bags are as good as packed, and I'm outta here."

He stayed where he was, thank God.

She walked faster, leaves crunching under her boots, and she was shocked by the sudden wetness on her face as tears washed hot down her cheeks. She hadn't cried in years. She'd dried up and died inside, becoming a hollow husk. But Cole had cracked something open in her. Emotion. Need. Desire for human contact. And it was killing her because it hurt. It hurt like all hell. And she couldn't have it.

———

Cole stormed back into the library. His father was near the fire, nursing a tumbler of scotch. The pill container was on the table at his side, the whisky bottle next to it.

"Needed something stiffer than Carrick's tea," he said as he swallowed another two pills and chased them down with a heavy gulp of spirits.

Cole stared at the booze bottle. He could do with a shot himself. Instead he went to the buffet, poured a cup of tea, helped himself to a sandwich. He took a seat by the fire, opposite his dad.

"You need to tell me about her." Cole took a bite, wolfing down half the sandwich in one go.

"Nothing much to tell, son."

A knee-jerk spasm of irritation chased down all-too-familiar neural pathways that had been forged over time. He delivered the other half of his sandwich to his mouth, swallowed, and took a gulp of tea. "You leave her this ranch, this McDonough legacy that has been in the family since the mid-1800s, and you have nothing to tell about the person you're leaving it to?"

"You and Jane abandoned this legacy. I have no obligation to you—"

"Oh, spare me. This isn't about me or Jane, and you know it. This conversation is about that woman and your relationship with her. Where is she from? What do you know about her?"

His father looked away, stared at the fire.

Cole washed down the last of his tea, set his cup down. He leaned forward, arms resting on his knees. "That's rough stuff, that murder. A woman, disemboweled, eyes gouged out."

Myron nodded.

"You believe Olivia tried to kill herself shortly before arriving here?"

His father took another deep gulp of scotch, nodded, his eyes going watery from the drink, drugs. Or something sneakier.

"You've seen the scar around her neck, too?"

Myron's eyes flashed up suddenly.

"You haven't? It's like a choker right around her neck." Cole paused. "As if she was rubbed raw by a rope, or a collar that cut deep and long."

Myron stared. Several beats of silence swelled between them. "She always wears a bandana," he said finally. "Or a turtleneck. I never knew."

"She's hiding it. I only saw because I took off her bandana to help ease her breathing when she fainted."

"Shit," Myron said softly. He took another deep sip.

"What do you remember about the Watt Lake Killer?" Cole said. "All I recall is that he was some sexual sadist who'd preyed on women up north, abducting and confining them over a winter, before setting them out for a spring hunt. The whole thing was just breaking when I was in the army, leaving for a peacekeeping tour in Sierra Leone."

Myron pursed his lips. "After he hunted and shot them dead, he hung his victims like deer meat to bleed out. He carved out their eyes. Kept body parts in a freezer. Consumed some."

"Like the Birkenhead victim was hung by the neck," Cole said. "Eyes also missing."

"But they got the Watt Lake Killer," Myron said. "They arrested and charged a man. The trial was big news. He died in prison some years back. That was in the news, too."

Cole sat back, inhaled deeply, exhaustion suddenly pressing down on him again. He closed his eyes for a moment and the sensation of Olivia in his arms immediately filled him—the way she'd resisted his embrace, then slowly melted into his body as if she needed him. It felt good to hold her. To be needed. To feel as though he could protect someone. Not let them down, like he'd let Holly and Ty down.

Shit.

Maybe it was him who'd needed that embrace, not the other way around.

"Well, whatever it was about the Birkenhead murder story and that fishing lure," he said quietly, "it triggered something in Olivia, catapulted her right into some kind of a flashback out there. She went for me with her knife—thought I was someone else. My guess is she's suffering from severe PTSD."

"I know she's got issues, Cole, but I've never seen her have a flashback. Nothing like you describe. Not in all the time she's been here."

Cole leaned forward again. "But you *were* worried she'd try to hurt herself again. What *has* she told you about her past, and where she's from?"

His father regarded him intently, something inscrutable entering his eyes. "You like her," he said quietly.

Oh, Jesus.

"I'm curious."

"That all?"

"Yeah, that's all. I'm curious because you're leaving this ranch to some whackjob who flips into flashbacks and threatens to kill me with a mean-ass hunting knife. What do you think?" Cole came to his feet. He set his cup and plate back on the buffet. "She has searchable references up until eight years ago. Before that she's a blank slate, like she didn't exist at all."

"You checked?"

"Yes, I checked. Some strange woman calls my cell phone at midnight in Florida, tells me my father is dying? Of course I'm going to try and find out who she is." He hesitated. "Besides, Jane asked me to follow it up. Like I said, she's worried Olivia is playing you."

Myron snorted. "Where in the hell did Jane get that idea anyway?"

"Forbes."

"And Forbes got it from where, exactly? He's full of shit."

"Seems Forbes was on the money—you *are* leaving her the estate. I'm guessing this news is going to get right up both his and Jane's noses, because *if* Olivia stays, this place is not for sale."

Myron ran his tongue over his teeth. "She'll stay."

"I wouldn't be so sure."

His father's eyes flickered. He drained the last of his scotch, setting his glass down with the careful concentration of a man on the fringes of inebriation and not wanting to show it. A state Cole knew all too well. His dad turned to look at the flames again. Silence shimmered into the library. The shutter banged in the wind. When his father spoke again, his voice was thick and distant, his words slightly slurred.

"When she first came here, I saw in Olivia a love for this wilderness, the fishing, the rivers, mountains, all echoes of Grace's passion for this place. Olivia blossomed here, Cole," he said, uncharacteristically gently, talking to the fire. "Like a desiccated flower on the vine she was when she arrived. This place healed her. Those scars on her wrists that were so red and angry, they began to fade."

Cole's stomach tightened. He was unused to this. He was programmed to lash back at his dad's bellicose belligerence. He didn't know how to deal with this evidence of compassion, or the fact his father had earlier admitted a role in destroying their family. It put Cole on the back foot, like he had to make the next move.

Myron looked up at his son with distant, clouded eyes. "She began to laugh. Her and that dog . . . they wormed their way right into this place. Into my goddamn heart. She became my friend. My only friend. And I . . ." He faltered. "Last night I thought that if I could do right by her, I would also do right by Grace."

The specter of his mother again.

This was still all about Grace. About his father not letting her go. About the fact he'd killed her and Jimmie.

Now he was even trying to secure Grace's dream from beyond the grave.

"It could be right for you, too."

Surprise rippled through Cole. "What do you mean?"

"Leaving the ranch to Liv might give you time to see that this place is what you want. That without my presence, it could once again become something beautiful. A home."

Cole felt hot. Awkward. A response eluded him.

He glanced at the pills and the bottle. It was the drugs talking. His old man needed some sleep—wasn't making sense.

"I need to go," he said, making for the door. His intention was to fire up his laptop and conduct a search on the history of the Watt Lake killings to see if they could shine any light on the Birkenhead murder.

At the door, he stopped. "You got any objections to me using the old barn in the east field for my plane? Wind is picking up. I need to stash it somewhere safe for when the storm hits."

"You flew here? You still got the Cub?"

"Yeah."

His father rubbed his whiskers. "The barn—no one's been in there since . . ."

Cole's stomach tightened. He waited for the next words: *Since the truck wreck was stored in there twenty-three years ago.*

But the words never came.

"Use my vehicle if you need one." He turned his wheelchair so his back faced Cole. "It's the black Dodge Ram in the garage. Carrick will get you keys from the office. Not like I'm going to be using it."

Cole stared at the back of his old man's gray head, the gnarled, veined, liver-spotted hands on the armrests. His gaze lifted to the image on the fireplace above his father. The strong younger McDonough posing atop a conquered peak. The old McDonough crumpled with age and creeping death in his wheelchair below the image. Time elastic and twisting.

You'll be just like him . . .

Cole didn't want to be just like him. Bitter and twisted. Shoring up his loss and pain because he was too afraid to open up, try again.

He left his father alone in his library and clomped down the stairs in search of the housekeeper with the keys.

———

Adele hunched over in the dark stairwell closet, her cell phone pressed to her ear, the door open a wee crack to let in some light.

"He's going to leave it *all* to Olivia," she whispered. "The whole damn ranch. I *told* you we couldn't trust that woman. She's been after the old man's land since the day she arrived. She was snooping around his study the other night, too, where he had the will on top of the desk. I know what was in that will—I read it. And it wasn't this."

She stilled at a creak on the stairs. Someone was coming.

"We've *got* to stop this," she whispered quickly. "If Olivia leaves Broken Bar, the place reverts back to his kids. You've got to find a way to get rid of her."

Light suddenly exploded into the dark space.

"Adele?"

She blinked and jerked her head up, banging it on a broom. Pain sparked through her skull as Cole McDonough loomed in a black silhouette at the door.

Heat rushed into her face, heart banging. She killed the call and slid the phone quickly into her apron pocket.

CHAPTER 11

Tori got up onto her knees and peeked over the windowsill, making certain her father was gone. Satisfied, she curled back down onto the bed and opened her e-reader, keeping an ear attuned for the sound of her dad's return. She began to read.

> Can you pinpoint the exact instant your life starts on a collision course with someone else's? Can you trace back to the moment those lives did finally intersect, and from where they spiraled outward again, yet from that point they remained forever entwined, two lives locked one with another?
>
> That moment came for the Watt Lake staff sergeant one cold November day up near Bear Claw Valley in remote Indian country, on a gravel bar at a fork in the Stina River, which wends its majestic way down from the interior to enter the Pacific under the Alaskan panhandle border.
>
> The sergeant was somewhat young to head up a detachment for the Royal Canadian Mounted Police, but he was a rising star on the federal force, and Watt Lake was a remote northern community, not a terribly large detachment. It was a good place to test the ropes of management after some acclaimed detective work in Alberta.
>
> Unlike the meandering river, the sergeant had a straight life plan. He'd recently married a crime reporter from the *Watt Lake Gazette*. She'd been working her own way up a journalistic career ladder

when she interviewed him regarding a court case. They'd fallen in love, tried to keep the affair secret. But when they decided to get engaged, she quit the town paper, gave up her dream of working one day for a big-city daily, and turned her talents instead to features for magazines, true crime stories, and she was trying her hand at a novel.

Then came the fated meeting on the river.

Tori's heart beat harder, and something dark and invisible began prowling along the fringes of her brain.

The sergeant cast his line out, spooling it into hazy sunshine that danced with tiny insects like dust motes over the river. The sun had no warmth. Ice still covered rocks in the shadows, and moss crunched with frost. Towering Douglas firs, some as old as the Notre Dame Cathedral in Paris, hemmed in the green-gold water like omniscient gods watching over him. He set his fly at the edge of an eddy, allowing it to drift down with the current to a deeper pool where the water was mirror still. Perfect for big steelhead.

Gently, he tugged on the line, making his fly dart like a living thing atop the surface.

When the sergeant got no bites, he brought in his line, moved farther downriver. The November cold breathed out from the shadows between the trees, and his fingers felt frozen in his fingerless gloves.

He cast again and was letting his fly drift when he became aware of a presence. A sensation of being watched. His first thought was grizz. He'd seen a big one upriver yesterday, near his camp. The bear had given him the eye, then disappeared. It wouldn't be the first time he'd been stalked by a bear.

Slowly, he shifted his gaze over his shoulder. A man stood in water about fifty yards down from him. He'd not made a sound in his approach. It was as if he'd simply materialized from the fabric of the forest.

The man wore a black jacket over his waders and a balaclava against the cold. The sergeant watched mesmerized as the man cast out his line. Perfect, languid loops rolled out above the water, doubling back one loop over the other, sending sparkling droplets into sunshine. It was mastery, sheer perfection.

The man landed his fly. Bam! He had a fish on. His rod tip arced down and the line went taut. The fish exploded from the surface of the water, leaping in a silvery flash against the line. It slapped down on the surface, running deep. The man let the fish take the line. The cop watched him play it until finally the fish was spent, and the man brought his catch in, flapping weakly.

The man crouched down, released his fish, then looked the cop's way.

The sergeant raised his hand. Acknowledgment of mastery.

The man gave a brief nod. He waded a little farther downriver, repeated his cast. And bam, another one.

Tori turned the page.

This time the cop moved close to better see the fish as the man brought it in.

"That's got to be close to thirty pounds," the cop said as the man crouched down and opened the fish's mouth, revealing rows of tiny sharp teeth.

The man glanced up at him. Through the slit in his black balaclava his eyes were the color of the water where it ran coppery over rocks and was filled with shafts of sunlight. And in his eyes was an intensity that gave the cop sudden pause. It was the kind of feral cunning one glimpsed in the eyes of things wild. He was suddenly cognizant of the fact that he was all alone in deep woods and mountains. People went missing in the wilderness all the time. Like Sarah Jane Baker, who'd simply vanished almost a month earlier.

The sergeant couldn't quite articulate the chill that crawled suddenly under his skin.

The man reached into the glistening pink mouth and extracted the hook. The lure was a big gun. Larger than standard winter steelhead lures. Bigger even than some of the newer Intruder designs.

The man clubbed the fish on the head.

"You're keeping it?" the cop said in surprise.

The man pointed to where the adipose fin had been removed. It was a hatchery fish in the Stina River system. The only kind of steelhead one could keep. Others were released by law.

"The fish," he said very quietly as he came to his feet, "is my brother, and I love him. Yet I must kill him, and eat."

The sergeant blinked. Then slowly, he smiled. "Like Santiago, in *The Old Man and the Sea*."

The man's eyes crinkled in the slit of his balaclava. "One of my favorites."

It was a pleasant surprise indeed, he thought, to find a man's man of a reader on the river wild.

"What are you using?" He nodded to the lure.

The man handed it to him.

The fly was tied with shimmering holographic thread and tufts made from shredded strips of lime tape. Three shining red beads for eyes.

"Surveyor's tape?"

The man nodded.

"Three eyes?"

"One extra for additional weighting at the front."

The cop examined the fly, the way the hook was tied to a leader and hid sneakily at the rear among the shreds of green.

"The Predator," said the man.

"It's a step up from the Invader concept," the cop said, turning it over in his hand, committing the design to memory. "A three-eyed Predator."

"Take it," the man said. "It's yours."

The cop's eyes flared up in surprise. The man met his stare with a placid steadfastness. He had the eyes of a mountain lion. Watchful, calm, yet calculating. With dark rims and dense black lashes. The cop returned his attention to the lure in his hand. Tying flies was an esoteric art, especially when it came to steelhead. There were always backwoods rumors about secret designs, and these were closely guarded by furtive anglers. They were not things you simply handed to a stranger, at least not in the sergeant's experience. A soft suspicion began to uncurl inside him along with the sense that he'd be making some Faustian bargain if he took this fly. That he'd be beholden to something dark.

"I can make many more," the man said, watching him closely.

"You designed this?" the sergeant asked.

"It was a gift." The man paused, something unreadable shifting into his eyes. "From a special friend."

A chill crawled over the sergeant's skin. Was it something in the way the man said this? Or was it the sun slipping behind the peaks?

"Just try it."

The cop tied the fly onto his line. He waded upriver, and within seconds the water exploded with a fish. His line zinged and his rod tip arced. He battled that sucker until the light started to fail. By the time he landed it, his arms shook and his skin was drenched with sweat. A whopping silver fighter close on forty inches.

Busting with exhilaration and pride, he looked up to see if the man was watching.

He was gone.

Just shadow and light. Dapples on the water. A ripple here and there. And a soft sigh of wind.

As silently as he'd appeared, the man had dematerialized back into the forest.

Gently the sergeant removed the Predator from the fish's glistening mouth. He crouched down and cradled the fish in the cups of his hands, holding it upright just under the surface, allowing the gills to move, to circulate oxygen. He felt a mystic connection to this creature of river and sea. Then, with a sudden powerful flick of its tail, it flashed out of his hands and ran upriver into the green current.

Feeling blessed, he packed up his gear.

On that day, Sarah Jane Baker, a young wife from Watt Lake who helped run the local sporting goods store with her husband, had been missing for three weeks.

The sergeant didn't know until the following spring that it was Sarah Baker who'd tied his three-eyed fly.

And that she'd given it to a monster.

———

"Everything all right, Adele?" Cole said as the housekeeper stepped out of the closet, hurriedly pulling the door closed behind her.

"Yes, of course, what can I do for you?" she said crisply, smoothing down her apron pocket, then her hair. Her face was flushed.

"I heard you talking in there."

She gave a terse smile. "Cursing, more like. I was looking for the vacuum cleaner bags—someone has misplaced them."

Cole's gaze went to her pocket, where he was sure he'd seen her put a phone.

You've got to find a way to get rid of her . . .

Those were the words he'd heard Adele saying as he'd opened the closet door to investigate the sound. He gave her a measuring look, suspicion unfurling inside him.

"Can I help you?" she said.

"My father said you have access to the key cabinet in the office. I need the keys for his Dodge."

"Oh . . . oh, of course." She dug her hand back into her apron pocket and extracted a ring of keys. "His truck keys are with the other keys in the safe. Come this way."

As they entered the office and Adele unlocked the key cabinet, he said, "How is Mr. Carrick?"

She cast him a sideways glance, selected the car keys. "He's doing fine. Retired from his municipal job now."

"Nice. He must be doing a lot more fishing and hunting, I bet."

She hesitated. "He was on long-term disability before taking the retirement. He took a knock on the head at work, got a bad concussion."

"He okay now?"

"He has his good days." She handed him the set of Dodge keys.

"And how is Tucker? Last I heard he was studying for a business degree, I think."

She smiled, and this time it reached into her eyes. "Oh, he got his master's some years back. He's back home, working in Clinton now."

"In town? I'm surprised there are any non-ranching or logging jobs around."

She closed and locked the key cabinet, cleared her throat. "He's doing investment consulting and financial management. The Dodge is parked in the garage out back, where the ATVs and snowmobiles are kept. Mr. McDonough hasn't used it in a while."

"Thanks." He hesitated, then called after her as she bustled out. "Adele?"

She paused in the doorway, turned to face him, a nervous flicker through her features.

"It must be unsettling, my father's prognosis, the future of what'll happen with Broken Bar and the staff."

Unguarded emotion chased through her face, but she tempered it quickly. "Yes. I . . ." She sighed. "It's been almost forty years here for me. A lifetime of memories. I've put everything into this place. I met and married my husband here. Tucker was born and raised on the ranch. But I suppose everything has its season." She offered a rueful smile. "Anyway, it's high time I retired, don't you think?"

"You guys going to be okay, financially?"

Her features turned inscrutable. "I have a pension coming. Mr. Carrick has his. We'll make do."

"What if the ranch keeps running? Might you stay on longer?"

Her eyes widened. "I . . . It will be sold. Won't it?"

He regarded her. "Not necessarily."

"I just assumed that it would. A sale would be of great benefit to the whole region."

"How so?"

She swallowed, hot spots suddenly riding high into her cheeks. "There's talk of a development—it's just a proposal, mind, for high-end estate lots and some commerce. It would bring jobs and tourism . . ." She glanced at her watch. "Goodness, look at the time. I really should get on with my work."

She scurried off, and Cole watched her go, his pulse racing. He needed to call Jane tonight.

—

Gage returned to the cabin, having scoped out the ranch and catalogued the guests and vehicles in the campsite. He was searching for something out of the ordinary, something that sparked his long-honed detective senses. He was uneasy about the camper with the generator-powered freezer. Something felt off there. But would *he* hide in plain sight? Or would he squat in the woods somewhere?

Would he be prowling around the ranch at night? When would he make his move?

Gage had noticed the cut fence along the campsite border. He'd followed the tire and boot tracks through the hole into the dense bush and then marsh, but whoever had gone in there wasn't there right now.

Was *he* even here at all?

His mind went to the Birkenhead murder. The location was en route to the interior. It was on First Nations land. And the body display sounded identical to the Watt Lake Killer's signature. He felt certain it was connected, that he'd lured the killer out.

He located the hillock where he'd gotten cell reception earlier, and he dialed Mac Yakima again.

Geese honked overhead. Gage looked up at the pulsating V of birds starting their long journey south. It was almost twelve years to the day that Sarah Baker was taken. Nerves rustled through him. He felt as if things were closing in. He was worried about controlling things now.

Mac picked up. Gage wasted no time on preambles or platitudes.

"You working the Birkenhead case?" Gage knew that the homicide investigation unit would have pulled a task force together. It would include cops from Pemberton and tribal police from Mount Currie. They would have IHit members both on scene and working from the head office in the city.

"Yeah. What's up, Burton, where are you calling from?"

"Which location you working from?"

"City," he said. "You okay?"

"Anything on the vic's ID yet? Any leads?"

A pause. "Burton, let it go. Take the time with your kid, enjoy the fishing. Leave this to us."

Irritation sparked. Wind gusted. A line of dirt rose above the trees across the lake—someone was driving through the forest to the campsite. His chest tightened.

"I saw it on the news," Gage said. "It's the same signature as Watt Lake—the display of the body, the gouged-out eyes. Strung up by the neck. Also on Indian land."

Silence.

"C'mon, Mac, you *must* have something."

"Remember that last time we all had dinner—you, me, Melody, and Karen. And Melody broke the news about your illness?"

Gage closed his eyes. His hand tightened around his phone. The four of them had been close friends ever since he and Mac had been stationed together at Fort Tapley.

"Remember how Melody mentioned that . . . symptoms might have been manifesting for a while. A long while. Small signs, changes in behavior not immediately apparent at the time, but in retrospect they could have been little markers, warnings." Mac paused, as if struggling to find the right way to plead his case. "It made no sense at the time, your insistence that Sebastian George was the wrong guy. In retrospect, this—"

"Jesus, Mac—is *that* what you think? That I was suffering mental delusions back up in Watt Lake?"

"It could be."

A buzzing began in his ears. "Listen, this has *fuck all* to do with my illness."

"Sebastian George was the right guy," Mac said with the kind of level tone he reserved for idiots. "And now he's dead. This Birkenhead case is something else. Let it go. Please."

Gage ran his palm over his head.

Fuck.

Quietly, he said, "So, there are no leads on the Birkenhead homicide, no ID on the vic?"

"Privileged information now. I'm sorry."

"Just tell me one thing—yes or no. Was there a bite out of each of her breasts?"

Silence.

Gage's pulse quickened. This was holdback information from the Watt Lake killings that never made it to the media. This was something only he and the immediate investigators on the old case knew. Not even Mac knew this about this.

"Was there a message?" he pressed, quietly. "Like a tightly folded note secreted into the right eye socket, a note that said something like 'It's not sport unless both sides know they're playing.' Or 'A hunt is a marriage between hunter and prey.' Or 'There is no hunting like the hunting of man, and those who have hunted armed men long enough and liked it, never care for anything else thereafter.'"

Dead silence.

"So there *was* a note."

Still nothing.

Blood thudded in his ears.

When Mac spoke again, his voice was crisp. "Burton, if you know something about this Birkenhead case . . ." Then, as if something hit him suddenly, "Where are you? Where did you take Tori fishing?" he demanded.

Gage glanced over his shoulder at the cabin.

Keep her safe. You're doing this for her . . .

"Listen." Mac's voice was sharper. "Can you tell me where you were the night before the retirement party?"

Jesus. Mac was thinking that he knew too much, that *he* had something to do with this?

"Gage? Tell me. Where are you and Tori now! You need to come in. I need to speak—"

He hung up quickly. His heart kicked against his ribs. So there *had* been a note. In the eye socket. Only the old task force members had known that. And him. He'd watched the interrogations, the interviews. He'd never told anyone about the holdback evidence. Not even Mac.

He was here.

Had to be here.

The Watt Lake Killer was back. Anxiety, adrenaline, fear stampeded into him. What had he done? Could he control this now? Finish the job?

His phone buzzed. Mac. Trying to call back.

Sweat prickled over his lip. If Mac took him in now, they'd tie him up, cost precious time, and it would be too late. The killer would finish his job before Gage could convince them he wasn't mad.

Quickly he cracked the back off his phone and removed the battery. He didn't want to be traced. No time. If the killer was going to act, it would be soon. Before the snow. Before Monday night.

Hooves thundered behind him. He spun around, quickly pocketing his phone and battery.

Olivia West rode up on a gray mare, her hair blowing in the wind, her face pinked with the cold.

"Gage, hi." She was breathless. And she was beautiful, especially up on that gorgeous creature. The horse stomped as she reined it in. Her dog approached over the rise behind them, tongue lolling out.

She hesitated then dropped down off her horse. From a bag at her saddle she removed a crumpled newspaper and plastic bag.

"Did you perhaps leave these in the office?" She held out the newspaper. The headline was the Birkenhead murder. Her name and the ranch address were printed above the headline. Slowly, he turned his attention to the small plastic ziplock bag. His mouth went dry. He felt hot. Dizzy.

He's here. The Watt Lake Killer is here. This is his first calling card . . . The game is on . . .

His eyes flared to hers. She was watching him intently. Clearly edgy. He knew why.

He reached out for the newspaper and bag, taking both from her hand.

"Thank you. I wondered where I might have left these."

Olivia's brow lowered. She regarded him intently, as if waiting for further explanation. Sweat prickled under his shirt. He glanced at the cabin. Tori's head peeked up into the window, watching them both.

"I . . . jotted your name and the ranch address on top of the paper I bought on the way up," he offered, "when we refueled at the Petro-Can in Clinton. The attendant at the gas station gave me directions to the ranch, said you were the manager."

Her frown deepened, as if she was unsure whether to believe him.

But he met her eyes directly, smiled. He did not want to spook Olivia. Instilling fear was the Watt Lake Killer's MO—the man fed off it. Letting his prey know that he was out there, hunting, was his game. Gage would not let him win the first steps in the hunt.

"Where did you get the lure?" she said. "Because it's not going to work here on Broken Bar trout. That's a steelhead fly."

He nodded. "A friend gave it to me. It was one of my retirement gifts, along with a spey rod. My buddy said this design was doing the rounds on the steelhead runs up north last fall. Apparently it works like a bomb."

"It's an interesting design," she said, her eyes still probing his, looking for a lie.

"Yeah, it is."

She hesitated, then put her foot into the stirrup and swung back up onto her mare. She stroked the animal's neck, a smile easing tentatively over her mouth. Gage read relief in her eyes.

"Thanks," she said as she nudged her horse forward.

"Wait—"

She reined her horse back in. It shuffled sideways.

"Could we perhaps book a guided session with you on the lake, maybe for later this afternoon?"

"We're actually done with the guided outings for the summer."

"Just an hour, max." He shot another look at the cabin. "Tori could do with the female company."

Olivia wavered, then smiled. "Of course. I have a few errands to run first. How about four o'clock. I'll meet you down on that dock." She pointed to a dock that lay beyond a gazebo. "We'll be back in plenty of time for drinks and a hot lodge dinner."

"Sounds good." Gage smiled, patted her mare's neck. "More than good."

"Tell Tori to bundle up. Gets really cold out on the water when the sun starts going at this time of year." There was warmth in her eyes. She spun her horse around and trotted off. Gage felt a clutch in his chest as he watched her go, her dog running behind.

She had been so much a part of his life, albeit from a distance, he felt he knew her. Intimately. She was like family.

You're doing the right thing. You're going to fix all this. For her. For Tori. You just have to stay sharp, because if he's here, he's watching . . . and he'll make another move soon . . .

———

Dry grasses grew tall along the approach track to the old barn and rustled softly in the wind. Vines clambered up the outside walls. The door creaked as Cole drew it open wide. He hesitated a moment before entering.

This was where he'd spent a good part of his youth, tinkering with machines, taking them apart to see if he could put them back together. Where he'd sneaked beer, and then vodka.

This was where he'd kissed his first girlfriend. Amelia from school. Where Clayton Forbes and Tucker Carrick had hunted them both down one hot afternoon and delivered a right jab that broke Cole's nose for "stealing Forbes's girl."

He stepped inside, air currents disturbing spiderwebs that wafted softly in his wake. A *whoosh* of barn swallows made him duck as they swooped down from the rafters and scattered through the door. His heart hammered. Dust motes danced in the shafts of light spooling from gaps in the beams and siding. The loft was full of old straw. He could smell it. Mold.

A cat meowed and skittered behind an old tin drum. Cole opened the other door wide so he'd have enough room to maneuver his Piper Cub through.

The additional light illuminated the rusting old wreck that still hunkered at the back of the barn. Surprise punched through

Cole. It was still here—the old truck that had been pulled from the river with his mother and Jimmie inside. Drowned. He walked slowly up to it, a dark cold leaching into his gut.

The fact that it had not been towed away and dumped bore stark testimony to his father's grip on the old bitterness and pain. As if getting rid of this wreck might somehow diminish Grace and Jimmie's memories. Or absolve Cole of what he'd done to cause it.

Cold tendrils of the past feathered into his mind like fingers of hoarfrost. He could almost smell that day. The air had been crystal, sharp, the snowbanks thick. He'd driven along the frozen river, showing off his work on the 1950s truck he'd restored so lovingly. Suddenly he heard Jimmie's laughter in the barn rafters, and he saw his mother's smile in the lodge kitchen. He swallowed. There were ghosts in here. He'd disturbed them.

And they reminded him that his life as he'd known it had ended that day. There was before the accident. Then there was everything that came after.

Almost against his will, he reached out and placed his palm against the rusted old body. The metal was rough and blistered, the paintwork peeling. He was thrust even further back into time. To his little brother sitting on a hay bale in this barn. Swinging his skinny legs with skinned knees as he watched his big brother play wrench monkey. There'd been the sound of crickets outside, the day hot, muggy.

Cole's heart clutched so hard that for a moment he couldn't breathe.

A glimmer in the straw caught his attention. He reached down and picked up a button.

His mind wheeled to another day past—that afternoon he'd brought Amelia to the barn. Nothing had tasted so sweet as her mouth, or felt so deliriously good as the firm swell of her breast under his palms. The bliss of sexual discovery had consumed him.

He'd not heard Clayton Forbes, backed up by Tucker Carrick, coming into the barn to fight him over "stealing" Amelia.

That day had marked the beginning of a deep rift between himself, Forbes, and Tucker, an animosity none of them had given a chance to heal. Clearly Jane still got on with Forbes. Cole pocketed the button and shoved the memories aside. He preferred not to dwell. He had no place for the past, or his roots in this place. He reminded himself that he had no intention of staying long.

But as he rolled up his sleeves and got to work moving bales out of the way and clearing out a small place for his plane, he wasn't so certain. Something subtle inside him was shifting.

As he worked, even though the wind was increasing outside, it got hotter in the barn. He shucked off his shirt, tossed it onto a bale, and bent down to muscle a tin drum out of the way.

Olivia let Spirit have full throttle as they bolted across the meadow, Ace falling way behind. Exhilaration raced through her chest. The riddle of the newspaper and fishing lure had been sorted, and it filled her with indescribable relief. The thrill of suddenly feeling free again pumped through her veins as she allowed the wind to tear through her hair and draw tears from her eyes.

Sure it was an odd coincidence for Gage Burton to be in possession of a fly she'd designed and given to her abductor, and for that fly to be tucked in between the pages of a news story that referenced Sebastian. But coincidences happened.

It was only in her paranoiac world that her subconscious continuously sought negative patterns, saw shadows where there were none. It was just survival mode, she told herself. When you'd been hunted before, you were bound to be a little more cautious than most.

As she passed the field where Cole had landed his bush plane, she reined Spirit in and slowed. The plane was gone. Myron's Dodge was parked there by the trees instead. Wind buffeted her hair across her face, and she noticed a dark band of cloud building on the south horizon. She nudged Spirit forward and rounded the grove of cottonwoods that had served as protection for the tiny yellow plane. The old barn doors had been opened.

She dismounted, tethered Spirit, and waited for Ace to catch up. Leaving her dog to sniff about in the cottonwood grove with her horse, she walked up the overgrown track toward the barn. Dry grasses rustled in the wind around her.

Freshly flattened vegetation—wheel tracks—led up to the barn. She came round the side of the door.

Cole was inside, tinkering with his plane. Shirt off. It was warm; the scent of old straw was strong. His skin gleamed with perspiration.

Olivia stilled, snared by something atavistic. She watched as his muscles rolled smoothly under deeply sun-browned skin. His dark hair was damp and sticking up in odd places where it looked like he'd run his fingers through it. His jeans were slung low at the base of his spine.

Heat pooled in her stomach. It shocked her. She'd not had this kind of reaction to a man in twelve years. And it rooted her to the spot, made her mouth dry. She seemed unable to command her brain to make her body move, to say something, let him know she was here.

He'd unpacked his tools and other gear from the plane. At his side lay a spanner and some other things she didn't immediately recognize, along with a set of small snow skis that could be attached to the wheels of his Cub. Wind gusted through the eaves, and dry branches scratched against the barn roof. The shafts of light spilling down from the cracks painted his skin gold.

She couldn't help but stare. Time stretched, became elastic. She felt dizzy.

Cole closed the hatch and got to his feet. He stood a moment, then turned and stared toward the back of the barn as if contemplating something.

He walked slowly to the old wreck at the rear. Tension snapped across her chest. She edged forward. He reached into his back pocket and removed his wallet. From it he took what appeared to be a creased photograph.

His shoulders rolled forward as he studied the image, as if he'd taken a punch in the gut. He brought the photo close to his face, softly kissed the image.

Olivia's pulse quickened. Panic licked. She'd intruded on an intensely private moment, but she was fixated by the emotion in his body, the shape of the pain in this big, bold man who conquered mountains and flew skies. He was physically bent by it. She needed to leave, now. Carefully, she tried to back slowly away. But she stumbled, crashing against the old door. Swallows swooped out around her.

He spun around. Stared.

His eyes met hers, simmering. Raw.

CHAPTER 12

"Thank you for seeing me on such short notice," Sergeant Mac Yakima said as he seated himself across from Dr. Julia Bellman. He'd assumed, when Melody had mentioned the name of Burton's neuro doc, that Dr. Bellman would be male. She was clearly not, but a rather disconcertingly attractive older woman.

"You of all people should know that I cannot discuss a patient, Sergeant." Dr. Bellman glanced at her watch. It was Saturday, but she had a patient waiting in her home office.

"I'm not here solely in a professional capacity," he said. "I'm also a good friend of Gage Burton. Both my wife and I knew him and Melody as a couple. Melody's death—it's had a devastating impact on him. I'm worried it could have precipitated some sort of . . . psychosis, or even dissociative identity disorder."

Her perfectly arched brows hooked up. But she said nothing.

Mac leaned forward. "All I'm asking is whether this is possible in a patient with a brain tumor like his. Hypothetically speaking."

She met his gaze, her features inscrutable. "People grieve in varying ways. Sometimes they do things that don't make sense to others at the time. Now if you'll excuse me, I really do have a patient waiting." She got up, made for her door.

"I fear for his daughter's well-being." Mac remained seated. "He's packed up his camper, taken her somewhere, and no one knows where they've gone."

She regarded him, her hand on the doorknob.

"Please," he said. "Time could be critical. All I want to know is, *hypothetically*, can someone with a tumor like Burton's develop a severe psychosis? Lose touch with reality? Could extreme stress caused by grief, perhaps, make a cancer grow suddenly faster and manifest in this way?"

Something shifted momentarily through her eyes, and Mac thought he'd gotten through to her. But she said, "I'm sorry. You'll need to find another medical professional to help you."

He came to his feet. "Dr. Bellman, I have reason to believe that in addition to endangering his daughter, Gage Burton might be responsible for a serious crime."

"Such as?"

"Murder."

She paled, removed her hand from the door and brushed it over her blonde hair, which was secured in a smooth bun at the nape of her neck.

"I believe he *thinks* he's hunting a serial killer. A killer he believes got away twelve years ago. I also have reason to think that Burton might act out the killings himself, using the same signature as the perpetrator from twelve years ago, and that he might have started with a first victim already."

She moved back behind her desk, took a seat, her eyes narrowing. "Continue."

"He has knowledge about a very recent homicide that no one but the killer could have."

She inhaled deeply, but her jaw tightened. "I really am sorry, but I can't give out information about a patient. You need to ask this question of another medical professional." She hesitated, then opened her drawer and removed a card. She slid it across her desk toward him.

"Dr. Greenspan. He's a colleague of mine. He'll give you what you need."

———

"What did that woman want?" Tori demanded as her father reentered the cabin.

"That woman has a name, Tori. It's Olivia."

"What did *Olivia* want, then?" She glowered at him, arms folded tightly across her stomach.

"I booked us a guided outing with her. For later this afternoon."

"I don't want to go."

He looked tired as he dumped a newspaper and a small plastic bag on the table, and shrugged out of his jacket. She thought of what Aunt Louise said on the phone, and fear surged back.

She latched onto anger instead. "Why did she faint in the lodge?"

"She was shocked by the terrible news on TV. You shouldn't have seen it, either." He filled the kettle in the kitchenette as he spoke.

"Why do you think that killer hung his victim up by the neck and gutted her like that?"

He stilled, his back to her, and he took a breath, as if straining for patience. She knew she was poking him, and she couldn't help it. "Sometimes a bad guy wants to send some kind of message, or fulfill a fantasy. He's not a well person."

He put the kettle on and took two mugs from the cupboard above the sink.

She got up and went to see what was in the bag lying atop the newspaper. Through the window she'd seen Olivia giving these things to her father.

The story about the murder was on the front page of the crumpled newspaper. A smaller headline questioned whether the Birkenhead murder held echoes of the Watt Lake killings.

That dark thing prowling along at the periphery of her mind circled a little closer. She frowned and touched the small plastic bag. Inside was a fishing lure.

A lurid lime-green fly with three shining red eyes.

Her heart started to stammer. She glanced up at her father. "Dad, weren't you a staff sergeant in Watt Lake?"

His head jerked around. "Why?"

She felt a punch in her stomach at the sudden, hot intensity in his face.

"Were you?" she said a little more cautiously.

"Yes, of course. You know that I was. Watt Lake is where I met your mother. Why is this coming up now?"

"No reason." Her gaze went back to the lure.

. . . The sergeant didn't know until the following spring that it was Sarah Baker who'd tied his three-eyed fly. And that she'd given it to a monster . . .

Something sinister started to unfurl inside her.

"Where did you get this fly?" she said.

"It was a retirement gift. I left it in the lodge office. Olivia returned it to me."

She looked up. His eyes bored into hers.

And inside Tori felt scared. A real dark, confusing kind of scared.

———

"What the *fuck*?" Fury crackled into Cole's features as he reached for his shirt. "How long have you been standing there?"

Olivia recoiled at his explosive reaction, aware of the open door at her back. Of escape. Then the light caught the wetness on his cheeks, the dark gleam in his eyes. Her heart crunched at the visible emotion on his face, his obvious humiliation at being caught in a private moment of memory.

"Why in the hell'd you go sneaking up on me like that?" He stuffed the photo back into his wallet, pocketed it, and punched his arms into his sleeves. His pecs were defined, his abs taut. His chest hair was dark and ran in a tight whorl into the waistband of his jeans. Cole McDonough might have been drowning his sorrows in Cuban and Florida bars, but that clearly hadn't yet gotten the better of his physique.

"I didn't. I was riding by and saw that someone was in the barn." Her gaze went to the old wreck at the back. "No one comes in here," she said softy.

"Weather is picking up," he said curtly, buttoning his shirt. "I needed to batten down my plane before the storm blows. Sorry I didn't get your *permission* first."

"That's not—"

"That's exactly what's going down here," he snapped. "You bloody run this place. This, all of this—" He cast out his arm. "All yours when he goes." His voice was thick, rough, full of frustration at having been caught half naked in more ways than one.

"I don't want it, damn you," she hissed under her breath. "I *told* you already. His decision was as much of a shock to me as it was to you."

"Is that so?"

"Oh, for Chrissakes. As soon as Myron passes I'm outta this place. So you and your sister can do or take whatever you want. Sell the land. Carve it up into tiny pieces for a development."

She turned and marched out of the barn, a strange emotion pounding through her chest.

"Olivia!"

She kept going. She didn't trust herself. Didn't trust him.

"Stop. Just wait. Please."

She stalled, something in his voice snaring her. She turned.

He came out into the sunlight. "I'm sorry."

Her gaze flickered reflexively to his jeans. Faded and worn in all the right places. She flushed at the sudden hot sensation in her belly, the way her pulse raced.

"That barn is . . . full of mixed-up memories. Unhappy ghosts. They bring out the worst in me." He tried to smile, but in the bright sunlight his face was bloodless under his tan, the lines around his eyes drawn deep. He was tired—the kind of deep soul-tired that was born of grief. Compassion mushroomed inside her chest.

He raked his fingers through his thick mop of hair, dust and perspiration making it stand up further. He looked suddenly defeated. He came closer.

Olivia tensed, an urge rising in her chest, warning her to step back, pull away, leave now, before it was too late. But it was coupled with something trickier, darker, a whispering physical awareness, an excitement that made her mouth dry. And she was besieged by an impulse to reach up and cup her hand around his strong jaw, to comfort, ease his pain.

She stuck her fingers into the front pockets of her jeans.

"I know about the accident," she said quietly.

"Who told you? My father?" he said, looking at his hands.

"Adele, mostly. Everyone in town knows the story. You were driving with Jimmie and Grace in the truck, lost control on an icy bend, and went over into the river ice. They say the brakes failed."

He snorted softly, looked away for several beats. When he turned to face her the rawness in his eyes made her breath catch. "The brakes did fail. But they didn't tell you I'd also been drinking, did they?" He heaved out a breath. "Only my father and I knew that."

Shock rippled through her. "So that's why he blames you?"

He seated himself on a rock in the lee of the barn, where it was warm. It was as if everything had suddenly been walloped out of him.

"I used to stash booze here in the barn. I was drinking, listening to music while I tinkered with the brakes. I'd put in new pads, drums, rotors. Brake fluid was fine. It appears I screwed up. Maybe if I hadn't been drinking . . . maybe if I hadn't been so pleased with my work and offered to show off to Mom and Jimmie by taking them for a spin along the river. Maybe if I'd been sober I'd have seen the ice was too bad . . ." He fell silent for several beats.

"Did you tell your father you'd been drinking?"

"He suspected. He came up here, found the bottles." He moistened his lips. "He never told the cops. By the time emergency services got up here in the snow, by the time they pulled the truck out, by the time they realized there was nothing they could do for Jimmie and my mother . . . They eventually checked out the truck, and did find the brakes faulty. So that and road conditions went down as the cause."

"Was that a photo of your brother and mother you were looking at?"

He took it out. Showed her. "I carry it everywhere."

Olivia took it from him. In the photo Jimmie was a little echo of the McDonough men. Grace as beautiful as in all the other photos she'd seen. But the image was marred with white creases, worn with use. As if it was looked at often. She glanced up at him. This man was consumed by remorse. Guilt.

"That was a long time ago," he said quietly, holding her eyes. "So long. But coming back to Broken Bar, going into this old barn, it's like stepping right back in time. As if it were yesterday and I'm still the stupid-ass kid who makes poor decisions." He rubbed his brow. "It makes you wonder, what does it all mean? What does it mean that you had a partner, and a stepchild—your own family? That you traveled as far away from this place as you possibly could, only to find yourself back, and it's all concertinaed down to nothing? Just that wreck in an old barn, and yourself, and the guilt."

Olivia lowered herself onto the sun-warmed rock beside him. "I heard about your family. I'm sorry."

"Adele told you about that, too?"

"Your father did."

He held her gaze for several beats. "What did he say?"

"Only that your relationship with your partner and her son faltered because of an incident in the Sudan, and that you were on some sort of guilt trip, drowning your sorrows in Cuba because of it."

He gave a snort. "Ah, I see, so *that's* where it came from—that 'wallowing in your own self-pity, all you know is your own narcissistic pursuit' comment over the phone."

Heat burned into her face.

"My stepson—that's how I think of him—his name is Ty." He paused, then gave a wry smile. "He's Holly's son from her previous marriage. He's around the same age as Jimmie was when he died. Sometimes life really makes no sense."

"I know."

His gaze collided with hers. Then very slowly, still holding her eyes, he reached over and took her hand in his. Softly, he traced his thumb across the scar on her wrist. Olivia started to shiver inside. Her eyes began to burn. But she fought the urge to pull away, fought the shame.

They sat like that, touching, in tremulous silence. Unspoken words heavy and pregnant between them. A kestrel wheeled, cried up high.

"Jimmie," he finally said, "used to come into the barn and sit on one of the hay bales, or on the tack box. He'd watch me working on the truck for hours, drove me nuts with his questions." A sad smile curved his lips. "I think I secretly loved the adulation—the fact little Jimmo actually wanted to learn things from me. I would come straight here after school, and I'd spend most of my time here during vacations, after I'd done my ranch chores." He paused, looking into the barn, watching the shadows, the interplay of sunlight and darkness. The flock of swallows *swooshed* back in under the eaves, and she realized an orange cat was sitting next to a bale, watching them.

He was right. She could feel it. Ghosts. As if this place were suspended in time. As though his words, his memories, were unspooling the years so that she could almost see a young Cole here, shirt off, working on the vintage truck, the clunk of metal tools. Little Jimmie swinging his legs, chattering away.

Cole traced his thumb absently across her wrist again, and Olivia's heart quickened. The instinct to escape began to pound louder through her blood.

"I used to like to take things apart just to see if I could put them back together," he said.

"You still do, but with people. In your books. You deconstruct motive, figure out what drives people to do things like climb mountains. To risk life. To live on the edge of existence. You take them apart to examine why they do the extreme."

He shot a look at her. "You really have read my books?"

This time she smiled. "Truth? I've skimmed, mostly. And I've read the jacket copy. But I'm reading your latest right now. The one on survivors. I sort of borrowed it from your dad's desk."

"It was on his desk?"

"In his drawer when I went looking for your number. It was bookmarked."

"He'd been reading it?"

"Appears so."

His gaze burned into hers, as if he were trying to see right inside her. Deconstruct her. See what fired her. His mouth was so close, his lips chiseled to perfection. Wide mouth. Strong mouth. She imagined it against hers. Heat seemed to swell and shimmer between them. Tangible. She swallowed at the intensity but seemed utterly incapable of looking away. So she filled the space with words instead.

"Sven Wroggemann—he was a guy you mentioned in the chapter about bush pilots. You said he was driven by survivor's guilt. That he believed he should have died in his wife's place, and that's what kept him chasing death, tempting and daring it to take him at each turn. You wrote that you thought part of him actually wanted to die, to be punished for having survived."

She turned her body to fully face his. "Is that how it is with you?" She tilted her head toward the barn. "You feel it should have been you who died, not Jimmie or your mom? Is that why you tempt your own fate, and chase others who do, too?"

He stared at her for a long while. Leaves clattered in the wind and branches scraped against the siding of the barn. He then scrubbed the dark stubble on his jaw.

"I suppose it's absurd, but I never thought about it that way," he said.

"Sometimes it's easier to deconstruct others." She paused, then said, "When I started reading of your pursuits, I envied your free- dom to live life at such full throttle, but I see now it might not have been freedom at all, but a kind of prison."

Ace came snuffling at their feet. Cole reached down, scratched behind the dog's ear. Ace repaid him by sitting on his boot and leaning into his leg for a deeper scratch.

Olivia was suddenly conscious of the time and needing to complete her chores before the guided fishing session with Burton and his daughter. But she was also deeply curious now. "What *did* happen in the Sudan?"

His features tightened, and his eyes darkened.

Inhaling deeply, he said, "It was also my fault. I should have had a better read on how volatile things had become." He paused. "Truth was, I did have a read. Yet I was in this rush, amped with adrenaline." He met her gaze. "And yeah, maybe that was the drug I was chasing, the drug that numbed the memories. It gave me a kind of tunnel vision. I'd scored a one-on-one interview with one of the rebel leaders. Holly and Ty were with me. She was doing a shoot for *National Geographic* and was going to capture the whole thing on film. But we let slide one fundamental thing—that we were parents. And that we should have been parents before report- ers. That our son was more important than showing the world the atrocities in a foreign land."

"That's a tough call."

"It's not. Not when you dig deep and ask yourself what it is, really, that drives you to bring these stories and images to the world. Is it outrage? Is it exposing the atrocities, shining the light on egregious injustice, a tool to fight it? Or how much is about your own thrill, the excitement that you could be nailing a blockbuster story, something that's going to make you famous, a journalistic hero, land you another movie deal. Blot out the past." He met her eyes. "How much really *is* narcissistic self pursuit?"

Olivia met his eyes, realizing in that moment how her comment must have sliced him.

"I wrapped up the interview. That afternoon we were in a small rented room in Wadi Halfa. We had Ty with us. We were liberal. Bold. Acclaimed in our circles. We were homeschooling and giving our son a radical world education. We were self-righteous and smothered with hubris, which made us feel . . . invincible. And that's how it happened. The attack came in the streets of Wadi Halfa. Short end of it all, we were trying to flee when Ty fell and got caught up in the melee. Holly and I were swept one way in the crowd, and Ty the other. He tried to run across the street to us."

He stopped talking. His features changed, and his eyes went distant.

"Ty was almost taken down by a machete, got cut across the upper arm. I managed to run into the melee and grab him away. I carried him back to Holly, to the doorway where she was hiding. Ty's blood was hot on my hands, my face, my arms." His voice caught. He took a moment to marshal himself. "We got him to safety. We're both first aid trained and managed to bandage him up. We made it to a doctor. We were all more shook up than anything. It was a close call. The warning knell. The end of our relationship."

"Why?"

"Holly and I fought. We blamed each other. We tried to go on. But Ty's scrape with death became an irreparable rift, a symbol of everything we were doing wrong as a family. Every time Holly and

I looked at each other, touched each other, we saw blame in each other's eyes. With it came the associated self-recrimination, the bitter words, the questioning about where we were going and who we really were as a couple, a family. She left. A break, she said, to think. It became permanent."

"Maybe you both just need some more time," Olivia said.

He gave a soft, derisive snort. "Holly's moved in with her ex. She took Ty back to his real father. A stable environment, she said. She's moved on. I'm the bad memory. I am the face of her own guilt. I'm the 'affair' she regrets having. She couldn't look into my eyes without seeing it. Nor can I look into hers. We can't go back, Liv. She's pregnant again." He seemed to struggle for a moment. "Oh, fuck, who am I kidding? I hate her for that. It's as if having another baby, a new kid, is in defiance of our memories. Of me. As if she can blot it all out."

"Or it's her way of coping, just moving forward."

He flattened his mouth.

She looked away, thinking about motherhood. Children, babies. Loss. The pain could be big and breath-stealing. It had been utterly crippling for her. It still was.

She ached with every molecule of her being to know what had happened to her baby. But she also knew she'd done the right thing in sacrificing her child to adoption. She would not have been a fit mother. Only once she'd reached Broken Bar and begun to find a measure of peace had she begun to believe she could be sound enough to raise a child. Until now. Until the flashbacks returned. And she knew it wasn't possible—she'd forever be haunted by *him*. Dead or not, he lived inside her. At least she'd freed her baby.

She wanted to tell Cole that she understood. That she'd lost family, too. That her daughter—wherever she was—would be just a little older than Ty and Jimmie.

"Be careful, Cole," she said quietly. "You don't want to hold on to it too hard." She paused. "You don't want to be your father."

His mouth opened. He stared at her. Then he snorted. "Funny, how sometimes you can see so much about others, but not yourself." He paused. "What about you, Liv?"

Liv.

It was the second time he'd called her that.

"You try to outrun it?"

"What do you mean?"

"Your past. You almost killed me back there, yet you won't talk about it."

She got up suddenly, dusted off her jeans. "I really should go. I have errands to run, a fence to fix before a guided fishing trip later this afternoon. And there are several guests booked for dinner at the lodge. I should give Jason a hand."

She tried to walk smartly down the rutted track, but her legs felt like water, as if they didn't belong to her. He was unraveling her like he unraveled the people in his books, peeling the layers away, exposing things she'd managed to keep hidden for years.

She stopped suddenly and swung around.

"I found out who left the newspaper and lure," she called out, trying to reassert her ground, show she was sane. "It was the new guest I signed in. They belonged to him."

He got up. "Let me help you with that fence."

"No."

"I don't like it. A woman alone with armed squatters or poachers."

"Says he who profiles people who live on the edge."

He opened his mouth, but Olivia turned, breathing in deep and focusing on long, steady strides as she made her way back toward her horse. Ace came running to her heels. She could feel Cole's eyes burning into her back—feel his need. She felt she owed him more comfort, after he'd shared like that. But she couldn't offer more. It brought him too close to the fragile part of herself—the very human part that ached to share, to touch and be touched, to be held.

So she refused to look over her shoulder. She wasn't sure what had just happened back there, but the paradigm of her world had tilted dangerously.

She mounted Spirit, and as they cantered up over the ridge, she saw a plume of dust rising down the valley. A gleaming black SUV was barreling down the dirt road toward the lodge. Norton Pickett. Myron's lawyer. He had to be delivering the new will. Tension twisted, and she kicked Spirit into a gallop.

———

After the sergeant left her office, Dr. Bellman leaned over, pressed the buzzer, asked for her assistant to bring in Gage Burton's medical records.

She paged quickly through her files, studying again the location of his tumor, the growth progression. She noted, too, that Burton had blown off his last appointment.

She rolled her pen between thumb and middle finger, debating what the cop had just told her.

I have reason to believe Gage Burton might be endangering his daughter . . . time could be of the essence . . .

She reached for her phone, dialed Burton's home number.

It rang three times before going to voice mail. Probably because he was out of town, as the cop had said. Bellman then tried Burton's cell. It clicked directly to voice mail, saying he was out of the service area. She sat for a while, rolling her pen between her thumb and middle finger.

Once before, early in her career, there had been a time when, if she had intervened, she could have saved a child. Instead she'd adhered rigidly to her code of ethics. The child had died. At the time she'd promised herself if it came to a child's life again, she would risk it—she would warn someone. She'd circumvent the bureaucracy.

She could not live with letting it happen again. And Burton had been showing signs that worried her.

She dialed Burton's cell again, and this time she left him a message, telling him he needed to come in.

Then she reached for the card the cop had given her. She dialed Mac Yakima's number.

———

Mac Yakima stared at the Tim Hortons sign through the rain-spattered windshield. They were parked in the lot outside. Martinello was one of those cops who actually did like donuts. She munched one now, powdered sugar on her chin.

"Is Raffey attending the postmortem?" she said, taking another chomp. That woman had a metabolism like nobody's business. She ran at least forty miles each week, and swam. Mac always got the idea that she was running from something. Like if she stopped long enough it might catch up with her. Maybe she ran just so she could thumb her nose at the cliché and eat donuts. That would be Martinello's style.

She was young for homicide. She had come to policing by way of a wealthy upbringing and a doctorate in criminology, which didn't ingratiate her easily to the other officers who'd slogged up through the ranks and beat the streets in order to earn a place on the integrated homicide team. Mac figured she made a big deal out of stopping for donuts because she wanted to be more like a blue-collar cop. Or something.

"Yeah. He'll call if anything comes up." Mac started the engine. "How was Burton when you drove him home after the party?" he said, looking over his shoulder as he reversed the cruiser.

"Edgy. Probably pissed that everyone bailed on him." She delivered the last of the donut to her mouth. "I would've been edgy, too. I mean, how often does a guy get to retire after a lifetime of service? Once. And no one can stick around long enough to finish a beer and see him off properly? They leave you standing in their dust while they rush out, all amped up about the next big call?"

"Did he press you for information on the call?" Mac pulled out of the parking lot and joined the throng of traffic along Fourth. He shot her a glance.

Her features had turned unreadable. Her cop face. Mac knew it well.

"He was curious, yeah. Why?"

"He mention anything about the bandage on his hand?"

"He told me he hurt it while moving a bookshelf."

"I want to know where he was the night before the retirement party."

"Jesus, Yak, you can't think—"

"I don't know what in the hell to think," he snapped. "Burton knows about the bites out of the breasts. He knows about the note in the vic's right eye socket. He even fucking knows what the note says."

But as she was about to speak, Mac's cell buzzed. He pulled over to answer it.

"Sergeant Yakima."

"It's Dr. Bellman. Listen, I understand time could be crucial, and that you could potentially use this information to secure a warrant. But what I'm going to say, for the record, is theoretical. Purely conceptual. It does *not* pertain specifically to any patient of mine."

"I got it." His gaze cut to Martinello. He mouthed the name: *Bellman.*

"The answer is yes. Stress can undermine the body's immune system. This in turn can exacerbate the growth of a lesion. Also, it's fairly rare, but a relationship has been demonstrated between structural intracranial lesions and mental illness. Psychotic manifestations cannot be dismissed as a possible symptom."

"Okay, just so we're clear in lay speak, that means someone with a brain tumor in a specific location of the brain could develop psychosis."

"It's been demonstrated."

"And what could this psychosis—hypothetically—look like?"

"In layman's terms, psychosis is an umbrella tag for a number of mental illnesses of which schizophrenia is one, dissociative identity disorder another."

"Schizophrenia—that's when you hear voices in your head telling you to do things?"

"It's a loss of touch with reality. And yes, often patients do hear voices giving them orders. Often it is not clear to the patient that this is something unusual, or that they're ill. I hope this helps."

"Thank you, Doctor, it does." He hung up. "Shit," he said quietly. "Burton could be a very sick man."

He tried Gage's cell again. No response. Or no service.

Mac put the cruiser back in gear and reentered the stream of traffic. "The pathologist puts the time of death around eight p.m. on the night before Burton's retirement party. The crime scene is a two- to three-hour drive from Burton's residence. We need to know where Burton was that night. We need a warrant on his phone to find out where he is now." He hefted out a heavy breath.

"You and him go way back?"

He nodded. "Right back to Fort Tapley up north. He was stationed there after Watt Lake, a lateral move that he never explained to me fully, but I understood it to be a result of his problems with the Watt Lake case. There was big political pressure to wrap that one up smoothly. He was a burr under the brass's saddle, from what I understand. He would not—could not—drop this idea that they had the wrong guy. Despite all the evidence, he maintained the killer was still out there. He's been obsessed with it ever since, and it's cost him some major career moves. The deputy commish job could have been his, I reckon, had it not been for this obsession. Instead it went to Hank Gonzales, who was on the Watt Lake Killer task force back in the day."

"So this could be personal for Burton on a whole other level," she said. "And what better way to keep the game going? To finally get everyone hunting again. To prove to Gonzales he was wrong all those years back. Is that what you think is going down here? That Burton's having issues with retirement, grief, illness, and it's made him psychotic—capable of killing?"

"All we know is that Burton is a person of interest in the Birkenhead homicide. Our *only* one so far. And we need to find him, even if just to rule him out."

CHAPTER 13

Through the scope of his bolt-action Remington .308 he studied the trio in the boat, the evening air chill on his ears. The snow was coming sooner than forecast. Of this he was certain.

He zeroed in on his prey. His lovely, skittish, wounded deer. It intrigued him, really, how even a gut-shot deer would not stray too far from home territory in spite of the fact the hunter was near. The familiarity of home always outweighed the danger. Deadly mistake, that.

Her hair caught the sun as it sank toward the tree-lined esker. She laughed. It was like a punch to his chest. The boat angled closer to the shadows and scrub along the shore where he hid. He could see her face clearly. Heat hummed through his veins.

He slid his forefinger into the trigger guard, softly caressing the trigger. Then he gave it slight pressure as he exhaled. *Poof.* In his power. He could so easily just squeeze the trigger all the way through, crack the .308 into her skull. And she'd be gone. He slid his scope a little lower. Or he could put it right there, through her heart. He had the control. All the choices. Once again he was beginning to own her.

Memories surged through him. The taste of her mouth. Her smell. The feel of her bare skin as he drove his cock up deep in between her legs. How he'd kept her shackled, the rope around her neck, as he'd forced her onto all fours like an animal. How he'd slapped into her, driving deeper and deeper until she screamed in glorious pain. Which made him wilder. His penis hardened at the thought.

She'd stopped screaming one day.

Even though he'd known he was still causing her pain, she'd fallen silent. He'd thought it was insubordination, a battle of wills, because she'd discovered that her screams only drove him wilder. He'd thought it was her trying to wrest back control.

But then he'd learned different. A smile curved over his mouth. He panned his scope over to the man in the boat.

Big man. Strong body with thick neck. Balding brush cut. A whisper of a memory feathered into his brain, but he was unable to grasp it.

He moved over to the child.

Long jet-black hair spilled over her shoulders, the ends lifting in the wind. She was not so much child but a creature reaching that special place between childhood and womanhood. That elusive memory feathered a little deeper into his brain, cold and unpleasant, like growing hoarfrost. But still he couldn't shape it, hold on to it.

He heard a voice.

Eugene . . . come here. Leave your father be . . . Come sit on my lap and read to me, my favorite boy . . .

A sick, dark change of mood twisted into him. His head began to hurt. Slowly, he lowered his scope.

———

Tori was bundled up in her down jacket with a flotation device strapped over the top. She felt like the Michelin Man, stupid and uncomfortable, and she was still cold in the boat, especially in the forest shadows at the calmer end of the lake. The boat had a flat bottom with wet carpet in it. There were two bench seats, and a seat at the rear where the motor and tiller were. Olivia stood at the rear, casting. Ace slept on a towel at her feet. He wore a doggie life jacket, which Tori supposed was cute. Her dad sat in the prow where he dangled out his line and watched an orange bobber. She was shivering in the middle.

Her gaze slid up to Olivia's profile. She'd glimpsed the mean-ass scar around Olivia's neck when that man had removed her bandana after she'd nearly fainted. It was impressive, that scar—she wondered what could have created something like that.

Olivia cast her line out in graceful arcs over the water, settling her fly far out along the edge of a shoal. She held her rod with her right hand while she slowly pulled the line in with her left. It pooled in big coils at her feet. Tori noticed scars on the inside of Olivia's wrists. Her pulse quickened. Had she tried to kill herself? Tori had read in novels about how it was more effective to cut lengthwise rather than across the vein if you wanted to commit suicide properly. Sometimes she thought of killing herself. If she was religious, and if she truly believed she would see her mother in the afterlife, maybe she'd have the guts to actually carry it out.

Olivia flicked her line out farther. Water droplets sparkled in the rays from the sinking sun.

The words from her mother's manuscript crept into her mind...

The sergeant watched mesmerized as the man cast out his line. Perfect, languid loops rolled out above the water, doubling back one loop over the other, sending sparkling droplets into sunshine...

Those unarticulated questions lurking at the periphery of her brain crowded in a little closer as she thought of the Watt Lake sergeant. The three-eyed fly in her mother's manuscript. She stole a look at her dad. He was intently watching Olivia, something unreadable in his face.

Tori's chest went tight. Her stomach hurt. She looked away, fighting a sudden surge of hot tears. She focused on the loon nearby. The bird watched them with a red eye, its beak like a razor.

Her dad took out his hip flask and offered it to Olivia. She said no thanks, but he said, "Go on. It's cold. It'll warm you up."

Olivia hesitated, then reached over and took the flask from him. She swallowed a mouthful and returned it. Tori felt blackness boiling up around her. She thought about her beautiful mom. Her mom would have packed a flask of cocoa. With cookies, or home-baked banana choc-chip muffins. The darkness boiled higher about her, drowning out the hurt, the pain, filling the great big hollow in her chest with anger.

Anger at Julia Borsos for telling her she was getting fat, and claiming that's why boys didn't like her. She *was* gaining weight—she knew that. She'd been eating everything in sight since her mother died, as if trying to fill that empty hole in her life. Her skin had gone bad. No one loved her anymore. She was lost. Alone. Dangerously angry underneath it all.

"Where did you go?" she muttered, not looking at her father.

"What?"

"Earlier, when you went for your walk?"

He took another swig from his flask and replaced the cap. "I went to the campground for a look-see."

"Why?"

"Just to get a lay of the land."

"Why did you take two guns?"

Her father's eyes flashed up. Tori felt a smug punch.

"I didn't—"

"You did. What's that in your boot right now, and in the holster under your shirt?"

Her father swallowed slowly, a hot glint entering his eyes. Olivia was staring at him.

Another smug punch. She'd forced her dad's hand. Now the suicidal guide-woman wouldn't like him.

"Not easy to get a permit for handguns," Olivia said, casting her line out in another series of long graceful arcs over the water.

"You're right. It's not."

Olivia flicked another glance at him but said nothing more.

"Why do you keep phoning Mac?" Tori pushed, unable to stop herself now.

Her father met her gaze in silence. Then he reached over. "Here, why don't you hold this rod. Watch the bobber out there. If it dips suddenly underwater, lift the rod tip up, and tug the line gently like this." His voice was dark and low, his eyes narrow.

Tori swallowed. "I don't want to fish."

"Go on. Hold the rod."

"No."

Silence. Their gazes warred.

"I don't understand fishing, anyway." She wrapped her arms tightly over her stomach.

"What do you mean?" Olivia said as she reeled in her line.

"You just throw them back into the water, so why bother catching them in the first place? I don't see the point. I'd far rather kill them. And I don't see why we needed to come on this stupid trip."

An iridescent bug landed on her knee. It had a thin, stick-straight body marked by bands of black and blue—a deep, luminescent blue that didn't seem natural. Its wings were a translucent gossamer, its eyes big round balls at the tip of its head. Its little body pulsated, and its wings quivered.

"Wow, look at that," her father said. "A damselfly this late in the season—that's unusual."

Some exchanges are as subtle as the touch of an iridescent damselfly alighting on the back of your hand. Some are seismic, rocking your world and fissuring into your very foundations and setting you on a new path . . .

Tori reached for the bug and squished it dead. She flicked the gunk off her fingers into the water.

She felt shock radiate from her father.

"Goddammit, Tori. What is *wrong* with you?"

Olivia watched them both. "Your father was right," she said calmly as she cast again, settling her fly like a live insect on the surface of the dark water. "It's really unusual to see a damselfly this late in the year." Wind gusted and the water spiraled in patterns across the lake. The sun was sinking toward the far ridge, streaking the sky with violent pinks and oranges. "They're usually all gone before the first frosts. This one must be special—I'm surprised the cold nights didn't kill it and that it lived long enough to visit you like that."

Tori swallowed.

It started, as all dialogues do, when a path crosses that of another . . .

She began to shake inside. It was as if her mother were here, whispering the words of her book into her mind.

"A damselfly nymph can live deep underwater for two years," Olivia said. "A whole lifetime for a nymph. Then when it's ready, it will swim to a plant and crawl up the vegetation into the air. Its skin then breaks, and it unfolds delicate little wings. That's a vulnerable moment for the damsel. It must pump body fluids into its abdomen and wings, which causes both to lengthen into the form you saw on your knee. And once the wings are dry it takes flight and starts a whole second life cycle outside the water. It's like getting a second chance where everything is new again." She smiled. "Or that's what I like to think—that there can be stages in life where you become a whole different creature. Where there are new possibilities."

Olivia gently tugged her line, making her lure swim like a bug over the surface. She seemed to be considering something deeply as she watched her fly. Then she said, "When I was a little girl, when I got really down about something and felt like there was no hope, my mother would take me aside and say, 'Just when the caterpillar thought the world was over, it became a butterfly.'"

She flicked the tip of her rod, looping her line and setting the lure out even farther, at the very edges of the dark water in the forest shadows.

"Damselflies and dragonflies are like the butterfly—symbols of new beginnings. Some people even feel they're spiritual totems." Olivia glanced down at Tori. Her eyes were the same green as the water, and Tori thought about her scars again. She wondered if Olivia had gotten a second chance when she hadn't managed to kill herself. Something shifted slightly in her.

"Adult damselflies are not really a big food source for the trout," Olivia said. "But the fish predate heavily on them while they're in the nymph stage. But those little nymphs"—she met Tori's eyes again—"they're just as predacious themselves. They lie in wait for other aquatic bugs to get in range, then grab them with jaws designed especially for chomping. That circle of life thing—" She stopped, and her gaze flicked to the water as her rod tip bent slightly.

"That's why I like to fish," she said, her attention still on the rod tip. "It teaches you to watch and understand the insect life and cycles of the lakes and rivers and seasons. When you try to mimic nature by designing a fly, it gives you a respect. And yes, you kill and eat the fish you catch. But you only take what you need. The rest you learn from and put back." She paused as her rod tip dipped slightly again. She raised the tip, but again, it must have just been a nibble.

"I can teach you to tie a damsel if you like?"

Tori looked away. She felt her father watching her. She felt sick. She could imagine the damsel pumping up its little body. Wanting a second chance at life. A strange sort of thick emotion bubbled inside her.

Olivia's rod tip suddenly bent over hard.

"Oh, got a bite!" She lifted the tip high, keeping the line taut. "Here," she said, thrusting the rod into Tori's hand.

Tori took it in shock.

"Stand up," Olivia said as she grabbed the tiller. She started the engine and moved them slowly into calmer water.

Tori got to her feet, wobbling as the boat rocked a little.

"Keep the tip of the rod up. Keep your feet planted wide apart and flex your knees. You'll balance easier."

Anxiety whipped through Tori as the line started to zing.

"It's running. Diving down deep. Let it go, but keep that tip up, keep some tension on the line."

The coils of line on the boat floor started rapidly feeding back into the rod eyes and out into the water. Her mouth went dry. She was shaking.

Suddenly there was no tension on the line.

"Bring in some line! Pull it in with your hand. The fish has changed direction and is swimming back to the boat. It'll spook when it sees us and run again. Be ready."

Tori swallowed, frantically pulling in line. Her skin felt hot.

Suddenly the fish leaped out of the water, all sparkling silver, twisting its body in the air and flipping its tail, spraying droplets. Tori gasped. The fish slapped down on the water, and the line started to zing again—everything she'd pulled in spooling back out into the water. Her eyes started to burn with the adrenaline now thumping through her body.

"Let it run, Tori, let it run!" her dad barked.

"I'm doing it, Dad!"

"Good job, Tori," Olivia said. "As soon as you feel it going slack, pull it in again, keep the tension on."

She nodded, eyes riveted to the water. She felt the line go slack and rapidly drew a handful of line in.

"If you hold the line with your fingers of your right hand, keeping it taut, you can reel in the slack."

She did. Her arms were shaking with excitement. Suddenly she saw the silvery fish in the green water. Her heart kicked. The fish saw the boat and tried to dive again. Tori let it go. When her line went slack, she reeled again, until once more she glimpsed the silvery creature.

"It's getting tired," Olivia said. "I think you can start bringing it in."

Tori reeled. The fish flopped feebly toward the boat, pulled by the hook in its mouth.

Olivia reached for the net as Tori brought the trout up along-side the hull.

"Don't forget to keep that rod tip up." Olivia crouched down and gently scooped the net under the fish. "Reel in some more . . . that's it."

Tori got onto her knees and carefully leaned over the side of the boat while still keeping the rod tip high and the line taut.

The fish looked up at her with a terrified eye. Its pink mouth was gasping. Her chest tightened. Her heart was beating so fast she thought it might bust out of her ribs.

Her first fish on a fly.

It was truly beautiful. So shiny and silvery with a rainbow blush down its side. Tori could see the tiny lure in its glistening mouth, the hook through the delicate cheek. And as she looked into that fish's eye, something happened inside Tori. She felt a connection.

"Here," Olivia said, reaching her hand into the net and cup-ping it under the fish's belly. "Hold it like this."

Her father took the rod from her, and Tori reached into the cold water with her bare hands. Tentatively she grasped hold of the trout.

It was firm, and slippery, and it smelled briny-fresh. In its pink mouth were teensy little razor-sharp teeth.

"It's above size," Olivia said. "Would you like to keep it?"

"Keep it?"

"For dinner," said Olivia. "Or breakfast, or lunch. Nothing like fresh Broken Bar trout. They have really pinky-orange flesh, almost like a salmon. The color comes from all the micro shrimp they eat in this lake."

Olivia took a Leatherman tool out of her fishing vest pocket as she spoke. She brought it down to the fish. "We'll just give it a sharp bonk on the back of the head with this, and it'll die quickly."

Tori stared in mild shock. It was the first time she'd ever thought about killing her food, really. It was the first time she'd experienced this thrill, this having connected with a secret creature from down deep. This poor creature who'd been foxed by an imitation insect. Very quietly she said, "Can we put this one back?"

"Sure we can." Olivia returned her Leatherman to her vest pocket. "You remove the hook like this." She opened the mouth and carefully extracted the hook. "When I tie these lures I press down the barbs so it makes them easy to remove, and there's less damage to the fish."

She got something else out of her pocket. It looked like a big eyedropper. She squeezed the rubber bulb at the end and stuck the tube part of it into the fish's throat, releasing the bulb while Tori continued to hold the trout just under water.

Olivia squeezed the contents of the dropper into the palm of her hand. Water filled her cupped palm. It was full of little black things.

"Chironomids."

Tori peered at them. Some were still alive, squiggling.

"Now we know what the fish are feeding on right now, so we know which lures to use." She emptied her hand. "You ready to let her go?"

Tori nodded.

"Hold her like this, move her gently so she can get water going through her gills."

Gently the sergeant removed the Predator from the fish's glistening mouth. He crouched down and cradled the fish in the cups of his hands . . . with a sudden powerful flick of its tail, it flashed out of his hands and ran upriver into the green current . . .

And just like that, her own fish flicked its tail, and she saw the silver burrowing deep into the green.

Tori felt tears in her eyes. It made her embarrassed. She didn't want to look up.

"It's getting dark," her father said gently. "Perhaps we should head back in."

Olivia packed in the rods and started the engine again. She steered them across the lake into the choppy waters. On the opposite shore, in the distance, glowed the warm lights of the lodge.

It wasn't really dark yet, just that the sun had gone behind the ridge and leached the color out of the landscape.

Silence descended on the occupants of the small boat as they puttered back to the shoreline in the dusk. Tori glanced over her shoulder to where the campsite was located on the west end. There were dots of flickering orange campfires among the dark trees. She could smell wood smoke. The Cariboo night chill was descending. Tori looked up at the sky.

The first star.

Her father was looking too.

They both knew what Mom would have said.

Star light, star bright, first star I see tonight—make a wish, guys!

I wish on that star that you could come back, Mom.

But Tori knew now that some wishes were impossible. They could never come true. No matter how hard you wished them.

Her mother was gone.

There would never be a second chance for that.

———

Cole came out of the bathroom and entered the kitchenette rubbing his wet hair with a towel. He hooked the towel around his neck, poured himself a mug of coffee, and took his mug to the small table in front of a window that overlooked the lake.

Dusk had settled and wind was whipping up small whitecaps, but the water on the far side of the lake in the shadows was still. An angler in a float tube moved slowly back toward the campsite. A small boat was returning across the lake. In it were three people. It looked like Olivia and Burton with that kid. Her guided outing.

Cole paused, thinking of her words back at the barn. She'd read him like a book. A smile tempted his mouth. She had indeed read him—in his book. Yet while she probed his secrets, she kept her own guarded tight.

He seated himself at the table and powered up his laptop. Her mystery had him hooked, and it struck him—Olivia had reawakened his interest in something outside of finding the next bar or mindless lay. His muse was starting to whisper.

His monitor came to life, but his battery was almost out of juice. He didn't have much time before he'd have to head up to the house to charge it again.

He typed in the ranch's wireless code and opened up a search engine. He entered the words: *Birkenhead murder.*

He reached for his mug and took a sip as the results populated his screen.

While he'd conducted a cursory search on Olivia West from O'Hare Airport, he was now approaching things from a different angle. Something about that murder on the news had freaked her, and he intended to find out more.

He clicked through the links, reading. But there wasn't much more than he'd already seen on TV or read in that *Province* article and op-ed piece. It appeared the police had still not identified the victim, a woman in her fifties. Again there were references to the signature killings from Watt Lake over a decade ago.

Cole took another sip, and this time he entered into the search engine the words *Watt Lake murders.*

A long list of links came up, most of them to archived news stories. And there were plenty.

He scanned the stories one by one as he sipped his coffee. Over a period of eight years, seven women had gone missing. The first four were sex trade workers, vulnerable women who'd vanished along a highway to the north. It was only in retrospect that a pattern had been identified. The women all disappeared around Thanksgiving, just before a big snowfall. The fifth had been a young married mother whose car had broken down on a remote road north of Watt Lake. Her car had been found abandoned. At the time it had been presumed that she'd tried to walk for help and had gotten lost and perished in the snowstorm that had blown in. The sixth woman was an angler who'd gotten separated from her fishing party. The seventh was a forestry worker who'd disappeared in the woods. And then there was the last victim. The one who'd survived. Sarah Jane Baker, 25, married to Ethan Baker, owner of the local sporting goods store.

Baker had gone missing the afternoon before Thanksgiving on the cusp of a severe early winter storm. Search teams and dogs had yielded nothing. The searches had been hampered by heavy snow and low cloud.

At the time no one truly suspected foul play. The wilderness around Watt Lake was vast and endless. People easily vanished, and did often enough—hunters, mushroom pickers, fishermen, hikers, climbers, snowmobilers. The weather, wild animals, violent rivers, treacherous terrain all presented hazards. No one connected her disappearance with the seven other missing women.

The following spring, on a misty morning, a truck driver came across a wild-haired, mad-eyed young woman stumbling through snow along the remote Ki'ina logging road. She was pregnant and wrapped only in a rancid bearskin and burlap sack. She wore hiking boots and no socks. She carried a rifle, was severely hypothermic, badly cut, bruised, frostbitten, and babbling nonsense. She had a frayed rope secured tightly around her neck. Sarah Baker. Miraculously, she'd survived.

Cole swallowed, slowly setting down his mug.

As Baker recovered in hospital, the horrors of her abduction were slowly revealed. She'd been held prisoner in a shack somewhere in remote wilderness. There had been other women there before her. She'd seen a flayed body of a redhead on a meat hook. Her abductor had carved it up and put meat in his freezer.

The female forestry worker who'd disappeared the preceding fall had been a redhead.

Media swarmed Watt Lake. The story quickly went national, and then global. Homicide investigators came up from E Division in Surrey, taking over the case from the local RCMP unit. Political pressure came to bear on the federal police force.

Five months later—after Sarah Baker had given birth to her child, after a lengthy manhunt—a joint RCMP and tribal police emergency response team finally took down Sebastian George and brought him in.

At least, "Sebastian" was what he said his name was. He was, in effect, a man with no formal ID. His birth had never been registered, and he'd never been entered into any official system. In the eyes of the bureaucracy, he quite simply did not exist.

Forensics identification teams descended on his land, where gradually the scope of the depravation was revealed. The remains of the seven missing women were all found on his property. Two other bodies were found buried farther away. Those of a male and female in their late sixties—his parents, who, it appeared, had lived in squalor in an abode in the woods near the main buildings of the property.

It was pieced together that Sebastian George was the son of a drifter who'd moved up from California in the sixties and decided to go off-grid when she met and took up with Peter George, an aboriginal hunter and trapper born in Bear Claw. They'd built a completely self-sufficient homestead in the remote Bear Claw Valley on First Nations land, and lived off the forest and rivers. They'd given birth to Sebastian, raised the boy entirely off-grid.

It appeared he'd one day repaid them by abusing and killing them.

Shit. Cole scrubbed his fingers through his damp hair. This was heavy stuff. He'd been on tour in Sierra Leone when all this had broken. George had later been tried, convicted, and then found hanged in his cell just over three years ago.

Cole clicked open a photo of the killer.

A striking man. Gaunt, tall. Wild dark curls the color of ink, amber eyes offset by a dusky complexion. Cole opened another image—that of George's mother.

It was a photo supplied by her kin in California. Her remains had been formally linked to her California family through DNA. This photo had been taken shortly before Jenny Burch had renamed herself Nightingale and left on a walkabout, never to return. Her family had eventually presumed her dead, and stopped looking.

Cole could see where Sebastian George got his looks. Jenny Burch had been a stunner—angular features, wide amber eyes, and thick, pin-straight hair the blue-black color of a raven's feathers.

He clicked open a photo of Sebastian George's father. It showed Peter George as a big, bold-looking man with dusky skin, liquid black eyes, and flared cheekbones.

Scrolling further down the search results, Cole found a page with photos of the eight victims. One after the other he clicked them open until he reached the thumbnail of the last one. The one who got away. He opened the link.

A face filled his screen.

Cole caught his breath. Ice speared through his veins. Slowly, numbly, he stared.

It was her.

Different, but absolutely her. Not a question in his mind.

Sarah Baker was Olivia West.

Cole hurriedly hit another link—this one about the extensive trial and DNA evidence used to convict Sebastian George. But as it opened, his monitor went black.

His battery was dead.

———

Mac Yakima replaced the phone receiver on his desk as Martinello appeared in the doorway.

"That was Raffey," he said, looking up. "He's still with the coroner. Apparently our vic recently had left knee arthoplasty—knee replacement surgery. We've got the identifying number on the orthopedic device."

She gave a fist pump. "Finally, something. And"—she wiggled the pieces of paper in her hand—"we've got the probable-cause warrant to search Burton's residence and a warrant to track his cell." She plunked the warrants on his desk.

Mac scanned them. "Day execution for Burton's residence. We can get in there with a full team first thing in the a.m. And we can get going right away for a trace on his phone." He stood, grabbed his jacket. "I'm starved. Chinese or Italian?"

"Turkish."

"What?"

"There's a new place off Main. It's Turkish. I'm sick of Chinese and Italian."

They exited the building, the energy between them palpable. They had the scent of their quarry. The hunt was on.

CHAPTER 14

Tori showered before her dad and was snugged back into her down jacket, finally toasty but ravenous after being out on the water and the excitement of catching her first trout. They were going to head up to the lodge for the seven o'clock dinner, but it wasn't time yet.

She waited until she heard the water go on in the bathroom before lifting the mattress and extracting her hidden e-reader. She stuffed it down the front of her jacket and pulled on a woolly hat. Outside, twilight lingered and the wind was cold. She walked down to the dock, where a bench in a gazebo overlooked the water. Small solar lights on stalks that had been sunk into the lawn around the gazebo were starting to glow. It was protected from the wind down here. She could read in peace for a while.

She settled onto the bench, switched her Kindle on. The page where she'd last left off filled the small screen. Coyotes called in the hills as she started reading in the gloam. But it was okay, the e-reader was backlit.

> She made him think the baby was his.
>
> It didn't stop him from raping her, but he did stop hurting her so badly, and she realized that he had an ego, a weak spot—he wanted to see "his" baby grow. He was interested in his own likeness. Her pregnancy was something he valued, which meant she had a tool.

She began to think he might even allow her to live. At least until the baby was born. It fueled her hope, her belief she would make it out.

But one dark morning, when everything seemed frozen in deep winter silence, this grown man came into her shed and told her that his father had never permitted him to shoot a pregnant doe. He'd always wanted to hunt and kill a pregnant doe, he said. To field dress it, to stick the knife in, rip into the belly, and split it, to see the baby hoofs come out of the sack.

She knew then, on some subterranean level, why he'd stopped hurting her, and why he was letting her baby grow . . .

An owl hooted softly.

Tori glanced up.

Dry leaves rustled over the lawn. Reeds whispered. It was getting duskier and spooky out, things taking strange shapes. She leaned closer in the fading light. But as she recommenced reading, a man materialized on the bank with a fly rod. She started in shock.

He stopped along the water just below her and cast his rod, spooling out long swirls of line. He wore waders and a fishing vest over his jacket. A ball cap hid his face.

As if sensing her gaze, he glanced up.

Tori tensed.

The memory of the words she'd read earlier shimmered into her mind.

He cast again and was letting his fly drift when he became aware of a presence. A sensation of being watched . . . Slowly, he shifted his gaze over his shoulder. A man stood in water about fifty yards down from him. He'd not made a sound in his approach. It was as if he'd simply materialized from the fabric of the forest . . .

"Sorry. I didn't mean to startle you," the man said, moving a little closer to the gazebo along the edge of the water. Tori still couldn't see his face, his eyes.

"Is that a good read?" He nodded to the e-reader clutched in her hand.

"Uh . . . yeah." She glanced up toward their cabin. It was just out of sight from the gazebo. A wolf howled in the mountains. It gave her goose bumps. She got up to go, but the man turned his back on her, ignoring her as he played out his line. She watched for a moment. He was an even better caster than Olivia. It was like a ballet. So beautiful, the way the wet line arced and droplets sprayed like little diamonds in the dusk.

Intrigue edged away her caution. Tori climbed down the small steps of the gazebo and inched closer to the water, e-reader clutched in her hand. The man moved slightly away from her, going farther along the bank, closer to the trees as he recast his line. He waited and watched his fly out on the surface, his hands still. An owl hooted softly again.

"I saw you out in the boat, catching a fish," he said. "I was in my pontoon, a little farther down the lake. At least, I think it was you guys in the boat."

"Olivia, our guide, caught the fish. I just brought it in."

"Well, bringing it in is just as challenging as getting it on a hook."

He raised his rod, and the line went taut. The end of the rod bent sharply. Her heart started to patter. She moved closer, excitement trilling through her as she recalled the sensation of catching her own. A huge trout leaped free of the water and smacked with a loud crack onto the surface.

"It's a big one!" she said. "A fighter."

He didn't say a word as he played it. He let it run, dive down deep, allowed it to think it was safe. Until finally it was exhausted and he brought it in, flopping weakly.

"Just like that," she murmured, incredulous. "You just put the fly out there and you got one, bam, right away."

"It's the time of day that helps." He pointed to the water. "See those bugs hovering low, just above the surface? The way the bats are going crazy, darting to get them?"

Tori blinked into the gloaming. She hadn't realized they were bats. Tiny. Like darting swallows.

"Action like that—it also means there's cold coming. Big weather."

He reached into his pocket and came out with a silvery tool. He smashed the big trout on its head.

Shock rippled through Tori as the fish went still. "You killed it," she said softly.

"Yup. Dinner." He stuck his fingers into the gills and lifted it out of the water. "A man's gotta eat."

She swallowed.

"So, was that your dad in the boat with you and the guide, Olivia?" he said.

"Yeah."

"Do you come up here often to fish? Do you use the same guide? You know her well?" He watched her intently as he spoke, but she couldn't really see his features in the shadows, nor his eyes, which were hidden below the bill of his ball cap.

Nerves whispered through her. It was rather dark all of a sudden. She glanced up to the cabin. She was out of sight down here.

"I've been wondering whether to hire her," he offered in way of explanation for his questions.

"No," Tori said. "This is the first time we've come here, and the first time we've been out with Olivia. My mom died in April, and my dad just retired, so he brought me here." The words just came out of her mouth. "I also burned a kid's books at school."

Something seemed to quicken through him.

"I'm sorry. That's terrible."

Emotion surged into her eyes. She averted her gaze. Stupid tears were always so close to the surface whenever she thought of her mother.

"Don't let it worry you," he said gently, his voice a smooth, low, and comforting sound. "I get it—that need to hurt something when you yourself are hurt."

She looked up at him.

"Say, why don't you come around to the campsite tomorrow and find me and my wife. I'm going to smoke half this trout—you ever tasted smoked trout?"

She shook her head.

"You're in for a treat then. *If* you come visit." He smiled slowly, his teeth glinting in the fading light. He bent down to put his fish in a creel that she only just noticed was there. "What did your father do, then? Before he retired?" he said, securing the lid of the creel.

"He was a cop."

His head ticked up. "A Mountie? Or another force?"

"Mountie. In Vancouver. He was with homicide. Before that he was stationed in Fort Tapley, where I was born. And before that he was the staff sergeant up at Watt Lake."

Something shifted in the air. His gaze seemed to pin hers. Wind gusted.

A chill suddenly crawled over her skin.

"Tori!"

She jumped. Her dad. Quickly she stuffed her e-reader down the front of her jacket.

"Where are you, Tori?!" He loomed around the side of the gazebo and came down the bank, breathing hard. "Jesus, Tori, you scared me . . . what in the hell are you doing down here?"

"I was watching the man fish."

"What man?"

She turned. There was no one there. Just shadows, branches swaying in the wind, ripples along the water where he'd stood. Her father peered into the shadows.

A *clang, clang, clang, clang* sounded. A duck fluttered and a loon called in a haunting warble. Leaves clattered down the bank in a gust of wind.

He grabbed her arm. "Come. That's the dinner bell. Guess they still do it cowboy style out here."

He marched her up the bank, his fingers digging into her arm. "Ouch." She jerked against his grip. "You're hurting me."

"Who was the man down there?" he demanded, his voice rough.

"I don't know. Just a fisherman. From the campsite."

He stopped dead in his tracks. "Did you talk to him?"

She said nothing.

"What did he say to you, Tori?"

"Nothing. He saw me catch a fish earlier. He asked about you and Olivia."

He tensed. She felt a dark, weird energy rolling off him in waves. The little solar lights glinted on his face, and she saw he was sweating. Something was wrong. Her father seemed afraid, panicky.

"You didn't give him your name or anything, did you?"

"No."

"You don't dare go near him again, you hear me? You don't go near anyone out here."

"Why?"

"Just don't."

"I don't know what your problem is! He seemed like a nice guy."

"Lures appear nice to fish, Tori. And look what happens to the fish. We don't know the people up here. This place is isolated. There are woods around us for miles. Hunters with guns. Anything could happen."

"You're just saying that because you're a cop, because you always think everyone is up to something nefarious, and it makes me *sick*!"

"That's because I've seen what people are capable of. You need to be more aware. Horrible, horrible things can happen to very good people."

She thought of the poor woman in the shed in her mother's book. But that was just a story. Fiction. Yet her mother also ripped stuff straight from headlines—that was what the reviews always said. That dark, cold thing crawling at the edges of her mind came a little closer.

"Come." He marshaled her along the path toward the lodge where the lights glowed yellow and warm into the darkness. But her father took only two steps before he gasped and bent over, clutching his temple.

"Dad? What's wrong?!"

He opened his mouth, as if trying to make words. But nothing came out.

Tori clamped her hand over his arm. "Daddy, please, tell me what's going on."

He waved his hand, trying to get his tongue around words. "I... it's fine." His words came out breathless. "It's nothing, honey, it's... okay." He stood slowly up, swayed a little, and caught onto her shoulder for balance. Her great big dad leaned heavily on her for support. "I... I'm fine. Just... really tired."

He forced a smile and took several deep breaths, then tried to walk again. But she grabbed his sleeve and held him back.

"Are you sick?" she demanded.

He looked down at her for several long beats. An owl's *whoo whoo whoooo* sounded in the trees above them.

"Tori, love." He reached down and pushed a strand of long hair out of her face. "Everything's going to be okay. Just—"

"I heard you talking to Aunt Louise on the phone," she snapped. "I heard you say that you were too young to retire, and she said something could go wrong any day now, and that I'd have to go and live with them back east. Coming to this ranch wasn't about what I did at school, was it? It's about you being ill and needing to spend time with me. Are you going to die? Are you going to leave me, too?"

He cursed softly and glanced up toward the lights of the lodge, as if they offered escape from a conversation he wasn't prepared to have, if he could just get there, but he was trapped here with her in the dark.

"Yes," he said finally. "I am sick."

Her lip started to wobble. "What's wrong?"

"I have a kind of cancer."

"What kind?"

He reached for her hand and led her over to a bench along the side of the path. Seating himself, he drew her closer, looked into her eyes. In the pale glow of the solar lanterns his eyes were dark holes, and his face was drawn.

Tori could scent fire smoke on the breeze. She focused on the smell, on the sounds of dry things crackling in the dead leaves under the trees. She wanted to run away, to not hear the horrible truth.

"I was diagnosed in January last year with what they call melanoma." His voice was low, quiet. He sounded defeated. "It starts out as a small mole on your body, but it can metastasize and spread cancer very quickly to other parts of your body if you don't catch it in time."

Her gaze fixed on him, she said, "Did it spread?"

Footfalls sounded down the path. Someone was coming. Tori's heart started to race.

"Gage? Is that you?" Olivia's voice reached them as she came up the path from the staff cabins.

Tori gripped his hands iron tight, her body vibrating. "Tell me," she hissed. Squeezing his fingers. Desperate. "Tell me quickly before *she* gets here."

"It had already spread when they found it. To my lymph nodes. Other places. It had moved into my brain. I have a tumor there."

"What does that *mean*? Can they take it out?"

Olivia was coming closer along the path.

"Yes," her dad said quickly. "It's going to be fine, but let's talk about it some more after dinner, okay?"

"You're lying. Because if they can fix it, why would I have to go live with Aunt Lou?"

Olivia emerged from the shadows. "Gage, Tori, is that you guys?"

"Later, okay?" he whispered. "I'll tell you everything."

Tori yanked away and stormed up toward the lodge.

"Tori!" he called after her.

She clenched her fists and jaw and just kept marching up the path.

"Hey, Tori," Olivia said.

She bumped aggressively into Olivia, pushing past her.

———

"Tori!" Gage struggled to his feet as Olivia appeared through the trees.

Olivia hurried forward. "What's going on? Are you okay?"

"Yeah. I was just a bit out of breath. Happens sometimes."

"I just saw Tori tearing up the path," she said.

He drew his hand down hard over his mouth, emotion hot in his eyes. He once felt so much in command, powerful. A good cop. A good provider and protector of his family. He'd felt blessed. Now he was unraveling like a ragged ball of twine. Inside he felt like the scared, small Alberta farm boy he once was, a lifetime—fifty-six years ago. All those years spent clawing himself out of the prairies, becoming a police officer, a top detective, working homicide, running a detachment, and it came down to this? The End. How did one deal with The End when you could see it coming like a freight train?

Melody had helped him plan it out. They'd spoken about how they would deal with it, had a strategy. Tori was to have been left with her mother. Melody was not supposed to go first.

Olivia placed her hand gently on his arm.

"Do you want to talk about it, Gage?"

And it was all he could do not to break, to tell her everything. This woman he'd been watching from afar ever since she'd been found on that logging road. Half naked, delirious. A fighter. A woman who knew pain and understood trauma. This woman who was so closely intertwined with his own past, and now, the future. His need to share everything with her, confess it all right now, was suddenly fierce and consuming.

"Is there anything I can do to help?"

He met her eyes. Beautiful eyes. Even in the dark, he could feel her beauty. Inside and out.

"What you did today with Tori on the boat . . . it was more than I could have hoped for. Thank you."

His sincerity, gravity, appeared to stall her a moment. She held his gaze in the dark.

"The violent streak I've seen in her since her mother's death really worried me. But the way you pulled her around, showed her with that damselfly, the fact she chose to release her fish in the end . . ." His voice caught, thick with emotion. Embarrassing.

"Anytime," she said softly. "And I do mean that. Come." She hooked her arm through his. "I'll show her how to tie a damselfly tomorrow, if she wants. Or maybe she'd like to help Ace with his tracking. I think they like each other," she said with a smile.

It cracked Gage's heart. There was love out there in the world for Tori. There *would* be a way forward for his daughter.

You're doing the right thing, Gage, by bringing her here. By seeing this through to the end . . .

A twig cracked in the bush. They both stilled. Listened. A cat may have run through the shadows.

Cole plugged in his laptop to charge. It was dim inside the library, just the glow from the fire and one animal-hide lamp. He was eager for his computer to juice up so he could resume his research on the Watt Lake case, learn more about Olivia.

He walked over to the big picture window in the library and dug his hands deep into his pockets, losing himself in thought as he looked out into the darkening evening.

When the clang of the old dinner triangle had reached him in his cabin, it had hurled him back in time, way back to when Jimmie was alive. To when the two of them had been allowed to work alongside the wranglers, and come dusk they'd been as hungry as little wolves. Being permitted to eat with the big cowboys had been thrilling. His dream at the time had been to ride with the guys full time, herding the cattle, working this ranch alongside his father and brother. Nostalgia rode hard on the back of the memories.

He wondered for a moment about choices, and whether he could really make a go of it on the ranch, if he put his mind to it. A wry smile twisted his lips. The irony wasn't lost on him. Now that he was toying with the idea of actually trying to stay, the land was going to Olivia.

The woman who'd once been Sarah Baker. A true survivor.

You're no survivor, you know that? You know dick about surviving . . .

Yeah, he fully got where she was coming from, now that he knew who she was.

Everything else about her made sense, too. Her scars. Her awkwardness about being touched. Her flashbacks, and why the Birkenhead news had triggered them. His thoughts turned to his father's words about how Broken Bar had helped heal her. And he wondered what had transpired with her husband, Ethan. Her family. Had she so thoroughly expunged her past in an effort to obliterate all memory of her ordeal? Had she needed to excise everything associated with her life in Watt Lake, including her name, in order to forget? He understood that need to forget. He'd left Broken Bar and this house in an effort to erase negative memories, too. Nothing compared to hers, though. It made his issues feel almost trivial.

It was almost full dark outside now, little solar lanterns weakly lighting the paths through the trees. And as he looked out into the dark, it struck him, the truth of it—why he'd favored selling the ranch when Jane asked. Because even though, deep down, this place still held magic for him, selling it was just another way of obliterating bad memories, of thumbing his nose at his father.

But something almost imperceptible had started to change in him. He remembered some good times, too, along with the bad. And those good times had been core, character-shaping times, things he'd forgotten about himself. And now that he'd been brought back to Broken Bar while at a crossroads in his life, it almost felt like a sign.

Yes, the ranch was falling into disrepair. Yes, it would require major effort and a serious investment of capital if they were to attempt to rebuild the livestock side of the business. But the possibility of a new chapter held allure.

What else did he have to go back to right now? If the muse ever did grab him by the balls again, he could still write from Broken Bar.

His thoughts returned to Olivia, and he gave a soft snort. If he wanted to stay now, it was going to have to be by her grace. It was her place to run. So why did that not bother him? Because she deserved it, that was the hell why.

The image from his laptop filled his mind—the photo that had been taken just before she'd disappeared twelve years ago. The one used for the "Missing" poster.

Same thick brown hair, prettily shaped, full lips. Mossy-green eyes. But in that photo she'd possessed the clear fresh-faced innocence of a young woman with promise in her life. Hopes. Big dreams. Before she was taken, maimed, marked, owned, terrorized.

Goose bumps crawled over his skin as he thought about the choker of scars around her neck.

She was found with a frayed rope still knotted around her neck.
Frostbitten feet . . .

The last victim. The lone survivor. The one who'd fought back hard enough to get away and take him down. But at what cost? Her life in Watt Lake? Her husband and family?

At what low point had she tried to kill herself?

Like a desiccated flower on the vine she was when she arrived.
This place healed her. Those scars on her wrists that were so red and angry, they began to fade . . .

He glanced at his watch. He should go down for dinner. The laptop would have to wait until after. He wouldn't confront Olivia about his discovery, either. He wanted the truth to come voluntarily from her. His new goal was to win her trust to a point where she felt comfortable, safe enough, to share her past with him.

He was about to leave his post at the window when a movement down among the darkened trees caught his eye. A couple emerged from the shadows and stepped into the light spilling from the porch. Olivia with that Burton guy. Her arm was crooked into his, their heads bent low as they conversed intimately. Cole's body flexed.

He stared down at them, curiosity and a possessive twinge of jealousy curling through him. But before he could think further, the phone on the long low table in front of the window rang.

Attention still fixated on the scene below, Cole reached over and snagged up the receiver. "Broken Bar Ranch."

"Cole? It's me, Jane. Do you know how long I've been trying to get hold of you—what in heaven's name is going on there!"

He glanced at his watch again. It was an ungodly hour in London. "Jane? What's the—"

"I heard the news." Her voice was pitched high. "Why didn't you call me at once?"

"I was going to. I—"

"I *told* you to watch out for that woman. I *warned* you she was manipulating him, exerting undue influence. That's potentially a criminal charge, do you know that? Exploitation of the elderly and the infirm. And now he's leaving her the entire bloody ranch? You have *got* to do something. You've got to get rid of her."

Cole inhaled a long, slow breath, his gaze still locked on the couple conversing under the trees below the window. "How did you hear about this, Jane?"

"Clayton Forbes phoned me. He suggested we sort this out before Dad dies, that we get him to amend the will. Because if we don't, it's going to cost a fortune in protracted legal battles to fight that woman. We could be in court forever."

"How," he said quietly, "does Forbes even know that Dad changed the will?" He leaned forward, watching as Olivia and Burton came up to the porch and disappeared under the eaves, entering the lodge. Mistrust curled through him. Along with a surge of testosterone-fueled protectiveness. His feelings for Olivia were growing complicated. He wondered again about the newspaper and lure that Burton left in the office. It took on an ominous light now that he knew who Olivia really was.

"I don't know how he found out. One of his employees told him, I think."

Adele's odd words from the stairwell closet suddenly sprang to his mind.

You've got to find a way to get rid of her . . .

His thoughts leaped to Adele's words a few minutes later as she'd handed him the Dodge keys.

A sale would be of great benefit to the whole region . . . there's talk of a development—it's just a proposal, mind you, for high-end estate lots and some commerce. It would bring jobs and tourism . . .

Suspicion braided into him. Adele had been standing in the library doorway with a tray. She'd overheard his father saying that he was leaving the ranch to Olivia.

"This should have nothing do with Forbes, Jane. It's not his business."

"It has *everything* to do with him. And with us. If we don't inherit the property, there is no sale. The financing for the development . . . the up-front fees, it all falls through. Do you realize what a big deal that is at this stage?"

His hand tightened on the phone. "He's securing investment on a nonexistent deal?"

"He has our legal letter of intent that we'll enter into good-faith negotiations to sell. That's something you can take to the bank. Jesus, Cole, you're not taking this seriously—do you understand this is serious? Do you know what kind of money we stand to make here?"

"Maybe I no longer want to sell, Jane."

Dead, deafening silence.

"Cole?" Her voice cracked. She cleared her throat. "You're messing with me."

"I'm in no rush. I have no place I need to go."

Another crackle of silence.

When she spoke, her voice was changed. "You signed that e-document. We both did. I had lawyers vet it on both the British and Canadian ends. It's binding."

He cursed inwardly. He needed to speak to Forbes, and a lawyer, figure out how to wangle out of this thing.

"Listen to me, if you try to pull out now, I *will* fight you on this. Clayton and I both will. We'll contest the validity of Dad's new will in the courts. Clayton will rake you and that Olivia woman through a protracted legal nightmare. It'll break you both financially. I promise you that."

"God, Jane, listen to yourself."

"Oh, don't go all high and mighty on me now. Toddy and I need that extra financing. I. . . it's a long story. We need that windfall. And you sure as hell don't need that ranch—you never wanted a thing to do with it."

Cole thought of Adele and her husband and his small disability fund. Jane needing money. Clayton Forbes up to his neck in house-of-cards financing. The Clinton community being promised jobs, tourism.

How many people's dreams were resting on the sale of Broken Bar, and the promise of development?

He thought of Olivia.

"I need to make a call. Good-bye, Jane." He hung up.

Cole was now ready to draw his battle line in the sand. Whatever in the hell his father did with this ranch, it wasn't going to Forbes, not on his watch. It was the principle of the thing. Before, Cole didn't care. Now he did. This ranch fell under the Agricultural Land Reserve. By law it had to be used for farming. It couldn't be developed without government maneuvering. And he suddenly couldn't bear the thought of it being sliced and sold off in pieces.

Maybe it was his own long-held animosity toward Forbes. Or maybe it was Olivia. He didn't the hell know, but the fire was back in him. And he liked the feel.

He looked up Clayton Forbes's home number on his charging computer. He dialed. The call went straight to voice mail.

He left a message. "Forbes, it's Cole McDonough. I'm back on Broken Bar. Our deal is off. We need to speak."

Almost as soon as he hung up, the library phone rang. It was Forbes.

"Cole! Welcome back, buddy. I heard—"

"Listen, don't waste your breath, there's no deal. At least not from my end. I don't care what you've arranged with Jane, but should part of the estate ever fall into my hands, there will be no sale."

"Now, now, McDonough. Take it easy. Hear me out. I have a legal document, vetted by my corporate legal team. And—"

The line went silent.

"Hello?"

Nothing.

Cole tapped the hook switch. "Forbes, are you there?"

The phone was dead.

Cole moved quickly to the phone in his father's office. No dial tone, either. Landlines must have gone down. Wind gusted on cue, ticking branches against the library window. The loose shutter banged repeatedly. The storm was closing in, and they'd lost contact with the outside world. He peered out the window into the dark.

An eerie green glow rippled across the sky, reflecting on the black surface of the lake. Northern lights. He stilled a moment as he caught sight of someone moving around the side of the house. But perhaps it was just a trick of light and dark.

———

Eugene fingered the cables and glanced up the wall to be certain he had the right ones for the sat dish. He'd already taken care of the phone lines. He reached for the bolt cutters slung at his hip, but stilled as he heard someone come out the kitchen door. He ducked back into the shadow of the wall, waiting while a garbage can clanged as refuse was emptied out. The lid banged again, then the kitchen door shut. It went quiet and dark again. He moved back to the cables. He didn't need a flashlight thanks to the soft green-blue haze that was now billowing gently across the sky. It wouldn't last long. Along the horizon a blackness grew, marching closer. It carried snow. Urgency crackled like soft electricity over his skin.

He reached for the bolt cutter . . .

CHAPTER 15

Cole entered the open-plan lounge and dining area. Ace lay in front of the fire on an old Persian rug worn thin over the years. Cowhide lampshades and flickering candles cast a warm glow through the room. Wood paneling, heavy log beams along the vaulted ceiling, the bleached antlers above the kitchen entryway all added to the old hunting lodge ambience.

At the far end of the hearth his father was parked in his chair, staring into the flames and nursing a rather large tumbler of whisky. On the sofa sat the daughter of Gage Burton, looking burdened by a serious chip on her young shoulder.

Two older couples conversed animatedly at the bar. One pair Cole recognized from the campsite—the owners of the de-barked poodle. Gage Burton joined them.

Behind the rustic bar, a man in his late twenties poured drinks for the guests. A slender blonde woman about the same age as the bartender was busy setting wineglasses on the linen-covered dining tables. Music in the background was a soft jazz.

Cole went up to his dad. "How're you doing?"

Myron just grunted. He was clearly well into his cups, and his cheeks appeared even more sunken than earlier.

Cole inhaled deeply, worry worming through him. His dad was taking a turn for the worse. He needed to call the doc, find out what next steps were required in the management of his father's care.

The flat-screen television that had earlier shown news of the horrific murder was muted and set to the weather channel. He watched for a moment the meteorological images of a massive storm cell moving in fast from the south. The pilot in him cringed at the sight of that weather hump. It was going to be a big one. And it could hit by morning. Already he could hear the wind moaning eerily and continuously in the top of the old stone chimney flue.

The Burton child was giving him the eyeball. He turned and smiled at her. She was quite beautiful under the carapace of her foul mood. And he wondered where her mother was—why she and her father were alone at a lodge for Thanksgiving.

"Hey," he said, deepening his smile. "I'm Cole. I grew up on the ranch."

Her eyes narrowed. She seemed to be weighing whether to answer him at all. "I'm Tori Burton."

"I saw you guys out in the boat with Olivia this afternoon. You catch any fish?"

"Olivia did. She let me bring it in."

"Big one?"

"Big enough to keep," she said. "But I released it."

The television screen flickered suddenly, then died to black. Cole went up to it and turned it off, then on again. No life. He checked the wires. Everything was connected.

"Is it dead?" Tori said.

"Stone cold," he said. "That weather heading our way must be interfering with our sat signal as well as the phones."

Which likely meant no Internet. No more laptop research on the Watt Lake Killer, or Sarah Baker, until things were up and running again. So much for charging his laptop. And with phones down, too, they were pretty much cut off from civilization now, with a serious storm closing in around the wilderness.

As if on cue, the wind moaned again, and shutters banged somewhere.

The kitchen door swung suddenly open. Olivia exited, carrying two bottles of wine. She paused as she caught sight of Cole. His pulse quickened as their eyes met.

She'd applied some makeup, and her hair fell in glossy waves to her shoulders. A soft cashmere-looking polo-neck sweater hid her scar. She wore a fresh set of slim-fitting jeans and cowboy boots.

A quick smile lit her eyes, and his stomach zinged, a whirlwind of feelings surging through him—respect, admiration, compassion . . . a desire to protect. And just plain old desire. He wanted her. Pure and simple. It struck him bold in the face.

But this was not the kind of woman a man could rush. Not with her past.

She carried the wine to the tables. As she set the bottles down, Gage Burton approached her from behind and touched her elbow. She spun around, gave him a big smile.

Cole's chest tightened with a sense of proprietorship. Tori had also stiffened on the sofa, her gaze riveted on her father and Olivia. Her eyes darkened.

Wind howled again, and a deepening, unearthly moan funneled down the flue as if the weather was seeking its way inside.

"My mom died," Tori said suddenly, her attention still locked on her father and Olivia.

His gaze flared to Tori.

She turned to look up at him, and the combination of anger and despair in her eyes, her face, crushed through his chest.

"She suffocated in a tree well in April. It was my fault. I was skiing with her when she went in, and I couldn't pull her out."

Oh, Jesus.

He lowered himself slowly onto the sofa beside her. "I'm so sorry, Tori." He hesitated. "But you cannot blame yourself for an accident like that."

Her eyes filled with emotion. Her hands clenched.

Cole could sense his father watching him, and he suddenly

had a surreal sense of time spiraling inward. Was his father think-ing of Jimmie? Of Ty, whom he'd never met?

"I also had an accident once," he said quietly. "I was only six-teen at the time. I drove my truck into a river with my mother and little brother inside. We crashed through the ice. I managed to get out the driver's window, but I couldn't get them out. I tried. God, did I try. But . . ." His voice faded as the cold memories swallowed him. "I have blamed myself my entire life for that day, Tori." He stole another glance at his father. "And I'm only just coming to realize that hanging too hard on to that guilt, it just stops you from living. *And* it won't bring your mother back." He leaned forward, arms resting on his knees. He held her deep green eyes. "You need to forgive yourself. You *need* to find a way."

A tear glistened down her cheek. He dug in his jeans pocket for a handkerchief but came up empty handed.

"Here."

Startled, he glanced up. His dad was holding out a fresh kerchief. Cole got up, took it from his dad. Their eyes met for a moment. And history, words unspoken, surged between them.

"I'm sorry, son," Myron said, very quietly, his eyes rheumy with drink. "For never letting go."

Cole felt a twist of pain, compassion. Warmth mushroomed through his chest. Love. Dammit. He cared for his dad. He really did. He needed his father's forgiveness like he needed air to breathe. He swallowed, Olivia's words filling his mind.

I thought that you might be big enough to take the initiative, to say sorry, make peace before he passes . . .

His father had beaten him to it.

"I'm sorry, too." *More than you can ever know.*

Myron looked away and reached for his drink, his hand fisting around the tumbler as he took a deep swig.

Cole gave Tori the hanky. She wiped her eyes, and blew her nose.

"Better?"

She glanced down at the kerchief balled in her hands, then her gaze flickered back to her father and Olivia. Cole's gaze followed Tori's.

Burton was leaning close to Olivia as he spoke in her ear. Her head was bent toward him as she listened. Slowly she smiled, then put her head back and laughed.

Cole was suddenly mesmerized. It was the first time he'd seen Olivia laugh. Even from across the room her eyes caught light and sparkled. Her cheeks were a healthy flush. In this brief moment she was relaxed, glowing, exuding a vital energy. Happy. And she looked magical. Maybe she'd somehow managed to compartmentalize her earlier flashbacks, the survivor in her triumphing tonight.

A combative surge of testosterone pulsed into his blood, and Burton was suddenly a rival. Cole also understood what was troubling Burton's kid. She missed her mother, and seeing her dad like this with another woman was killing the child. Distaste filled his mouth.

He turned to Tori. "Will you be okay if I leave you for a sec? I need to talk to Olivia."

Her eyes held his for a long, beseeching moment, and she nodded.

Cole got up, and as he walked toward them he had to consciously tamp down the militant energy that had ignited him.

Olivia looked up as she saw him approaching.

"Cole," she said, reaching her arm out for him to join them. "Come, let me introduce you to everyone and give you a rundown of who's who."

She really was sparkling tonight. Was it this Burton character? His company was that remarkable? What had happened in that boat this afternoon to get them from there to here?

He felt a tightening in his chest.

"This is Kim," Olivia said, as the young blonde who'd been setting glasses on the table came by with a tray of condiments. Kim smiled, nodded.

"And that's Kim's fiancé, Zack, behind the bar. Both recently graduated from the University of the North and have been working at Broken Bar over the past summer. Thanksgiving will be their last day on the ranch, and then they're off to Europe. Jason Chan, as you know, is the mastery behind the kitchen. Nella over there, helping Kim set the table, is Jason's daughter."

"We met earlier," he said. She'd been the kid sitting on the sofa with Tori when they'd seen the terrible news on TV.

"Nella's mom and dad are separated. This Thanksgiving is Jason's turn to have her. And that's Brannigan at the bar, chatting with Zack. He's our groom, the last of the Broken Bar wranglers, so to speak. The others are all guests from the campsite and two of the cabins. You met the couple who own the poodle—they're from Kelowna. The older pair with them are from Russia. And the tall man with them is a forester from Hundred Mile House."

Cole regarded the taciturn forester, who seemed to be watching them in return.

"And this of course is Gage Burton. You were speaking to his daughter, Tori, on the sofa." Olivia turned to Burton. "And this is Cole McDonough, Myron's son."

"We spoke briefly earlier." Cole reached forward to formally shake Burton's hand.

Burton's gaze met his. The man had an iron grip of a handshake, direct clear blue eyes. He possessed a presence that put Cole instantly in mind of a military man—possibly an allied paramilitary professional, or law enforcement officer. He had a radar for this kind of man. Burton was the kind of alpha male he often wrote about. He had on a wedding band.

Animosity mushroomed hot in Cole as he released the man's hand. With it came a whispering unease.

Burton seemed to be assessing him in return, as if weighing up a foe.

"Can I get you something to drink?" Burton said with a smile that didn't quite reach his eyes. He was taking control in what was essentially Cole's territory. And he clearly had something going for Olivia. Tension swelled thick and static between them.

But instead of resisting, Cole said, "Thank you. Scotch on the rocks. Make it a double."

Burton went to the bar. Cole's gaze tracked him.

"Gage was the one I told you about who left the newspaper and fishing lure in the office," Olivia offered.

Cole turned to face her. Her eyes were deep green and clear. He dropped his gaze to her lips. Softly glossed. She stood close enough that he could scent her shampoo again, and a hint of some other fragrance. Her pale-pink polo-neck sweater looked candy-floss soft and came almost to her chin, fully concealing her scar.

And as she met his eyes, her own pupils darkened, and Cole felt a clutch of desire and almost delirious pleasure. She was physically interested in him. This knowledge, the fact he could read approval in her gaze, inflamed the carnal thoughts and lust already ribboning through him.

Yet warning bells clanged. *Go slow. Think this through.* Was it right to even pursue this? While he might read interest now, he'd seen her react under stress. He'd witnessed firsthand her aversion to being touched, the terror it had sparked in her eyes. And he knew why. Her sexual abuse had been horrendous.

Shit. This was heavy. He hadn't expected to come home and find this.

"Odd," he said quietly, "that lure of Burton's. More like a steelhead or salmon fly."

Hesitancy flickered almost imperceptibly through her eyes. Her hand tightened around her wineglass. Cole was reluctant to push further, because that lure had really set her off earlier. But why? His curiosity outweighed his caution.

"It was a retirement gift, apparently," she said. "Along with a spey rod and some other flies. It had been given to him just before he came up. I guess that's why he had it on him."

He held her eyes. "Came up from where?"

"Vancouver."

"Have you met him before?"

A frown creased her brow. "No. Why?"

He shrugged and turned to watch Burton at the bar ordering drinks. "He works fast."

"You have a problem with him," she said.

"I have a problem with how he's fawning over you."

Her mouth opened in shock. Then a slow smile of understanding curved her lips. "If I didn't know better, Cole McDonough, I'd say you were acting proprietary."

"Perhaps I am."

A wariness entered her eyes.

"Perhaps I don't like what his interest in you is doing to his kid back there."

The smile died on her lips. She held his gaze for a beat, then turned slowly to look at Tori. She swallowed.

"His wife died in April," Cole said. "I suppose that's plenty of time to heal and chat up another woman in front of a child still deeply grieving her mother."

Indignation flared in her eyes. "It's not what you think. You're right, Tori *is* suffering, but Gage asked me to help her out today—"

"You're not helping her now. Not by encouraging Burton."

"Christ, you really are like your father, you know that." She turned to go.

"Maybe I know what it means to lose a kid," he called quietly after her.

She stalled, turned slowly back to face him. He continued.

"Maybe I just want to tell them to hold on to what they've still got because it doesn't last forever."

She hesitated, uncertain. Her gaze flickered toward Burton at the bar.

"Did he tell you what he did for a living before he retired?" Cole pressed.

"No. And I didn't ask. I don't give all my guests the third degree. All I know is that he needed help with his daughter this afternoon. Some female company, he said. Tori had demonstrated a violent streak at school—her way of reacting to her mother's death. He just asked if I could spend some time with them."

He crooked a brow.

Irritation flared through her features.

"Look, I was able to help a man and his daughter today. Both lonely and hurt. I made them seem just a little bit happier, even for a moment. And that made *me* feel good, okay? That's *all*. I don't know what you have against him. I don't have to listen to this."

She was about to turn away again, then added, "Grief isn't linear, Cole. I'm sure you know that. And I'm not even going to grace your comment about me encouraging him with an answer. If you'll excuse me, I—"

Impulsively, his hand shot out and he caught her arm. She stilled, tension tightening her face. A cool flint entered her eyes.

"Be careful, Liv, I don't trust him." He paused. "I don't believe in coincidences."

"What does that mean?"

But before he could answer, Adele approached them, sans apron, purse in hand.

"Unless there's anything else," she said to Olivia, "I'll be on my way. I heard on the kitchen radio that it might start snowing as early as tomorrow morning. I might have to take one of the rooms in the lodge tomorrow night if it gets bad."

"I tell you what," Olivia said. "Why don't you call in early tomorrow before you leave Clinton. If it looks as though the snow will be heavy by tomorrow evening, we might not be having anyone for our Thanksgiving dinner anyway. Might end up canceling. And if the storm sticks around, you could get stranded here for a while."

"You might have trouble calling in tomorrow," Cole said. "The landlines have gone down. As well as sat reception."

Both Adele's and Olivia's eyes shot to the TV. It was blank.

Another sharp gust of wind rattled at the shutters and howled up high in the chimney. Adele went over to the phone on the wall near the bar, lifted the receiver.

"You're right," she said, coming back. "No dial tone."

"Okay, maybe it's best if you don't drive up at all tomorrow," Olivia told Adele. "Just stay home. Stay safe and warm. I'll handle things here."

The housekeeper hesitated.

"Honest." Olivia smiled. "We'll be fine."

"All right then. I'll call the phone company from Clinton tomorrow," Adele said. "Just to check that it's a regional problem and not a ranch-specific issue."

"Thank you."

"Well, good night then." She nodded at Cole.

"Regards to Mr. Carrick and Tucker," he said. Then on impulse, "Will you see Tuck soon?"

She looked fidgety. "He often comes around to our house. So, yes, probably."

"You mentioned he's in finance. Who does he work with? Clinton is such a small town."

"A development company."

"Forbes, perhaps?"

Her face reddened. Her gaze cut to Olivia. "Well, yes, he's doing some work with Clayton Forbes's real estate business. He's helping on his mayoral campaign as well."

"*Forbes* is running for mayor?"

She nodded and gave a quick, forced smile. "Like you say,

small town, not many opportunities outside of ranching. Got to take what one can get." She turned to Olivia. "Jason said he'd be ready to serve in five minutes. Well, good night, Olivia, Cole." She gave a quick nod without meeting his gaze again.

Cole watched Adele head into the hallway. The housekeeper removed her coat from the hook, cast a quick backward glance. Their gazes met for a brief instant. She opened the door, a draft of wind flapping her skirt, and she slipped out into the night. Cold washed in along the floor, and the flames in the hearth shivered. The door slammed in the wind.

Olivia turned abruptly to him "What was that about?"

"Did you know that Tuck Carrick works for Forbes?"

"No."

"But you know Forbes wants to buy the ranch."

"Everyone in Clinton knows that." She frowned. "Do you always observe a room like this? Like you're doing some sort of analysis? Are you always so damn suspicious of everyone's motives?" Irritation laced her voice.

"Old habits die hard, Olivia," he said quietly, holding her eyes.

"It's as if you're searching for reasons to dislike everyone."

Gage returned with Cole's drink.

"If you'll excuse me," Olivia said coolly, "I'm going to check with Jason to see if he's ready to serve."

Olivia strode toward the kitchen, back stiff. Cole noticed again her slight limp.

. . . wrapped only in a rancid bearskin and burlap sack. She wore hiking boots and no socks. She carried a rifle, was severely hypothermic, badly cut, bruised, frostbitten, and babbling nonsense. She had a frayed rope secured tightly around her neck. Sarah Baker. Miraculously, she'd survived . . .

Cole absently sipped his drink as he watched the kitchen door swing closed behind her.

Great, buddy. You sure blew that one. Right out of the water. Way to build trust.

Burton was watching the door where Olivia disappeared, too. He met the man's eyes, and something dark and malignant swelled between them.

CHAPTER 16

Myron hunkered at the head of the table like a sick old raven, his eyes sunken and bleary from drugs, drink, illness, or all three, as he poked at his dinner. He seemed in an odd mood, his gaze darting restlessly between Olivia, Cole, the kid, Burton. And he was being more reckless with his drink tonight. Something had altered in him, and as the wind outside howled, bringing the storm closer, Olivia felt the *tick tock* of a metaphysical clock.

Cole was seated to his father's right. Gage had taken the chair beside Olivia. Tori sat across from her. Rancor seemed to percolate around the child as she fiddled with the corner of her white linen napkin.

Guilt clutched through Olivia. She glanced at Cole. He was watching her from below his dark lashes as he ate and sipped his glass of Burgundy. And while the food was excellent as usual, while sounds of merriment rose from guests at the other tables, the mood at their table was off.

"Compliments to the chef." Cole wiped his mouth with his napkin, setting it beside his plate.

"The trout starter was from the lake," Olivia offered, trying to lighten the atmosphere. "The venison is from the neighboring ranch, and the roasted autumn vegetables came from the kitchen garden."

"A vegetable garden your mother started," Myron muttered to Cole, reaching for his third glass of red wine. "Back when we took delivery of the first chickens. She tilled that soil by her own hand. Grew peas up the back fence, right to the top. Watered from the rain tank."

Cole's hand stilled, glass in midair as he regarded his father.

"Jason Chan tends it now," Olivia cut in, trying to break the tension.

Kim cleared the starter plates and brought in the main course. Zack came from the bar and set two more bottles of wine on the table, one white, one red. Music was good. Conversation at other tables grew louder, and there was more laughter. The wind rattled insistently at the shutters and keened plaintively down the flue.

Olivia glanced up, saw that Tori's gaze was fixed on her. Their eyes met for a moment.

"You doing okay there, Tori?" Olivia said. "Did you like the trout?"

"Yeah," she said, glancing at her father before she returned her attention to pushing food around her plate. Olivia met Cole's gaze. Something surged between them. Unspoken.

She swallowed.

"Gage," Cole said suddenly, reaching for the wine bottle and topping up the man's glass, "Olivia mentioned that you recently retired."

Gage braced slightly. "Yes."

"What did you do?" he said, offering Olivia more wine. She shook her head, casting him a hot, questioning glare.

"Consulting," said Gage.

Tori's knife clattered to the floor. Everyone jumped. She stared up at her father, mouth agape.

"Pick it up, Tori," Gage said curtly.

"No, no, it's okay," Olivia said quickly. "Leave it, please. Kim?" She called Kim over from the bar. "Could you bring us another knife?"

Kim bustled off into the kitchen.

"Consulting?" Cole cut into his food, delivered a forkful of venison to his mouth. Olivia scowled at him. He ignored her.

"Security systems."

Tori shoved her chair back abruptly and came sharply to her feet.

"What are you doing?" her father said.

"I'm going back to the cabin to sleep. I'm tired." She started for the hallway.

"Tori," he growled. "Get back here. Mind your manners."

"Why! Why should *I* pretend? Why should *you*? I don't want to be here."

Olivia surged to her feet. "Tori, come here. Why don't you come sit by the fire. Kim can bring your dessert there."

Her gaze shot daggers at Olivia. "And why should I listen to *you*? You're not my mother. How did you get that ugly scar around your neck anyways? The one you try to hide?"

Everyone around the table fell dead silent. The fire crackled, popped. Even the chatter at the other table fell quiet. Wind battered the house.

Cole got to his feet, about to interrupt, when Olivia said quietly, "It was a crab-fishing accident. I worked a season up at Dutch Harbor. I got a cable from one of the crab traps around me when they were about to drop it overboard." She forced a smile. "I was lucky to live."

Tori stared, something warring through her features, as if she wanted to think Olivia was cool but she needed to honor her mother. Mouth flattening, hands tight at her sides, she turned and marched over the wood floor into the hall. She grabbed her jacket and yanked open the big door, slipping out into the night. The door banged shut behind her.

Gage hesitated, then got up, slapped his napkin on the table. "I apologize. She's having a rough time after losing her mother."

Olivia said, "If there's anything we can do—"

"It's fine."

"I'm sure you're *both* having a rough time," Cole said.

Gage met Cole's eyes, hostility flashing through his own. Choosing silence, he strode for the door, his boots loud on the wood.

"What in the hell did you have to go and do *that* for?" Olivia snapped.

"You know why. His lavishing attention on you is hurting his daughter. It's as obvious as day."

"And *you're* the ranch shrink now? The arbiter on how one should experience grief?" She stormed off and slapped through the kitchen door with both hands.

Plates of blueberry crumble were lined in rows on the kitchen counter, ready to serve, dark purple berry juice bleeding into ice cream as white as snow. It was as if Olivia had smacked straight into a wall. Berries. Blood. Thanksgiving. Storm coming.

He leaned closer, and my mouth turned dry. And he told me about the wild blueberries. Down by the bend in the river.

I took the lure.

I went in search of the berries.

I never came home.

She tried to swallow, to catalogue her surroundings in order to stay present.

Nella was busily unpacking the dishwasher. It was warm in the kitchen. Jason had a glass of wine on the windowsill. Kim came in behind Olivia, snagged four dessert plates, balancing them on her arms as she backed open the door.

Music played softly on the radio.

She tore her eyes from the "bloodied" ice cream, cleared her throat. "Jason, you outdid yourself tonight."

"Wait until the big meal tomorrow," he replied with a grin.

She glanced at the window. There was a green glow in the dark sky, which meant it was still clear. "If that storm does hit tomorrow, we might have to cancel."

"We'll play it by ear." He reached for his glass of wine, took a sip. "Whatever I prepare can always go into the freezer if we call it off. You could be having turkey pot pie well into the winter."

"Can I help clear up?"

"All under control."

"You guys must be getting excited," she said to Nella. "You all packed?" Her mother was taking her away for a week to Mexico. And Jason would be leaving after the weekend for his summer job cooking for a tour group in New Zealand. It was doubtful he'd return. Olivia wondered if there'd even be a ranch next year this time.

"Just about," Nella said. "Still need to buy sunscreen."

"We'll miss Broken Bar." Jason's eyes held hers, reading her mind. There was a shift in the warm kitchen atmosphere.

"I know," she said quietly. "Me too. Well, I'll call it a night then, once the last guests have left." She paused on her way out. "Oh, Nella, thank you for the berry basket."

"What basket?"

"You know . . . the one left outside my door."

"I didn't leave any berries." She grinned. "Now I wish I had. We picked tons for the dessert and had plenty to spare. They were growing all over the forest. Ripe in perfect time for Thanksgiving blueberry crumble."

"Oh. Okay . . . thanks." Olivia backed up a few steps, turned, and woodenly pushed through the door.

There had to be a simple explanation, but her mind was suddenly messing with her again. Cole's words curled through her mind.

Be careful, Liv . . . I don't believe in coincidences . . .

The warning suddenly felt sinister. She wanted to ask him what he meant. He never did get a chance to explain.

———

Shadows darkened the porch. Eugene reached for the door handle, surprise washing through him as he found it unlocked. His quarry was still too bold. Disquiet trickled through him—had she not received his lure? The newspaper? Why was she not more fearful? She would be after tonight.

Trees bent and groaned in the mounting wind as he stepped inside, eyes adjusting to the dark interior. Concern sliced afresh through him as he thought of her with the kid and father in the boat. Things were not quite what they seemed there. The kid brought unsettling thoughts about his mother. And while he didn't personally recognize the father as a cop from Watt Lake, it gave him pause for thought.

Who was the game and who the hunter?

Urgency prickled through his blood.

He found her bedroom, entered with his mouth slightly open as he breathed in her scent. Tasting her. Refamiliarizing himself. He moved to her bed. Wind rattled branches outside. He froze, listening for the approach of footfalls. None came.

He reached for her bed cover.

———

Kim placed a plate of blueberry crumble in front of Cole and one in front of his dad.

"What's gotten up your ass?" Myron grunted at Cole as Kim left.

"I don't trust Burton." Cole picked up his spoon, poked at the ice cream.

"It's not like he's going to abscond with the silverware."

"Something's off." He glanced up. "About the way he is with Olivia."

He had his father's attention now—his bushy brows hunkered in a low frown over his eyes.

"Off, like how?"

"Burton was the one who left that newspaper in the office with her name on it, and the lure inside that freaked her. It's a big-ass steelhead lure. Got nothing to do with local trout."

"So?" But a glimmer of interest peered through the inebriated haze.

"The coincidences are weird, that's all. Burton arrives on Broken Bar right as the news breaks about a woman found hanging by her neck from a tree. This freaks Olivia, who also has scars around her neck. Then he leaves that newspaper with her name right over the story." He couldn't say more, not without revealing Olivia's past as the Watt Lake Killer's last victim. That was hers to tell.

"Doesn't sound terribly nefarious to me."

"You saw how his kid reacted when he said he worked in security. She dropped both her jaw and her knife. Then she spoke about pretending. I think he's lying."

"Probably means nothing," Myron muttered into his beard. "Just coincidence."

"That's the thing," Cole said. "I don't believe in coincidences."

"So what do *you* think he wants? What are your hyperaware journalistic observation skills and conspiracy theories telling you?"

Cole raised a brow. "I don't know," he said quietly.

His father swirled his drink with his gnarled hand, spilling a few drops like blood onto the white linen. "You found something out about her past, didn't you," he said, words a little more slurred. "Something you're not telling me."

Cole didn't reply. He reached for his own glass, took a sip.

His father held his eyes a long time. "Something's changed— what is it? You going to tell me or not?"

"I'm not."

His father took a deep swig, and drew in an even deeper breath.

"It *has* to come from her," Cole said. "It's not mine to tell."

"But you've got her back, right? You're going to see her straight. You're going to see that she's okay running this ranch on her own."

Emotion—something close to affection—sideswiped Cole as he looked into his father's rheumy eyes and saw a raw earnestness in the old man's craggy features. Guilt snaked through it all as he thought about Forbes, Jane, the document he'd signed. His mind turned to the big fight he and his father had had thirteen years ago, when Myron had yet again thrown at Cole the fact he'd killed his mother and brother and destroyed this family and the ranch because of it.

It suddenly all seemed distant. Trivial. He should have been man enough to realize that his father had become mentally trapped inside his own grief. That he'd been incapable of forgiving Cole his sins, incapable of trying to move his family forward. In retrospect, Cole could have approached it all differently.

And right on the spot he made a new goal. Downed phone lines be damned, he was going to drive into town tomorrow morning, find Clayton Forbes in person, and draw his battle line in the sand. He was going to fight for what was left of this farm and family.

"The ranch will be safe," he said quietly. "I'll do my best by her."

His father stared at him long and hard. He reached abruptly for his wheels, spun his chair around, and wheeled off toward the hall. "Going to bed," he called over his shoulder.

Cole surged to his feet. "Here, let me take you up."

"Over my dead body. Zack!" the old man barked, "Zack—get me the hell out of here."

Cole stared as Zack wheeled his father out into the hallway and toward the elevator, a mix of hurt, compassion, love, an unfamiliar cocktail of sensations ebbing and pulling like a tide inside him.

"What was that about?"

He spun around. Olivia. She'd caught him unguarded again. He pulled his features back in line.

"He's just being a jerk."

"You should go easy on him. It's the medication."

"You need to stop making apologies for him."

Eyes like flint met his.

"Pour me a drink?" she said. "I could use one, and I need to ask you something."

———

Tori marched faster into the darkness and wind, outdistancing her dad, her heart banging in her chest. Her skin was hot. She wanted her mother.

A sharp cracking of twigs sounded in the brush next to her. Something big moved. Scared, she froze on the spot. Ghostly aurora played over the sky. Wind swished leaves. Then her dad came running over the lawn.

The noise sounded again, like a large animal crashing away through the dry brush and leaves. Bear, or deer.

Her father placed a hand on her shoulder. "Who's there?" he demanded, peering into the shadows as his other hand went for his holster.

Wind gusted. Leaves curled and swirled. Nothing more moved in the bush.

"Come," he whispered, his gaze still probing the dark shadows in the scrub.

"Why?" she said as they moved toward the cabin. "Why did you lie? You said you were in security. You lied about being a cop."

They reached the porch, and he crouched down, took her shoulders in his hands, his attention still flicking into the darkness behind her, watching for whatever had made the noise.

"Sometimes it's just easier *not* to say you're a cop. When you tell people you're in law enforcement, everything changes. I didn't want to talk about my job. I didn't want to talk about your mom. About

. . . things that hurt." He inhaled a deep, shuddering, shaky breath. His eyes glimmered with wetness in the dark. "Sometimes it's easier not to have to tell strangers over and over again. Just to be private."

She stared at him, her own eyes burning. Lip quivering. "Why are you so nice to her? To Olivia. What about Mom?"

Water slapped against the dock below the gazebo.

"Oh, Tori . . . it's nothing like that. Not at all." He smoothed hair back from her brow. "Someday you'll understand. Someday soon. I promise."

"You didn't tell me why I might have to go and live with Aunt Lou if they can operate and fix you."

"I know. And I was going to. I never wanted to hold anything back from you or make you worried. I thought it would be good to get away for Thanksgiving before explaining it all. Because I first wanted some time to put things right between us. And about Aunt Lou . . ." He hesitated. "After the operation there could be a couple of months of recovery getting my brain and motor functions back to full speed. There could be physiotherapy . . . There are variable outcomes for this kind of surgery. So, during that recuperation period, it would make sense for you to go east and stay with Lou and the family, go to school there for a while."

"I don't want to."

"Do you really want to go back to your old school in Vancouver? I'm not so sure it will be easy after that fire incident. Or the fight with Julia Borsos. You certain you want that?"

She glanced at her boots. "Maybe not."

He cleared his throat. "And then, when I'm back to full speed again, I can come out east, and stay there too. Lou and Ben have that big, big house on the lake. A cabin where you and I could live. You could finish school out there."

"You'd move, too?"

He smiled, his teeth glinting in the dark. "Yes. There's little I wouldn't do for you, Tori. One day you'll see that."

A fresh start. Like the damselflies—a second chance. It held a faint and distant promise. She really didn't want to return to her old school. Or the old house, even. It hurt.

He put his arm around her shoulders. Warm. Comforting. Her safe, invincible dad again. "Look. Look up there." He pointed.

The stars in the dark vault of sky were endless. Soft green and blue light with tinges of peach at the edges waved across it in silent curtains. The curtains of gods.

"I think she's watching us from up there."

Tears leaked silently down her face. And in that instant she was certain that from up there, everything must look like it had a plan. A reason. A pattern. She just couldn't see it from down here.

———

Olivia rubbed her knee—a nervous tic—as she sat by the fire waiting for Cole to bring her drink.

He set a bottle of scotch and two glasses with ice on the low table in front of the fire, poured two drinks and handed her one.

She took the glass, and their fingers brushed. Heat crackled up her arm, and she felt a clench of desire that was at odds with her nerves. This man did things to her.

"I'm pleased to see that you're still talking to me." He seated himself on the sofa beside her. Close. He smiled but his eyes were tired. He looked rough again, the firelight casting hard planes over his face. He seemed edgy, a little drunk perhaps. Yet there was something solid and safe about him.

"I need to wait for the last guests to leave," she said. "And I have some questions."

He watched the fire, cradling his glass in his big hands. "Shoot."

She'd been going to press him over his concerns about Gage Burton, but she also didn't want to tell him why that newspaper and fishing lure were such a trigger.

"What happened with Myron?" she said instead, chickening out. "You goad him again?"

A wry smile curved his gorgeous lips, and he was silent for a while, as if weighing something. He sucked back his whole drink, reached forward, and poured another.

"I told him that I had concerns about Burton and his interest in you."

She felt the blood drain from her cheeks. Her pulse quickened. *"That's* what upset him?"

He snorted. "He wasn't upset. He just asked if he could count on me to have your back."

She sipped her drink. "And you said what?"

He glanced at her. A beat of silence. "I said yes."

Olivia swallowed at the intensity in his eyes. It was as if he were devouring her, owning her. She fought an urge to shift slightly back in her seat.

"Do you like him—Burton?"

"I think he's . . . kind. I believe he's trying to do his best by Tori, even if he's making mistakes. But I feel he's genuine."

I don't feel about him like I feel about you.

"Yet you seem worried now," he prompted. "You're asking questions now."

She glanced away. Tori's words in the boat came to mind.

Why did you go with two guns . . . what's that in your boot now . . .

Olivia owned a pistol herself. But it wasn't legal. Handguns were restricted firearms in this part of the world. They required a special "authorization to carry."

"Has anything . . . odd happened, Liv? Beyond the episode with the newspaper and lure that rattled you so badly?"

Her heart beat faster. She felt trapped. *Shit.* She wanted to talk about this as much as she didn't. She thought about getting up to go, but he placed his solid hand over her knee, halting her.

"Look, we both know something bad happened in your past. And I don't want to press you on that, unless you want to tell me. I just got a vibe about Burton and wondered if there was some link between him and your past."

Moth wings of panic fluttered through her stomach. Her thoughts turned to the berries, the scarf, the tracks, the sense of being watched, followed. The coincidence of this freakish Birkenhead murder with so-called echoes of the Watt Lake Killings. If she turned it all one way, she could see them as coincidences. Turn them another and she was no longer so sure. Pressure mounted in her to tell him. But she couldn't.

No matter how tempting the need for comfort, or the allure of having someone truly at her back, she couldn't become Sarah Baker again.

Olivia took a deep sip of her drink, holding her glass tight so he wouldn't detect the tremble in her hands.

"So, just be careful about him, okay?"

Her gaze flicked back to him. Nerves deepened at the gravitas she saw in his eyes.

"Also, know that I'm here if you need me."

She swallowed. Her skin grew hot. She felt she was at a crossroads, on the razor's edge of telling Cole everything, of wanting to lean into him, be with him in more ways than one, but she was unable.

Laughter from the table near the bar startled them both. Her gaze shot across the room. The last of the guests were getting up to leave.

They waved and called out their good-byes. The room fell silent as the door closed behind them, just the roar of the fire and the battering of the wind outside.

"There's something else I want you to know." He reached out and took her hand in his. Olivia's muscles snapped wire tight. Her body warred between the urge to pull away and an impulse to turn her palm faceup under his, to lace her fingers through his. Her mouth turned dry. A buzz began in her head.

"I agree with what my father did. I want you to have the ranch in trust. I want you to run it."

"Cole, I told you, I don't want—"

His thumb moved under the hem of her sweater sleeve, inching gently along the ridge of her scars. Their eyes met. She tensed, almost pulled away but didn't, her world narrowing. She was vaguely conscious of Kim and Zack heading into the kitchen with the last of the dishes.

"It's the right thing," he whispered.

"Why?" Her voice came out thick.

"Because I'm thinking of staying, helping. You said it yourself, ranching is hard work, and getting the livestock side of things up and running again is going to require an injection of capital. I could handle that end of the business, if you concentrated on the year-round tourism-destination side of things."

She stared at him in silence for several beats. "It's the drink talking. You really *are* like your father."

His eyes darkened, and his energy changed. She could feel a dark electricity crackling off him in silent waves. He inhaled, deep, as if drinking her in, absorbing, consuming, trying to decide something. He glanced away, still holding her hand, his calloused thumb softly stroking against her palm. She could barely breathe. And she did it, she turned her palm up against his, lacing her fingers through his. He tightened his hand and his gaze snapped to hers. In his eyes she could read desire, fierce need.

She felt it in her own.

Slowly, he ran his hand up the outside of her arm, up to her neck. He cupped the back of her neck, fingers threading into thick hair. He drew her closer as he leaned toward her. He brushed his warm lips over her mouth.

A bolt of fire cracked through her.

She pulled away abruptly. Got up, heart stampeding. She stared down into his gray eyes. He stared back. Unspoken things surged between them. Things she did not want to broach. Too close, too intimate—not on just a physical level. She could not go there. Wherever he was going.

"Olivia?" His voice was thick, dusky.

"We can lock up the dining room now. The guests have all gone," she said abruptly. "Unless you want to stay and have another drink, then please close up behind you." She clicked her fingers, and Ace lifted his sleepy head and reluctantly rose from his slumber in front of the fire.

"I'll walk you." He got up, came after her.

"No. I'm fine." She was shaking like a leaf.

He touched her arm. She snapped tight. "You are fine, Liv. More than fine, but I'm not letting you walk back alone."

"Cole—" Her voice caught. Her eyes burned. Need throbbed painfully through her body, her nipples tight and screaming for touch, her groin hot and throbbing. It was overwhelming. She . . . she didn't know how to handle this.

"It's okay," he said, raising his palms. "No pressure. No obligations. Just a walk back through the dark woods." He smiled. "I understand."

"I've managed on my own for years, you know."

"But you don't have to."

CHAPTER 17

They reached her porch.

His boots sounded heavily against wood as he came up the stairs.

"There you go." Cole smiled in the darkness and stuck his hands deep into his pockets. But he didn't leave. He appeared to be waiting to be invited in. In more ways than one.

Tense, Olivia placed her hand on the knob, opened the door.

He cocked his head. "You don't lock it?"

"I have nothing to fear here." But her voice sounded bolder than she felt. Ace skirted into the cabin through the crack she'd opened in the door.

Cole went to the porch railing, placed his hands on the banister. He looked out over the lake and into wilderness and the blackness of the mountains beyond. Ectoplasmic curtains of light billowed across the sky, a dance of the cosmos.

"They're like magic," he said quietly. "I always imagine that they should make a sound, something crackling or electrical, or whispering, but they're so silent."

The wind wasn't silent, though. It chased through dry branches, chinked the halyard against the flagpole down on the shore, slapped waves against the dock that creaked and groaned with the heave of water dotted with ghostly whitecaps.

Olivia couldn't help it. She gravitated to his side, her shoulder almost touching his arm as she stood beside him. She zipped her jacket up higher and turned the collar up against the increasing chill. Side by side in silence they watched the interplay of light against sky and water. A black blot of weather grew on the south horizon, and it ate steadily toward them.

He moved ever so slightly closer, so that the sides of their arms touched. And he allowed his little finger to connect with the edge of her hand on the banister. Her heart stuttered.

"I missed this," he said.

She swallowed. God, she missed this, too. Touch. Physical contact with another human being. She'd fought it off so long— this need to be held, loved, just accepted for who she was. And now his touch opened a great, yawning chasm deep inside her that just seemed to grow, and ache.

"You must have seen aurora elsewhere," she said, voice thick.

"It's more than lights," he whispered.

Heat washed softly through her belly. Tentatively, he touched her pinkie with his little finger, then hooked it through hers. Breath snared in Olivia's throat.

She held herself dead still despite the desire quivering down through her. Her vision seemed to narrow, spiraling in to just this moment, to them. Alone. Touching. Under this haunting light display. It felt as though every molecule in her body was straining toward him, drawn by an invisible but powerful magnetic north as the aurora crackled in an electrical storm around them.

She closed her eyes for a moment, struggling to marshal logic, but her thoughts darted into the trickier carnal shadows of her mind.

"It's also about missing a sense of home, you know, real home. Roots. The place you grew up in. Those lights symbolize this place for me. Not everyone has a place like that. Sometimes you don't realize that you were missing it until you return." He fell into contemplation for several beats, then said, "To think this same view over that water, looking out toward that Marble range, has been burned into the eyes of my lineage for over a hundred years—you wonder if something like that can leave a DNA fingerprint of sorts. Something that creates a physical longing in one for a place in order to feel whole." He paused a long while.

"I wish I'd brought Ty and Holly here. To meet my dad. I've made mistakes. Big ones that can't be fixed."

She inhaled deeply, almost afraid of speaking, because while he was being so candid with her, she didn't want to open personal doors of her own.

"But you can start over," she said, cautiously. "You can grow out of those mistakes."

He turned suddenly to her. "As in a second chance?"

She moistened her lips, held his gaze in the eerie light.

"Tell me about your family, Olivia."

"I don't get on with my family."

He regarded her for a beat, then a smile curved his lips. "So, you just throw stones from a glass house, then? By trying to tell me how to get on with mine?"

"Touché," she said quietly. "You're right. I'm in no position to tell you how to act with your father. But in the same way Burton got up your nose with how he was treating his daughter, you and your father got up mine. You were both being idiot bulls, each refusing to back down first. And when you know how one 'sorry' could have changed everything in your own life, it makes you want to interfere in the lives of others where there is still opportunity to make things right. You ache to tell people they can still salvage what family they have left."

"This happened with your father, your family?"

She glanced up at the magical sky. "I really don't want to talk about them."

She was allowing him to skirt too close.

How long before he—before they all—figured it out? Adele had now also seen her neck scar. Adele, the town gossip. Adele, whose son worked with Forbes, who in turn was connected to everyone. Nella had seen, too. Unless this Watt Lake Killer news died down, someone was going to figure out how she was connected. It wasn't that hard if one dug into the Watt Lake news archives. Her identity had been safe until now because no one ever had reason to probe her past from that angle. Until this bizarre fresh murder. Until she'd gone and reacted like an idiot. Until Cole had exposed her terrible scar.

"Look, I called you in Florida for the same reason you interfered with Gage and Tori. And now that it's done, now that you're here and can take care of your dad, it's time for me to think about new plans."

"Such as?"

"Moving on, finding a new place to stay."

"I told you—I want you to stay. This is your place."

Her gaze flared to his. "Why? What *has* changed your mind about trying to make this place work? You arrived here gung ho to sell."

He laughed. The sound was deep and guttural, and it tightened something in her belly.

"Like you have so sweetly pointed out, Olivia, I *am* like my father. Stubborn. And I've gotten into my mule head that I really don't want Forbes to get his claws into this place, to carve it up into ritzy estate lots. I mean, look out there, look at that view . . ." He fell silent. Then he exhaled deeply. "Truth? This is something that sneaked up on me."

"So, you really are serious, about trying to build the ranch business up again?"

"I'd like to angle for that second chance. I'd like to dig my fingers into the soil, to feel grounded, to feel my roots." His voice hitched on a dark thread of emotion. He gathered himself. "I got lost over the years, Liv. I want to see what happens if I stop running now. If I try to settle a bit. I want to see if I recognize myself when I wake up morning after morning in the same place, sober."

"You finally want to stop cheating death?"

He was silent for a long moment.

"I'm at a crossroads. I'm in no rush. No one to go back for. I have funds." He paused. "Maybe this is about my father. About regret. And forgiveness. Maybe it's about a knee-jerk dislike for Forbes." He looked down at her. "Maybe it's about you."

She swallowed, hearing the subtext of his words. And it confused and secretly thrilled her a little. It also terrified her.

She cleared her throat. "What about your sister?"

"If you stay under the terms of my father's amended will, there should be no problem. If you leave, Jane would get her share. But I'm hoping you won't, and that you'll have me here, to help." He smiled. "See? I'd be here by your grace."

He turned to face her fully and ran his hand slowly up the length of her arm. Dry leaves whispered. Water slapped harder at the dock.

She wanted to resist, to tell him to leave her the hell alone, but couldn't. Because as much as she didn't want this, she did. And the two sides of her were at full-out war.

He cupped the side of her face, his other hand going behind the small of her back, drawing her slowly, inexorably closer. He was strong, warm, and his eyes were dark pools. But she also felt the question in his touch—he was asking if this was what she wanted. Not pushing, yet making clear his design.

The aurora pulsed, soft hues shimmering over the rough planes of his face, and his silent question hung, visceral, in the air between them, soft and crackling with promise and danger. For a moment Olivia dared dream forgotten dreams. All she had to do was yield, give herself over to it. Take what she wanted from this man.

But in spite of her desire, she felt fear coiling low and serpent-like into the heat of her belly.

He slid his hand around the back of her neck and lowered his head, angling his face, and tentatively feathered her lips with his.

Heat exploded through her brain, zinging down latent neural pathways, sparking forgotten muscle memories of desire into life. And it was delicious, consuming, and also harrowing because the serpent stirred comfortably and dangerously into the heat, bringing to the surface a dark recall—of the times Ethan had tried to make love to her once she'd healed, many, many months after, and long after the baby had gone.

But while she might have healed physically, her mind had remained broken. Her heart had ached with the loss of the child Ethan didn't want. A child he'd reviled.

And so had Ethan's desire been broken.

His perfunctory sexual advances ripped open raw memories of her assaults. She'd recoil from his touch no matter how she tried not to. And he from her. Because even on the occasion she had managed to quiet the flashbacks, she'd glimpsed disgust in her husband's eyes when he looked upon her naked body. And fear of what one human could do to another. Of what one man had done to his wife. And of what that had done to him, and their marriage.

She could see, also, in his eyes, the doubt, the questions— would this have happened to them if she hadn't encouraged a killer?

The end of their marriage had begun the day Sebastian George had walked into their store and chosen her as his next victim.

Neither could look into the other's eyes again without Sebastian George being present. Neither could live with Sebastian George present. So they parted.

Olivia had not been with a man since.

Cole drew her more firmly against his body, his mouth pressing down harder. Blinding desire swelled through her, obliterating all thought, all memories as she opened her mouth under his. His tongue slipped into her mouth, tasting, devouring her, and she leaned up into his kiss, into his solid body, her tongue tangling furiously with his as her own hunger consumed her.

His stubble was rough against her face. It made her more fierce, hungrier. She felt the hard length of his erection press against her pelvis as he backed her toward her cabin.

He backed her in through the slightly ajar door, and it crashed open wide. He kicked it closed with his boot as his tongue tangled and slicked and mated with hers.

It was warm inside the room, embers in the stove pulsing a soft orange, casting a coppery glow through the interior. He edged her toward the sofa. Her knees buckled as they connected with the furniture, and he was lowering her down, his weight on top of her.

—

Through the branches Eugene watched as they entered the cabin, locked in embrace. His pulse pounded. His cock was hard. Painfully hard. His fists clenched, and he gritted his teeth. A complication. That was all. This didn't have to change a thing. He would correct her later for being a traitor. Females were fickle in heat. A good hunter should expect the unexpected with the female species.

He'd just kill the male first.

—

Tori waited until the strip of yellow light under her door went out and she knew that her father had gone to bed. She reached under the mattress, found her e-reader. The green glow wavering through cracks in the blinds was spooky. Wind ticked a branch against the tin roof, and cones bombed down from the trees.

She turned on the e-reader. Snuggled deeper into her duvet, her mother's words coming to life.

> The sound of the returning geese reached her. On hands and bare
> knees she scrabbled over the floor to the crack in the chinking. She

strained against the rope to glimpse a slice of sky. Then she saw him. In the clearing on old snow, his legs planted wide and strong.

All around him the forest dripped, cracked, popped. Sounds of thaw. His breath showed in white puffs. He glanced toward her shed.

She scuttled back into her corner, careful not to clink the shackles or to rub the rope further into her neck. Curling into a ball on the skins, she wrapped around her baby like a protective carapace, pretending she was asleep,

The door creaked open. She felt the light cut in.

"It's time," he said.

Her pulse kicked. She turned her head slowly and blinked into the shaft of white light that sliced into her hut.

"Get up."

"Time for what?" Her voice, thick with disuse, came out like a croak. The sound scared her. Who was she, really? What had she become?

He didn't answer.

He crouched down in the center of the floor, watching her. His scent filled her nostrils. Her mind began to close in on itself, drifting out and above the cabin. But he didn't undress. He placed a pair of boots in the middle of the shack. She blinked. Her boots. The boots she'd been wearing the afternoon he took her.

He came closer, in a crouch. Like an animal. She held her breath as he moved the burlap off her bare legs. He touched her foot. She braced. Jaw clenched. But he unlocked the shackles. The chain clinked on the hard floor. He came even closer, his breathing heavy as he brought out a knife. Her heart raced. Sweat beaded. The blade glinted in a sliver of light that sliced through a hole in the rafters. This was it. This was what he meant by "It's time." She coiled her body tight, ready to kick, ready to fight for her life, for her baby's life. He raised the knife . . . and sawed through the rope that bound her to the wall. The cut end of her noose dropped to the ground. She stared. Started to shake.

He left. The shed door banged shut.

Silence. Just noise from outside. Dripping. The burble of a small creek somewhere that had grown louder with the thaw.

She waited for the familiar grating sound of the bolt being slid home on the outside of the door.

It didn't come.

Tension, confusion whispered through her.

He hadn't locked it?

Something had changed.

It's time.

She waited. No idea how long. Until she could no longer hear him outside. Would he return? Should she run? Where to? Was he waiting outside for her to try? She got onto her knees, crawled over to her boots, touched them, bracing for his entry.

He didn't come.

Panting, she struggled with stiff fingers to get her swollen, cracked feet into the cold leather boots. She fumbled, shaking, sweating to tie the laces.

Carefully, she tried to stand. Pain seared. She braced her hand against the shed wall, wobbly as hell. She peered through the slats. Trees. Endless trees. Up high, glimpses of blue sky.

Freedom?

A kind of mad ferocity seeped into her terror.

Raw adrenaline pounding in her blood, she hobbled quickly over to her corner, gathered up a burlap sack, wrapped it around her naked, swollen waist, securing it with parts of the rope she found on the ground. She was thinking of Ethan. Home. Getting home. The child inside her. Hope. She began to shake. Tears streamed down her face.

Hope could be a thing of extraordinary power. It fueled her then.

She draped a bearskin around her bare shoulders and stood there for a long while. Unsure.

Then, carefully, she edged open the door and blinked like a mole into daylight.

A rifle was propped against the shed wall, just by the door. Within her reach.

Where was he?

What did he want?

What game was this?

———

Cole kissed her deeply as he shucked himself out of his jacket, letting it fall to the floor as he unzipped hers.

Dizzying kaleidoscopic swirls of red and black obliterated Olivia's thoughts as heat rushed up through her chest. She ran her hands along his waist, across his abs, feeling the iron-like solidity of his muscles. She drank in his scent, his taste, filling herself, drowning herself in a place of deep vestigial pleasure.

He lifted the hem of her sweater and slid his hand onto her belly. His palm was hot, his skin rough. He moved his hand up higher and unclasped the front opening of her bra. Her breasts swelled free. A moan rose from deep in his chest as he cupped her breast, his thumb finding her nipple tight. Then his fingers neared the crater of a scar—the bite mark Sebastian George had left in her.

A shaft of ice speared to her core.

She froze.

It was the mark forensics techs had matched to Sebastian's teeth. Just one of many traces he'd left on her body that had convicted him. A suffocating blackness filled her lungs. Olivia clamped her hand over Cole's, halting him, as memories raced through her mind.

She couldn't breathe. Couldn't see. Claustrophobia tightened. Her heart started to palpitate.

She held tightly onto his wrist, fighting against the images, against the past, sweating, starting to shake. No.

No!

She would *not* let Sebastian back in. She would fuck the living daylights out of the past. She would *own* this, take it all back. Be whole, a woman. Have this man. Show herself she was free, because if she couldn't do this now, she never would. She'd be forever a half person.

And Olivia's dearest dream, her deepest hope, was to be whole again. She'd fought so hard to get this far, but she hadn't yet gone all the way. On some level she knew that only then would she be truly free.

"Liv?" he whispered, breath warm against her ear.

She released his wrist and began to squirm out from under him, wildly undoing the zipper of her jeans, wriggling out of them and her panties. Her jeans bunched around her boots. She kicked one leg of her pants free. With a feral kind of madness, with shaking hands, she pushed Cole down onto his back on the sofa and straddled him. Panting, half blind, she grappled with the fly of his jeans. Sweat was beginning to drench her body. Her breathing turned ragged. *Don't think, don't think, don't let him back in . . .*

She yanked his jeans partially down his hips. His erection swelled free in her hands. Big, hard. Hot. Damp at the rounded tip. She couldn't breathe. His hands clamped over her wrists.

"Olivia," he whispered darkly, voice thick, raw. There was question in his features, concern in his eyes. "What're you doing?"

Tears began to stream down her face. She fought against his grip as she maneuvered her hips, opening her thighs wide above him as she sought the smooth, hot tip of his erection. It met her skin. Anticipation, anger, fear—it all smashed through her as she closed her eyes tightly and angled down onto his cock, opening her legs wider as she sank inch by inch onto the delicious length of hard, hot shaft. Her breath caught at the shock of the sensation of him inside her. But she pushed against pain until he was in to the hilt, right up against her inner core. And she felt a sweet, quivering explosion of wetness as she adjusted to the size of him. It was an exquisite, titillating kind of hurt that just drove her higher, wilder.

Breathless, she scrabbled to undo the buttons of his soft flannel shirt as she rocked her pelvis against his hips, sliding up and down on him, wetter, slicker, hotter. Faster. Buttons popped off, pinged to the wood floor, some rolling under the sofa. She slid her hands over his chest, drinking in the roughness of the hair on his pecs, the way it ran in a tight whorl to his groin where it flared out in an even rougher, springy mass. The rub of it on the sensitive skin of her inner thighs fueled the fire inside her, and the softness of his balls was sweet against her butt.

In the next instant she was blinded as her vaginal muscles tightened like a vise around his cock, screaming for release. She banged harder, faster, her hands going to his shoulders, her nails digging into his skin. Somewhere in the distance of her mind she felt his large hands on her bare hips, trying to control her, slow her down. Stop her. But she fought him. She dominated and owned him. She obliterated the past with each pelvic thrust until she froze. Her spine arced.

A wild roar began in her ears.

She threw her head back, and her muscles released suddenly in an explosive spasm that took hold of her entire body, forcing her to cry out loud and gasp until she was spent.

She collapsed onto Cole's bare chest, tears wetting her face, her heart racing, her skin slick with sweat. She was shaking.

He wrapped his arms around her. Held.

Then, slowly, the edges of consciousness began to crawl back in. Olivia stilled.

His cock was still inside her. Still hard. But he wasn't moving.

Reality seeped in fully, along with a cold thread of anxiety. She lifted her head, looked into his eyes. He took her face between his hands and studied her in the eerie undulating light from the window. The shadows of trees moved across his features.

But still he made no move for his own release.

She swallowed, becoming aware that he was fully dressed. And she was in her sweater and socks, her jeans half on.

And although she couldn't read the expression in his eyes in this light, she felt it. The concern. The questions. And she felt him going soft inside her.

Hot embarrassment washed through her.

Shame.

"Liv," he whispered.

Desperately she tried to move her hips, to vaginally massage and coax him back to desire.

"No, please. Wait. Let me take you to your bed. I want to be with you there. Properly. I want you naked, all of you, in my arms."

"Just . . ." She swallowed, trying to rock against him, tears coming. "Just come . . . please . . . like this . . ." Desperately, she tried to milk his dying erection, rotate her hips, a sob building in her chest. *Please, please.*

She felt his penis slip out of her.

"Please . . ." She clenched desperately with her muscles, trying to hold him in. But couldn't. Tears swelled into her eyes, ran down her face.

He held her hips firmly now. "Olivia. *Stop.*"

Her body trembled.

He didn't want her. He hadn't come. He'd softened inside her . . . she'd turned him off.

Like she'd turned Ethan off, disgusted her own husband, who couldn't get it up when he looked at her.

She scrambled off Cole, extracting her limbs from his, hopping on one socked foot as she stuffed her other foot into the leg of her jeans, emotional walls slamming up. Cold. Hard. Safe.

He sat, reached for her hands. "Liv, come here. Let's go into your room."

She couldn't.

She didn't have the courage that she'd thought she had a moment ago. She felt humiliated and unable to strip herself fully naked, expose herself and her scars to this man. She was unable to reveal to him that she was Sarah Baker.

She'd been mad, insane. Blinded by something irrational. How could she sacrifice eight goddamn years for a moment of stupid hot lust?

She took a step back, zipping up her pants, her hair a wild mess hanging in front of her eyes. "This was a mistake. Please, get out."

She was going to crack. She was shaking against her own foundations, against every ounce of control. The line between Sarah and Olivia, the past and present, was glass thin, with hairline cracks fissuring out in all directions, and she was going to shatter in a nanosecond. She would not let him witness that.

"Listen to me, Olivia, I know what—"

"Please, just get the hell out. Now!"

CHAPTER 18

"No," Cole said, eyes lasering hers. "This was *not* a mistake. You're beating yourself up here. Tell me what's going on."

"You made it pretty damn clear what's going on. You couldn't even fuck me. Now please, do me a favor, and don't humiliate me further. Just leave." She tossed his jacket at him. It landed in his lap.

"It's not like that."

"Oh, then what was it?"

Cole stood, zipped up his pants. "Don't pretend here. Do not try and turn this around on me." He reached for her hand, and she stepped back sharply, bumping against the table. Hot panic flared in her eyes.

Shit. This *was* a mistake. A major one.

"Listen to me. I want to make love to you, all of you, slowly, in your bed. I want to be with you the whole night, not go to combat with you." He pointed to the couch. "You didn't want *me* back there. You were screwing something else. I was just a sexual punching bag. That's not how I want you."

She swallowed, eyes gleaming. Feral. Afraid.

He raised both his hands. "It's okay. I'll go. I . . . I just don't want to leave you like this, that's all. I want—Whatever it is, you can tell me. I can help."

She said nothing, just glared at him, mouth in a tight line.

He cursed to himself, reached for his jacket. He went up to her and kissed her on her cheek. She held herself stiff as steel, hands braced against the table behind her.

Cole stepped out into the night, closed the door gently behind him. He pulled on his jacket against the bracing cold.

He paused on the deck as he heard the *snick* of a dead bolt sliding home.

I have nothing to fear out here . . .

And now she did.

She was afraid of him. Of what he represented.

But as Cole made his way down the stairs and along the dirt trail to his cabin, he realized it wasn't him. She was afraid of herself, and what she was feeling inside.

—

Tori turned the electronic page.

Secured with a string through the trigger guard of the rifle was a drawstring bag. Her gaze darted around the clearing, then warily she crouched down and grasped the gun. Inside the bag was a box containing several rounds of ammunition.

Confusion chased through her. She peered into the forest, took a tentative step. Nothing happened. Heart thudding, she moved in a crouch with the rifle into the center of the clearing, her senses bombarded with stimuli from not having been outside for an entire winter.

Somewhere behind her he racked a pump-action shotgun. The sound made a tha-thunk that echoed into the woods. She froze. He fired. A boom that scattered birds from trees. With a scream she raced for the woods. She scrambled through leafless budding willow brush that tore at her bare white legs.

She heard him crashing after her. She ran deeper, deeper, into the forest, breath going ragged in her lungs. When she could breathe no more, she crouched down in a ditch of rotten snow, sharp corn crystals slicing into her bare shins.

She waited, panting, mouth open, hair tangled in front of her eyes.

He was waiting, too. Just listening. Or had she lost him? What was his game?

Cautiously, in the gloam of the deep forest, she checked the rifle. Loaded. He'd left her armed with spares.

"There is no hunting like the hunting of armed men." He'd told her that once.

She got into a wobbly crouch. Then, slowly, quietly, trying not to allow her boots to punch too often through the deep, rotten snow crust, she aimed for ground where pine needles lay thick and soft. Where she'd make less sound, leave less trace.

It was twilight when he found her. She was cowering against the giant buttress roots of cedar.

He materialized silently in the shadows among branches, his eyes trained on her like a mountain lion. Slowly he raised the stock to his shoulder, fired to her right. She gasped, scrambling away on hands and knees, bushes tearing free her burlap sack, leaving her buttocks flashing naked at him as she burrowed into a tunnel of brush. She heard his footfalls approaching.

She was trapped.

"What do you want!" she screamed, tears streaking with dirt down her face, blood oozing from the cuts on her shins.

"Run!"

"Go to hell!"

"Run!" He fired a 12-gauge shotgun slug into the ground near her feet. Loam and stones exploded around the bullet, stinging into her skin. She screamed . . .

———

Olivia closed the bathroom door. Locked it. Undressed. She stared at her body in the long mirror. Ripped, bitten, cratered by Sebastian

George. Branded. Owned. She couldn't look at her naked self without reliving *him*.

Slowly, she reached up and touched the bite marks on her breasts, then she fingered the rope scar around her neck. Her gaze lowered, taking in her scarred legs, her frostbitten toes—two missing, another two amputated at the joint. Her attention went to the suicide scars on her wrists.

She felt the swell of shame and disgust. She hated to look at herself. How could she expect the love of anyone else? How could she hope to actually turn anyone on?

Her deepest need was to be free, normal, a real woman again, but she saw now that to be free would mean fully exposing herself, stripping naked in a way that would trap her again. Because it would mean exposing her past as Sarah Baker to Cole. It would mean exposing this body.

Cole was a ticking time bomb of questions. Already he'd seen enough to clue him in, if he looked hard. He was gallant and wonderful for not pushing her.

But she'd not had enough goddamn courage to reveal herself in the hopes that even after seeing her like this, he'd still find her attractive. It was madness to think he wouldn't ask the hard questions when he saw the full extent of her maiming.

What was it worth anyway? One moment of lust? How badly did she really need sexual affirmation? He was a rolling stone. Sure, he was at a crossroads right now, but once he got his bearings back, what then?

Was it worth the cost of facing the media again, her family, the town? The looks, the curiosity, the questions . . . reliving it all again? And again. Because she knew it would also bring the flashbacks. It would mean a return of the very things she'd tried to obliterate by attempting to kill herself.

Panic, claustrophobia choked her, and bile surged up her throat. She lunged for the toilet, her stomach heaved, and she retched. She braced herself, panting, sweating, until her stomach and chest stopped contracting.

Then she ripped back her shower curtain, turned the water on scalding hot.

Broken Bar had once been safe. Her sanctuary. Her dream of a future. But in the space of a few days ill winds had blown in with the winter frost and converged to change everything. That murder, the news. Myron and his will. Cole. She wished she'd never picked up that goddamn phone and called him.

But she had.

And now she had to accept that this chapter, this phase, this sanctuary, was over.

Because even if Cole left her alone, Adele had seen. Nella and Jason now knew about her scars and her flashbacks. There would be more news about the Birkenhead murder in the media, more references to the Watt Lake Killer. Some reporter, someone in Clinton would get curious and look up the old case, his last victim. And there she would be.

Ethan would find her. Her family . . . She couldn't do it. Could no longer stay here.

She climbed into the tub. Dry-eyed she sat on the tub floor, arms wrapped tightly around her knees, and let the water beat down on her head and back, scalding her flesh until it turned lobster pink and the gas ran out and the water began to run cold.

———

Tori's heart raced as she quickly turned the next electronic page.

Tiny snowflakes began to crystallize in the air and dust the ground.

It helped hide her tracks as she crept like a pregnant Neanderthal woman with animal skins and bare buttocks, weapon in her hand, a wild madness in her head. He'd allowed her to escape. That time. And now, as she crawled, she held her mouth open, and her nasal passages flared as she tested the breeze for his scent, listening for his sound.

She heard it.

The shrill chuk chuk chuk of a chipmunk warning someone away.

He was here.

Somewhere.

She stilled, turned around in a slow circle, heart hammering, mouth dry.

Then she saw it. Bear scat. Oily, green-black in color, the kind of stinking fecal plug released after a long winter of hibernation and not eating. Her gaze darted through the forest. She found what she was seeking—markings at the base of a massive hemlock, and more scat. Scrabbling on hands and knees, she ducked under the curtain of protective hemlock branches. She saw claw marks scratched down the trunk. The marking of territory.

And there it was—an opening into the decaying base of the big tree.

Tentatively she pushed her hand inside, felt around. A den. Warm. Padded and insulated with needles and brush and dead moss. No bear.

She squirmed inside, careful not to squeeze her baby bump. There was enough room for her to curl into a ball. She covered herself with the bits of bark, dry moss, and dead leaves that had been raked inside by the bear.

If the animal returned, then she would deal with it. Anything was better than dealing with him.

She curved her shoulders and spine around her baby inside her stomach. And finally, she stopped shivering.

Outside more snow began to fall. Heavy and muffling. Hiding her path into the den.

———

Cole entered his cabin. It was cold and dark. He considered starting the fire. Instead he lit a small gas lamp and poured himself a drink. He found a woolen hat in his duffel and pulled it low over his head. He took his drink and sat out on the porch in his down jacket. Looking out over the lake, he watched the fading aurora reflecting on the ruffled surface of the water.

The sky darkened in the south as the band of cloud boiled forward, blotting out stars.

He was an asshole to have even tried to kiss her.

He could see what was going on. She'd wanted him, all right, but she wasn't ready. She was full of shame and horrific memories. He sipped his drink, wondering if a woman who'd endured what she had could ever be ready. Maybe the kind of damage that had been wrought in her was something that would forever leave her crippled in certain ways—emotionally, mentally, physically. And what would that mean to someone who fell for her?

Shock rustled through him as he realized he *had* fallen for her. Wholly. He wanted to get to know her on so many more levels, and it wasn't just to do with this ranch.

It was also why he'd pulled back, why he wanted to take her gently to bed, to move more slowly. But now he'd blown it. And there might never be a way to retrace steps and start over.

He sipped, pondering a deeper question as the warmth of brandy blossomed through his chest.

What might it mean to him, to fall in love with a woman with whom he might never consummate a relationship?

He heard the wolves now, primal. The sound raised hairs on the back of his neck. Wind gusted harder, changing direction.

He glanced toward her cabin. Her lights were still on. He could glimpse them through the ghostly white-barked trees. And he snorted softly. Perhaps he'd finally, after all these years, found the *survivor* for whom he'd been searching—the person who'd survived against all odds, the one who could help him, on some subterranean level, understand why he'd survived, too, when he shouldn't have. Maybe if he could just be here for her, help her move steadily, comfortably forward, build something here with her on this ranch, he could atone in some way for having stolen the lives of his mother and brother all those years ago.

Being celibate might just be the cost of absolution.

He cursed softly, and took another sip. It was the drink talking. She was right. He was like his dad.

He'd clung to that twenty-three-year-old incident as bitterly as his father had. Or, it had clung to them. All of them. Even Jane.

———

Olivia yanked on a terry bathrobe and cinched the belt tight. Hair hanging in dripping wet strings, she went to her closet and hauled out her bags. Opening her drawers, she began to throw in her clothes. Everything. Fast, furious.

She zipped the bags closed and stood there. Ace was still fast asleep in front of the iron stove, oblivious, and she loved him for it. He was her sanity. She went over to him, crouched down, and just nuzzled her face into his ruff, drinking in his popcorn-doggie scent. He groaned and rolled over. She scratched his belly, exhaustion suddenly overcoming her.

She'd finish packing what was left of her meager belongings at first light. Then she'd load up her truck, warn the remaining guests about the storm arriving early. Say farewell to Myron. And hit the logging roads before the snow was too heavy. She'd call the ranch when the lines were back up to organize transport for Spirit. To wherever she'd found a new home.

She put out the kerosene lamps, leaving just the one by her bedside on. She cast back her covers.

Her heart stopped dead.

In the middle of the white sheet lay a sprig of rose hips.

Beneath it, in lurid red lipstick streaks, words were scrawled:

Time to finish the Hunt, Sarah

Run, run . . .

Olivia lunged forward and yanked the covers right off her bed. She stared. His scent seemed to rise up from her bedding to fill her nose. He was here. She could smell him. He'd been in this private place where she slept. She staggered back, crashed against her closet, the past spiraling up to swallow her.

The scream that rose from her throat didn't even seem to come from her.

She was back in the forest. Running on the numb stubs that were her feet in cold, wet leather.

He was behind her. Breathing heavily. She could hear his footfalls—soft thuds on the springy, mossy earth matted with needles. She fell. She couldn't go on. She had no clue how long she'd hidden in the bear den, but when she finally came out, he was waiting.

She rolled onto her back in the pine needles. He was up on the rise, peering down the barrel of his gun at her. She knew this was it. He was going to take the kill shot. He was going to slice the baby out of her belly. She was the pregnant doe his fucking daddy never allowed him to hunt.

She lifted her rifle. Shaking, she aimed, curled her finger through the trigger guard, didn't hesitate. She pulled. The recoil slammed back into her prone shoulder.

The bullet hit the trunk right at his face. Bark and chunks of wood exploded into him. He stilled, lowered his gun. Staggered sideways.

And fell like a log.

Her heart leaped to her throat. She waited. But he lay motionless. Slowly, she got to her knees, stood. He remained unmoving. All she could think was that shrapnel got him in the head. She had no idea whether he was dead, alive, or dying. She just ran. Down into an alder and willow-choked ravine. Scrabbling through branches and rotten snow deep in the ravine bed, she moved southwest. If she was right, if she was reading the direction of the sun correctly, she had an idea that southwest lay home.

A scream sliced the night.

Cole lurched to his feet, spun, slamming his drink onto the balustrade.

Olivia!

He raced down the path, through the grove of swaying trees, debris shooting down at him in the wind.

In one stride he was up on her deck. The cabin was in darkness now. He lunged for her door. But as he reached for it, an arm clamped around his neck like a vise, choking him backward. A cold blade pressed against his throat.

"Stay right where you are, you fuck. You think you can scare me, you bastard . . ."

"Olivia," he said quietly, calmly, his heart thundering in his chest. "It's okay. It's me. Easy, just lower the knife."

She didn't move. Breath rasped in her throat. She couldn't seem to think, either, as if unable to come down from whatever rush she was on, whatever place her mind had taken her to.

Slowly, he reached up and curled his hand around her wrist with the knife. He pulled it away from his neck. She had the iron strength of madness. "Easy," he said. "Easy does it."

He turned around.

Her arms were stiff at her sides, knife still clenched in her right fist. Her mouth was open. She was panting. Her eyes wild. Her hair a wet tangle.

Her bathrobe hung open. She was naked underneath. Warm wetness oozed down Cole's neck. He touched it with his fingertips. They came away sticky with his own blood. She'd nicked his neck.

She stared at the blood on his fingers, then at his face, confusion chasing through her features.

"Talk to me, Olivia," he said quietly. "What happened?"

She didn't seem to know or be able to register. She wobbled, as if she were going to faint.

"Here," he said, holding out his hand. "I'm going to touch you, okay? I'm going to take you back inside. Can I do that? Will you let me touch you?"

He moved slowly forward and put his arm around her shoulders. He escorted her back inside the cabin, closing the door behind him. He took the knife from her hand and placed it safely atop a cabinet.

Her living room lamps were off, just the orange glow from the fire lighting the interior. A whining, scratching noise came from behind her bedroom door.

Tension snapped through him.

"Where is Ace, Liv?"

"I . . . in there."

He went quickly to open the bedroom door.

"No!" she yelled, suddenly. "That . . . that's private. My room."

He paused, hand on doorknob.

Her robe was still hanging open. In the coppery gleam from the fire, he saw the big scars on her bare breasts. The ragged mark around her neck. The scars down her thighs and shins. His gaze lowered slowly. To her feet.

Oh, God.

Missing toes, parts of toes. It explained her awkward gait.

The horror of what Sebastian George had done to her was laid bare to him, mapped all over her body.

Muscles clamped across his chest. Emotion seared through him. Compassion and hot rage bubbled into him. And in that instant, he knew he'd do *anything* to protect this woman. This strong, incredible, beguiling, kind, generous woman who'd been shattered and shamed so that she couldn't even allow him to love her.

She registered his scrutiny, and shock visibly rocketed through her body. White-faced, she scrambled to tie her robe. The look of shame, embarrassment in her features killed him.

"What's inside the room?" he said, gently.

"It's nothing. Just get out of here. I'm fine."

He'd heard that one before. "Ace needs out. I'm going to open the door to let him out, okay? I need to see that he's all right."

Horror morphed back into her face as her gaze shot to the door. For a moment Cole feared she might bolt.

Carefully, he opened the door. Ace came wiggling out and went straight to her.

She crumpled down around the dog, wrapping in a human ball around him, burying her head into his fur as he licked her face.

Emotion filled Cole's eyes as raw adrenaline thumped through his blood. Quickly he entered the bedroom, then froze in shock.

Across the white sheet, scrawled in what appeared to be crude strokes of lipstick, were the words:

Time to finish the Hunt, Sarah
Run, run . . .

Next to the scrawl lay a sprig of rose hips.

Cole's gaze darted around the rest of the room. Her window was closed. Bags littered the floor. Drawers were empty. The bathroom was steamy-damp from a recent shower, the floor wet.

He exited her room, closed the door behind him, went straight to put the kettle on.

"Liv?" he said, coming back to her and placing his hand on her shoulder. She glanced up, face white, hollow eyes. Dry eyes.

"Come sit over here by the fire." He dragged an oversized stuffed chair closer.

"Cole, I—"

"Come," he said again, helping her up. "You *need* to talk to me, Liv."

Great big shudders took hold of her body, uncontrollable shakes. He sat beside her, wrapped his arms tightly around her, and just held her.

When finally she stilled, he said, "It wasn't a crab-fishing accident, was it?"

CHAPTER 19

Tori huddled under the bed cover with her backlit e-reader. It was getting colder in the cabin despite the burning woodstove in the next room, and the wind was moaning through the eaves. But she was unable to put away her device and sleep. She started on the next chapter of her mother's manuscript.

The truck driver put on his fog lights. Mist swirled and fingered among the dark conifers hemming in the steep logging road. Spring snow still lined the banks.

He blinked as he saw a shape in the fog. Right in front of his truck.

Jesus God. A woman? Bare legs, animal skin, matted hair. A rifle in her hand. He slammed on the brakes. His logging rig screeched and skidded sideways toward the apparition in the mist. He tapped the brakes, tried to steer into the skid, desperate to avoid jackknifing or spilling his load. Or hitting the creature.

He came to a stop inches from her. Sweat beaded his brow. The woman turned and looked up at his cab. His heart stalled dead. She was ghost white, dark hollows for eyes. Her skin was streaked with blood and dirt. She had a piece of rope around her neck, no pants on.

He scrabbled out of his cab and jumped down onto the road. She whipped up her rifle, aimed dead at his heart. He put out his hands, palms facing her.

"Hey, it's okay. I mean no harm."

She sighted him down the scope, unmoving.

Fear spurted through him.

"Please. It's okay. Can I help you?"

She stared at him for what felt like an eternity. Like a feral thing. Measuring whether to flee. Or kill. Mist swirled around her bare legs. She had boots on. No socks.

It hit him. The missing woman from last year. The posters.

"Sarah?" he said. "Sarah Baker?"

Her mouth opened. She lowered the gun, and she seemed to hang in the air for several beats before she collapsed in a pile on the gravel.

He hurried over to her. Pulse was weak. Skin ice cold. She stank. It was her, the Watt Lake woman—had to be. He'd seen the missing posters everywhere. That was five or six months ago, before the winter.

He struggled to lift her with his bad back and carry her to the truck. She was wrapped in a rotten old bearskin. He gagged at the smell of her. Inside the cab he removed the wet animal skin. Shock imploded through him. She was pregnant. She had large, festering wounds on her breasts, arms, legs. Quickly he wrapped her in a survival blanket from his first aid kit. He covered this with his down jacket. He put his wool hat on her head.

She moaned in pain as he took off her wet boots. His chest tightened. Her toes were blackened with frostbite. She was going to lose some.

Her ankles were chafed raw and bloody. Pus oozed from marks that had been cut deep.

He wrapped her feet carefully in a spare set of work pants.

With shaking hands he reached for his radio, called dispatch.

"Call 911," he told the dispatcher. "I think I found her—I found Sarah Baker. She needs an ambulance. I'm heading straight for Watt Lake Hospital—medics can meet me on the way."

Tori swallowed as wind keened outside. A branch *tick tick ticked* against the window, like something trying to get in.

Cole wrapped a blanket around her shoulders and brought Olivia some tea. She cupped her hands tightly around the hot mug. Her skin was clammy and cold, her breathing shallow, her pupils dilated. She was still in shock.

Quickly he stoked the fire up, added another log.

"I'm going to get you some socks." He went back into the bedroom.

Her drawers were completely devoid of clothes. He found socks in one of her packed bags. Clearly she was intent on leaving. It was his fault. He should never have tried to kiss her like that. Remorse, self-recrimination sliced through him.

Returning to the living room, he got down on hands and knees to rub some circulation back into her feet before putting the socks on. She squirmed, trying to hide her damaged toes. "Please," she said, voice small. "Don't touch my feet."

But he took them in his hand, gently massaging and warming them, not avoiding the stumps. He met her gaze. "You need to get warm. I'm getting circulation back."

Her gaze fell to his hands against her maimed toes, and Cole knew what she was feeling. Embarrassment. Shame.

He put her socks on.

"You've got blood down your shirt," she said. "I hurt you. I'm sorry."

"Just a surface cut. It's fine."

She stared at the blood.

"Drink that tea. It's sweet, hot, and will relax you a little, before the adrenaline shakes really kick in."

Her eyes held his as she sipped.

Cole's heart cracked at the vulnerability he saw there. This woman had been stripped naked before him, body and soul. Her physical secrets laid bare. And it was killing her.

"There's no shame, Liv," he whispered, taking the mug from her and setting it on the small table next to her. "No reason to hide yourself from me. You're the strongest, most beautiful woman I've ever had the privilege of meeting, and I mean it in more ways than one."

And for the first time since he'd barged in here, emotion pooled into her eyes and tracked down her cheeks.

Cole drew up a chair and sat beside her. He leaned down and scratched Ace's neck. "There's no need to finish packing those bags in there, no need to leave because of this. Nor because of me."

She swallowed, looked away. "You know who I am, don't you?"

He remained silent.

She turned slowly, looked into his eyes.

"I know there's a name scrawled on your sheet that's not 'Olivia.'" He still needed it to come from her. Fully. On some gut level Cole knew it had to happen that way, knew that it would be good for her.

"It's not me," she said softly. "Sarah Baker is not me."

"I know."

"I left her behind."

"Most of her," he said, quietly. "But you brought the strong parts with you. You brought the survivor in Sarah here to Broken Bar. And you've taught me something—you were right. I know dick about surviving." He smiled.

She stared at him. "It was my reaction to the news on TV that clued you in, wasn't it? You went and looked it up, the Watt Lake story. You found Sarah, and you found she was me."

"I did."

"Fuck," she whispered. She turned away, and for a long while she stared at the flames behind the glass in the little iron stove. Outside the wind increased.

He said nothing, just sat there, being there for her, letting her take the steps on her own. And there was no other place in this world that Cole wanted, or needed, to be right now.

"I built a new life. I . . . I don't want anyone to know." She began to shake—the adrenal aftereffects of shock. "He was *here*. Inside my cabin. My bedroom. My *bed*. How can he be here, how *can* he be back?"

"He's not back, Olivia. Sebastian George is dead. This is something—someone—else."

Her eyes flared to his, a desperation clawing through her features. "*Who* would do this? *Why?*"

She clutched the blanket tighter under her chin, and reached for her mug of tea. She spilled some as she sipped again, shaking badly now. "The rose hips . . ." She inhaled. "They're a sign of fall. Like wild blueberries and the cry of the geese flocking south, like the scent of coming snow. *Time to finish the hunt . . .*" Her voice cracked. She paused, gathering herself. "*He* said those words to me. How could anyone here possibly know this—about the rose hips, and berries, and what they mean to me?" She stared into the distance, into the past, eyes haunted.

"He kept me a whole winter. I knew it was spring by the lengthening light that was coming through the slats in the shack. By the dripping sounds of trees and the water leaking into the cabin. By the smell of the forest and soil around the shed. He kept me in the dark, and my sense of smell grew acute. I would smell him coming. I *know* his smell—I'd know it anywhere. I smelled him on my sheets in my bedroom."

"Transference, Liv. It's not possible that he was in there. He's dead. Someone else did this."

She slammed the mug down on the little table beside her chair. "Who! Dammit, *who?* Why?!"

"I don't know why, or who, but what I do know is this: I looked up the Watt Lake story and I saw an old photo of the last victim, and recognized you instantly. If I could do that, anyone can. And my guess is someone did, and is now using this fact to scare you. It's the *only* possibility."

"The rose hips?"

"There must be some reference in one of the archived stories about rose hips."

Doubt flickered through her eyes. "Why scare me—what have I done?"

He dragged his hand over his hair. "Maybe it's what my father has done. By rewriting his will. If you take over the ranch, it's pretty darn clear there will be no sale, no big development windfall. Someone might simply want to scare you into packing your bags and leaving, so that Broken Bar reverts to me and Jane. So that the development will go ahead."

And the document that I signed will ensure the sale . . .

Guilt twisted through Cole. With it came a bite of urgency. He had to get to Forbes first thing in the morning.

He splayed his feet and leaned forward, arms resting on his knees. "From what I understand from my sister, there's already big money invested in a future development proposal for Broken Bar land. Someone might have high stakes and really need the sale to go through. You can't let them win, Liv. You can't let them spook you off."

"Who would know about your father's amendments to his will? I mean, the change is so recent."

"Adele heard about it. She came into the library, remember? She also saw your neck scar and your visceral reaction to the television news of the Birkenhead murder. And you heard what she said before dinner—her son is handling investment for Forbes Development. If Adele told Tucker what she knew, Forbes might also know about the will, and about you."

A more sinister thought struck him. Jane knew about the will. Jane and Todd had big stakes hanging on a sale. His sister was a little Machiavelli, always had been. Acquiring physical things had been her way of handling their mother's death and life on this ranch with a bitter father. He would not put it past Jane to hire someone to do something like this, and the idea hardened Cole's resolve. He felt responsible.

"Look, I'm going to sort this out. I'm going into Clinton first thing in the morning to lay down the law with Forbes, make it clear there will be no sale. I'll inform him that he needs to pull the plug and start damage control. And I'll find out who did this. Someone must have come in here while we were all at dinner. So it could have been Adele—"

"She wouldn't."

"I think she has a lot at stake here. Her husband is on disability. Her job at the ranch is in question with my father dying. She feels she's put her whole life into Broken Bar. She likely believes she has some right to at least part of it. And her son's neck might be on the line with the investment. Desperate people can be driven to do very desperate things. And you made it easy—you didn't lock your door."

"I never locked my door because I *refuse* to be scared. After the news that Sebastian George had hung himself, I made a commitment to be free. I felt safe here. It was my way of taking a stand, fighting back." She gave a weak, self-deprecating snort.

"And look at me now—" She opened her hands, palms up. She rubbed at the dried blood she saw there. His blood. Her wrist scars caught the coppery gleam from the fire. "I'm a pathetic mess of PTSD, jumping at my own shadow. Losing periods of time." She looked up slowly. "I almost killed you. I . . . I thought you were him. I . . . hadn't had a flashback in years. The therapist said there was a risk they could return, if exacerbated by stress or a traumatic incident." She rubbed her temple, as if in pain.

"But I honestly began to believe they were over. Until I felt an acute sense of being followed the other morning. There were boot prints paralleling mine when I laid a track for Ace. And someone dropped that scarf on my track." She nodded to where a soft-looking scarf was draped over a hook by her door. Cole glanced at it.

"When I returned to my cabin, I found a basket of wild blueberries outside my door. Berries were how Sebastian lured me to the river. Then came the news about the Birkenhead murder, and the flashbacks started."

She swallowed.

"And then there was the fishing lure in the newspaper. The Predator. I created that design. I gave Sebastian that fly . . ." Her voice faded again as her face twisted with dark memories.

Cole's chest tightened. "Who else knew about the fly?"

"Only the homicide investigators who came up from Surrey, and a criminal profiler—a consultant from Ottawa. They questioned me for hours over a period of days, about how he came into the store, stalked me. What he said and did. I told them about the Predator, and how, after I gave it to Sebastian, he responded by sharing his own secret about where the blueberry stash was."

She shook her head. "Blueberries. He lured me with simple blueberries. Because I wanted to bake a pie for Ethan."

She fell silent for several long beats. The wood in the stove cracked and popped as it burned. "It was because I loved Ethan, who could never love me again afterward. Not after what had been done to me." She rubbed her hand over her mouth. "He couldn't even look at me."

It hit Cole—*that* was part of her shame. Her own husband had made her feel ugly. Responsible, even, in some way.

"And what was Gage Burton doing with the Predator?" he said gently. "How did that happen?"

"I told you—he said he got it as a retirement gift just before he left."

Cole chewed on the inside of his cheek. "And he just happened to leave that particular lure inside a page with reference to the Watt Lake killings?"

"It could just be a coincidence. I mean, once people start copying a fly design, it could end up anywhere."

He nodded. He also needed to talk to Burton—something still wasn't jibing about the guy. Like his father had said, Burton could be totally innocuous, and this whole scenario was far more likely a scheme backed by Forbes to scare Olivia with her own past—threaten her with the revelation of her true identity—run her out of town. Sick bastard.

But he was going to sound Burton out when he returned from Clinton.

He reached over and moved a lock of hair that had fallen across her face. It was drying in a soft, dark spiral. He hooked it behind her ear.

"I'll get to the bottom of this, Liv," he said, softly. "I'll find who did this. But one thing you can't do is let them win and chase you away. You need to unpack those bags."

"I can't live here with people knowing who I am. If you figure Forbes knows, the whole bloody town will know. I can't do this. I need to go where I can bury Sarah Baker again."

"Then you'll forever be running," he said. "He—Sebastian—even in death will always have power over you."

"Says the man who's been running his whole life?"

"I've stopped."

She held his gaze.

"I have. I'm serious about staying here, putting down some roots. And remember this: You are beautiful. You are strong. You are enough. You don't need to be anything more. Or less."

Her eyes flooded, and she swiped tears away with the sleeve of her robe.

He got to his feet. "Where do you keep spare bedding? Or have you packed it all?"

"That closet over there." She nodded toward the far wall.

He opened it and removed a fresh fitted sheet.

"What are you doing?"

"Making your bed." He smiled. "Then you're going to get some sleep."

Horror widened her eyes, and her gaze flared to her bedroom door. She opened her mouth to protest. But he placed two fingers on her lips, bent over, and kissed her ever so gently on the forehead.

"Don't worry," he whispered against her hair. "I'll stay with you until morning."

———

Olivia woke with a shock to find a man's arms locked around her body. She blinked rapidly into the dark, holding her breath, before she became fully cognizant and realized where she was, what had happened. She was in her own bed, in clean sheets, with Cole, fully clothed, spooned around her.

His nose was buried into the crook of her neck, in her hair, against her scar, and his breath was warm. His arms were hard muscle, and she could feel the steady, comforting, solid beat of his heart.

Slowly she breathed in deep. It was almost overwhelming to just be held like this. Loved. No pressures. Accepted. Not reviled for the grotesque mutilations on her body.

You are enough . . .

———

Tori's vision was blurring, and she could hear her father's deep, rhythmic snores coming from the other room. But she was unable to put her e-reader down.

A man who said his name was Sebastian George was arrested after a fifteen-hour standoff at a remote homestead deep in the Bear Claw Valley. George was a man with no ID—invisible to the system. A man with the same strange amber eyes that the staff sergeant had looked into on the gravel banks of the Stina River when he'd accepted the Predator lure.

George now sat opposite two homicide investigators at a table in the Watt Lake interrogation room.

From behind two-way glass the staff sergeant watched as one of the officers placed on the table the fly the man had given him on the Stina River. Sarah Baker had already said it was exactly the same as the one she'd designed and given to George when he'd come into her store.

"Do you recognize this fly?" the officer said to George.

The suspect shook his head. Eyes blank.

"Is this the fly you gave to a fisherman on the Stina River?"

George remained silent.

The staff sergeant leaned forward and keyed a mike that fed into the earpiece of one of the interrogating officers.

"Ask him about the books in his cabin."

The interrogator's brow furrowed—the staff sergeant was not supposed to interfere. The big homicide guns had taken the case over, that much had been crystal clear to him.

Yet the interrogating officer acquiesced. Leaning forward, he said, "Tell me about your books. You have a lot of heavy literature in your cabin."

Sebastian George stared in silence at the interrogating officer. His eyes were empty. Not even a glimmer of the feral fire, the deep, intellectual crackle that the sergeant had glimpsed in the eyes of the man on the river.

"You must like reading," the interrogating officer prompted.

"Can't read," said George.

"But you can write," the interrogating officer said.

"Can't write," George said.

Yet written messages had been secreted into the right eye socket of each skull they'd excavated from the graves around George's property.

"He's lying," the staff sergeant snapped into the mike. "Press him!"

The interrogating officer shot him a hot warning glare through the two-way mirror, and the line of questioning was dropped.

George's claim to illiteracy—despite his cabin shelves being stocked with well-thumbed books, including tomes by Hemingway, Thoreau, Algernon Blackwood, an old William Godwin treatise on libertarianism—never made it to discovery.

The jury never learned about his books.

It was deemed a minor anomaly better swept under the carpet in the face of all the other overwhelming evidence—DNA, fingerprints, dental impressions. George had already admitted guilt in each count of murder. Sarah Baker had also identified him in a lineup. He was the same man captured on security camera footage visiting Sarah in the Watt Lake sporting goods store.

When the staff sergeant, beyond his purview, questioned this omission, he was reminded that Sebastian George was a slick, lying sociopath who was trying to con them all. The case had become political. The Mounties needed a smooth conviction. A stamp against crime before the next federal election. The less that could complicate a trial, the better.

A clean conviction was also the horse that homicide team leader Sergeant Hank Gonzales, a peer of the Watt Lake staff sergeant's, was riding toward a promotion.

Tori glanced up, a chill crackling down her spine. Gonzales was her dad's boss in Surrey. He was the assistant commissioner now. How much had her mother ripped from the headlines? Heart galloping, she read further . . .

But the staff sergeant continued to press Gonzales. Yet again, he was told to back down, toe the official line. This time the order came direct from big brass in Ottawa, which irked the hell out of the sergeant, and made him even more determined in his assertions that the Mounties had somehow gotten the wrong man.

Then came transfer papers to a remote detachment in Fort Tapley. He was being reassigned, stripped of his managerial role because of his apparent insubordination.

Even so, beyond overwhelming evidence or rational explanation, the sergeant continued to believe the man from the river was still out there . . .

———

Vancouver. Early Sunday morning. The day before Thanksgiving.

Dawn broke with a low, leaden sky and monsoon-like rain. It was the brunt of a series of storms blowing in from the Pacific and powering north, where it would dump as snow. Mac stood with his coffee in the doorway of Burton's home office, fighting down a sense of guilt in being here. This was his buddy's residence. Melody's home. But Burton was not well. Possibly experiencing psychotic episodes. And he was their *only* person of interest in the Birkenhead River slaying so far. He had perverted motive, and opportunity. They needed to find him.

"You're gonna want to see this." The forensic tech called him over to Burton's computer.

Martinello joined Mac. They peered over the tech's shoulder.

"Appears Burton was using a fake account to trawl adoption reunion sites. He's been using the tag 'Olivia West'—seems he's been posing as a mother searching for her child surrendered in an adoption."

"What the . . . ?" Mac bent closer as the tech brought up another page from the system cache. "Bring it in," he said crisply. "All of it. Computer from Burton's deceased wife's office, too."

He reached for his cell, hit quick dial.

"Jerry, you got that trace on Burton's phone yet?"

"Negative. Either he's out of cell range, or he's disabled his phone."

Mac killed the call, looked at Martinello. But before he could speak, her phone rang.

She listened, nodded. Then said to Mac, "They got an ID on the vic from her knee replacement. Recipient is a woman from the US, Washington State. Her name is Mary Sorenson. Age fifty-three. She and her husband, Algor Sorenson, were on a camper trip around the States. Part of their early retirement. Their kids haven't heard from their parents in weeks—not since a photo of Mary Sorenson was sent from Arizona, via Algor Sorenson's cell. The kids didn't think this was unusual. Their parents often traveled a few weeks without calling in, so they never reported them missing."

"So how the fuck did Mary Sorenson end up gutted, partially flayed, and swinging from a tree on the Birkenhead River this side of the border? And where in the hell is Algor Sorenson now?"

"And where is their camper and trailer?"

"We need to speak to Border Services."

CHAPTER 20

Sunday morning. The day before Thanksgiving.

Tori woke early. She got up onto her knees on the bed and peered through the blinds. It was barely dawn outside, low cloud. Tiny crystals of snow wafted on the wind. She snuggled back into her bed and powered up her e-reader. As she started to read, the *tick tick tick* of the branch against the window grew more insistent. And so did the black beast of questions prowling around her mind. Her heart hammered faster.

"Tell me what it was like during the first days in the shed?" the journalist said, speaking with a measured calm, so as not to agitate Sarah Baker. The journalist was lucky to have been granted access to this last victim of the Watt Lake Killer—the lone survivor who was going to help put Sebastian George away for several lifetimes. The journalist was one of the few people Sarah would talk to at this time. Sarah was having trouble communicating with her husband, Ethan, and with her mother and father. The journalist liked to think that their interview sessions were therapeutic for Sarah. She liked the woman. Admired and respected her. And Sarah's pain had slowly become her own over the days she'd visited, listened, and written down her story, reliving the trauma piece by terrible piece with her.

The journalist had once been a newspaper reporter, but she now made her living from true-crime features, and she was trying to write a novel. Her plan was to use these interviews for a book.

But there came a moment during her sessions with Sarah when the journalist didn't think she'd be able to write this book in the end. Or at least publish it for financial gain. It had begun to feel too personal.

"In the early days of that winter," Sarah said, staring blankly out of the window, "I sometimes heard choppers, thudding behind cloud . . . then came silence. Darkness. I'd thought hearing them searching for me was the worst. It wasn't. It was when the silence came, and I knew they'd stopped looking." She paused. "In the end it was the baby that kept me alive. I'd have done anything for Ethan's baby, and to get back to him."

Sarah fell silent, her gaze going more distant.

The journalist grew uncomfortable, warring with something personal inside. "Would you like me to bring her in?" she said. "Would you like to see her?"

"No."

"She's just an innocent, beautiful little baby girl, Sarah, just a day old."

Sarah's mouth tightened, and her hands tensed on the bed covers. She focused intently on a tiny hummingbird hovering outside the hospital window. The trees were in full leaf. It was a hot July day out.

The journalist leaned forward in her chair. "Please. Just look at her. She needs you. She might have been conceived out of violence, but there's not a drop of bad blood in that tiny little body. She's innocence embodied."

Tears pooled in Sarah's eyes. Her fists bunched the sheets. She was fighting herself.

The journalist got up and called the nurse. Possibly she was making a vital mistake—involving herself like this. Yet she was unable to stop, already too emotionally vested.

The nurse wheeled in the crib. Sarah had given birth barely a day ago. Her breasts were hard lumps, swollen against her stitches and leaking patches of wet into her hospital gown. But mentally she was dead to her child. She'd been like that since DNA from amniocentesis had shown the baby was not Ethan's. The tests had been done after the logger brought her in at about five months pregnant, and an infection of the amniotic fluid had been suspected. Doctors also wanted to determine how developed the baby's lungs were, in case she went into early labor. The prosecutors and cops wanted the test, too. Results had revealed Sebastian George was the father. She'd been doomed from that moment to knowingly carry to term the baby of a monster. The fertility treatments prior to her abduction had made her ripe for it.

The cops and lawyers were pleased with the test results. The baby DNA would convict Sebastian George on the sexual assault counts, no question.

But Ethan had been devastated by the news.

The day Sarah went into labor, Ethan hadn't come to the hospital. The journalist had seen him outside, through the window. Under the oak tree. As if trying to come in. But he never made it. Sarah's mother and her God-fearing pastor of a father hadn't come either. This enraged the journalist.

What true man of God would turn his back on his own daughter at a time like that? How could he minister to the souls of this town and instruct them about good when he couldn't support a young woman— his own flesh and blood—in dire need?

The journalist nodded to the nurse, who quietly left the room. The journalist then wheeled the crib to the side of the hospital bed. She seated herself next to the cot and silently watched the baby, an ache growing in her own chest, in her own breasts. She knew what Sarah and Ethan had been going through in trying to have a child. She knew it with every fiber of her own body, that need for a baby.

Slowly, Sarah turned her head. She swallowed, stared at the little creature in the crib. Then very slowly she reached out her hand.

Trembling, she touched the infant. It had dark, soft hair. Rosebud lips. Dark lashes. Like his.

The baby's miniature fingers curled tightly around Sarah's forefinger. Her breath hiccupped in her throat. Silent tears leaked down her face.

The journalist didn't say a word. She tried not to cry, too. Her arms, her chest burned to hold them both. Meld them together forever. Make this right.

"She's beautiful." Sarah whispered.

"Your daughter."

Her lip wobbled.

"Do you want to hold her?"

She nodded.

The journalist placed the swaddled baby in Sarah's arms. After a few moments just gazing into the infant's eyes, Sarah said, "Will you help me? Will you help me feed her?"

The journalist helped slide the gown off Sarah's shoulder, and she assisted her in latching that little rosebud mouth to the mother's nipple. Sarah still had bandages over the wounds on her breasts. She was clearly in pain as the baby started to suckle. She leaned her head back against the pillow and closed her eyes. Tears leaked from beneath her lashes.

"Dear God," she whispered. "Dear God, please help me. Please help my child . . ."

But God had long ago deserted Sarah Baker.

Hope had deserted Sarah. The journalist believed hope died in Sarah the day Ethan was no longer able to hold her, love her. The day her own husband showed his revulsion and confusion. She had survived thus far, in part for him, but when he rejected her, that was the day she stopped trying.

The journalist still believes to this day that Sarah would have kept that baby had the world left her alone. Had Ethan opened his heart to the child. Had her father led the way and shown others how to forgive, accept . . . how to welcome this innocent baby. Instead Sarah made the decision to surrender the infant, nameless, to the system.

"I only want the best for her. I can never be free of him, but I want her to be free. The only way I can do that is to let her have a fresh start. To never know."

"During captivity, did you not once, ever, consider the baby might be Sebastian's?"

"Never," Sarah whispered. "I don't think it was possible for me to entertain the idea." She paused. "I don't think I—we—would have survived."

Tori set her e-reader down, got out of bed, and edged open the living room door. Her father was still snoring soundly. She crept over to where he'd tucked the crumpled newspaper onto a shelf. Carefully she smoothed it open on the table and read the teaser for the opinion piece inside. *"Birkenhead murder—echoes of the Watt Lake Killer? See page 6."*

She opened the paper to page six. Her father grunted. Her gaze shot to his slightly ajar bedroom door. But he spluttered and turned over, resuming his deep breathing. There was just enough light coming in from the window for her to read. She scanned down the piece with her finger, checking the names of the victims who had been abducted and killed by the man they'd dubbed the Watt Lake Killer. Her throat closed in on itself as she saw the final name.

Sarah Baker.

The name in her mother's work of fiction.

————

The scent of freshly brewed coffee and the sound of logs being tossed into the stove roused Olivia from deep slumber, the kind of heavy sleep where it takes a minute or two to orient oneself. She lay there a moment, reliving the comfort of having been wrapped in Cole's embrace. He'd stayed the whole night. His side of the bed was still warm. Yet as she came fully awake, a subterranean unease grew in her.

She got out of bed, grabbed her robe and tugged it over the pajamas she'd put on before climbing under the covers with Cole last night. She hesitated as it dawned fully on her again, in the light of day, that he knew who she was.

He was privy to everything that had happened to her.

The sense of nakedness, vulnerability, was suddenly stark. Olivia went into her bathroom, rinsed her face, dried it, and looked into the mirror. She felt a clutch in her chest.

She didn't know if she could do this—go out into the world as Sarah Baker now, the last victim of the infamous Watt Lake Killer—after coming so far to hide from it. She cursed suddenly, violently, as she caught sight of the defiled sheet bundled up on her laundry hamper.

He wasn't the only one who knew. Whoever crept in here and left her that scrawled message knew, too.

She had to face him. She had to go out into the living room and look into his eyes.

One step at a time . . .

Cole dwarfed her tiny kitchenette. He stood with his back to her. Ace lay near his feet, waiting, no doubt, for crumbs to drop. Cole had stoked up the stove, and her home was toasty and filled with the scent of freshly brewing coffee. Dawn was flat and gray outside. Tiny snowflakes drifted past the window.

Olivia stalled a moment, absorbing the scene. She'd never imagined a man in her tiny cabin. In her bed. A memory chased through her—the sensation of him under her, inside her, his muscular body, the roughness of his hair against her bare skin. Her cheeks flushed. That subterranean unease grew louder, tension seeping into her chest.

He turned.

"Hey, sleepyhead." A grin creased lines around his eyes and

deepened the brackets around his mouth. Dark hair fell in a lock on his brow. He wore a white T-shirt that was well-fitted and defined his abs, his pecs. His biceps rolled smoothly under toned, sun-browned skin as he reached for two mugs and set them on the counter in front of her. He looked more delicious than before, and rested, too, his gray eyes intense, lambent. Alive. Yet he also appeared more imposing. Bigger somehow, in her tiny home. Crowding her space.

"I was going to leave you to sleep. It's started snowing, barely, but I would like to make it into town and back before it really comes down," he said. Her radio was on, playing music softly in the background as they faced each other across the small expanse of her kitchen.

Conflict twisted through Olivia, and she almost allowed her gaze to flicker toward the sofa where she'd embarrassed herself. She knew he was thinking about it too. Her heart began to pound, and her skin felt hot. What next? What to say?

She felt as if she were balanced precariously upon a fulcrum where one word or action could sway her life in one direction, and another could have exactly the opposite effect. The urge to scuttle back into her safety zone was suddenly overwhelming.

He seemed to read her indecision. "You doing okay?"

She drew her robe closer over her chest and cleared her throat. "Yes. Thank you for . . . everything."

He held her eyes a moment. Her pulse beat even faster.

"I'm going up to the lodge first to check on my dad, and to see if the phones are back up. If they're working, I might not need to drive into Clinton. If they're still down, I'd like to get going right away before there's too much snow and the roads shut down."

Just like that. Easy. She'd undergone a groundswell that was rocking the very foundations of her identity and life. And he seemed so relaxed.

Olivia walked over to the door, called Ace, and let him out.

She went to the living room window, folding her arms over her stomach as she watched him sniffing his way down to the lake.

"Liv?" Cole came up behind her and put his arms around her, resting his chin in the curve of her shoulder. His breath was warm against her cheek. Her muscles constricted. Her heart began to gallop in her chest.

She wanted to push him away. She suddenly couldn't cope with the intimate reminder of the night before, standing here, right beside the sofa where it had happened. Having him in her bed, his compassion, suddenly felt even more intimate than sex. She struggled against her rising claustrophobia. But it was too much, too fast, and panic swamped her, black and smothering. Her heart started to palpitate, a dark inky tide suffocating her brain with the kind of blackness and anxiety that had always preceded a serious flashback.

She pulled away sharply, spun round to face him.

"You're not really okay, are you?"

She dragged a shaking hand over her sleep-tangled hair, glanced away, then met his eyes again. "I wish I were. I wish I was normal. God knows I try. But the truth? I don't really know how I am right now." She paused, then said, "Or who I am. Or who I can ever be."

He reached for her hands, but she backed sharply up against the windowsill, another shard of panic slicing through her.

She clenched the windowsill behind her. "I . . . I'm sorry, Cole. I can't do this with you. Not right now."

"This?" he said, crooking his head.

Her face went hot. She didn't even know what "this" was. "Us," she said, tentatively.

He held her gaze, his stormy eyes unfathomable for a moment. Then a smile slowly curved his mouth, crumpling that gorgeous, rugged face and fanning lines out from his eyes. "How about some coffee?"

Relieved, she nodded.

He went to the counter, poured a steaming mug. "How do you take it?"

"Just a dash of cream."

He found the coffee cream in her fridge and splashed some in. He brought the mug over to her by the window. She felt naked in the harsh dawn light, without her bandana or polo neck. But he managed to avert his eyes from her choker of scars.

As she took the mug from him, he said, "A friend of mine, Gavin Black, who quit war photography because of PTSD, once told me after our near-death incident with Ty that you've just got to keep living one day at a time, until you're living again." He paused. "I didn't give those words any credence until your phone call pulled me out of the bar that night. Because I wasn't living one day at a time—not even close. I was blotting it out. But I think I get it now. And it's not easy. It involves exposing oneself to feelings that hurt. I don't want to rush anything, either, Liv. Just one day at a time. And right now, the only pressing thing, my one step for the day, is to confront Forbes and make it clear where I—we—stand. I'm going to make it clear that his development proposal is no go." He paused. "You're okay with that?"

She nodded.

"Then that's *our* job for the day—our one step." He smiled, reached for his jacket hanging by her door. "You should take the Sunday off, just hunker down in the cabin, stay warm. Relax."

"Why? You think I should be worried th—"

"No," he said firmly. "I don't think there is any danger out there. I believe Forbes and his cronies are being jerks about this development, but I can't see that they'd physically harm anyone. Still, there's nothing wrong with a day off."

"I need to make sure the guests are leaving, with this snow."

"Okay, so once you've driven around there, you come back and stay in the cabin. Or in the lodge with Myron. Until I get back—promise me?"

She gave a soft snort and couldn't help a smile. "I don't know whether to be affronted at being ordered around, or grateful to have someone watch my back."

"That's what friends are for—they watch out for each other."

Her smile faded.

He shrugged into his jacket and exited the door with a cool blast of air.

From the window she watched him marching over the grass, and she was reminded of how he'd appeared in the sky over the southern horizon in his little yellow airplane. And how everything had changed.

Keep living one day at a time . . .

Except, she didn't know if she had time. Her secret would soon be out all over town. Taking her coffee, she went into her kitchen to make some toast.

She popped a bagel into the toaster and bumped up the volume of the radio as the signature tune for the hourly newscast sounded.

Snow was coming down a little more insistently now, clouds darkening over the lake, which had turned gunmetal gray. Across the water, spruce marched like black soldiers with spears in the sky.

You are strong. You are enough . . .

Cole had given her a gift in those words. They were words that should have come from her family, her husband, her community, and never had. Not even close.

Apart from that journalist, Melody Vanderbilt, who'd sat with her over so many days and just allowed her to talk. Melody had listened—*really* listened. She'd offered such nonjudgmental compassion that Olivia had been unable to stop talking to her. She'd just bled it all out. With Melody she'd never felt like a freak or a terrible human being. Melody had shown her a way forward.

For that, Olivia could not have been more thankful. As she waited for her bagel to pop up, she sipped from her mug, wondering where Melody was now.

You can always contact me. Look me up. Either through the adoption agent, or via this number on my card . . .

Melody had given Olivia her business card.

Never feel afraid to call, even if just to know how she's doing . . .

Olivia hadn't kept the card. She'd kept nothing of the past. But as she stared out the window now, at Ace snuffling along the frosted scrub that lined the shore, she wondered where her baby girl was. How she'd grown. Who she'd become.

An ache swelled in her chest, and Olivia was consumed with an acute and sudden sense of aloneness. Regret.

She shook it off, as the bagel popped up. She spread cream cheese on it, listening to the news about the coming storm, reminding herself she'd done it for her daughter.

It sounded like the front was much more intense than anticipated, and arriving sooner. Snow was already heavy in southern regions of the interior plateau. Olivia glanced at the clock. She needed to get moving and inform any campers who hadn't already left, give them time enough to decamp and drive out before the roads became treacherous. Clearly the Thanksgiving dinner planned for tonight would have to be cancelled.

Then the news cut to the murder.

"IHit spokeswoman Constable Isla Remington says police have scheduled a news conference for 10:00 a.m. CBC has learned that police will release the ID of the Birkenhead River murder victim at the conference and will update the public on the progress of the ongoing investigation. According to a CBC source, the victim had recently undergone knee replacement surgery, and police have traced the surgeon through the serial number on the artificial joint. Remington would not comment further on the similarities between the Birkenhead case and the Watt Lake killings that occurred over a decade ago. The only surviving victim of the Watt Lake Killer was Sarah Baker, the young wife of Ethan Baker who identified her assailant as Sebastian George. Baker later testified against George, who was found dead in his cell just over three years ago. According to criminal analyst Dr. Garfield Barnes, the Birkenhead case could have been the work of a copycat, someone who identifies with—"

Olivia reached up and punched the radio button off. Her hands shook. Her mouth was dust dry. Blood began to boom in her head. *Thud, thud, thud, thud* . . . the shovel hitting dirt as she peered through the chinking in her shed. She could see him, digging in the black loamy earth. She could smell the soil, the dampness of the forest, the rot of the siding on her shed.

He turned and looked toward her shed. His eyes, pale amber, met hers through the hole. Her stomach roiled.

Olivia grabbed the counter, braced herself, her brain spinning as she fought to stay present.

Tick, tick, tock, tock . . . the sound of water dripping. Spring coming.

Time for the hunt, Sarah . . . never hunted a pregnant doe, Sarah . . .

She spun around, knocking her mug of coffee off the counter. It crashed and shattered on the floor. Hot coffee burned down her leg. Pain, but nothing like the pain in her memory.

Olivia bent over and braced her hands on knees, trying short, shallow breaths, panting like an animal, stressed. Head down. Blood rushed back into her brain. Slowly she came around and stood up. Her skin was wet. She could smell the acrid scent of fear on her own body. She swallowed and steadied herself by holding the back of the chair.

How in the hell was she going to control these flashbacks? They were coming closer and closer together now. She had a real and sudden fear that she would actually go mad. End up in an institution. Rage erupted inside her. *No.*

No way on goddamn earth was she going to succumb, or remain a prisoner of her past. She'd almost killed herself once—would be dead if some paramedic hadn't found her and interfered. Now she wanted to live. Someone here on Broken Bar had conspired against her and was sending her back into a living nightmare, and she was not going to let them win. She could *not* live like this.

She marched into her room and began to thrust what was left of her belongings into her bags. She changed rapidly into jeans and a sweater, and dumped her toiletries into another bag. She stood in the center of her room for a moment.

Focus.

You can do this.

Move on.

Leave this ranch.

Myron was dying—it was over anyway. And she had one little window of opportunity before the snow locked her in. Before she'd be stuck here for days, even weeks on Broken Bar.

Where to go?

Didn't matter where. East. Drive east. Alberta. Next province. Over the Rocky Mountain divide. Lots of ranches and rivers and lakes. Wide, wide spaces. People who didn't know her.

She pulled on clothes. Shucking into her jacket, she gathered her bags, and began to lug her belongings up to her truck. Once everything was inside, she covered the back with a tarp and then ran through a mental checklist. All she had to do now was talk to Brannigan at the stables and tell him that she'd call with a plan to transport Spirit to wherever she ended up. She'd pay him to care for Spirit in the interim. She'd give Spirit one last ride before the storm set in, take her around to the campsite, where she'd kill two birds with one stone and check to see all the guests were gone. Then she'd say farewell to Myron and be on her way.

Olivia stalled. *Cole.* She dragged both hands over her hair. She had to leave him a note, explain.

Hurriedly she made her way back down through the grove and reentered her cabin. She found a pen and a piece of paper. On it she wrote:

Thank you for everything. Thank you for showing me that I was enough. You gave me back a piece of myself, and I will take that with me wherever I go now. With all my heart I wish you well with Broken Bar. Look after it for me . . .

Olivia paused, besieged suddenly with raw emotion. She gathered herself.

I know he probably won't ask you this himself, but Myron made me promise him something. There's a place up on the esker, the highest point where the grasses grow tall. It looks out over the entire forest canopy and lake. It's where I promised Myron I would scatter his ashes, next to the stone memorial he built in your mother and Jimmie's memories. I will think of him there. Please do it for me. For him . . .

Emotion snared. *Shit.* She stopped, rubbed her brow, wincing as she connected with the bruise from where she'd hit her head on the picnic table earlier.

I'm sorry we did not meet at another juncture in life, Cole. I like to think things could have been different had we crossed paths in another way. Thank you again. Take care of yourself. All my love, Olivia.

She stared at her hastily scrawled note.

All my love.

She could love a man like him. Maybe she already did, a little. With a twist of regret she tucked the corner of the note under her cactus pot on the kitchen counter so it wouldn't blow off when the cabin door opened.

Stepping out into the cold, she went down the bank toward the water.

"Ace!" She waited for him to pop out from the bushes as tiny snowflakes drifted about her. Ace didn't appear.

She whistled and called again.

The wind had died down, things had grown still and colder, whispering frost fingers appearing on the grasses. One day to Thanksgiving Day—always on Monday. Today was the anniversary of her abduction. Anxiety whipped through her, feeding into the adrenaline and urgency already strumming through her blood. She had to leave.

Ace was probably still busy down in the scrub somewhere doing his business. He'd be fine while she sorted Spirit out and gave her a quick run around to the campsite. Ace's legs were better rested, anyway. She'd been working him too hard of late.

She started along the path, heading for the stables, snow crystals pricking against her face. Thoughts of Cole dogged her. The memory of his arms around her, the way he felt, the look in his eyes. She liked him. Too much. Too soon. She blew out a shuddering breath as she neared the paddock.

It would make things easier for him and Jane if she left. That much she could give him. And she'd brought him home to Myron. She believed she had actually made a tiny, tiny difference. Because now Cole might stay. He might fulfill Myron's dream. Too little, too late, but she had given them that.

———

Tori shivered as she read, but it was more than the cold. A dark sensation was building in her chest. Sarah Baker was real. She'd been mentioned in the newspaper, and she was also in her mom's manuscript. A journalist from Watt Lake had taken down Sarah's story. A staff sergeant who was being transferred to Fort Tapley believed the police had caught the wrong man. Fort Tapley was where Tori had been born . . .

The journalist dished scrambled egg from the pan onto two plates that already held toast and bacon. She carried the plates to the table where her husband was reading a newspaper.

She placed one plate in front of him. He smiled up at her. He was in his uniform, and handsome. His smile always seemed to light up her life. She loved him.

Taking a seat beside him, she set her own plate in front of her and reached for the teapot. She poured tea for them both. The window was open wide to a summer morning breeze, fat green leaves clattering in the tree outside.

"How're the sessions going? She still talking?"

"Her therapist agreed with her that it's cathartic." She sat silent, looking at the food on her plate.

"Not hungry?"

"She's giving the baby up for adoption."

He delivered a forkful of food to his mouth, chewed. "I know. It's best under these circumstances."

"We could take it."

He stopped chewing, stared at her.

She leaned forward. "We've spoken about adoption. We agreed . . . since the tests. We'll never have a child any other way. Why not this baby?"

"This is—"

"We can give her the life she deserves. We know her story, the whole background. When she's old enough to understand, when she's had the best start we could possibly give her, we'll be in the best position to help her through it."

"You're serious," he said quietly.

"Never more.

"The optics . . . the case—"

She placed her hand over his. "You're not technically on the case. And you have this transfer coming up. We could use it for a fresh start. All three of us. We can go through an agent, a private, closed adoption. No one really needs to know at all."

He opened his mouth, but she saw in his eyes he was listening, receptive, and it excited her.

"I can leave right away with the baby," she said quickly. "I can set up home in Fort Tapley, and you could join us there. We can tell everyone she was born there."

He stared into her eyes, conflict in his own. He shook his head and cupped the side of her face. "I don't think—"

"Please," she whispered. "That child is going to need all the love she can get. Sarah needs this, too. There's no one else. We've been trying for a child—"

"You've already spoken to Sarah, haven't you?"

She swallowed.

The journalist had her heart set on that little baby now, those tiny fingers that had clutched hers, that soft, black hair, the little rosebud mouth, her scent . . . She ached for that baby. She ached with all her soul to give that little infant the life and love that Sarah Baker couldn't.

"I think her eyes are going to stay green," she said. "Like Sarah's. She's going to be beautiful. Like her mother."

The staff sergeant glanced away.

"I know what you're thinking, but there's no reason she should turn out like him."

The staff sergeant had been unable to say no. And when he did finally make it up to Fort Tapley, and his wife placed their newly adopted baby girl into his big, solid arms, he was overwhelmed with emotion. The world was suddenly different, big and vast, and it struck him that this smidgen of humanity cradled in his arms was the definition of innocence and vulnerability. She cut to the very core of all the reasons he'd joined the force, wanted to become a cop. A Mountie.

Defend and protect. Stop the innocent from being hurt. To put away the bad guys.

And on that day the sergeant made his baby girl a pledge. He vowed to the tiny, innocent, vulnerable being in his arms: "I'm going to get him," he whispered. "I'm going to find that man from the river no matter how long it takes me. And I'm going to kill him . . ."

Tori threw back her covers and rushed to the bathroom. She gagged but couldn't throw up, just dry heaved, which hurt her stomach and burned her throat. Trembling, she washed her face with cold water, flushed the toilet.

She stood in the bathroom, bare feet on cold floor, looking into the mirror. In her eyes she saw fear. The dedication in her mother's book swirled into her mind.

For my dear Tori, a story for the day you are ready . . .

She began to shake. Fear, confusion smothering her brain as she felt another punch of nausea.

Rushing back to her room, she yanked on her clothes and a jacket and hat. She took her e-reader and hurried quietly through the living area. She turned the door handle, waited until she heard her father snore again, then she stepped out in a land that was cold and shrouded in shades upon shades of gray. Snow swirled softly. She raced down the steps and along the grass, and just started running faster and faster until her breath burned her chest.

CHAPTER 21

Gage put the kettle on and crouched down to open the stove. He added wood to the embers and poked the flames to life before securing the small door with a window of smoke-stained glass.

"Tori?" he called out as he got up to make tea.

Silence.

He stilled, suddenly sensing the emptiness of the cabin. A small kick of panic went through him.

"Tori, where are you?" He pushed open her bedroom door. The room was empty. Her jacket and boots were gone.

"*Tori!*" She wasn't in the bathroom.

Panic tightened.

She was gone. It was cold out, snowing. Why would she leave? Where would she go? He told himself to focus. Before he started hearing voices in his head again. It was probably fine. He'd overslept—in fact he'd slept as if drugged. His health was worsening. He knew it. It was creeping up on him now. She might have gone up to the lodge house in search of breakfast or company.

Then he saw the newspaper spread out across the table. It was open on the page with the editorial speculating about the similarities between the Birkenhead and Watt Lake murders. He was convinced he'd tucked that paper onto the bookshelf. He flung open the cabin door, his gaze darting across the grassy bank, down to the water, the dock. Snowflakes swirled in frosty air. Cloud was low, the sky dark. Mist sifted through trees.

"Tori!"

The campsite. That man she'd been talking to—she could have gone there! He checked his weapons, laced on his boots, grabbed his jacket, and rushed out into the cold.

Voices called after him, swirling and laughing in the snow.

What have you done? What were you thinking, bringing her here? He's got her! He took her! You brought her right to his feet ... it was he who lured you ...

He spun around, hands going to his ears. "Tori! Where are you?"

He began to run, tripped, stumbling forward as he fought to regain his balance. He had to hold it together. He had to reach his truck, get around to the campsite.

———

Cole drove down the main street of Clinton, searching for the Forbes Development Corp building. He'd managed to call Forbes on his cell once he neared town. Forbes said he'd be at his office even though it was Sunday, the day before Thanksgiving—a day many families chose to cook a big celebratory meal together. Snow was just starting to fall in town, which was at a far lower elevation than the ranch. The street was blazoned with orange and blue banners declaring *Forbes for Mayor—vote jobs, industry, growth, tourism.*

He found the building on the corner of Poplar and Main and pulled into an off-street parking space next door, beside the old museum, which was filled with gold rush memorabilia. Displayed in the window of the Forbes Development Corp offices were slick artist's renderings of a major development. Cole left his father's Dodge parked on the side of the street, and, shrugging deeper into his jacket against the cold, he walked up to the windows. Another jolt of surprise ran through him when he made sense of the images and renderings. They depicted a high-end boutique hotel and a private plastic surgery clinic right on the shores of Broken Bar Lake where the campsite now lay. Clustered around the main clinic building were patient "cottages." There was another building marked as a spa, another as a fine dining restaurant, another as a gym. He whistled through his teeth. This was massive.

Literature beneath the renderings detailed a private clinic that would attract "guests" from around the world who could fly in, or drive, to seek discreet "treatment" in the "clean Cariboo country air" where they could thereafter recuperate in the privacy of their cottages. "Medical tourism" was the catchphrase. There would be horseback trail rides, swimming, birding, guided hikes, and in winter there would be sleigh rides, snowshoeing, and cross-country skiing for those who desired. A shard of irritation sliced through him.

He moved to the next window, which displayed the rest of his family's ranch carved into long estates of several acres each, some with lakefront, some with lake views. Prices for the smallest parcels of acreage started in excess of one million.

What the fuck had Jane gotten him to sign on the dotted line for? *This*? His father would have a heart attack if he saw this shit. Was Forbes already securing deposits for land that was not his to sell?

He pushed open the glass door to Forbes Development Corp. The interior was plush in comfortable tones of blue. His next shock was recognition of the woman at the reception desk.

"*Amelia?*" he said.

She looked up, smiled, then her eyes went wide, and she lurched to her feet.

"Cole? My God, I . . . How *are* you? What are you doing back here?" Her cheeks pinked. "Heavens, I can't believe it. I've read all your books. Seen your movies."

As she was talking, Forbes came out of a door behind her desk. He stalled dead in his tracks. "Good Lord. It's McDonough.

In the flesh." A flicker of something sharp chased through his eyes, but it was followed by an easy smile with a row of whitened teeth as he came around the reception desk.

"How are you, man?" He reached out and clasped Cole's hand with his right, placing his left on Cole's forearm. "Good to see you."

"Clayton," Cole said as he glanced at Amelia—the woman he and Clayton Forbes had once tussled over in the barn. The first woman Cole had ever kissed. And the body language that passed between Amelia and Forbes did not escape his notice. Old-history dynamics were still at play. And it told Cole these two still had something going on. His gaze went to Forbes's wedding band. He noted Amelia did not wear a ring. He wondered why she was here, working alone with Forbes on a Sunday.

"You better come into my office," Forbes said, holding his arm out, leading the way. His suit was slick, a slate gray with faint pinstripes, ice-blue dress shirt, red tie. Pointed designer shoes.

A large flat-panel television was recessed into a shelving unit along the left wall of his office. The television was on mute and tuned to the news channel. It showed satellite images of the storm closing in. A ticker tape of text across the bottom informed of an official storm warning. Behind the desk was expensive-looking art showing a ranch scene with rolling gold hills.

Forbes indicated one of the leather chairs in front of his desk. "Please, take a seat." He closed the door, went around to his side of the massive, gleaming wood desk.

Cole remained standing. His gaze went to a framed photo on the desk of a blonde woman and two young kids. "Married?"

Forbes moistened his lips, and his gaze wavered, almost imperceptibly, toward the closed door behind which Amelia sat. It confirmed Cole's thoughts—Amelia had not become the bride. Just the mistress. He wondered which was the closer confidante to Forbes. He wondered why Amelia had settled for this.

"Indeed," Forbes said. "And loving it. How about you?"

"Never married."

"Look, about your call last night—" Forbes started to say,

"I'm not going to waste time on a preamble. I came in person to tell you there's no deal."

Forbes's smile remained unchanged, but his complexion paled slightly and his eyes flattened. Cole understood why—judging from the display in his storefront windows, and from the election banners blaring down the main street, Forbes had a helluva lot riding on a Broken Bar Ranch sale. Cole even felt a small twinge of guilt. He had, after all, signed papers helping pave the way. Then he thought of Olivia. And his father. And the land itself. He thought of the McDonough legacy, his ancestors who'd homesteaded the place.

"Look, I have a legal document signed by both you and Jane— an official letter of intent to enter into good-faith negotiations with me on the sale of Broken Bar Ranch if and when it comes into your hands. It's as good as a legal option on the property. Something I have taken to the bank."

"I'm sorry. I'm retracting my end of the bargain."

He laughed, then his smile died. "You can't do that."

"You can't do what you're doing—preselling a development on land that is not even yours?"

"Yet."

"Even if we did sell to you, Broken Bar Ranch falls into the Agricultural Land Reserve. By law it must be used for farming. It cannot be zoned for commercial development. The back half of the property is also environmentally sensitive wetland. I don't see how you can even begin—"

"I have assurances from the minister of the environment that the rezoning process for the property will be smooth. Approval to remove Broken Bar from the ALR will be forthcoming, as will impact assessment approvals from all the necessary departments for rezoning."

Cole stared at him, a darkness growing in his gut. "And how can any minister give that kind of assurance without the proposal first going through the assessment studies, appeals, public hearings, due process?"

Forbes leaned his knuckles on his desk, barely masking the fact that his patience was wearing thin. "This is in *your* interests, McDonough. Don't push it. You stand to reap a bonanza, and the way Jane tells it, you wanted nothing to do with that run-down hovel of a ranch to begin with."

Cole inhaled deeply. "You'd best start damage control," he said quietly. "Because that development is not going to happen on my watch."

"I'll fight you in court over it. I'll break you. Mark my words."

Cole gave a dry smile. "You might have to wait a long while to get your day in court, because as things stand right now, the ranch will go in trust to my father's manager."

"Not if she leaves. If she leaves, it reverts to you and Jane."

"So you *do* know about the changes to the will?"

Forbes's eyes narrowed.

"Who told you?"

"That's immaterial. If—"

"Was it Adele Carrick? Or Tucker?"

Forbes's brows lowered farther, and his eyes turned to flint. A muscle pulsed in his neck.

Cole leaned forward, palms pressing flat on Forbes's desk. "Because that's the other thing I came to say. If you're trying to scare Olivia off the ranch with those stunts, if you or your people set one foot on McDonough land, or you go anywhere near Olivia, you're dead, mate. I'm going to see that you're buried by the full brunt of the law on this one."

Forbes raised his chin, looked blank. "What stunts?"

Something shifted in Cole. "Stalking. Leaving . . . things."

"What in the hell are you talking about?" He truly looked ignorant.

On the wall to Cole's left, the television news segued to the Birkenhead murder. A banner across the top said the broadcast was coming live from a police press briefing. A female cop took a podium in front of a bank of microphones. A photo of a middle-aged woman came up in a window to the left of the screen. They'd identified the victim. The name underneath the photo said *Mary J. Sorenson.* Cole's attention was momentarily distracted from Forbes. There was something familiar about the woman. The ticker tape underneath was saying that the photo had been shot in Arizona by her husband and sent to her children via cell phone. It was the last picture taken of her alive.

Cole frowned, something faint ticking against his memory. Mary Sorenson looked average enough. Squarish face. Nice eyes. Healthy and tanned. Brown hair flecked with gray framed her face. She was dressed in a black tank top, with a soft scarf in tones of gold and yellow and bronze around her—

"I don't know what the fuck game you think you're playing, but hear this—if your father leaves his ranch, even in trust, to Olivia West, Jane and I will drag her backward through the courts. And I *will* see to it that you are held to your end of the deal."

Cole was filled with a sudden sense of urgency as his attention flared back to Forbes. *If Clayton Forbes was not messing with Liv's head, someone else was. And she was out there alone on that ranch with the storm coming.*

"I've said my piece. And I'm telling you, back out now of your own volition and start damage control before I talk to the press about my intentions *not* to sell the ranch. That'll give your investors serious cold feet. And journalists will have a field day when I tell them about the prime acreages you've promised in government kickbacks for rezoning approvals of environmentally sensitive land."

Forbes paled. "Who told you?"

He snorted. "That, my friend, was a good guess. Thank you for confirming it. Quit while you can still avoid prison." He turned and made for the door.

"That a threat, McDonough?"

"A promise." He reached for the door handle.

"This is some stupid-ass vendetta—is that what this is about?" Forbes called after him. "You're trying to take me down because of that day in the barn. It's about that truck. You couldn't let that go, could you? You've gone and addled your brain like some wasted old fool in Cuba, and this is all you've got left?"

Cole stilled, hand on doorknob. He swung around.

Forbes's face had turned thunderous, his skin stretched tight across his cheekbones, his shoulders rigid. He had the look of a coiled serpent. Lethal, as his gaze pinned Cole's.

"What truck?" Cole said, voice low, level, cold.

Forbes quickly began to backpedal at Cole's pulsating intensity. "Look, whatever Tucker and I did, it's buried history. Let it go."

Cole surged across the room, reached over the desk, and grabbed the man's collar and tie. He hauled Clayton Forbes halfway across the desk.

"*What truck?*" he growled. "What did you and Tucker do?"

Forbes's gaze darted around the room, his face going puce. "You can't prove anything now—"

"Did you and Tucker Carrick mess with my truck that day?! Did you touch the brakes? Was this because of Amelia?"

"Unhand me. Or I'll call the cops." His hand fingered along the desk, reaching for his phone.

"Oh, I'd like the cops to hear this. That you and Tucker Carrick sabotaged the brakes on my truck, right before they failed and I lost control on that bend and drove my mother and kid brother into the river!"

"You going to tell them you'd been drinking, too?"

Cole shook inside.

Tucker had always done Forbes's bidding, since school. He'd lived in the shadow of Cole on the ranch. It was likely him who'd told Forbes about his father's new will, about Olivia getting the ranch.

"Is he still your grunt? He messing with Liv now, too? Trying to scare her off Broken Bar so he can get the piece of the land he thinks he and his mother deserve? Is that what you've promised him?"

Another photo came up on the television screen to the right of the cop behind the podium. An image of a man with close-cropped white-blond hair. Cole barely registered it, his attention focused solely on Forbes. Yet a subterranean stirring started deep somewhere in his brain.

"Where is Tucker now?" he said through his teeth.

Forbes laughed. "What're you going to do? Go after him? Kill him? Beat him to a pulp? Bury me? Maybe you should, huh? After all these years. All that blame carried on your shoulders. For little Jimmie and your mother. Drowned in an icy river."

Rage blinded him. Almost.

It took extreme power to hold back. It was what Forbes wanted—for Cole to lose it, assault him. Cross the line of law. He was goading him, and Cole couldn't be certain it wasn't a lie, that he wasn't being set up. He held Forbes's gaze for several long beats, then slowly released him. Forbes scrabbled back over his desk, pulling his tie straight. Fury crackled in his face.

"You're a dead man," Cole whispered. Then added, "Metaphorically."

He stepped out of the office, closing the door behind him.

"Cole?" Amelia said as she got up. He brushed past her and pushed out the glass door into the cold. The entire framework upon which his world had been constructed was on its ear.

Was it possible? That he had not been totally responsible for the truck accident? For his mother's and brother's deaths? Or was Forbes just messing with his head, trying to goad him?

Snow was coming down heavily now. Big fat flakes. It was settling on his father's black Dodge. He thought of Olivia. Urgency mounted. He needed to get back. To her. To his father. Because another thought niggled him as he climbed back into the Dodge and fired the ignition. What if it *was* Tucker scaring Olivia? Doing Forbes's dirty work? Could he do worse? Kill?

People had died for lesser things than a multibillion-dollar medical tourism development, and the political careers that hinged on it.

———

Olivia galloped through the snow on Spirit, heading around the west end of the lake on her return to the lodge. There'd been no one at the campsite. Cabins were all cleared out. Winter had come, settling a white hand over the dry grasses, red berries, gold leaves. And for a while the wind had stilled, and everything felt frozen and eerily silent and isolated.

Mist rose off the black water as Spirit's hooves thundered on packed earth, and the mare's snorts crystallized white in the air. Olivia felt focused, emotionless. It was as if she'd come over the mental hump of autumn and now had clear direction into the new season, and little was going to sway her.

Her next step was to stable Spirit. Already she'd spoken to Brannigan. Her mare would be in good hands. She had enough time to say farewell to Myron and hit the logging road before too much snow had accumulated. She could be in Clinton two hours from now, where she'd refuel her truck, then drive southeast for the Rocky Mountains. The bad weather was heading north. If she was lucky it would still be dry to the east. She could make Alberta by nightfall.

She caught sight of tracks in the fresh skiff of snow. Smallish footprints. And bigger ones alongside. She reined in Spirit, an eerie sensation crawling over her skin. The bigger boot prints seemed to be about the same size and stride as the ones that had followed her when she'd laid a trail for Ace to follow. The same size as had led into the swamp through the cut fence. She looked up, could see no one. But the tracks were fresh, given the falling snow.

She detoured her horse, following the prints toward the water. The big prints veered abruptly off into the trees while the smaller prints continued to the dock in the isolated bay at the west end of the lake. As Olivia rounded a clump of brooding evergreens that grew tightly along the shoreline, she saw a small dark shape huddled at the very end of the long, narrow dock that jutted out into the lonely west bay. She squinted through the mist and softly falling crystals.

Tori?

Olivia's gaze chased quickly across the dock, water, treeline. No sign of anyone else. Perhaps the big prints had been Tori's father's tracks. She dismounted, tethered Spirit, made her way along the dock, foreboding sinking into her bones.

"Tori? Is that you?"

The girl turned.

Olivia felt a gut punch. The child's face was ashen in this light, her eyes black holes. She'd been crying.

"What's the matter? Where is your father?"

"Sleeping."

Olivia lowered herself to her haunches beside Tori, who was sitting with her jeans in wet snow, feet dangling over the side of dock, boots almost in the water.

"What's the matter?"

She picked at a thread along the end of her jacket. Snowflakes grew thicker, prettier. They settled on the dock, on Tori's black hair, on her jacket.

"Come, let me take you inside. We can ride on Spirit. Would you like that?"

No response.

"Tori, talk to me."

Wind gusted, sending a dervish of swirling snow over the water. It was beginning to settle fast now. Olivia's window to get out was closing. Fast.

"Please, let me take you inside and get you something warm to drink. I'll find your dad. Was he with you earlier?"

"He's not my dad."

"Excuse me?"

Tori's lip wobbled. "I think it's all a lie. They were lying . . ." Emotion pooled suddenly and glimmered in her green eyes.

"Who was lying?"

Tori reached down the front of her jacket and pulled out an e-reader in a pink cover.

"I was reading my mom's last work in progress. She was a writer. She wrote ripped-from-the-headlines fiction. Thrillers and mysteries. Dark books. She didn't let me read them, but I got them out of the library. She was writing this one before the accident. She dedicated it to me. It says in the front, *For my dear Tori, a story for the day you are ready.* I . . ." Her voice hitched. She bit her lip so hard it drew blood. Shock twitched through Olivia.

"I don't understand, Tori."

She sniffed and swiped at her eyes. "I think . . . I think . . . in the story . . . in the hospital. Up in Watt Lake . . ."

"Watt Lake? Your mother set a story in Watt Lake?"

She nodded.

"What's it about?"

"The character in the story . . . it's not her baby. It's the baby of a terribly bad man. A serial killer. And the victim's husband doesn't want to look at it . . . and . . . she gives it away, up for adoption. Because she doesn't want to look at it either. She's confused. The journalist brings the baby to the mother's bed in an incubator thing . . . and she, the mother holds it, and breast-feeds it, and asks God to help it. And then the journalist goes to her husband, who's a cop, and says she wants to adopt it. I don't think it's fiction. My dad was the cop there."

Olivia went cold. Her memory spiraled violently back to the day she'd lain in the hospital bed and Melody had brought her baby daughter in. And she'd held the infant in her arms.

"A cop? *Where?*"

"Watt Lake. He was the staff sergeant, like in the book. And my mom was a journalist before she turned to fiction. All the stuff—it could be about them. And . . . I'm scared because they told me I was born in Fort Tapley."

Olivia couldn't breathe. The curtain of snow and mist grew thicker, time leaking away.

"What . . ." She cleared her throat. "What was her name? Your mother, what was her full name?"

Startled at her intensity, Tori glanced sharply up, met her eyes, and said, "Melody. Melody Vanderbilt. She used her maiden name for her job."

Olivia's stomach lurched bile up her throat. Sweat prickled over her skin. Snow wet her face. Confusion tightened around her, closing, encircling, trapping, time folding in on itself, inside out.

"Did . . . did the victim in the story have a name?"

"Sarah Baker, like the lady in my father's newspaper." Tori held Olivia's gaze, wide-eyed, vulnerable. "Sarah's baby . . . the journalist and cop adopted her and took her up to Fort Tapley. But it *has* to be fiction, right? My mom was just drafting this thing. She always worked in drafts. She used ideas, true things from the headlines, from reality, and she braided them with fiction—that's what all the write-ups and reviews always said. She'd use facts as a base, and then wove her own stories around them. That's what she was doing, right? She was using that situation in Watt Lake as inspiration."

"*Show me.*"

Tori flinched slightly, then tentatively held out her e-reader.

With shaking hands Olivia brushed snow from the cover

and opened the e-reader. Sliding the "On" button, protecting the screen with her body, she began to read.

> It started, as all dialogues do, when a path crosses that of another. Whether in silence, or greeting, a glance, a touch, you are changed, irrevocably, by an interaction. Some exchanges are as subtle as the touch of an iridescent damselfly alighting on the back of your hand. Some are seismic, rocking your world, fissuring into your very foundations and setting you on a new path. That moment came for Sarah when he first entered the store.
>
> The bell chimed, and in came a cool gust of air. Sensing something unusual had entered, she glanced up.
>
> From across the store his eyes locked on to her face—the kind of full-on stare that made her stomach jump. Ordinarily she'd smile, offer a greeting, but this time she instinctively averted her gaze and continued with her bookkeeping. Yet she could sense his eyes on her, rude, brazen . . .

Her words. Her story. The one she'd told Melody Vanderbilt.

Olivia's gaze shot to Tori. She stared, her mind wheeling. Tori's green eyes looked back. Mossy green, like her own. Blue-black hair, the color of Sebastian's . . .

"You're Melody's daughter?"

Tori nodded, confusion in her eyes.

"You're an only child, their only child?"

She nodded again.

"Melody was married to a *cop*?"

Tori swallowed, fear darkening into her eyes. She started to shiver. "My dad is—was a cop."

"Not a consultant, for security?"

"He lied."

Olivia's voice came out hoarse, thick. "When is your birthday, Tori? How old are you?"

"I'll be twelve on July seventeenth."

Twelve years ago, on this day, the day before Thanksgiving, Sarah Baker was taken by the Watt Lake Killer. Their baby was born the following summer. A hot muggy day in July.

July 17 . . .

———

He watched close by from the trees. The woman and the child's words carried clear like crystal on the cold, fragile air, through the stillness of snow. That child was his. It was her likeness that had brought to mind his mother as he'd watched them in the boat earlier. He could see it fully now, in his mind's eye, in his memory of the old photographs that his mother kept of her youth. Her straight black hair.

The cop had raised *his* baby. And now the cop had brought her back here, to her mother's arms.

A sickening oiliness slicked through his belly and bowels. Had he been lured here by the cop? Was the Internet adoption site a ruse? Was the cop using Sarah Baker as the lure? Why?

To catch him?

For how long had the cop been playing this game? Since he'd taken in the child?

Gamos. A lure has to be something important to the prey . . .

Adrenaline thrummed into his blood. Excitement. Thrill. Finally, a real hunt. A fitting challenge to the very end. All were on stage now. As if by supernatural design, all paths predestined to lead here.

So where was the cop now? Watching? From the shadows?

Awareness crackled through him as he listened for the telling crunch of footfalls in scrub, dead leaves breaking under the snow, the action of a weapon. He could sense an ambush. He swallowed slowly. He had to move now. The snow was getting thicker, closing them in. He must act while it would cover his tracks, and while he could still get out.

He stepped from the shadows and started down the long, narrow dock toward the two of them perched on the end.

It was time.

Time to go home.

———

As Cole drove the return trip to Broken Bar his mind reeled with the possibility that he had not been responsible for the faulty brakes. Snow was already an inch or two thick on the logging road as he crossed the halfway point between Clinton and Broken Bar Ranch. The wipers battled to carve arcs into the snow accumulating on his windshield. He could feel the tires beginning to slip every now and then.

His mind circled back to the conversation with Forbes in his office, then further back to the fight in the barn with Tucker and Forbes all those years ago.

Tuck and Forbes had driven up from Clinton together to confront Cole over Amelia. The animosity between Cole and Forbes had been thick over the rest of the summer and into winter. They'd had two more physical dustups; the last, right after Christmas, had been particularly violent. Forbes had jumped him, and Tucker had provided backup. That time Cole had broken one of Forbes's bones. Tucker had lived with his mother and father in one of the ranch houses at the time. He could have gotten into the barn anytime and tampered with the brakes. Cole smacked the Dodge steering wheel with his hand and swore.

He *knew* he couldn't have screwed up the brakes. He'd been forced to doubt himself. Then to finally believe he'd killed his mother and brother. That some sick twist of fate had saved him while it took them.

Sure, he'd had a few drinks, but at the time he'd felt fine. He wouldn't have driven his mom and Jimmie if he'd thought he'd had too many. Still . . . while it might explain the brakes, it didn't excuse him. But it made him ask, *what if.* What if the brakes had been fine?

Can't prove a thing now . . .

All these years, and it could have been sabotage? Because of a girl? All that grief, the loss, the guilt, his family dynamics crumbling as a result—Cole's father sinking into a bitter shell. Cole and Jane becoming who they were now, the ranch business failing.

Anger fisted Cole's hands around the wheel as he negotiated a curve on a steep decline. Wheels slid sickeningly sideways at the bottom of the turn. His heart faltered. He steered into the slide, tapping brakes, controlling the skid. He brought the truck back in line just before the edge of a ditch.

Focus.

His worry now was that Tucker might be handling not only Clayton Forbes's questionable investment deals but that he could be involved in scaring Olivia. Who else could it possibly be? If Cole was a betting man, he'd put money on the fact that if things went to shit, Tucker would also take the fall as Forbes's scapegoat.

This man—these men—were dangerous.

The truck radio segued from a country-and-western tune into a news jingle followed by a weather alert. The first wave of the storm was hitting the plateau. There could be several feet of snow before nightfall. Cole's tires slid again. If he'd left any later, he'd have been stuck back in Clinton.

The news switched to the Birkenhead murder.

"At a press briefing this morning, police released the identity of the victim, Mary J. Sorenson, aged fifty-three, a resident of Blaine, Washington." Cole reached over and turned up the volume, his mind going to the image of Mary Sorenson that he'd seen on the television in Forbes's office.

"We now have additional breaking news to bring you. CBC has learned that Mary's husband, Algor Sorenson, crossed the US border into Canada alone in the couple's AdventureCaper camper and trailer at the Peace Arch crossing five days ago using a NEXUS card. The camper is mounted on a gray Ford F-150 pickup truck with a long bed. Police have released their Washington State plate number, and are asking anyone who sees the camper, or Sorenson, to immediately call 911."

Cole's mind raced as the anchor read out the plate number.

Sorenson. The name was vaguely familiar. Something about the woman's image had also seemed familiar. AdventureCaper camper . . . His heart stopped. He negotiated another bend, his body going hot. What was the name of the guy Olivia had checked in the other day? He'd had an AdventureCaper camper mounted on a gray Ford F-150. Long box. But his truck had BC plates. Cole had a near-total-recall memory for these things—honed from years of journalistic, on-the-spot observation in tense situations. Then it hit him.

The ham radio plate on the back—it had been issued in Washington State.

Snow came down in a heavy curtain, and he was forced to slow as he headed into another bend on the logging road. His heart jackhammered suddenly.

The scarf.

That was what had felt familiar! The scarf around Mary Sorenson's neck in that photo taken in Arizona looked identical to the one he'd seen in Olivia's cabin last night. It was the scarf she said had been dropped on her tracks by someone she'd thought was following her. The scarf of a slaughtered woman. A woman whose body had been displayed with similar signature mutilation to the Watt Lake victims.

All of a sudden there was nothing that felt innocent or coincidental about the newspaper with her name on it, the lure inside, the berries. The scarf. The scrawl on her bedsheets. Nothing.

He reached for his phone in his pocket, hit 911. He could recall the number on the ham operator's plate. If the cops had that, they could look it up, see if the amateur radio operator's license was registered to the Sorensons from Blaine, Washington.

But he had no bars, no reception. He cursed. He was already out of Clinton cell-tower range. He was over halfway to Broken Bar. Going back to town would take too long, and he might not even make it in this storm now. He hit the gas. He had to reach Olivia, stat.

He drove fast along the dangerous logging roads, snow coming down heavily, the dead pines spearing like ugly, blackened skeletons into the mist.

———

"Why did your father bring you to Broken Bar? Why *now*?" Olivia demanded, her voice coming out low, urgent, as she thought of the recent murder, the fact Burton had left her the newspaper, the lure. Trickier, more painful and poignant emotions surged under her sense of biting urgency. Her child. Her baby girl. Right here in front of her. After all these years. It all felt as fragile as delicate glass.

"Why did he bring you fishing, Tori?"

"He's dying," Tori said quietly. Snowflakes melted on her hair, face, lashes. "He's got a brain tumor, melanoma. He . . . he said we had to come here and finish something. He told me they can operate and fix him . . . but I don't believe it now."

A creak and sudden motion of the dock made them both look up.

Approaching them was a black figure materializing through the gauzy gray snow and mist.

His face was obscured beneath a ball cap, his jacket hunched up around his neck, his hands deep in his pockets. He blocked their escape route off the narrow dock. Irrational panic, claustro-phobia whipped through Olivia.

Then came relief as she recognized the man. Algor Sorenson from the campsite.

She got to her feet. Flustered, she pushed wet hair back from her face. "I thought you'd left," she called out to him. "There was no one at the site when I went round."

"Olivia, hi," the man said as he neared. "I've been looking for you. You have a German shepherd, right?"

Ice dropped like a stone through her stomach. "Yes. Why?"

"Is he missing?"

"I . . . *why?*"

"My wife and I saw one chasing something along the trail into the marshland. We heard a yelp, and then crying."

Ace.

Where was Ace?

CHAPTER 22

"Where exactly did you see him last?" Olivia demanded, adrenaline stampeding through her. She'd left Ace outside her cabin, snuffling about in the willow scrub along the shore. Ordinarily Ace wouldn't wander far. He'd be waiting on her deck, on his raised bed outside the door.

"My wife and I were hiking through the otter marsh—a last walk before we headed out. We're all packed." He dug his hands deeper into his pockets, looked up at the sky. "It's really coming down now."

"Where?!" she demanded.

"Near the marsh trailhead. We heard excited barking. Then we saw what looked like a German shepherd chasing after something. Then a cry. Whining. I think he might have gone over the bank somewhere on the east side. We went in a little way, but couldn't see. We need to leave now, but I wanted to find you and let you know."

Shit. Ace's eyesight. She'd been worried about something like this.

"Will you show me?"

"We're worried about getting out now before it's too thick and—"

"Please."

He looked conflicted.

"Tori," she said quickly, putting her arm around the child's shoulders. "Where is your father now?"

"In the cabin. I left him sleeping."

"Okay, you're coming to the lodge with me. I'm going to leave you there with Myron while I go find Ace. Okay?"

"I want to help," she said, gripping Olivia's arm, a desperation swelling into her green eyes. Her eyes. Her child. Olivia's throat closed in on itself. She looked deep into Tori's eyes.

"No. I want you with Myron. Algor can help me." She glanced up at the tall man, his ball cap shading his eyes, snow settling along the bill. "You show me where Ace is," she said. "You can wait for just a few minutes before driving out. It'll be fine."

He glanced up at the sky again, then at the deck with the settling snow.

"*Please,*" she said. "If you could just point the way. I'll only be a minute. I need to get Tori to the lodge."

"Sure. Okay. I'm parked around the trees, all set to leave. I'll let my wife know." He glanced at Tori. "I'll wait at the trailhead for you."

———

Myron pulled the piece of paper closer to him and tried to put his pen to it. He was attempting to write to Cole, to say good-bye. To say he was sorry for never stopping trying to punish his boy. To say he loved him, and that he forgave him. But he doubled over in excruciating pain, sweat thick on his brow in spite of the cold snow and wind coming in through the wide-open window.

Shivering, he dropped the pen and grasped for his pills. It was time. He had to do it now before they took him into a hospital, before he became incapacitated and they hooked him up to machines, and he'd be unable to say he forgave his son. If he took some pills first, he might stop shaking long enough to write his note. He'd opened the window in an effort to let Grace in. He ached to feel her presence on the cold wind. He wanted to feel her arms calling out to him.

"Myron!"

Shock, confusion raced through him. He glanced up. It was Olivia. With the Burton child. Both wet. Standing in the doorway to the library.

"Myron—what's going on?" She rushed over to him.

"Are you okay?" Her hands were on him, helping him. "You want medication?"

He nodded.

She opened the bottle, tapped two pills into her palm, put them in his mouth, and brought a glass of water to his lips. He swallowed. "Another . . . two . . . please."

She hesitated, looking deep into his eyes. Then she tapped out another two and helped him drink them down.

"Tori," she said briskly. "Can you shut that window?" She crouched down, hands on his knees. The beautiful Olivia he'd come to love. He wanted to touch her face. Couldn't move from pain.

"I *need* you, Myron. I need your help. Can you help me?"

Something in her features pulled him into sharper focus. He slid his gaze to the girl. She stood by the window. Shivering. White-faced. Something was wrong. Very wrong.

He nodded. He could feel the painkillers kicking in. Maybe this time they'd just touch sides. Maybe he could hold on.

"Listen to me—I need to go find Ace. Before the snow gets too thick. I think he's gone down a bank and can't get back up somewhere along the marsh trail. I want you to watch Tori for me. Just be with her."

She shot a glance at the child, then back to Myron. Clearly she was worried about what he'd been trying to do with the pills.

"She's got something I want you to read, Myron. Something important. Please, read it if you can. And just be here with her. Do not leave her—do not let anyone into the house, understand?" She hesitated. "Not even her father."

"What's going on, Olivia? What's wrong with Burton?"

"He's not well. Please, I've got to go. Just keep the doors locked. Keep her safe. And you stick around until I get back, you hear me?

We'll talk later."

And she was gone, just him and the dark-haired girl staring at him. Alone in the house.

"You okay?" he said.

She didn't reply.

"What have you got for me to read?"

"He's not my father."

"Who's not? Burton?"

"My father is the Watt Lake Killer."

Myron's jaw dropped. He gathered himself. "What makes you say that?"

She held out a pink thing.

"What's that?"

"E-reader."

———

Olivia galloped on Spirit to the marsh trailhead. No one was there.

"Algor!" she called out into the snow, her mare stomping as she reined her in.

Not a sound. She saw boot tracks leading into the trail. They were quickly becoming obscured by snow.

"Ace!" she yelled, following the tracks into the marsh. She whistled, then called again. "Ace! Where are you, boy?" She kept her eyes trained on the tracks, going deeper and deeper into the narrowing, twisting trail through tall moss-draped trees. The ground was marshy here. A beaver had dammed the stream. There was lots of deadfall.

"Over here!" She heard his voice suddenly. "He's this way!"

She stopped, listened as she tried to ascertain which direction the voice had come from. Mist and snow swirled. Spirit snorted softly, edgy beneath her.

"This way!" She heard Algor's voice again. "I found him! He's over here! Down the bank! Not moving."

Panic, the worst kind of fear, speared through her. Olivia kicked Spirit forward into a trot, bending her head to avoid branches drooping low with snow. The trail widened a little, and she kicked up speed, going too fast for conditions, driven by a sheer desperation at the thought of losing her Ace. It hit like a bolt.

Across her neck.

Rope.

Olivia gasped as she was flung backward off her horse.

She landed with a hard thud on her back, so hard she couldn't breathe, couldn't move. Pain and white pinpricks of light sparked through her brain, blackness swirling at the edges of her consciousness. Spirit fled through the trees.

It took a few moments before Olivia could wheeze in a breath. Her ribs felt like they might be broken.

Trying to understand what had just happened, she struggled to reach her arm over her body and to roll onto her side. She managed to edge onto her stomach, push herself up onto her hands and knees. Spirit had spooked off down the trail. All was silent around her.

She got onto one knee and reached for a branch to pull herself up when something cracked up the side of her head, so hard, with so much force she felt her ear rip from her skull. The blow reverberated through her nasal passages, her brain, sending a bitter taste of bile into her throat. Confusion swamped her. Hot wetness gushed down her neck. Pain was blinding. Dazedly, she put her hand to her ear. It was partly torn from the side of her head. Weakness buckled her knees. She fell forward, into the red blood pouring from her ear into the snow. She grasped out with her hand, tried to crawl, to pull herself forward.

But someone clutched a handful of her hair and pulled her by the hair to her knees. She screamed in pain, roots tearing from her scalp. Another blow cut across her face, crunching her nose. She gagged, spat out a glob of blood and spittle. Her assailant tossed her backward, onto her back.

A shadow loomed over her. Blurry.

Him.

Algor.

She reached up, tried to mouth the word *help*.

But he crouched down and pressed a gloved hand hard over her mouth. She choked, blood going down the back of her nose. She shook her head wildly, flailing with her arms, desperate for breath. He brought his face lower. Close. She stilled. His breath was hot on her face. She looked into his eyes, right into his eyes. They were no longer blue. They were the pale yellow eyes of a mountain cat. A hunter. A carnivore.

"Did you miss me, Sarah?" he whispered into her bloody ear, before raising his hand and delivering another blow to the side of her head. Her vision faded to black.

—

Cole drove under the wooden arch with the bleached bull moose antlers into the ranch. Heavily falling snow obliterated the view toward the lodge. Within the next twenty minutes or so, the roads would be impassable via ordinary vehicle.

As he approached the lodge, a horse came barreling out of the mist and across the road. Cole slammed on brakes, his heart speeding. Quickly he wound down his window. *Olivia's horse?* Saddled and riderless. It galloped up the ridge and disappeared into the shroud of snow and cloud along the crest.

Cole hit the accelerator and raced down the track to the lodge. He saw Olivia's truck parked near the trail through the alders that led to her cabin. A blue tarp covered the back. He hit the brakes, flung open the door, and raced over to her vehicle. He cast back a corner of the tarp. The bed of the truck was packed with her bags and other gear.

She was leaving.

What about the horse?

He ran down the path to her cabin. Her door was unlocked, her cabin empty.

Closets empty.

He spun around, saw a note tucked under a cactus pot. He grabbed it.

> . . . Thank you for everything. Thank you for showing me that I was enough. You gave me back a piece of myself, and I will take that with me wherever I go now. With all my heart I wish you well with Broken Bar. Look after it for me . . .

He swore. She *was* leaving. But her truck was still here, her riderless horse fleeing in fright. Something had happened.

He raced back to the Dodge, drove over snow-covered grass, and skidded to a stop right outside the lodge front entrance. He flung open his truck door, took two stairs apiece up onto the porch, and tried to open the door.

Locked.

Cole peered through the side window.

Dark inside.

He banged loudly on the door with the base of his fist. "Hello! Open up! It's Cole!" Nothing. Dry grasses from the harvest wreath on the deck behind him rustled and whispered in the breeze.

He banged again, harder, louder, another kind of fear biting, eating into his panic. *Was his father all right?*

"It's me, Cole! Open up!"

The sound of the dead bolt drawing back stopped him. The door edged open. He looked down. Through the crack, the dark-haired Burton kid peered up at him. She looked . . . wrong.

"Tori? Is . . . is Myron okay? Who's here?" He pushed the door open past her and stepped inside. He started up the stairs. "Dad!"

"In here, son. Library."

Tori rushed up the stairs and into the library after him.

"I just saw Olivia's horse! Where is she?" He stalled dead in his tracks as he registered the look on his father's face. "Where's Olivia?"

"She went on her horse to find Ace. In the otter marsh."

"What?"

"Ace fell down a bank in the marsh," Tori said. "The man from the campsite saw him go in there and came to tell us. He's helping Olivia find him."

Cole dropped to his haunches, grabbed her shoulders. Her jacket was sodden, her hair wet. "*What* man?!"

"Algor," said Tori. "The one with the wife."

Panic struck like a hatchet. Adrenaline exploded into his system.

———

Olivia came around and coughed blood and saliva out her mouth. It pooled, slimy and sticky under the side of her face, which was pressing into something soft. A mattress. Her body was being rocked about. Fading in and out of blackness, she realized she lay trussed up in the back of a moving camper—hands bound behind her, feet tied at the ankles. Her head was swallowed in pain. The mattress beneath the side of her face was hot and wet with her own blood.

Confusion swirled around and around in her brain. She tried to recall what had happened. She'd ridden into some kind of ambush. He'd tied a rope across the trail. She tried to recall his words as he'd dragged her by the hair through the snow to the waiting camper, which he must have driven into the marshlands via the cut fencing and deactivated track.

You weren't searching the Internet for your child, were you? It was the cop who brought me to you. Sublime, don't you think? Design. There is a pattern to all things in nature. What do you think of her—rather beautiful child we made . . .

She gagged again, spitting out more blood. He'd been in disguise. A chameleon. She hadn't seen it. But she could now—he was older and had grown gaunt. He'd dyed his hair white-blond and shaved it into a buzz. He'd shaped the Balbo beard and goatee. Blue contact lenses had disguised his pale eyes. The sociopath in him had smiled and conned them all.

But it was him. She knew it now. His smell. Those eyes that had haunted her darkest nightmares for over a decade. But how? How could it be him, when he was dead in that prison cell? She'd identified him in the lineup. It had been him without a doubt—the man who'd tortured her throughout an entire winter. His DNA matched the child in her stomach.

Oh, God, how could this be happening again? It was not possible.

It was him, and it wasn't.

It struck her suddenly.

The wife.

Her gaze darted around the interior of the camper. Did this belong to the dead woman? Had he assumed the identity of a dead husband? The credit card—it had read Algor Sorenson. What had happened to the real Algor Sorenson?

A true predator knows how to melt into his environment, Sarah. He knows how to blend, how to fashion a lure. Nature designs things this way. Even prey can camouflage itself in order to try and hide, isn't that so, Sarah?

The camper lurched and rolled. She was securely strapped to the bed. She felt the truck tires skidding. They fishtailed. The engine revved. They were going uphill. Along a rugged, unpaved road. He must have turned north along the logging road at the back end of the marsh. He was taking her north. Away from civilization. Storm closing in. Like last time. Tracks being wiped clean.

On the anniversary.

All over again. Back to the beginning.

Tears burned in her eyes. Pain rolled over her in suffocating waves. For over a decade she'd been running. She'd thought she was finally safe.

She'd thought it was over, but it was only just part of a contin-
uum still playing out.

Tori, her child. Gage Burton, a cop who'd adopted her baby, a
killer's baby. Why? Melody had said that she and her husband had
been trying to conceive. She never knew Melody's husband was a
cop. Melody had kept that from her. She felt betrayed. Consciousness faded in and out. She was unable to pull pieces of logic together.

She ran through events leading up to her attack in the marsh.
He'd lured her with Ace. Her eyes burned and adrenaline surged.
Had he killed her dog? Had he taken from her the most precious
thing in her life? Olivia struggled wildly against her bonds in
a spurt of frustrated panic. She tried to reach her belt with her
bound hand, before recalling he'd taken her sat phone. He'd put it
in his own pocket. He'd taken her knife.

Olivia rolled in and out of consciousness with the sickening,
yawing, nauseating sway and skid of the truck.

Would he keep her for another winter? Would he put her out
for another spring hunt?

She just didn't have the strength to fight it all over again . . .

———

Cole grabbed a shotgun from the gun safe, along with several
boxes of ammunition. Mind racing, he busted out the front door
and ran around the side of the house to the garage that housed the
snowmobiles—he'd seen them in there when he'd found his father's
Dodge earlier. As he neared the garage, he caught sight of the sev-
ered wires leading up the side of the wall behind the kitchen. He
stalled. His gaze shot up, following the cables to the roof. They led
to the sat dish. A sinister chill snaked through him. This had been
done purposefully. Had the same thing happened to the phone lines?

The phones had gone dead around the same time as the television set when they were having dinner. Around the same time someone had entered Olivia's cabin and scrawled that note onto her sheets.

The entire ranch had been cut off on the cusp of a major storm.

He slung the shotgun across his back and swung the garage doors open wide. He'd seen several jerry cans of fuel on the back shelves.

Hurriedly he gassed up one of the snow machines, tested the engine. It roared to life. He swung his leg astride the seat and released the throttle, feeding the machine juice. The tracks rumbled and scraped over concrete as he squeezed past a tractor, sending up sparks as he bumped along a metal frame and shot out of the doors and into the snow. He goosed the machine, kicking up speed, blinking into blizzard-like flakes as he raced toward the otter marsh—he hadn't had time to search for helmet and visor.

As he neared the narrow trailhead to the marsh where he and Jimmie used to play, time curved and warped and doubled back on itself. He swung the machine into the narrow trail and bombed along the dense, twisting track. Snow was thick here. It had covered whatever trace Olivia might have left. Then he caught sight of indentations that could have been made by hooves. He slowed to a stop, and cut the engine. He tried to control his breathing as he listened for a sound—anything that might show him direction.

He heard nothing.

Restarting the engine, he traveled a little farther into the densely wooded marsh, following what he believed could be horse tracks.

He cut the engine again, listened. This time he heard a sound. His heart jumped. He slowed his breathing further, waited. He heard it again, a yap—it came from the west, from a ravine tucked behind dense growth.

He dismounted and scrambled through the scrub to where the ground dropped down a sheer bank. He got onto his stomach, peered over.

Ace.

"Hey, buddy! Hang on. I'm coming!"

The dog barked.

He scrambled down the bank backward, using branches for support, dislodging small stones from beneath his boots, sliding through snow. He dropped down beside Ace. The dog licked him all over. Cole ran his hands over his fur, checked his legs, paws. He didn't seem hurt. Then he saw the bone lying in the snow with bits of raw meat still attached. He'd been lured here with food.

To trap Olivia?

"Where is she, boy? Can you help me find her? Can you show me her trail?" Cole glanced up the snowy bank, trying to figure out how to get Ace back up. He unhooked the shotgun from his back and removed his jacket before resecuring the gun.

He wrapped his jacket under Ace's belly, tying the sleeves around his body to fashion a harness.

"Okay, you ready, big guy? All you've got to do is hold steady while I haul you up, bit by bit."

Cole reached up for a branch and pulled himself up the angled slope, kicking the toes of his boots into the bank for leverage as he carefully lugged Ace up, bit by bit, with his other hand.

He scrambled over the lip of the slope, muscles burning, sweat mixing with melting snowflakes in his eyes. He helped edge Ace over. The dog scrambled wildly, then licked Cole's face as he untied the makeshift harness. The animal was stressed, panting.

"Okay, where's Olivia, boy? Find her!" he said as he shrugged back into his jacket and once again secured his shotgun across his back. "Find Olivia!"

Ace snuffled the air, nose held high, nostrils waffling as he tested air currents. His head jerked sideways, as if he'd been yanked by a bull ring in his nose. He scrambled through bushes, making a snorting sound. *He was on her trail.*

Cole ducked and pushed scrub and branches aside, going on hands and knees at times in order to clamber over roots and under deadfall. The dog was following scent wafting through air, not tracks, and scent didn't care about accessibility. Twigs snared in Cole's hair and slashed across his face. Dislodged snow dumped down his neck.

"Go, boy! Keep at it!" He was breathing hard now, bare hands frozen.

They popped out onto a trail. Ace stilled, then gave a weird whimper and lay down in the snow.

Horror filled Cole as he stepped out of the dense scrub into the trail.

Blood—great big gouts of it—covered the snow. It was surrounded by depressions, broken branches, drag marks. His heart beat a tattoo against his ribs, anxiety almost blinding him. He ran through the snow to the end of the trail, following what appeared to be deep prints and drag marks, more blood. Along the way were clumps of hair. Olivia's hair. Roots attached.

He reached the edge of the trail and burst out onto a wider track. It was the deactivated road that led from the cut fencing they'd seen earlier. Whoever had taken Olivia had been plotting this a while. Her assailant must have surveyed the scene, cut the fence, and driven a vehicle in here, parked it to wait while she was enticed into the marsh using the most treasured thing in her life as a lure—Ace.

The drag marks ended where fresh tire tracks gouged into snow and showed black dirt.

She'd been taken.

Where?

He knew that this disused track popped out at the back end of the marshland. From there a driver could either turn south on the logging road and head back toward Clinton. Or north onto lesser-used dirt roads that would eventually come out onto the interior highway to the north.

He ran back and mounted the snowmobile, calling Ace to heel. He helped Ace up onto the seat, where he wedged the dog between his legs and arms. "Hang on, buddy. I'm going to need you."

And if he found Liv, she would need her dog.

Cole goosed the throttle and bombed along the trail to where he'd seen the tire tracks. He followed the tire marks up to the logging road and stopped.

The vehicle with Olivia had turned north. He swore, overcome by a moment of indecision. He could chase those tracks for miles and miles through wilderness and ranch land, but he'd run out of gas long before a four-wheel-drive truck did. And then what? He had no form of communication on him, no way to call for help. He'd lose her.

There was only one option. He revved the gas, released the throttle, and gunned back around the lake toward the lodge.

Vancouver. Sunday around noon.

"You need to see this." The forensics computer tech motioned for Sergeant Mac Yakima to come over to where he was going through Gage Burton's system.

"Burton wasn't just using an alias on these adoption sites that he'd been trawling, he was using the name of a real woman." The tech sat back in his chair to show Yakima an image on his computer of an attractive, dark-haired woman with green eyes.

"Olivia West," the tech said. "She works as a fishing guide at Broken Bar Ranch. In his last message, Burton, posing as West, told a child apparently searching for her mother, that he—Olivia West—had surrendered for adoption a daughter born July 17 at Watt Lake. He gave West's address as Broken Bar Ranch. This photo is from the ranch website."

Mac Yakima stared at the photo, his blood going cold.

"Watt Lake," he whispered.

The tech glanced up at him.

"It's her. That photo. Olivia is Sarah Baker, the last victim of Sebastian George. The woman who put him away. Burton was obsessed with her and that case." He swore. "And Burton had to have known it, all this time, that she changed her name and was working up there. Jesus Christ. He's been tracking her and creating fake accounts in her name, pretending he's searching for the baby fathered by Sebastian George."

Martinello came up to his side, peered at the image of the tech's shoulder.

"Fuck," she whispered, then glanced at Yakima. "What in the hell is Burton trying to do?"

"I don't know," said Yakima as another officer approached the computer station.

"Sarge," said the officer, "we have two recent hits on Algor Sorenson's credit card. It was last used in Clinton at a sporting goods and logging supply store three days ago to buy duct tape, a skinning knife, and what appears to be fly-tying equipment. It was used before that at the Broken Bar Ranch and Campsite about an hour north of Clinton. And we have records showing the card was used in Arizona, Nevada, Oregon, and Washington for food and drink items, colored contact lenses, hair dye, and several times to fulfill Algor Sorenson's prescription for sleeping pills."

Yakima swung to face Martinello. "Get the Clinton detachment on the line. We need to get someone out there stat. Put in a call for a helo."

"There's a major storm hitting the interior," she said.

"Place the call anyway. We'll be ready on standby."

Cole left the snowmobile parked outside the lodge and ran up the stairs. Ace followed. But as he was about to open the door, he saw a figure staggering toward the lodge through the mist and snow. He lurched over to the deck railing, raised the shotgun stock to his shoulder, peered down the barrel.

"Stop right there! One foot closer, I shoot."

Hands shot up into the air. "It's me—Burton. Gage Burton. I . . . I need your help." He stumbled forward onto hands and knees, crawled several feet through snow, then staggered back onto his feet.

Shock slaked through Cole. He lowered the weapon.

Burton wobbled drunkenly up to the deck. White-faced. Cheeks gaunt.

"What happened?" Cole demanded.

Burton pressed his hand to his temple, face contorting as if in great head pain. "It's . . . my fault. I . . . I lured him here. The Watt Lake Killer. He's on the ranch somewhere. I don't know where. He's got Tori."

"What do you mean, the Watt Lake Killer?" Cole's brain scrambled. The cops were looking for Sorenson, or possibly a man posing as Sorenson. "Sebastian George is dead."

"I always believed they got the wrong man. I—" He reached up and grabbed the deck railing from below, holding himself up. "I was the staff sergeant up at Watt Lake when Sarah Baker was taken. I believe they put away the wrong man. I've been hunting for him since. I lured him here, using Sarah. He's out there."

Urgency sliced through Cole. "But the proof—"

He shook his head. "Help me, please. He's got . . . Tori. She's Sarah Baker's child. God help me . . ." He fell into the snow.

Cole raced down the steps and hauled Burton up. He hooked Burton's arm over his shoulder, supporting his weight. "Can you make it to the stairs, can you make it inside?"

Burton nodded.

Cole assisted the man up onto the deck.

"Talk to me," he said. "How can you say they got the wrong man?"

"They buried something—the fact Sebastian couldn't read, which means he couldn't have written notes stuffed into the eye sockets."

"What notes?"

"Notes with literary quotes about hunting..." Burton struggled for breath. "It... was holdback evidence. Press never learned about it. Only core investigators and I knew. Never... made it to trial."

They reached the door.

"They wanted a clean conviction. They shut me up, shipped me out to Fort Tapley. My wife and I—we adopted Sarah Baker's baby, took her to Fort Tapley. I... I *knew* one day the real killer might come looking."

Cole leaned Burton against the wall. "You're telling me you kept her baby all this time as a lure? You wanted him to come back for the child, for its mother?"

"It's not like that—"

"What in the hell *is* it like?!"

Burton flinched.

"Tori's safe," Cole snapped. "She's inside with my father. But whoever you're hunting has got Olivia. And yes, I know she's Sarah Baker."

Burton closed his eyes. He was silent for a beat, as if saying a prayer of thanks for his daughter's life. Then he said, "How did he get Sarah?"

"Olivia. Her name is now Olivia. He lured her into the marsh using her dog. She's been hurt pretty bad, judging by the amount of blood on the trail. He's taken her in a vehicle, probably that truck and camper that was in the campground. He's gone north."

"At the first scent of snow..."

"What?"

Burton's eyes opened. "He always hunts right before a big snowfall. I know where he's taking her. He's going home, back to Bear Claw Valley. He's going to finish the job."

CHAPTER 23

"Where's Bear Claw, exactly?" Cole demanded.

"About sixty klicks northwest of Watt Lake, in Indian territory. Deep valley, other side of Pinnacle Ridge."

"Are you hurt, sick? What's going on with you?"

"I get headaches. I have a brain tumor. The episodes come and go in waves. I'm dying." He pushed himself off from the wall against which he'd been leaning. He swayed a moment, then managed to stand upright unassisted. "I need to see Tori."

Cole's gaze lasered the retired cop's. "You lured a killer using Olivia and your kid?"

He swallowed. "I made a pledge to Tori when she was a baby." His voice was thick, shaky. "I vowed to find justice, get this guy, make the world safer for her. When Tori's mother died, I had to do something—Tori was acting out, violent. I feared that when she learned who her father really was, after my death, she'd be all alone in the world. She'd think the blood of a violent sociopath ran through her." He stumbled forward, and Cole caught his arm, steadying him.

Gage took a deep breath, refocusing. "I . . . I needed her to meet her mother. I wanted her to see that she had a good half. A beautiful, kind, and just half. I needed her to see what else she *could* be. I also believed that once Sarah met her daughter . . ." His voice faltered. "What have I done?"

"You're fucked in the head, you know that?"

"I do know. I have been for a long time. Maybe longer than I realized."

Cole stared at the man. His brain spun. He glanced at the snow, the direction of the wind. In his mind he ran through the meteorological images he'd seen on television, the way the storm was moving. Could he risk it? Maybe once he got up, he could even outrun the worst of it. *If* he was lucky. He could also die, which was more likely.

For the first time in his life the thought of death terrified him—he didn't want to perish. Not this time. He wanted to survive to save Olivia. He wanted that goddamn second chance. For her. And himself. For this ranch. He wanted it like he wanted air to breathe.

"How certain are you that he—whoever he is—is going to Bear Claw?"

"Even a gut-shot deer goes home—he told Sarah that many times. She said so in the interviews I watched. This guy is all about the ritual of the hunt, the kill. He's going to want to finish his ritual where he started. Where he always kills. On First Nations land, preferably in his home territory. He's animal in that way."

He had to risk it. Doing nothing was worse than dying.

"You're coming with me," Cole said suddenly.

"Where?"

"We're taking the dog. We're going to Bear Claw. We're going to stop him."

"How?"

"My plane."

Burton glanced at the swirling snow. Worry tightened his face. There was fear in his eyes. "Tori?"

"She'll be safe here. You go get on the snowmobile. Take Ace. Wait for me. I need to tell my father where I'm going. I need to give him that ham operator's plate number in case he can get word out."

As he ran up the stairs to the library, Cole prayed to every god he could think of to protect Olivia from too much pain.

Hold on, Liv, just long enough for me to reach you. Hold on . . .

———

The Royal Canadian Mounted Police SUV turned off the highway from Clinton at the sign to Broken Bar Ranch. The officer driving struggled to navigate through the snow on the logging road, his tires slipping as four-wheel-drive action kicked in. They made it only 2.4 klicks in before the vehicle stalled in a drift. Snow was falling thicker than ever, cloud socked low over the forest canopy.

The four officers exited the SUV and took the two snowmobiles from the trailer hitched to the back of their vehicle. One officer called in their location and new ETA for the ranch as the others donned helmets, thick gloves. The coordinating officer pulled on his own helmet and swung his leg over the seat of one, tucking himself in behind the driver.

The four jetted along the logging trail, aiming for Old Man McDonough's ranch.

They were responding to a call from Sergeant Mac Yakima of the integrated homicide team investigating the Birkenhead slaying. The credit card of Algor Sorenson, husband of the Birkenhead victim, had last been used at the ranch. There were stark similarities between the Birkenhead slaying and the Watt Lake killings, and the ranch manager was Sarah Baker, the Watt Lake Killer's last victim. The one who got away.

Additionally, Detective Sergeant Gage Burton, one of IHit's own, recently retired, was possibly on the ranch. He was a key person of interest in the Birkenhead murder. He'd been the staff sergeant in Watt Lake at the time Sarah Baker had been abducted. Burton apparently believed against all evidence that the RCMP had put away the wrong man, and he might have been hunting him since. Medical professionals, according to Yakima, felt Burton could now be psychotic. And dangerous. It was unclear at this point how it was all connected, but Burton had his child with him. Clinton RCMP were advised to proceed with every caution.

—

Cole crouched down and took the kid's shoulders in his hands.

"You look after Myron, okay, Tori?" Cole knew Survival 101—caring for someone else in a life-threatening situation bettered your own odds a hundredfold. "Make him tea, something to eat. For yourself, too. Can you manage the kitchen?"

She nodded.

"Keep the doors locked. Keep putting wood on the fire. Anything you don't know, or need, you ask him, you hear?"

Her eyes were big and dry, her complexion wan. She nodded.

He hesitated. "And his pills, only two at the top of every hour, no more. Understand? Even if he gets mad, okay? This is important."

Because Myron needed to be here for Tori, too. He *needed* his father to hang on until he got back.

"Cole," Myron called from his chair.

Cole glanced up.

"You're only licensed for visual flying."

"Yep."

"It's not safe."

"We have to try."

His father's gray eyes lanced his from across the room. A beat of silence hung.

"I'm sorry," he said. "I was a shit dad. I'm sorry I couldn't let go, that I kept on trying to punish you."

Cole went over to his dad, dropped to his haunches, hand on the wheelchair armrest. He was about to tell his father that Forbes and Tucker might have tampered with the brakes, but he backpedaled. It didn't change the fact he'd driven drunk with his mother and Jimmie in his truck. He had to own that. And he would. Forbes and Tucker would get their comeuppance when Cole alerted the cops to the kickback scheme they were running with top government officials. That would be Cole's justice. That would be his absolution for having pulled out of the deal he and Jane signed.

"Dad," he said quietly. "I need you to know, before I go, just in case, I am so sorry. And your forgiveness . . ." His voice hitched. His eyes burned. "It means everything."

Myron stared. Paled. He swallowed. Then slowly his eyes pooled with tears. They leaked from the corners, following wrinkled tracks in his skin, down his face. He reached out with his gnarled, liver-spotted hand. He placed it against his son's cheek. Cold. He opened his mouth, but no words came.

"I need to go."

Myron nodded. When he spoke his voice was hoarse. "Just fly that damn thing, okay. And come back in one piece. Bring Olivia home. You both get your asses back here, because I'm not letting Forbes have this goddamn ranch."

A wry smile curved Cole's lips. He made a small salute sign. "Yessir."

He wanted to say something absurd, like *I love you, Dad.* He promised himself he'd do it when he got back.

And he headed downstairs to meet Ace and Burton.

There was not much room in the Piper Cub for both men and a dog, but he'd dump some other shit to lighten the load. He had to move fast to get the skis onto the wheels. He was going to need Burton's help. And they had to get into the air before the wind switched again and started to howl north. They needed to stay ahead of the brunt of weather or they'd be tossed like a cork in the violent sea of cloud.

Not much light, either. Not much room for maneuvering at all.

His only trump card was that the Cub was an iconic bush plane, designed with pitched propeller blades for incredibly short takeoffs and fast climbs, and high-set wings for rough bush landings. It was also fitted with low-pressure tundra tires, which could handle rugged gravel bars. With the skis wrapped around them, he'd be able to tackle snow, ground, and ice.

But it all meant nothing if he couldn't see. Or if the storm caught them in its grip.

———

"The Clinton guys are on their way. Our chopper is on standby." It was Martinello. She had two mugs of coffee. She set one on the desk in front of Mac. "They found something in Burton's files," she said, perching her butt on the edge of his metal desk.

By the look in his partner's eyes, Mac judged it was serious. He reached for his mug, watching her. "And?"

"Adoption papers," she said. "Tori Burton is the child of Sarah Baker and Sebastian George."

He stalled, the rim of the mug against his lips. Slowly he lowered the mug.

"Shit," he whispered. "He's taken her to her mother." Yakima glanced up at Martinello. "Just how sick is this guy? What the fuck is he doing? And where is Algor Sorenson?"

"The techs also found something in Melody Vanderbilt's laptop. A kind of memoir that she was drafting before she died. It appears to relate the whole story behind Tori's adoption, and it details Sarah's abduction. Most of it appears to be compiled from interviews she did in the hospital with Sarah Baker. The tech found all her notes. Apparently Melody was the only journalist granted interviews by Sarah, and it appears she never published a word of it. Instead, she and Burton adopted the baby and moved away."

———

Crosswinds buffeted the Cub as Cole gave the engine full throttle, pulling the nose high as they climbed into thick cloud. Snow plastered the windshield, and for a heart-stopping instant he thought he'd be totally blinded. Then the wind and velocity began pushing snow off the windshield, running it in watery rivulets down the side windows, giving him a small window of visibility. He battled to steady the wings as higher crosswinds tossed them like a tiny boat on waves.

He climbed higher, faster, in an effort to pop out above the weather. The engine whined in protest. They were carrying a lot of weight. The prop whorled. But the cloud was deep and dense. He leveled out, flying blindly into the dark, gray mass. His mouth was dry. He flew from memory and his compass. If he was right, the mountain range was to his left. If he was wrong . . . they'd crash and die before he even knew it.

A whip of panic hit him. He tamped it down.

Panic was a mug's game. It would kill them. If they died, Olivia died. Their staying alive was her only hope right now. But his fear continued to ride his back like a dragon.

Without fear, there cannot be true courage . . .

Did he not write those lines himself?

Reaching for his mike, he keyed his radio, put out a call.

No response.

He fiddled with the frequency, tried again. Still nothing. He replaced the handset. He'd try again farther north. If he could get through on the radio, he might find someone who could get word to the Watt Lake police. He also had his cell in his jacket pocket. Once they were closer to Watt Lake, there was a chance of reception.

He spoke to Burton through his headset. "You're certain that Tori is Olivia's child?"

Burton was strapped in the seat behind him, Ace wedged tightly between his legs. Myron had given Cole a tracking line and harness for Ace, which Olivia kept in the lodge.

"There's no doubt," came the voice through his headset. The man sounded defeated.

Another blast of wind slammed them across the flank. They seesawed wildly. Heart jackhammering, Cole struggled to bring his bird back under control. But he was still droning blindly forward into dense fog and cloud.

"I did it because I love her," said the voice in his earpiece. "I brought Tori here because she has nothing else. It was the right thing."

The man was trying to convince himself.

Cole clenched his jaw. *The things one does for love . . .*

What he and Holly had done for Ty was done out of love, too. They both thought at the time that they were doing the right thing by taking him on their travels, homeschooling him in exotic places. Dangerous places . . .

A dark shape loomed suddenly in front of the plane, rushing toward them. Cole's heart leaped to his throat. He opened the throttle, pulling the nose back into a sharp climb. Too sharp. The engine whined. They went up, up, but the black shape rushed closer.

Shit. They were heading into a cliff, they weren't going to make it—

———

Can you pinpoint the exact instant your life first starts on a collision course with someone else's? Can you trace back to the moment those lives did finally intersect, and from where they spiraled outward again . . .

Tori stared out the window, thinking of words in her mother's manuscript. The world outside was like a crazy-mad snow globe. Not much different from how she felt inside, her thoughts swirling like those fat, cold flakes settling white over the ground and trees and changing the way everything looked.

She rubbed her arms despite the warmth in the library. Her jacket was hanging over a chair, drying beside the fire, which crackled and hissed.

Myron hunkered in his wheelchair beside the hearth, his gray head bent forward as he read her mother's manuscript. She'd had

to show him how to turn the e-reader on, and how to turn pages—
he'd never seen an e-reader before.

Tori glanced over her shoulder.

He sensed her eyes on him and glanced up over the top of his
reading glasses. He looked uncomfortable.

"You want to put another log on?" he said.

In silence she went over to the fire and drew back the grate.
She took a split log from the giant copper scuttle at the side of the
hearth and tossed it into the flames.

"You could put a couple more on," he said.

She placed two more logs onto the fire. It hissed and spat and
smelled like pine resin. She drew the grate closed.

Myron studied the flames, deep in thought, then said, "Your
mother is a good writer."

Her lip started to wobble. She wanted to say that Melody was
not her mother, but couldn't.

He scratched his beard. "Can you make us some tea? And
sandwiches?"

She nodded.

"I take my tea black, strong, with three sugars."

She got up and found her way down into the kitchen. There
was a bread box, a kettle. In the fridge there were cold meats,
cheeses. She found mugs. She boiled the water and buttered the
bread, feeling numb. The house felt big and empty all around her.
Outside it seemed to be growing darker.

She carried the tray upstairs, balancing carefully so as not to
spill, and placed the tray on the buffet in the library.

Myron reached for the pills on the table next to him, tipped
four into his palm.

"You should have two," she said.

His gaze shot to hers, held.

She suddenly felt hot inside, but stood her ground. "Cole said
so. He said it was important."

He hesitated, put two back. He swallowed them with water, wincing as they went down.

She brought him a plate with two sandwiches and a mug of hot tea.

"What kind are these?" He lifted the top off one sandwich.

"Cheese and salami with some lettuce," she said, taking a seat opposite him.

"You like that kind?"

She shook her head. "Yes. I dunno. My dad likes cheese and salami."

He gasped suddenly and doubled over in his chair.

She lurched to her feet. "You okay?" Her gaze darted to the table. "Do you need more pills?"

He waved his hand, his eyes watering. He was trying to breathe.

Panic kicked through her. She placed her hand on his shoulder. "Mr. McDonough, please . . . what can I do?"

He gasped, coughed, sucked in a great big wheezing breath, and struggled to sit up straighter in his chair.

"Tea," he managed to say. "Hot tea would be good. It'll melt those damn pills faster."

She handed a full mug to him with both hands, ensuring his gnarled fingers were wrapped safely around it before she let go. Her eyes met his. He sipped. The warmth seemed to aid him, because color returned to his face.

"This is damn fine tea, Tori Burton."

She said nothing, just slowly backed up to her chair and reseated herself, nervous that he was going to die or something with her all alone here in this big hollow log house in the wilderness.

He studied her a while. "You not going to have some?"

She shook her head.

"You know something? This is going to be rough." He nodded to the e-reader on the little table beside him. "No one can kid you otherwise. It's going to take time, lots of time, to assimilate all this. But your dad did something incredible by bringing you here. Do you know why?"

She shook her head.

"Do you know what happened to Sarah Baker?"

"No," she said softly.

"I think I know what happened to her."

She waited, her heart quickening. But he turned and stared into that fire again, and he rubbed his whiskers. He shook his head slowly, his bushy brows lowering over his deep, gray eyes.

"Sebastian George died in prison," he said slowly, quietly, as if picking his words very carefully. He met her gaze again. "He was the one who took Sarah Baker."

She nodded.

"Well, when he died over three years ago, I received an application for employment from a young woman. She was a special person. I could see that right off. Don't ask me how." Creases folded around his eyes as he smiled a sad sort of smile under his whiskers. "I had grown into a crusty old codger who didn't care for much, but somehow she got to me. She had these really bad scars on her wrists."

Tori's heart beat faster. She held his eyes, intent.

"It looked to me as though this woman had tried to kill herself. She also had a beat-up-looking German shepherd, and I thought to myself, these two have been through the wars. Well, I checked out her résumé, and it all added up, but only to a point. Everything about this woman seemed to go back only as far as eight years. Do you know why?"

Tori shook her head.

"Do you know who I am talking about?"

"Olivia," she said quietly. "And Ace."

He nodded. "And I think her records went back only eight years because that's when she changed her name from Sarah Baker."

Tori stared. She tried to swallow.

Myron leaned forward in his chair. "I never asked her about her past, or her family, or where she was raised, not until recently. But I suspected terrible things, and slowly it's all started to add up. And you know what else? I think that's why your father brought you here. To meet her."

Tori's insides started to tremble. Her eyes started to pool with moisture. She wanted to look away, but couldn't. She held the old man's eyes.

"Olivia—Sarah—is one of the finest people I have ever met. A heart as big as those woods and wilderness out there. A brave and powerful woman. Courage like a mountain lion. All of that is inside you, Tori Burton, if what this book says is true. And that is why your father brought you here. To meet your mother. For you to see how much good is inside you, what kind of blood and heart runs through your body."

The moisture in her eyes slid hot down her cheeks. She couldn't breathe.

It took several minutes before she could speak again.

"I hate him."

"Who?"

"My dad. My . . ."

"I don't know exactly what is happening with that terrible murder news, Tori. Or who exactly has taken Olivia, but"—he glanced at the e-reader—"from the words in there, your father is a decent man. A man with principle. A man prepared to stand against the fierce current of a river when everyone else is trying to go the other way. Whatever your father has done now, I think he's trying to set it all right. For you."

"He's leaving me. He's dying. I have no one."

"All the more reason to set the world right for you, then. All the more reason to bring you home to your biological mother."

She rubbed the knee of her jeans, anger, fear darkening her thoughts, tightening her face, her neck.

"I know it's easier to throw up angry walls, kid. By God, do I know. Much easier to strike out at the world and cling to the bitterness. But it cost me. Instead of opening my heart and trying to build something stronger upon the foundations of a tragedy, I tightened up and cut off my own children, my own family. Look at me now."

Slowly she raised her eyes.

"An old badger with no friends. No family around him. No grandchildren. No legacy for my farm. What's it all worth . . ." His voice faded. He cleared his throat. "Sometimes life gives you a second chance."

"Like those nymphs," she said quietly.

He frowned. "You mean—"

"Damselflies. They get a second life."

"Olivia told you that?"

She rubbed her knee again. "You think she'll come back?" she whispered. "You think she'll be okay? Ace, Cole . . . my dad . . ." Tears pricked into her eyes again. She swiped at them angrily with her sleeve.

Myron was silent for several long moments. Wind moaned up in the chimney. She couldn't look at him. She felt his discomfort.

"There's a white plastic box in my study," he said suddenly. "It looks like a construction worker's toolbox. It's got a slate-blue bottom and a blue handle. It's on the bottom shelf nearest the window that looks over the lake. Bring it to me, will you?"

"Why?"

"I want to show you something."

She found the box and brought it to him. He asked her to move a bigger table closer and to draw up a chair.

She did.

"Now, pour me a whisky—from that bottle there. Not too much."

She went to the bottle. There was a glass beside it. She unscrewed the cap, poured.

"Yes, that's good," he said.

She brought the glass to him. He swallowed the whole lot in one gulp, inhaled, eyes watering. He wiped his brow with his sleeve.

"You in pain?"

"Yeah."

"What's wrong?"

"Old age, that's what. My time on earth is done. Wasted bloody time." He struggled to open the clasp of the box with gnarled fingers, blue veins standing out on the backs of spotted hands.

She watched him wrangling with the clasp for a few moments, then reached over and did it for him.

The box opened to reveal shelves that concertinaed out in stepped layers like a sewing box her mother once had. Lots of little compartments tucked into each shelf were filled with sparkling beads, a rainbow selection of shimmering threads on wooden spools. Hooks, gleaming silver, of different sizes. Feathers and animal-hair swatches, some of it dyed bright colors.

He reached for his reading glasses and set them askew on his craggy face.

He affixed a metal clamp device onto the table, and twisted the screw on the bottom to hold it steady. With trembling fingers he inserted a tiny silver hook into the pincer at the top, and tightened another screw, securing the hook.

He looked up, over the rim of his reading glasses. "'Nother whisky might help. For the pain, mind. A dying man's purview. Not every day, you understand."

She smiled. "I'm almost twelve." It just came out. A need to say it. Share something of herself.

"I know."

She topped off his glass, adding a wee extra splash for good measure. She brought it to him and he took another sip, smaller this time.

She angled her head, watching him. He was crusty. But she

decided she liked him. He said things like they were. Tori placed a high value on this.

"How old are you anyway?" she said.

He chuckled. Then his smile faded. "Old enough to have had a good run on this earth, kid. Take a seat next to me here."

She did. "What if they don't come back?"

"They will."

"I don't believe that you know it for certain."

"Kiddo, you *need* to believe. Now come, we're going to tie a fly."

"What kind?"

He peered over his glasses. "A damselfly."

He showed her how to pick the colors and wrap them tightly around the hook, forming the body with shimmering blue bars with black bands. He showed her how to make the wings. He let her have a go at winding thread and picking eyes. They made several flies, some really bad, but she was getting the hang of it. They worked and she copied, and the grandfather clock ticked. He drank more whisky, and she fed the fire.

"Do you think they watch down on us, Tori—the dead?"

"I . . ." She inhaled deeply. "I think my mom does."

He nodded. "Grace, too. My wife."

"I think the dead see everything. And from up there in the stars, everything makes sense. It has a design."

He crooked up a hairy gray brow. "Do they forgive you, do you think? From up there?"

She thought on this a while. "Yes. They do. They know that you don't have the same perspective that they do, so you make mistakes. You make wrong decisions even though you think they're right."

"You'll forgive your father, then? For any mistakes?"

She looked down at the shimmering gossamer blue thread in her fingers. In her mind's eye she could see the damselfly alighting on her jeans . . . but before she could answer, a great big booming thundered up the stairs.

She tensed. Myron's head snapped to the door, his eyes going wide.

The banging continued. Voices reached them. Men outside. Yelling, screaming.

Myron quickly rolled his chair over to the wall, took down his shotgun from a bracket. "Stay there."

"Where are you going?"

The banging sound boomed up the stairs again, reverberating through the big empty lodge house. Her heart raced.

Myron flung open the window, peered down.

Voices reached in through the open window. "Clinton RCMP. Police! Open up!"

CHAPTER 24

Cole braced for impact as he fought to pull the nose higher. Suddenly, wind slammed the Cub along the flank and they were thrust sideways, forcing him to bank sharply to the left. Another force of wind, big downdraft, hit them from the top, and the plane plummeted like a rock.

Just as he thought they were going to enter a death spiral, they were flung upward again by a rush of air deflecting off the mountain in front of them. It shot them way up, like a cork in a wild waterfall current. He struggled with the controls to keep his wings level, opening the throttle, racing with the wind, riding it like a wave, and abruptly, they popped out above cloud.

His heart hammered.

His skin and shirt were drenched.

The engine droned loudly in the sudden quiet. Behind the tail of his plane he could see the gray—a roiling, churning hump of air—the storm they'd just punched through. It curled and crawled behind them like deadly smoke trying to reach out and grasp them back in as they headed north. All he had to do was keep outrunning it now.

Yeah, right. And he had to find that truck and camper before the weather monster swallowed them up again.

He wiped his brow with his sleeve.

"Shit," came the word through his headset.

He gave a snort. "Got that right."

Below them lay a shining ribbon of road yet to be covered by snow. The northern highway. Vehicles moved steadily back and forth along it. Cole banked, descended, and began to follow the strip of road, watching for a camper on a gray truck. He figured whoever had Olivia would have ditched the boat and trailer long ago.

He tried to calculate distance from Broken Bar versus how fast the camper could conceivably have been traveling along the snowy logging roads. If Olivia had been abducted three hours ago, at a max speed of sixty kilometers per hour for the most part, then faster once the camper hit the highway, the bastard who took her could have made it well over 180 klicks north by now.

"There!" Burton barked into his headphones. "Camper! Heading north near that turnoff ahead at two o'clock."

He saw it. He banked again, descending and flying low over the highway, buzzing the tops of cars as he went.

"Binoculars are in the side pocket beside your seat," he told Burton. "We're looking for an AdventureCaper camper on the bed of a gray Ford F-150, BC plates."

Behind him Burton found the scopes, peered through them as Cole flew yet lower, keeping an eye out for hydro lines. There was thin, high-level cloud cover here. Tiny crystals were starting to form and hit his windshield. The storm was moving steadily in.

"Can you see BC plates?"

"Affirmative." Then he swore. "It's a Citation camper."

Cole lifted the nose. They continued to follow the gleaming ribbon of road. Tension twisted through him. With increasing cloud cover it could be dark in a few hours. They had to locate the camper before nightfall.

He took the plane down again as another vehicle caught his attention. But it was a camper on a red truck.

"That's the dirt road that leads off the highway and into First Nations territory." Burton pointed over his shoulder. "There, at about eleven o'clock."

"I see it."

"It bypasses Watt Lake and heads way up into the forest and mountains out the back. Toward Predator Ridge and then Bear Claw."

Cole's gaze flickered between the highway and the twisting thread of dirt snaking into dense forest. It was a gamble. Olivia's assailant might not have even come this way.

"It's the only place he'd go." Burton's voice came through the headset.

"Her life is on the line. If you're wrong—"

"I want to save her more than you can possibly know," Burton said, voice low, quiet. "It's the reason for everything."

Cole swallowed, then banked sharply to the left, leaving the highway to follow the logging road into dense, evergreen wilderness. Foothills rose in the distance. Beyond those, Pinnacle Ridge was hidden by cloud. He had to get Olivia before Sorenson took her through those Pinnacle mountains.

"There!" Burton yelled suddenly, right at the same time Cole saw the plume of dust rising above the trees. "Something's traveling along there!"

Cole swooped the plane down, and they buzzed over the top of a camper and truck, a cloud of fine, gray glacial dust boiling up behind the rig as it raced and rocked along the narrow road.

Burton peered through the scopes. Cole's heart was in his throat. He scanned the surrounding terrain. Not one fucking little piece of dirt to come down on, apart from that twisty road hemmed in by giant, dark conifers. Snow started to fleck a little more insistently against the windshield. He cast a quick glance over his shoulder. The monster of churning cloud was fast on their tail.

"AdventureCaper," Burton said. "Long box, gray Ford F-150. BC plates."

"I'm taking her lower. Look for another plate on the rear of the camper, to the left of the door. It's a ham operator's license plate."

He buzzed lower, skimming the towering tops of trees.

"Affirmative! I can see the plate."

Immediately Cole took the nose up a tad. The camper picked up speed. Dirt roiling as it raced through the trees. The road was approaching a canyon with a silvery river.

Cole tried his radio again, fiddling with channels. He wasn't getting any reception.

"You got a cell phone?" Cole barked.

"Negative. Left it in the cabin."

He dug in his pocket, found his phone. Handing it over his shoulder, he said, "Use mine. See if Watt Lake can send in an emergency response team, choppers, before that weather hits. Before it gets dark."

But as he spoke, the weather dragon behind him unleashed a tongue of wind that flicked his little Cub sideways. "Shit!"

He banked, struggling with the controls again. And the phone fell between the seats before Burton could grab it. It skittered all the way along the floor into the gear at the back.

They were on their own. Cole sucked in a deep breath, taking the Cub low again, adrenaline pounding through his blood as the camper neared the first bend at the canyon. It swayed precariously round the corner, too fast, sending a boulder tumbling and exploding down into the river.

The camper increased speed further. The driver clearly knew he was being chased from the air. Cole fought with conflict. Chase them, and they could crash. He could kill Olivia. Let up, and the camper could slip into that endless, dense forest and mountains, and once the weather and darkness hit, Olivia was as good as dead anyway.

Gritting his jaw, he kept over the camper. It rocked and swayed down a decline, approaching another bend that hung over the river. As the camper veered into the bend, the left side came frighteningly close to the drop. As if in slow motion, part of the road shoulder seemed to collapse under the left wheels. The rig seemed to hang suspended above a shower of clattering stones that tumbled down into the river. Dirt mushroomed up, billowing away in the wind. The camper tipped.

Cole felt his stomach drop to his bowels as the rig rolled, crashing onto its side and sliding with rumbling boulders and stones and uprooted saplings in a landslide, down, down, down toward the churning green-and-white water.

The wreck came to rest, precariously balanced on a rock ledge over the water.

Holy Mother of God.

He had to land. Now.

Cole banked sharply, taking his craft low over the water, flying upriver, trees rushing at their sides barely a breath away from the wingtips. Snow was starting to beat against his windshield. Through the blur of his prop he searched for a bank, a gravel bar, anything—even if it meant crash landing, he had to go down now.

———

"Olivia called him Algor," Tori told the cops, who were now inside with her and Myron in the library.

One of the officers showed her a photo on an electronic device. "Was it this man?"

She scrunched up her brow. "Yes. No. I mean, he looked sorta like that. Same whitish-blond short hair, same facial hair. I don't know." She glanced up at the officer. The cop seemed young. Nice.

"The man wore a ball cap," she explained. "With the bill pulled low over his face so it was mostly in shadow when I saw him. But it could have been him."

"How tall was he?"

She glanced at one of the dark-haired RCMP members talking to Myron. "About that officer's height."

"So about six two?"

"I guess. He said he had a wife, but I never got to see her."

The cops exchanged a glance.

"Thank you, Tori," the officer said.

He went to the window and looked out at the snow as he made a phone call.

"Sergeant Yakima," he said into his phone. "Yes. It could have been Sorenson, or a man posing as Sorenson—similar in appearance. He's abducted the ranch manager, Olivia West. She's apparently injured—lots of blood left on the trail where he took her. The belief is he's heading north, to the Bear Claw Valley."

He paused, then said, "Affirmative, that was the information that Cole McDonough, son of ranch owner Myron McDonough, left with his father. He also said that there were now BC plates on the truck, but there was still a ham operator's plate on the back of the camper, issued in Washington." He gave the number.

Another pause. "I know. Yes. It was Burton who insisted she was being taken to Bear Claw, and yes, I'm aware Burton's state of mind is questionable. But it's our only lead right now—everything here"—he glanced at Tori, then Myron—"points to her abductor taking her north. Possibly to finish the job started by Sebastian George."

Another pause. "Piper Cub. Yellow. No, I don't know." He cleared his throat. "Burton's daughter says that her father is armed with two pistols, and McDonough has a shotgun. She said her father came here to 'finish some business.' My recommendation is we alert Watt Lake detachment and get an ERT up into the Bear Claw Valley, stat."

———

Ahead was a narrow bar of gravel—an island around which the river flowed. It was short. Cole was skeptical that he'd be able to stop his Cub before they hit the water again at the end of the bar. The skis around his tundra tires were going to take a beating on the rocks, could flip the craft over.

"Hang on!" he yelled, making a split-second decision to take her down. "Hold the dog!" His wheels skimmed the churning water. He worked the flaps, kept the nose just so, and his landing gear smacked against rocks. The plane lurched up, flew, slapped back down, yawing wildly and bouncing as Cole did everything in his power to stop the perfect little bush craft on a dime. And then he saw the log. They crashed hard, and the plane tipped forward and sideways, crunching over onto the left wing as it came to a stop on its side. The prop whacked into rocks and splintered into shards of wood that smattered against the windshield.

Cole's shoulder hurt where he'd bashed against the side. His heart palpitated overtime.

"Burton?"

"Okay, I'm okay."

"Ace?"

"He seems fine, just panting . . . stressed."

Cole unbuckled his belt. The door flap was on the upended side. He bashed it open, climbed out.

He helped lift Ace out with Burton pushing and lifting the dog from behind. Burton clambered out himself after Ace. He had a nasty cut on his brow. Blood leaked down the side of his eye.

"You sure you're good?"

Burton nodded, white-faced.

Cole took hold of Ace's harness and clipped on his tracking line. He handed the line to Burton, then reached back into the cabin. He struggled to fold back the seat, eventually smashing it back, breaking the hinge, then he climbed in again. Leaning on his stomach over the broken seat, he fingered along the floor of the back of the Cub, searching for where his cell phone might have slid. He couldn't locate it. It must have gone right under the rigging and gear in the back, which was crushed. No time. Olivia might be alive, hurt, dying. Every minute was critical.

He unclipped the first aid kit from the side panel, removed it, and strapped it onto the belt of his jeans. He jumped out, wincing as a bolt of pain shot up his ankle. He reached into the front of the cabin, unhooked the shotgun he'd stashed along the side. It appeared to be in working order. He felt in the front compartment for the ammunition. He tucked the boxes of slugs into his jacket and slung the 12-gauge across his back. He held out his hand for Ace's line. Burton gave it to him.

"The water looks shallower along that fork." He pointed to water that jiggled over rocks. "We can wade across there, head downriver along the bank on the opposite side."

Snow was beginning to settle here too, now, the sky growing low and dark. Wind was gusting, carrying a deep chill.

With his first step into the water, his boot slicked out from under him, and he went down on his side with a splash. The ice-cold shocked his heart and stole his breath. Dripping, he pushed himself up, started again, more cautiously picking his way this time.

"Careful. Rocks are covered in slime," he called over his shoulder as he led Ace into the river.

———

A sea of pain. A red tide. She was drowning in it. Like thick paint being mixed, blackness swirled slowly with crimson in her brain, making her dizzy, nauseous. Somewhere in the distance of her mind she heard a creaking and grating of metal, then a crash of glass. She felt movement. Moaning, she tried to turn her head, open her eyes to see what it was. She felt the straps around her body being undone. A hand tightened around her upper arm and tugged.

She screamed in pain. The shrill animal sound that exploded from her own chest jerked her fully back into consciousness. Her heart pattered. Blood choked the back of her throat. A man was pulling on her arm, turning her over, and like a bolt of white lightning the memory hit her. Every muscle in her body jerked as her heart exploded with adrenaline, fear. She tried to open her eyes, focus, get up.

"Hey." He slapped the side of her face. "You need to get up." He slapped harder.

Olivia moved her head to the side, spat out bloody mucus, gagged. He tried to lift her again, and the wave of pain that slammed down the left side of her body was unbearable, almost making her lose consciousness again.

"Not . . . my arm," she managed to groan. "Arm . . . is broken. Leave my arm."

He hooked his hands under her armpits and hauled her up. Her world reeled. Everything was sideways. Then, as she blinked, struggling to orient herself, she realized they were in the back of the camper, and it was lying on its side.

"Easy," he said, trying to drag her out the back. "Whole thing could go over."

Panic kicked. She remembered—lurching over, rolling, sliding, crashing. Thank God he'd strapped her to the bed or she might have broken more than an arm.

He pulled her out the mangled door, her bound legs dragging behind. As her boots came free of the door, they thudded with the aid of gravity to the rocks. She gasped again. Pain was consuming. But it was real. It meant she was alive. If she'd learned anything, it was how much pain a human could bear without letting it kill you.

She struggled to keep her eyes open in what felt like blinding light that sliced into the back of her skull. He laid her onto rocks. Water. She heard a river. They were on a rock ledge above churning water. Her hands were still bound behind her back.

He crouched over her, untied her ankles. He took the rope from her ankles and tied it in a noose around her neck, like a leash.

Please. No. Not again . . . I cannot endure this all again . . . just let me die this time. I'm going to let myself die . . .

An image swam into her mind. A face. So crystal clear she felt as though it might have been put into her head by some outside force. Soft green eyes with darkly fringed lashes looked at her, right into her. They were filled with longing, need. Dead straight hair shimmered in a frame about her face, the blue-black color of a raven's feathers.

Tori.

Her daughter.

Her eleven-year-old daughter who was going to have no one left in this world if she died. Tears, hot and fierce, burned into Olivia's eyes. She'd fought to live for her baby once before. She'd fought like a rabid she-bear to give her baby life. Then she'd let her baby girl down—she'd bowed to Ethan and the pressure of her parents and the community. She'd not had the strength of character to fight them all and keep her infant. Even if it meant doing it alone.

She would *not* let Tori down this time. Never. One more time, she *would* fight for her child. And by God or the devil, she would win this time. She would kill this fucker.

Olivia sucked down a bolt of pain as he dug his hands under her armpits again and lifted her to her feet. She wobbled, trying to steady herself, trying to swallow back a surge of nausea and mucus.

"Move." He went ahead of her, tugged on the rope. It tightened around her neck.

"Undo my hands, you bastard! If I trip I can't break my fall!" She spat out more blood and spittle. It landed in a pinkish-red glob on the rock.

He swung around, glared at her. Power seemed to vibrate out around him. Then his mouth curved into a slow, wide smile. His teeth were the same—perfect white lines, eyeeteeth that dropped a little lower, giving him a feral air. Teeth that had eaten parts right out of her body.

His eyes were the predatory eyes of the animal who'd haunted her for twelve years through her darkest nightmares.

"You've changed, Sarah. You used to be so very sweet."

"Who the fuck *are* you?! You died! You're *dead*!"

He came up to her, close, so close his chest touched her breasts. He angled his head, bringing his mouth toward hers, and he breathed his words over her lips. "Not me, Sarah," he whispered. "Sebastian died, not me. Sebastian was the expendable one. He was the half-human my mother always said I should have consumed as a fetus in her womb. Sebastian should have become part of me, my body, before I was born—*fetal resorption*. You've heard about it, Sarah? The vanishing twin. But alas, he was born. And it appears there was greater purpose for him. He was to be my serf, and he was to be slowly absorbed by me in life. He was to sustain and nourish me, and he came through, right to the very end. Shadow brother. The servant brother. In the end there was supposed to be only one."

He flicked his tongue out and licked her lips like a snake. She recoiled, gagged.

He turned his back abruptly and yanked on the rope. Her neck cracked and she staggered forward, panicked suddenly about getting her feet under her, keeping her balance. If she went down with her hands bound behind her back like this, she'd smash her face into rock. As he jerked her up the bank, she cast a quick look behind her at the camper and truck.

The rig lay on its side right at the edge of a small rock plateau. It was a miracle they hadn't gone in. She glanced up, searching the sky for the plane she'd heard buzzing low overhead as the camper had sped up and started lurching. There was nothing in sight but leaden cloud and a bald eagle wheeling in and out of great soupy tatters of mist that sifted through the trees. Tiny crystals of snow kissed her face.

Another thing she'd learned—you could listen for planes for months. But it meant nothing. In low cloud, and in the approaching storm, she would be on her own.

Olivia turned her focus to placing one boot carefully in front of the other, keeping her balance as she picked her way through gravel and rock and other landslide debris. She concentrated on the pain, too. She'd learned this as a way of mental escape. Don't fight it, let it consume you. Let it pulse through to every nerve ending with each beat of the heart, each thrust of blood through veins. If she fought it, the pain would grow unbearable. She embraced it instead, cataloguing the places she was damaged. Possible fractured humerus. Ripped ear going crusty with dried blood. Torn sections of scalp. He might have also broken her nose. She stumbled, falling to her knees. He yanked on the rope, and she staggered back up.

She saw him looking up at the sky, too. He seemed worried.

When he found a path up a section of low bank, he led her up, then into the trees, where it was dark and cold. Snow was coming down solidly now. Darkness was encroaching. With it came a wave of despair. She tripped again and hit the ground with the right side of her body. She had no control of the scream that sparked out of her at the crush of pain. Her eyes watered. Blood leaked afresh from her ear. She wormed her way into a sitting position, panted, trying to catch her breath.

"How far?" she managed to say.

He didn't reply. He was regarding her intently, as if measuring something.

"You never did go hunting for our baby, did you, Sarah?"

She held his gaze, swallowed.

"I thought you would. Someone like you. I was so certain you would. I put out my lines, and I waited."

She challenged him with her eyes, her chest filling with a mix of guilt and regret and the kind of pain only a mother who'd lost a child could know.

"I wanted her to be free of you," she whispered. "I could never be. The least I could do was save her." She spat out more blood that was coming from the back of her nose. "Seems I did the right thing."

His lips curved into a wry smile. He angled his head.

"Ah, but the cop—the staff sergeant—the man I now believe I met on the banks of the Stina River one cold November day, he read me better than I read you. He knew I was out there, and that I'd keep looking. He cast out Internet bait of his own. He brought me to you, Sarah." His smile deepened. He bent over, bringing his face close to hers again. She continued to hold his eyes, refusing to back down.

Never again would she back down for him.

He reached for the rope around her neck, jerked it tight. She gasped for air. None came down her windpipe. Her eyes watered. He held her like that until her vision began to fade into tiny white pinpricks. Then he dropped the rope, and she fell suddenly back into a heap on the ground. She wheezed in great big gulps of air.

"Get up," he ordered, his voice suddenly flat and cold. "Walk. We need to find a place to spend the night and have a little fun."

As he tugged her forward into deepening forest, Olivia scrabbled furiously with the fingers of her right hand to undo the watch on her left wrist. She let it drop silently to the soft loam behind her. She dragged her feet, trying to leave as much trace as she could in soil and pine needles without alerting him, praying that the coming snow wouldn't obliterate all her effort.

CHAPTER 25

Snowflakes were settling like confetti on the wreck. Cole moved carefully inside, so as not to rock and tumble the rig down into the water.

There was no one inside the truck cab, nor in the camper on back. Blood soaked the mattress. He found strands of Olivia's hair. If there was any consolation at all, it was that she had to have been alive and mobile in order to have left here—her assailant would not have been able to clear out so fast lugging a body.

Ace suddenly started barking, whining outside the wreck. Cole tensed as he heard Burton yell.

He stuck his head out of the camper.

"Here! Ace is on to something! I think it's her scent."

The dog was whimpering and lunging against his line to scramble up the bank.

Cole jumped down, hurried over, and dropped to his haunches to see what had fired Ace up. Pinkish red blood and . . . it looked like spittle. More drops of blood spotted the rocks nearby. His jaw tightened, and he glanced up.

"You take him." Burton was struggling to hold on to Ace. His complexion was still sheet white, his cheeks gaunt. He was ill. Worsening.

Cole took the line from Burton, wrapping it around his hand for purchase as he braced against Ace's pull. The dog yanked and yipped in desperation to hit the trail he'd found.

"Ready?" he said to Burton.

The ex-cop nodded.

"Find her, boy," he said. "Go!"

Ace scrabbled up the bank, sniffing left then right, then *bam*, his nose went down, and he was off, heading downriver, below a cliff. Cole stumbled over rocks and talus, scree clattering out from under his boots as he tried to keep up. Snow fell heavier, making rocks slippery.

Burton lagged behind, breathing hard, using his hands to grab bits of scrub for purchase.

Ace stopped suddenly, raised his head, looking confused. He started snuffling in circles. His tail started to wag. He gave a little whine and lunged into the rope again as he relocated Olivia's scent.

By the time Ace led them up a low section of riverbank and into dense forest, they'd traveled almost a klick downriver. It was dark under the trees. They had no flashlights. From here they'd basically be navigating blind, led only by the dog's nose and a line attached to him.

Cole waited for Burton to catch up, but Ace suddenly burst against his leash, almost jerking his arm from his socket. He winced as pain from his shoulder sparked across his neck. Ace moved forward a few feet and suddenly lay down.

"What's the matter, boy?"

Burton caught up to them. "He's alerting." He bent over, bracing his hands on thighs, wheezing gulps of air in. Once he'd recovered a little, he said, "Had two Police Dog Service guys on my watch at Watt Lake. One a narcotics K-9. He was trained to alert like that when he hit scent. Lie down."

Cole crouched down and examined the loam between Ace's paws. And there he saw a watch. Olivia's. His chest crunched with a surge of emotion as he picked it up.

"Good boy, Ace," he whispered, stroking the dog's head. "You're such a good boy. You think you can do it again, huh? Find her—find Olivia."

The German shepherd surged to his feet, snuffled like a truffle pig through the loam, and was off through a gap in the trees. Cole and Gage took off in hot pursuit, leaping over fallen logs, ducking under low branches, tearing through brush, and tripping through tangled roots into the gloam of the snowy forest.

Ace abruptly lay down again. Cole crouched, feeling with his fingers in the gathering darkness between the dog's paws. He touched something hard, picked it up. Tensed. Olivia's truck keys. She must have had them in her jeans pocket.

"Can you search some more, boy? Find." The dog was amped, but clearly physically tiring. Behind him, Burton kept tripping, falling, and scrambling back to his feet.

"You gonna make it?" he said to the ex-cop.

Burton wiped his brow, breathing hard. "I'm going to make it. This is what I came to do." His voice was breathy.

Cole studied the sergeant in the dim light. "I need you," he said quietly. "We both need you."

He nodded. "I'm fine. Go."

Cole let Ace have free rein again, and once more they took off after the dog. Ace slowed a little, snuffling more carefully now as the snow was accumulating and wind moved through the forest. Cole guessed this might be messing with the scent, blowing it into different places. Ace led them up a ridge. They stopped along the tree line at the crest. Below lay a clearing. And although it was fully dark now, there was a little more visibility outside of the forest canopy. The settling snow also reflected more light, giving an almost eerie glow to the little valley. Silence was heavy, apart from drips and plops as snow and water fell from branches. At the far end of the clearing a grove of leafless alders clustered around what appeared to be a decaying and deserted log cabin and a scattering of rotting outbuildings.

A faint flicker of yellow light came from between the slats of one of the cabin walls.

Cole waited until Burton caught up and crouched down beside him.

"Looks like an abandoned homestead," Cole said softly.

"Or an old trapper's outfit."

Ace whined.

"Shhh." Cole hushed him, stroked him, and spoke softly. Sound carried in this kind of snowy weather in remote forest. But the dog was restless, making little moans in his throat as his nostrils waffled the breeze blowing their way from the cabin.

"They're in there," Cole whispered. "Ace can scent her."

"He's most likely armed," Burton said. "We don't know how badly either of them are hurt, but they made it this far in decent time, so I'm guessing they're both fairly mobile."

"And Olivia's clearly still thinking on her feet, leaving Hansel and Gretel clues like that for someone to find."

Which meant she had hope. Cole let this fuel him. But they had to do this carefully, not rush anything.

"Any ideas?" he asked the ex-cop.

"What have we got between us? Your shotgun, my Smith and Wesson, and a Taurus .22." He glanced at Ace. "And her dog."

"No," Cole said, squinting at the dilapidated hut, his heart racing. "The dog doesn't get hurt. He stays out of this."

Burton maneuvered himself into a more comfortable crouch. His right arm hung oddly limp at his side.

"What's with the arm?" Cole said.

"Gone a bit lame."

He frowned, trying to see into Burton's eyes in the dark. "Is it the illness?"

"I think so."

"What's it doing—the tumor?"

"The lesion in my brain is growing rapidly. It could manifest in motor coordination problems if it presses on certain neural paths."

Cole cursed softly to himself. Burton was failing in front of his eyes—he might not last physically through a takedown. He glanced at Ace. If he left Ace tied to a tree up here in the forest, the instant he and Burton headed down into the valley, the dog was going to start yapping, and any hope of cover would be blown.

Then it hit him.

"I have an idea," he whispered to Burton. "We do it like this."

———

The decaying building was powerfully reminiscent of the old shed in which Olivia had been chained for a winter—wet, cold. It stank of mold and moss. Her pulse raced so fast she thought she'd faint. She struggled to hold on to a shred of sanity.

Focus. Do it for Tori. Play his game, but do it better than him . . .

He shoved her into a corner.

"Like old times, huh, Sarah?" he whispered.

"What's your name?" she said, teeth chattering. She was trying to stay present. Trying to keep him human as long as possible. "If you're not Sebastian, you must have another name."

"Eugene," he said.

"Eugene George?"

He glanced into her eyes. A shiver shot down her spine.

"Yes," he said, holding her gaze as he tied the end of her neck rope to a heavy iron bar in the corner.

"So you're a twin? An identical twin?"

He snorted. "Sebastian was a genetic echo, an offshoot of myself. Expendable. He was born onto this earth to support me. My mother made me aware of this from a very young age."

"How come I never saw him?"

"You did. He helped butcher the bodies. Perhaps you thought he was me? He lived in another shed, far from the house. It was his business to stay on the periphery of my life. Like my parents, in the end."

"Is that why he said in court he couldn't read? Only you were taught?"

"Get down," he said once the rope had been secured.

She stood her ground, hands bound behind her back, blood leaking from her ear again. "Why did you never tell me your name before?"

He looked into her eyes, then said, low, slow, "A name is immaterial. Sebastian and Eugene, Romulus and Remus, Castor and Pollux, Sam and Eric from *Lord of the Flies*, my mother used any and all these from time to time. Names are just a symbol that have become a way of bureaucratic control. See, Sarah-Olivia? We are not bound by a name. We can become whomever we want. Like chameleons we can blend into new people, assume their identities. Like I long ago assumed the identity of a dead bush dweller living off-grid up north. I used his identity to enter the States twelve years ago, after they arrested Sebastian. I did time in prison in that dead man's name when I shot and killed an Arizona State Park Ranger two years later. It was finally ruled involuntary manslaughter. Little did they know I killed him because he witnessed what I was doing with a dear, sweet little victim with blonde hair and round breasts." He smiled. "I guess they never did find her body in the end, deep as it was down the ravine, where wildlife was plentiful and hungry."

Bile surged into her throat. Hatred, pure, thrummed her veins.

"Where," she said through clenched teeth, "is the real Algor Sorenson?"

"Ah. They might find him yet. Left in remote desert he was. Birds picking his bones, I'm sure. The lovely Mary—we know they found her, don't we, Sarah-Olivia? The Sorensons were perfect, of course. I selected them after we got talking in an Arizona campsite shortly after my release, and I learned he had a NEXUS card and traveled often to Canada to hunt. He had the right build, coloring. Equipment."

A shudder racked her body. Nausea swirled.

"Get down," he ordered again, voice flat, cold. Eyes unreadable.

Slowly she lowered herself to her knees. The floor was rotted wood. He unsheathed the knife he'd taken from her, and he sliced through the rope securing her wrists. She winced as her left arm fell free. Eugene reached for the jacket zipper at her neck. With a ripping sound he yanked it down and pushed open her jacket. He slid it off her shoulders. Her jacket fell to the ground. He punched her lightly on the sternum, forcing her to fall backward onto her butt on top of the jacket. Her pulse jackhammered. She scooted farther back into the corner, the rope grating around the scars at her neck.

His face split into a smile, teeth glinting in the light of the small fire he'd made in a circle of stones in the center of the hut. Smoke was being sucked up through a hole in the rafters above. Snowflakes came down through the hole, hissing and sizzling on the flames.

"We have a whole, long night ahead, Sarah-Olivia," he said, going down onto his knees in front of her. He brought the knife blade up close to her face. He feathered the cold tip down the bridge of her swollen nose, along her lips, her chin, down to her neck. She held her breath, trying not to swallow as he traced the sharp tip—she knew just how sharp, she'd sharpened it herself—down the column of her throat. With a jerk he grabbed and slit her sweater open down the front.

She gasped, scrunching her eyes tight as her sweater flayed open, exposing her bra.

He hooked the blade into the fabric between her breasts, lifted it sharply, and her bra split open. Her breasts fell free. She needed to go to the bathroom. Her bladder, her stomach had turned to water. Her nipples pinched tight and hard from cold.

"Oh, now look at that," he whispered, tracing a nipple with the blade. She began to shake. She knew what he could do. He lowered his face to her breasts, licked each nipple in turn. She braced for a bite, anticipating his teeth sinking in, puncturing skin, him sucking blood as he tore out a piece of flesh. It didn't come. The tip of his tongue traced the curve of her old bite scar, dipping, laving into the crater he'd left there. He resheathed her knife at his own hip, and placed a hand on each side of her naked waist. He ran his hands down to her hips, to the waistband of her jeans.

Olivia moved her head to the side, looking away, desperation rising like a suffocating tide in her. She knew he'd freed her hands because he liked it when she fought and hit and tore at his hair. It drove him wild, made him harder, made him hurt her more. Her heart stumbled as she caught sight of her knife hilt at his left hip. While he was sucking on her breast, she slowly fingered her right hand toward the hilt. His hands were undoing the button of her jeans, her zip. He pulled the front of her panties aside, and forced a finger up inside her.

She held her breath, gritting her teeth as she curled her fingers around the hilt. She yanked it out, and with a heavy grunt, she plunged it through his jacket into the side of his waist. He shocked still, his finger remaining inside her. She forced the blade in deeper, twisting it, her vision blurring as the rope pulled at her neck.

His left hand clamped down like a vise over her wrist. He pulled his finger out of her. She froze, chest heaving, sweat drenching her naked torso. And he fucking smiled, then licked his finger. Her heart dropped like a cold, heavy stone to her bowels. He raised his hand and cracked it across her face. The force flung her backward against the wood siding. She lay there, watching, blood leaking down her split cheek.

He extracted the knife from his torso. The blade came out red and glistening, and he clamped his left hand hard over the wound. Blood oozed through his fingers. He glanced at her again, and she braced for another impact. But he sheathed the blade. Lifting his jacket and the hem of his shirt, he examined the wound. Blood rushed down into his jeans. He reached for the sweater he'd cut off her, and balled part of it, plugging it tightly against the wound. He tied the sleeves firmly around his waist.

Then he turned to her, and the look in his eyes was death. He crawled closer. She edged backward, trapped by the rope in the corner, but a sound stopped him. His head jerked sideways, listening.

It was an animal—a wolf. No, a dog, yapping, barking, howling.

Eugene glanced at her, yanked on her rope to make sure she was properly tied, then lurched up for the shotgun he'd propped against the far wall next to a rifle. In a crouch, he moved toward the door of the cabin. He peered out into the darkness.

The animal howled again, the sound dying off into a series of whines. Olivia turned cold. She knew that sound. It sounded like . . . It wasn't possible. She closed her eyes a moment, dizziness and blackness swirling.

Eugene stayed crouched like an animal at the gap in the door for what seemed an eternity, watching, listening. Then slowly, he creaked the rotted door open wider and crawled out into the snowy night.

———

Cole crept silently through the snow along the forest fringe. His aim was to try and circle through the trees along the edge of the clearing, and come up in the gully behind the cabin. He stilled for a moment, breath misting in front of his face. He studied the building. The orange glow of a small fire flickered faintly through cracks. He could smell the smoke, but couldn't see it through the shroud of swirling flakes. It looked like a simple one-roomed structure. His bet was there was only the one door out the front. The windows appeared boarded up. Adrenaline crackled through his veins as he was besieged by a reckless urge to just run down there into the open clearing, and barge in headfirst.

If he did that, he'd be as good as dead.

Him being dead wasn't going to help her.

Controlling the ferocity of his impulse, he crawled back into the cover of trees, and made his way quietly toward the bank knotted with deciduous trees.

Once hidden in the gully among the tangled, dry aspen, willow, alder, he studied the back of the dilapidated building through the snowy gloom. He could make out one boarded-up window along the back wall. He judged himself to be almost two hundred meters out from the building. Still a big, open expanse between him and that cabin.

Ace threw up another plaintive howl on the opposite end of the clearing. It echoed through the forest like the voice of wolves. Cole tensed as he heard a rough creak. The front door was being opened? He couldn't see, or be sure from here.

He crawled a little closer to the edge of the clearing, lying flat in snow.

If things were going to plan, Burton would be waiting in a little hollow at the opposite edge of the clearing, not far below the forest fringe that hid Ace, who was tied to a tree. The intent was for the sound of the dog to draw Olivia's assailant out of the shed and into the clearing where Burton could get a clear shot. Cole had given Burton the shotgun and slugs. He himself carried the pistols.

The instant Cole heard Burton's shot, he was to race across to the cabin and try and come around from the back to free Olivia.

It was a crapshoot. But it was all they had. Sweat prickled across his lip, every muscle in his body coiled wire-tight as he waited for the signal shot.

Seconds seemed to tick by. Snow fell silently. It melted on his face, dripping into his eyes. More seconds passed. Then more. Fear licked through Cole. He heard no gunshot.

The dog cried again. Hairs rose on the back of his neck. Something was off.

———

Using her good hand for balance, Olivia crawled on her knees until the rope at her neck drew her up short. Still, straining against her noose, she had just enough line to reach a small hole in the siding. She peered through it. Eugene's shadow hunkered slowly through the snow toward the howling dog. A dog who sounded like her Ace. But it wasn't possible. Was it? How could it be?

She narrowed her eyes, trying to keep track of Eugene's shadow as he was absorbed by the silent shroud of swirling flakes.

He disappeared from sight.

All fell silent. Just snow, lots of snow.

Time stretched.

She tried to swallow, shivering, her bare skin tight with goose bumps. He'd be back before long. She had to do something—find some weapon before he returned.

Her gaze darted around the cabin interior. It settled on the lone rifle still propped near the door. With her right hand she yanked hard in frustration on the rope that secured her by the neck to an iron rod in the back corner of the room. It was tied fast. *Shit*—she'd never reach the gun tied up like this. Panting, Olivia scrabbled back into her corner. She grasped the length of rod, trying to jerk it loose from its moorings. But it was fixed solid into a slab of concrete. It cut her hand. That's when she noted how rusted and rough the iron was along the edges. Frantically she picked up the rope slack and started to work the rope against the sharp iron.

Very slowly, tiny strands of rope began to pop and fray. A gunshot boomed through the night. She froze, heart stuttering. Dust fell from the ceiling.

Quickly, she crawled back to the hole in the siding, peered through, trying to see what had happened. Had he shot the dog, or wolf? All she could see was soft, swirling snow.

Then suddenly his shadow materialized in the falling snow, a black, hobbling, injured shape.

Adrenaline, fear, exploded in her. She knew with every fiber of her being that if he didn't kill her tonight, he'd set her out to be hunted come first light. He was out of time for anything else, out of his comfort zone.

She scrabbled back into her corner, grabbed the fraying rope, and began rubbing with all her might against rusted iron, burning her fingers, blood from the cut on her palm wetting the rope. Sweat dribbled between her naked breasts.

A few more strands popped. Perspiration leaked into her eyes. Breath rasped in her throat. She could hear him now—the squeak of his boots in dry snow, the crunch of dead leaves beneath. She rubbed harder. Faster. Pain in her body was consuming. She panted, working even more frantically as the noise outside drew closer. Almost free. She tugged. It still held. *Fuck.* Almost blind with panic, she sawed the rope some more, and finally cut through.

Scrabbling on knees with one hand, dragging the frayed end of rope behind her, she made for the rifle at the door.

She grasped the weapon and crawled to the half-open door. She peered around the opening. *He was almost at the cabin.*

Heart in her throat, Olivia leaned her left side with her broken arm against the doorjamb for balance. She put the rifle stock to her shoulder, and, pressing her cheek against the butt, she curled her finger through the trigger guard and around the trigger. *Careful now. You have one shot. One good arm.* Part of her feared that even if she did hit him, he wouldn't die. He'd just keep coming like some monster in a nightmare movie.

On her exhale, Eugene's black shadow firmly in her sights, she aimed for center mass and carefully squeezed the trigger.

Click.

Her heart bottomed out in her belly.

It wasn't loaded.

In desperation, she squeezed again, and again.

Nothing.

Panic licked a hot flame through her stomach. No wonder he'd left the gun. It held no ammunition. Her mind raced.

If she tried to bolt out of the door in front of him and race for the forest, he'd shoot. If he missed, she might be able to outpace him in his injured state, but he was unlikely to miss at this range. He was a veteran hunter with an accurate eye. And he had 12-gauge slugs—enough to stop a charging grizz in its tracks. He'd blow a hole clean through her lungs before she took two steps.

For a moment, panic almost swallowed her brain, and blackness swamped in from the fringes of her mind. She felt her body going faint.

No! Think of Tori. You can't let her down. Not now . . .

She forced herself to focus. Slowly she edged up onto her feet as his shadow loomed into the quavering gold light spilling into the darkness from the doorway. She inched her back up the wall so that she was in a standing position almost behind the door.

Using both her good arm and broken one, she clenched her teeth against pain and raised the rifle high above her head. Mouth bone dry, limbs trembling, she waited.

———

As soon as Cole heard the shotgun blast, relief punched through his chest. He lurched to his feet and began to race across the clearing toward the boarded-up rear of the building.

He crouched down against the wall, heart thumping as he tried to peep through a crack. He needed to ensure Eugene had indeed been shot by Gage and was not still in the cabin. But from this angle, he couldn't see much of the inside other than the small fire in the center of the room. He heard a few noises. A scraping sound.

He was about to creep farther along the wall when he heard something else in the muffled night. A faint cough. He stilled, listening, breath misting around his face. His pulse quickened at another cough—it sounded like it had come from *outside* the front of the cabin.

Then he heard the crunch of leaves under the thin cover of snow.

Footfalls. His stomach clenched.

Burton?

But suddenly he had a bad feeling.

Quietly he crept around to the back corner of the cabin, his pistol held ready.

———

Eugene's body snapped wire-tight the instant he noticed Olivia was not in her corner. But as he took a step forward into the cabin, she brought the rifle down with a sharp crack on his skull.

The jolt of impact reverberated up her arms, and jackhammered into her shoulders, neck, teeth. She felt it in her broken nose.

Eugene went dead still, as if shocked by an electrical current. Then slowly he turned to face her.

Olivia caught her breath as pale amber eyes met hers.

Everything turned to elasticky slow motion. In the flickering firelight she could read every detail, every nuance of Eugene's features as the killer's eyes held hers. And Olivia was suddenly suspended in time, everything looping back on itself, taking her all the way back to the Bear Claw shed where he'd held her, raped her, all those years ago.

A quiet despair rose in her chest.

It was all over. All lost.

He opened his mouth, smiled, then suddenly stumbled sideways. In that blinding instant Olivia whipped the gun out to her side like a baseball bat. She swung with every ounce of might, with every inch of her desire to live, and cracked the weapon in a sideswipe across his cheekbone. She heard, felt, bone break, crush.

Bile lurched bitter into the back of her throat as Eugene staggered, a bemused look in his eyes, and he tripped backward. He landed hard on the floor, hand reaching out behind him to brace his fall. His hand went into the fire.

A roar of pain exploded from his chest, as he lurched back up onto his feet and came in a full frontal lunge for her. He bashed his body into hers, crushing her hard against the wall. Pain sparked through her brain, her ribs. He wrapped his big hands like a vise around her throat, lifting her feet off the ground as he squeezed. She couldn't breathe. Her eyes bulged. Her first wild impulse was to grab at his iron-like fingers and try to pry them away from her crushing windpipe, but instead she held her focus, and groped madly for the knife that she knew had been resheathed at his hip.

He pressed his body against hers and squeezed her neck harder. Her vision went red. Her consciousness slipping. On some distant level she registered his penis was rock hard, pushing against her hips where her fly was still open. A memory washed through her, the sensation of his sweaty, naked body atop hers, him driving his cock deep into her. Her mind suddenly sharpened with rage. Her fingers met the familiar hilt of her knife at his hip. She yanked it out of the sheath, and plunged it deep into his side, this time angling upward under his ribs toward the liver. He stilled. His fingers loosened slightly. Her vision flooded back. She ripped out the blade and plunged it in again. And again. And again.

He gasped. His hands dropped to his side. He staggered back, his lion eyes holding hers, his features twisting with disbelief.

As his hands went to the blood coming from his side, she lunged at him with the knife held high in her fist. Driven by a feral kind of madness to survive at all cost, to beat him down forever, she brought the blade down hard into his chest.

Steel met bone and sent a judder up her arm. She yanked the knife out, the shaft gleaming with blood. He crumpled to the ground, his skull cracking against stones around the fire. The ends of his hair met coals. The acrid scent of burning human hair filled the cabin as Olivia dropped down on top of him, and with small grunts, her mind black and unthinking, she plunged her hunting blade into his chest, his neck, his belly, his face. She was vaguely aware of blood. Everywhere. Hot and slippery. On her hands, face, her naked torso. In her hair. She could taste his blood in her mouth.

Those vile yellow eyes stared blankly up at her now. His body was limp, his head lolling with each ferocious stab of her knife. Somewhere, far away, she heard her name.

Olivia! Olivia—stop!

Vaguely she registered big hands on her shoulders, someone grasping her wrist that held the knife. Someone trying to stop her, yank her off the bastard.

She fought it. A gunshot cracked the air.

She stilled.

Shaking.

And for a moment she couldn't quite register what she was seeing, what she'd just done. She turned and looked up.

CHAPTER 26

Cole stared at the vignette in front of him—a scene from a horror movie.

Olivia, naked from the jeans up, her fly open, straddled a bloodied mess of a man lying dead on the floor, his wet hair singeing in a dying fire. She was splattered in blood, her eyes wild, unrecognizable, a mother of a hunting knife clutched in her fist.

"Livia," he whispered, holding her eyes, crouching down beside her, as he stuck the pistol he'd just fired into the waistband of his jeans. The smell of blood, burned hair, filled his nostrils. And something worse—guts. She'd nicked through to the bowel of this monster, and the stink was vile. He looked deep into her eyes as he reached gently for her shoulders.

"You can stop now," he whispered. "Look at me. Focus. He's dead. Gone. Long gone."

She looked blankly at him, mouth open, panting.

His heart wrenched. "Come, come to me, Liv."

He lifted her off her assailant and gathered her wet, bloodied body up into his arms. He held her tight, rocking slightly as he stroked her matted hair. "It's okay," he murmured against her hair. "It's over. You did it. You got him."

He cupped the side of her face, looked into her eyes. "Can you hear me, Liv?"

Her mouth opened, but she seemed unable to speak, great big

shudders taking hold of her body. Her ear was ripped. Bleeding. Her nose looked broken. Her face was cut and swelling. He quickly shed his down jacket, started to put it on her.

But she gasped in pain as he attempted to slide the sleeve over her arm. The pain seemed to refocus her a little.

"Where are you hurt?"

"Arm," she whispered. "Broken, I think."

He tried again, more carefully, conscious of her left arm. He edged the sleeve of his jacket onto her hand, moved it up until he could wrap the jacket around her and she could get her right arm into the other sleeve.

He zipped it up to her neck. Her gaze dropped to the massacred body on the floor.

"I . . . I . . . killed him."

Cole cupped the side of her face, forcing her to look at him, not the mess on the floor.

"Yes," he said quietly. "Don't think about it now. Don't look at him. He's in the past. Come here." He led her away from the body, into the corner of the cabin. He helped lower her into a sitting position. She leaned against the wall, going limp. Spent.

"I want you to tell me where you hurt."

She looked blank.

"Your arm," he prompted. "Your nose." He touched it gently. She winced. He dug in his pocket for his father's handkerchief, which was still there. Ever so gently he wiped the blood from her face. Most of it was her assailant's, by the looks of things, apart from the dried blood around her torn ear. His heart clutched. He smiled softly, relief, love, washing through his chest. "You're going to be fine, Liv," he whispered. "You're going to be just fine. You hear me?"

She nodded, swallowed.

Then she blinked. "How . . . how did you find me?" She frowned, her mind reaching back. "The plane—it was you?"

He nodded.

Heat crackled sharply into her eyes, and she grabbed his wrist. "Ace? Was that Ace? I heard gunfire. Did he shoot Ace?" She was suddenly sheet-white and shaking all over again.

"No," Cole lied. Because he didn't know. Yet. And he wasn't going to upset her into thinking otherwise. But he intended to find out, because right now, more than anything, this woman needed her dog. He was also worried about Burton. He shot a glance at the body, then scanned the rest of the cabin. An old rotting canvas tarp was bunched in the corner.

"Wait here."

Cole lurched to his feet, gathered up the canvas. Dust and debris fell from the folds as he draped it over the body. He dragged the covered body by the boots away from the fire. Quickly he fed more bits of wood onto the embers, stoking them to life.

He went back to Olivia. "I'm going to check on things outside, okay? Will you be all right alone, just for a moment?"

She swallowed. Her gaze locked onto his. He knew she was thinking about Ace. His heart and stomach were so tight with worry it stopped his breath. He took her cold hands in his. "I'll just be a minute. Don't look at him, okay? Don't even think about it."

She nodded.

Cole exited the door. It was still snowing heavily. Anxiously, he moved into the clearing, making his way toward the ditch where Burton was supposed to have been lying in ambush for the killer. As he neared, as his eyes adjusted to the gloom, he saw a black shape about twenty meters out, lying in the snow. He rushed forward. A chill washed over his skin.

"Burton?"

Nothing moved. No sound came. Snow was settling over him.

Cole reached for his shoulder, turned him over, and his heart clean stopped as the man's head flopped back, blood leaking from the corner of his mouth. And from a gaping hole in his chest.

Cole felt for a pulse, knowing full well it was useless. The cop was dead. His gaze flashed up. Olivia's attacker must have second-guessed them. The dog, while drawing him out, must have also piqued the suspicion of a cunning hunter. Expecting an ambush, he must have approached Burton from behind.

Shit.

He dragged his hand over his wet hair. Then fear suddenly lanced through Cole. *Ace?*

He grabbed the shotgun that was lying at Burton's side and ran toward the bank and up into the forest.

"Ace! Buddy! You okay?" he called out.

Silence.

Then as he entered the cover of trees he heard a yip. His chest near burst with relief.

The old dog yapped again, louder, his voice hoarse as he jerked against his line to reach Cole.

Cole dropped to his haunches in front of the dog. Ruffling his fur, he unhooked the harness. "Someone needs you now, bud. More than she ever will. Go! Go find Olivia!"

The dog bulleted out of the forest, down the bank, and into the snowy field. Cole ran after him, tracking line and shotgun in hand. They raced across the snow toward the cabin.

Ace wiggled into the door and found her in the corner.

Olivia gave a gut-wrenching sob as she grasped hold of her dog, burying her face into his fur, just rocking and holding him. Cole entered the cabin and stood there, watching woman and dog. Emotion flooded his eyes.

He let them be for a moment. Ace whined slightly, licked her face. When Olivia looked up, her eyes were hollows, her face white under blood and bruises and cuts.

He wasn't going to tell her about Gage Burton right now. That could come a little later.

He crouched down beside her and moved matted hair from her face. "You should let me look at those injuries now."

She held his gaze. Then she leaned into him, put her head against his chest. Cole's heart clean broke. She rested like that, as if drawing strength from his presence. Slowly, gently, he put his arm around her. She had hers around Ace.

"Thank you," she whispered. "Thank you for coming to find me, for drawing him out like that. I . . . I wouldn't have made it otherwise. He . . . he'd have taken me . . ."

"It's over, Liv."

She nodded against his chest. "My sat phone," she said as he stroked her matted hair. "It's in his jacket pocket. He took it from me and put it in his pocket."

"In a moment," he said. "I'll get it in a moment." He closed his eyes, just held her awhile longer, and said a silent thanks to the universe that this woman—*his* woman—had made it through. That he'd arrived in time. That maybe, just maybe, there would be a second chance. For both of them now.

CHAPTER 27

By the light of the small fire he'd kept going in the cabin, Cole listened to Olivia's recount as he patched and bound her up as best he could with the help of his first aid kit. He'd already called in with her satellite phone, which he'd retrieved from Eugene's jacket pocket.

"I've heard of dominance-submissive issues between twins," he said, "but this seems to take it to the extreme. Sounds like his mother was at the root of his problem. From what he told you, she fueled this notion in his brain."

He peeled open another butterfly suture and applied it to the rip under her ear, carefully drawing the edges of the wound together with the bandage. She winced, eyes watering.

"It sure explains the DNA evidence used to convict Sebastian. And how you thought it was him in the police lineup."

"Where is Tori?" she said after a long period of silence.

"With my dad."

"How did you manage to take off from Broken Bar in that storm?"

He smiled ruefully. "I suspect we had a helping hand—don't ask." He paused and sat back, examining the bandages, then the sling he'd fashioned for her arm.

"Sometimes," he said quietly, "I wonder if there is a greater plan, if things are just meant to be. If all my life I was supposed to circle back to Broken Bar, and meet you."

Her broken eyes met his. Her hand still rested on Ace. "That's what I asked Melody Vanderbilt once. She was Gage's wife, a journalist who used to come and sit with me in the hospital. I asked whether she thought we could pinpoint the exact moment our life first started on a collision course with another's—" Her gaze sharpened suddenly as it struck her. "If Tori is with Myron, where is Gage? He . . . he didn't come with you, did he?"

"Olivia—"

"Oh, Jesus, no . . . the gunshot . . ."

"He'd have wanted it this way, Liv. He was dying, close to the end. And he had this one thing in life to finish. All his life, the Mountie believed the real killer was still out there. And he proved it. He finally found him. The Mountie finally got his man."

Her eyes flickered toward the shape under the tarp, and a shiver ran through her body.

"He also brought you and Tori together."

"She's lost *both* her parents," she whispered. "How . . . how is she going to cope?"

"She has you."

He held her gaze. "We can do this, Liv. Together."

She stared at him, a range of emotions chasing through her features as she absorbed the subtext of his words. Tears, finally, filled her eyes. And when Cole saw them, his heart clenched. She was coming back. They were going to win this.

"I want to see him."

He thought about it a moment, inhaled, nodded slowly. "You think you can stand, walk?"

"Yup," she said quietly.

———

Cole took her arm and led Olivia outside. It was dawn, merely a lighter shade of night.

She blinked, feeling as though she'd stepped from one reality into another. She glanced up at Cole. His eyes were dark, stormy, intense, full of questions and worry. In his touch she felt his compassion, love. And in that moment, in that exchanged glance, with her arm in his, leaning on him like this, she believed she could, maybe, just love this man back. Maybe, one day, she'd figure out how to trust someone again.

"What?" he said quietly.

"I . . . nothing." He held her gaze a moment longer, then gave a quiet nod. As if he'd read her mind. As if he'd seen in her face what she was feeling inside. But he was not going to push her. Olivia believed now that Cole McDonough would never rush her. And in spite of everything she'd just been through, a sweet warmth filled her chest. It wasn't a sensation she could articulate. Didn't even want to. Not yet.

He led her away from the abandoned cabin. Away from Eugene's body. Ace followed at their heels. Cloud was low and heavy, mist thick. Snow had fallen several feet deep, and was still coming down.

As they neared the mound in the snow, Olivia heard the faint thudding of choppers above the clouds. Her heart kicked. She glanced up into the tattered swaths of mist—there was no way a pilot could put down here. Yet it was still good to know they were out there, coming. This time she was no longer alone.

Cole crouched down, dusted some snow off Burton's body.

"Take the snow off his face," she said.

He dusted the face free. Wide, frozen eyes looked up at them.

Olivia stared at the body. A long time. Finally, softly, she said, "I can't believe how inextricably our lives have been entwined. Gage's, Tori's, Melody's. Mine. Eugene's. All these years, and I didn't even know it."

Cole squeezed her hand. She let go of him and lowered herself painfully into a crouch. Ace sat at her side.

"I'll look after her, our baby girl," she whispered. "I promise." She reached out and gently closed Sergeant Gage Burton's blue eyes. "I'll make sure she's proud of you." Her voice caught.

Wind soughed through the snowy pines, and flakes stirred around them.

She came to her feet. Hesitated, then said, "I don't know what happened to me back there in the cabin." She looked at her hands that were still stained with Eugene's blood, "I don't even remember doing it, stabbing him like that."

"You wanted to live. It was self-defense."

"It was overkill, Cole. They'll come down on me hard for that."

"Liv, I doubt it."

She glanced up into his eyes.

"Whatever happens," he said, locking his gaze with hers, "you are not alone. I have your back."

As the distant whine of snowmobiles deep in the forest reached them, Cole put his arm around her.

"Ready?"

She nodded.

Cole loaded a cartridge into the pencil flare from the first aid kit.

He fired it up into the cloud. Pink light exploded into the misty snow, mushrooming into an umbrella of color that hung low and haunting among the dark trees.

Out of the woods and over the ridge they came, an army of law enforcement personnel, paramedics, search-and-rescue volunteers on snow machines.

He drew her closer to his body. "Time to go home," he said.

They stood in the glare of headlights, under the pink cloud from the flare as the cop on the lead snowmobile dismounted. He took off his helmet and came rapidly toward them, followed by another member. Two paramedics also dismounted and ran toward them.

Cole stepped forward to greet the lead officer. "I'm Cole McDonough. This is Olivia West—she needs immediate medical attention."

The cop's gaze darted around as he shook Cole's outreached hand. "Sergeant Yakima, homicide," he said as the EMTs surrounded Olivia. "This is Constable Martinello." He motioned to the cop behind him who took off her helmet. Blonde hair in a ponytail came free. Her face was pinked from cold.

The female cop nodded toward Cole, and moved directly to Olivia's side, joining the paramedics as other personnel deployed around the scene.

———

Tori held the old man's hand. He was in great pain as he lay in bed. His gnarled fingers clutched hers tightly, as if she were a lifeline. She swallowed, besieged by a sense of grave responsibility, and for a moment she felt as though she were a bridge, holding hands with the other side, and if she could just hold on long enough, she might keep him here until Olivia and Cole and her father returned.

The other cops were downstairs in the library, but one sat in the room with her—the nice, young-looking one. He was seated on a chair in the corner, near the heater. His phone buzzed.

He answered and spoke softly, then looked up and said to Tori, "They got him."

"Is Olivia okay?"

"Yes. She's safe. With Cole."

Tori stood up from her chair, still keeping her hold on Myron. "And my father?"

The officer was quiet a moment. He stood, came over to her, placed his hand on her shoulder, a strange look in his eyes. He seemed to be weighing how to tell her something terrible. And she knew. She just knew.

"Your dad would have known that this is the hardest thing a cop does—"

"He's dead?"

"I'm sorry, Tori."

She swallowed, her heart falling. She clutched the old man's hand tighter, moving closer to the bed.

"What . . . happened?"

"Your dad went down a hero, Tori Burton," the young cop said, a gleam in his eyes, a crack in his voice. "A real hero. He got his man. After all these years, after no one believing him, he got the Watt Lake Killer."

Tori tightened her mouth. The insides of her stomach trembled.

She felt Myron squeeze her fingers. Her gaze shot to him. His eyes were open. He was looking at her, right into her. Emotion clogged her nose, her throat. She didn't know what to do. What to say.

"How did it happen?" she asked again.

"In the course of rescuing Olivia West, he took a fatal gunshot wound to the heart."

She looked away. The day was dawning outside—cold and wintery. A new day. And the whole world was changed. She wasn't a kid anymore. She didn't even know who she was anymore.

"Tori," the old man whispered. "He's . . . a hero. He did it for you."

She looked at him, then the cop.

"Can I get you anything?" the officer said.

She shook her head, and reseated herself slowly on the chair next to Myron's bed, still holding his hand. After a long while the cop stepped out for a moment to take another call.

Tori felt something change in the old man's grip. The air grew suddenly cold in the room. She glanced up, sensing a presence.

Something moved like a breeze beside Myron. For a nanosecond Tori saw the shape of a woman, just like the one in the frame next to his bed, then she was gone. Then Tori saw another face. She saw her mother—Melody's face. She smiled and held out her hand to Tori. Warmth filled Tori's heart. And the image faded.

Tori's heart raced. She shot a look at the old man. He'd gone still.

"Myron?" she whispered, coming sharply to her feet. He didn't move. Cautiously she touched his cheek with her fingertips. His skin was ice cold.

And he had a smile on his face.

———

Thanksgiving Day. Evening.

The police had brought a victim services worker up from Clinton on a snowmobile to stay with Tori and talk to her.

The woman was cooking supper for them both in the kitchen.

Tori was in the library, which was the warmest room in the lodge right now with the big fire going. Myron's wheelchair was empty next to the hearth. She watched out the window, feeling hollow inside, unsure. Snow lay thick and silent under the eerie bluish light of evening. There was a gap in the storm—the whole world looked frozen and still. The social worker said another front would be blowing in around midnight.

She heard it. The distant chop of a helicopter. She tensed and peered down the side of the window. It came into view, making a loud *thuckthuckthuck* sound. Trees bent, and snow blew up in a dervish as the chopper lowered to the ground.

Tori turned and fled down the stairs. She burst out the front door, stalled. Suddenly afraid.

The helicopter set down a short distance from the lodge, clear of telephone and hydro lines.

The door opened as the rotors slowed. A figure jumped out. Cole. He helped another person out, lifting her to the ground. Olivia. She had an arm in a sling. Ace jumped out behind them.

Cole put his arm around Olivia's shoulder, and they ran in a crouch under the rotors. Once they were clear, Cole gave a thumbs-up, and the helicopter rotors sped up again. The skids lifted off the ground, then the chopper took off at an angle and disappeared into cloud.

Tori walked slowly to the edge of the porch.

Cole and Olivia started toward the lodge, Cole's arm still around Olivia's shoulders. Tori's heart tightened, and a spurt of tears came into her eyes. She ran down the steps and raced through the snow toward them. Olivia crouched down. She had bandages on her face. Tori hesitated. Their eyes met.

A long shivering moment of indecision seemed to trap them on the spot, all the questions about the future shimmering and multiplying silently between them.

Olivia held open her good arm. "Tori," she said softly. "Come here."

Tears streamed suddenly down Tori's face.

Olivia hugged her tightly with her good arm. So tight Tori could hardly breathe. She wouldn't let go, and she pressed her face against Tori's hair, drinking her in.

"Tori," she murmured against her hair, "the social worker told me that you know who I am."

Tori went still inside, nodded.

Olivia moved back, still crouched down in the snow. Their eyes met, and it struck Tori that they were the exact same color. A funny little quiver ran through her chest. This was her mother, her biological mother. She really was a genetic part of this brave woman who she'd read about in her mom's book. On the back of that quiver came a soft burst of pride. Olivia was a survivor. She was very cool that way.

"My mom, Melody, she loved you," Tori said quietly. "It was in her book."

Olivia's mouth tightened, and she seemed unable to speak for a moment.

"She wrote that book for when I was ready," Tori said. "I . . ." Her voice choked on a surge of thickness in her throat. " I . . . don't know what to do now."

Olivia reached for her hand. "We phoned your Aunt Louise," she said gently. "She's flying out to see you. She'll be here tomorrow morning. If the weather is really bad Cole will go and meet her at the highway pullout on snowmobile."

"Aunt Lou on a snowmobile?"

Olivia nodded. "She insisted. Come hell or blizzard, she's getting here."

"My dad . . . he would have thought it was funny. Aunt Lou on a snow machine. She's quite fat, you know. And bossy."

Olivia smiled, and her eyes gleamed with moisture.

"I don't want to go to Ontario," Tori said. "I . . . I don't want to live with Aunt Lou." Tears, hot ones, filled her eyes again, and she fought to hold them in.

"We're going to work this all out. All of us." Olivia glanced up at Cole. "Step by baby step. It's going to be your choice, Tori, all of it, but I want you to know that my heart, my home, this place, it's yours, too. If you wanted to stay . . ." Her voice caught. She swallowed, struggling with her own emotions. "But I'd really like it if you stayed. Cole would, too. Myron would also have wanted it that way, his ranch, the old house, full with a family."

And something whispered through Tori's mind, through her heart and body and soul, and it was, she realized with shock, her mother's voice, as if whispering through from the other side: *You're going to be okay, Tori. You're going to find a new home. Here. With these two people. I want it this way, too. We looked after you until you and your mom were ready to meet, until your father could be certain you were both safe . . .*

On impulse she hugged Olivia.

Olivia gave a sob, wiped her nose with her sleeve. She seemed unable to speak further, but Tori saw it in her eyes. Love. Raw, whole, consuming, the unquestionable love of a mother for her child.

Tori glanced up at Cole. He had a dark, intense look on his face, his features tight.

"Myron's gone," she said quietly.

Cole nodded. He placed his big hand, warm, on her shoulder. "I'm sorry about your dad, too," he said.

"I held Myron's hand," she said. "He tried to wait for you. He tried to hold on."

Cole's eyes shone.

"He had a smile," she said very softly.

Cole's mouth quivered, and he put his arm around Tori's shoulders. "Come," he said, voice thick. "It's getting cold and dark out."

And they walked together, the three of them and Ace, Cole with one arm around Olivia's shoulders, and one around Tori's, a tentative family forged by fate. They walked toward the big old Broken Bar lodge house, warm, golden light spilling out from the windows into the cool dusk and snow.

ACKNOWLEDGMENTS

At least once each summer my husband, Paul, and I load up our truck, camper, and trailer and head north with our Black Beast of a labradog, up into the interior to Cariboo country, where we spend days, sometimes weeks at Big Bar Lake—a slice right out of paradise.

Occasionally we stay in the campsite at the far end of the aquamarine waters, colored by white marl shoals, where we fish for darting rainbow trout. More often we stay on a very special piece of land graciously shared with us by Tom and Jennifer Cole. It was there, under big sky, surrounded by endless forests, the Marble range in the distance, the haunting cry of coyotes echoing at dusk, that Olivia and Cole's story was born. A very big thank-you for this novel's inspiration is thus due to Tom and Jenn, who introduced us to the place. And to my Paul, for helping me land my first trout on a fly line, and for drawing me into the esoteric art of fly tying and the magic of watching nature in order to learn what might make a fish bite (any errors are my own).

Thank you also to Deborah Nemeth for early editorial insight. To JoVon Sotak for bringing this book under the Montlake umbrella, to Kelli Martin for editorial shaping and polishing, and to the rest of the Amazon Publishing team who make books possible. A big thanks, too, to Joanne White for some wonderful artwork and promotional material. And as always, to my writing comrade, Mica Stone, for always kicking me in the butt (or head) when I need it most!

ABOUT THE AUTHOR

Photo © 2013 Paul Beswetherick

Loreth Anne White is an award-winning author of romantic suspense, thriller, and mystery novels. A double RITA finalist, she has won the Romantic Times Reviewers' Choice Award, the National Readers' Choice Award, and the Readers' Crown, and is a Booksellers' Best Award finalist, a double Daphne Du Maurier finalist, and a multiple CataRomance Reviewers' Choice winner.

Loreth hails from South Africa but now lives with her family in a ski resort in the moody Coast Mountains of North America's Pacific Northwest. It's a place of vast, wild, and often dangerous mountains, larger-than-life characters, epic adventure, and romance—the perfect place to escape reality. It's no wonder it was here that she was inspired to abandon her sixteen-year newspaper career to escape into a world of romantic fiction filled with dangerous men and adventurous women.

When she's not writing, you will find her open-water distance swimming, skiing, biking, hiking, or running the trails with her Black Dog, and generally trying to avoid the bears—albeit not always successfully. In the summer she will often be on the road, searching out remote camping and fly fishing spots with her husband or participating in tracking and air-scent courses with her Black Beast. She calls this work, because it's when the best ideas come.

Loreth loves to hear from readers. You can contact her through her website at www.lorethannewhite.com, or you can find her on www.facebook.com/Loreth.Anne.White or twitter.com/Loreth